HETTY FEATHER AND SAPPHIRE BATTERSEA

www.**randomhousechildrens**.co.uk

HETTY FEATHER AND SAPPHIRE BATTERSEA
A CORGI YEARLING BOOK 978 0 552 56786 2

HETTY FEATHER
First published in Great Britain by Doubleday
Text copyright © Jacqueline Wilson, 2009
Illustrations copyright © Nick Sharratt, 2009

SAPPHIRE BATTERSEA
First published in Great Britain by Doubleday
Text copyright © Jacqueline Wilson, 2011
Illustrations copyright © Nick Sharratt, 2011

This collection first published in Great Britain by Corgi Yearling,
an imprint of Random House Children's Publishers UK,
A Random House Group Company

This edition published 2012

3 5 7 9 10 8 6 4 2

Text in this edition copyright © Jacqueline Wilson, 2012
Illustrations in this edition copyright © Nick Sharratt, 2012

The right of Jacqueline Wilson to be identified as the author of this work has been
asserted in accordance with the Copyright, Designs and Patents Act 1988.

The Random House Group Limited supports The Forest Stewardship Council® (FSC®),
the leading international forest-certification organisation. Our books carrying the FSC
label are printed on FSC®-certified paper. FSC is the only forest-certification scheme
supported by the leading environmental organisations, including Greenpeace. Our
paper procurement policy can be found at www.randomhouse.co.uk/environment

MIX
Paper from
responsible sources
FSC® C016897

Set in New Century Schoolbook

Corgi Yearling Books are published by Random House Children's Publishers UK,
61–63 Uxbridge Road, London W5 5SA

www.**randomhousechildrens**.co.uk
www.**randomhouse**.co.uk
www.**totallyrandombooks**.co.uk

Addresses for companies within The Random House Group Limited
can be found at: www.**randomhouse**.co.uk/offices.htm

THE RANDOM HOUSE GROUP Limited Reg. No. 954009

A CIP catalogue record for this book is available from the British Library.

Printed and bound by CPI Group (UK) Ltd, Croydon, CR0 4YY

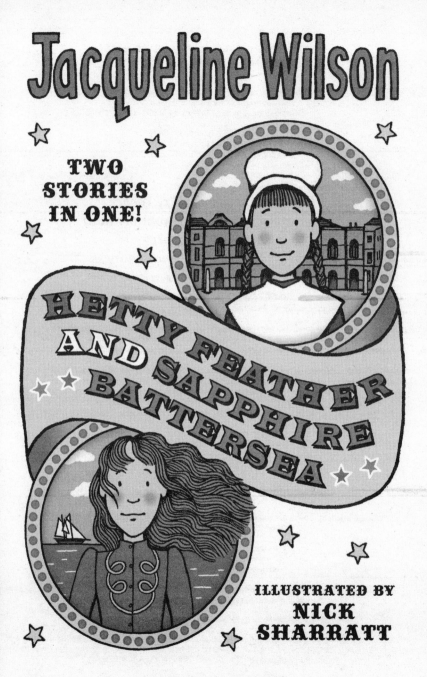

Jacqueline Wilson

TWO STORIES IN ONE!

HETTY FEATHER AND SAPPHIRE BATTERSEA

ILLUSTRATED BY **NICK SHARRATT**

CORGI YEARLING

For my dear friend Mary Vacher.
Thank you so much for all your brilliant
professional support –
and all your loving care and kindness.

Jacqueline Wilson

HETTY FEATHER

ILLUSTRATED BY
NICK SHARRATT

CORGI YEARLING

My name is Hetty Feather. Don't mock. It's not my *real* name. I'm absolutely certain my mother would have picked a beautiful romantic name for me – though sadly I have not turned out beautiful or romantic.

I shall picture her:

'My little darling,' my mother whispered, wrapping me up tightly in a shawl. She held me close close close to her chest, as if she could never bear to let me go.

'My little . . .' Rosamund? Seraphina? Christobel? My eyes are my best feature, as blue as the summer sky. Did she perhaps call me Sapphire? Azure? Bluebell?

I like to think my baby hair had not yet sprouted from my little pink head. A bald baby can still just about be beautiful. An infant with hair as scarlet as sin is an abomination, spawn of the Devil. So says Matron Bottomly, and she pulls my hair hard. Once when I cheeked her really wondrously, calling her

1

Matron Stinking Bottomly, she pulled so fiercely, a whole hank of my hair came away in her hand. She would have been in trouble if anyone had spotted my poor bald patch, but she crammed my cap down hard and no one saw. Well, two hundred foundling girls witnessed her assault on me, but Matron Bottomly didn't give a fig about them.

It took an entire year for my hair to grow back properly, but it was worth it because from that day onwards we *all* referred to her as Matron Stinking Bottomly – though not out loud. No other girl is as bold as me. I have a nature as fiery as my wretched hair.

I do so *hope* I was bald when I was newly born in 1876. Suppose I came into the world with little red tufts. Oh dearie, what a shock for my poor mother. Maybe she was tempted to call me Carrot or Goldfish or Marmalade.

No, I am absolutely certain my mother would not mock me. She held me close, she rubbed her cheek over my flaming head, she gently wound a little lock around her finger. She loved my red hair because it was mine. She cut off one tiny tuft to plait with pins and keep within a locket. That way she kept a small part of me for ever.

She didn't *want* to give me away. She loved me with all her heart. I know I was a poor, puny little thing, hardly weighing so much as a twist of sugar.

I'm sure my mother nursed me night and day, trying her hardest to build me up and make me strong. If I close my eyes now and hunch up small, I can almost feel her arms around me, hear her humming a lullaby, smell her sweet perfume, clasp her white hand with my tiny fingers. I cannot focus properly, but if I try really hard I can see her pale face, the tears in her own blue eyes.

Everyone says you can't remember back to babyhood. I've asked the nurses and the teachers and they all say the same. Even Jem insisted this is true, and he is the wisest boy ever. However, I'm absolutely certain they are all wrong on this point. I *can* remember.

I remember the worst day ever, when my mother bathed me and dressed me in my napkin and my petticoats and a little white gown she had stitched herself. She wrapped me up in a crocheted shawl and then carried me outside. She took me on a long, long journey. I'm sure I remember the roar and whistle of a train. Then I think we took a cab because I cried at the strange bumping and the clack of the horses' hooves. She held me tighter, rocking me in her arms, crying too.

Then the bump-clack stopped and my mother stayed crouching inside, shaking, so that I shook too. The cabman shouted at her and she gave me one last desperate kiss.

'I will always love you,' she whispered right into my ear.

Then she clambered out of the cab, clutching me close. She said a few words to the cabman and then walked over to a tall gateway. She murmured to the gatekeeper, so softly that she had to repeat herself. Then the gate creaked open and we stepped inside. There must have been other mothers, other infants, because I heard wailing all around us.

My mother and I stood in front of a long polished table where a line of solemn men sat and asked questions. My mother answered, while I whimpered dolefully. Then we were led to a little room with a bright gaslight overhead. I blinked and tried to burrow into my mother's breast, but large cold hands snatched me away from her.

I was laid on my back on a hard table. My shawl was tugged away. My beautiful white dress was unbuttoned and taken from me. Both my petticoats were pulled over my head. They even removed my napkin so I was lying there stark naked. The hard hands turned my head from side to side, prodded my belly, moved my arms and legs about while I protested vigorously, screaming my head off.

Then the hands wrapped me in strange coarse clothing, not mine at all! They picked me up and carried me away. My arms and legs were too small

4

and weak to punch and kick. All I could do was scream. I screamed and screamed for my mother, but she wasn't there any more. I was being carried down endless corridors in this vast building, away from my mother for ever.

I was bound so tightly within the scratchy woollen shawl that I couldn't move. I was laid on my back in an iron cot, still screaming. I cried for my mother, but she didn't come to rescue me. I cried for my own soft familiar clothes, but I stayed stuck in these harsh, worn garments reeking of carbolic. I cried for the comfort of my thumb, trapped inside the shawl. I cried for gentle arms and warm sweet milk.

'Now now, what a terrible noise! You're disturbing all the other babies. What are you crying for, hm?' said one of the nurses, picking me up.

What did she *think* I was crying for? I was only a few days old and I'd lost everything I loved. No wonder I howled. But she meant it kindly enough. She held me against her flat starched chest and patted my back as if my problem was just a little trapped wind.

'There, there, nearly time for your feed,' she said.

She put me down again and I cried harder. I only quietened for a few seconds when someone plucked me once more from my cot. I desperately hoped they were about to return me to my mother, but the hands that held me were coldly capable, not tender and stroking. A bottle was thrust into my mouth. My lips puckered and would not suck. It tasted wrong. It wasn't my mother. I choked and tried to spit it out.

'This one's a hopeless feeder – and she's tiny as it is. I don't know why they accepted her. She's not long for this world.'

'They'll have to christen her quick or she'll be off to Limbo-land,' said another. 'Let me try. I'll make her feed.'

I was passed over promptly and the bottle poked hard against my mouth. I kept my lips pressed together. She pinched my nose so I had to open my mouth to breathe. I yelled furiously at this mean trick.

'Temper, temper! Never mind Limbo-land, she's like a little imp from H-e-l-l,' she said, giving me a shake. 'Take the bottle like a good girl! You don't want to starve, do you?'

I did not care whether I lived or died if I could not be with my mother. I cried all day, until my throat was raw and I shook all over, but it was no use. She still didn't come.

There were other babies crying too, though not as loudly and insistently as me. I couldn't see them as I was stuck on my back, but I could hear them.

I heard their sucking and sighing after the hateful hands had lifted them from their cots.

'Won't you feed too, poor little lamb?' This was a gentler voice, with smaller, softer hands. She wasn't my mother but she cradled me almost as carefully. She didn't ram the choking bottle into my mouth straight away. She shook a few drops of milk onto her finger and stroked it against my lips. I opened my mouth and sucked.

'Ah, it's good, isn't it? Some more?'

She gave me more drops on her finger and I sucked it dry. She did this again and again. When I opened my mouth eagerly for more, she edged the bottle very cautiously against my lips. I could not resist sucking – and felt the sweet milk splashing down my sore throat. I still did not like the feel of the bottle, but I ached with hunger and thirst so I sucked and sucked.

'My, look at Winnie with 25629! She's got her sucking away a treat now.'

So the kind nurse was called Winnie. And 25629 seemed to be *my* name now. I was not old enough to understand numbers, but the long sound was harsh and I hated it. However, before long I was given yet another name. I was dressed in a gown so stiff with starch I was stretched out rigidly, scarcely able to draw breath. I was carried to a new place, vast and echoing, with strange windows that played patterns

7

of red and blue on the stone floor. There was solemn talk and then a voice addressed me.

'I christen you Hetty Feather,' he said, and sprinkled icy water on my forehead.

I cried, trying to tell him that I didn't *wish* to be called Hetty Feather, that wasn't my real name at all, my real name was . . .

But I couldn't speak yet so I simply screamed, and someone tutted and scolded, whispering that I was a bad example to the other babies. I paused for breath and heard thin copycat wails. I took satisfaction in the fact that no one else could achieve anywhere near my volume, for all that I was so small.

I was carted back to the sleeping room in disgrace. Gentle Winnie was there and rocked me gently.

'Hello, little Hetty! No need to cry so. There now. I'll take the christening robe off and fix a bottle for you.'

I was soon soothed, though I hiccuped a little as I gulped my milk. Winnie laughed and hiccuped too, teasing me. I peered up at her, trying hard to focus. She had a round rosy face with fair hair escaping from her cap. She wasn't special like my mother – but perhaps Winnie could be a second mother to me now? I was too small even to smile, but I fixed my blue eyes on her. She looked back, doing all the smiling for both of us.

Other babies were wailing now, demanding attention, but Winnie still held me, whispering my new name. 'Little Hetty Feather! Well, you're light as a feather and no mistake.' She whirled round and round so that I whirled too. We danced in and out of all the iron cots. It felt as if I was flying. I willed Winnie to whirl us right out of the door, away from this chill, puzzling prison, but another nurse spoke to her sharply and she put me back in my little bed, both of us breathless.

I did not cry for my mother that night. I still thought of her longingly, but I consoled myself with the thought that I'd see Winnie in the morning – and every morning after that.

I couldn't have been more wrong. The next day new hands fed me, bathed me, and then dressed me in my uncomfortable clothes. The shawl was wound extra tightly and knotted at the ends, so that I resembled a small woollen parcel – and like a parcel, I was picked up, carried along corridors, taken outside the huge door and posted into a waiting cab.

I was stuffed into a large basket padded with rags. I lay there, too stunned even to scream. What was happening to me now? I wanted Winnie. I wanted my mother. My heart started beating so fast it nearly burst through my shawl. *Were they taking me back to my mother?*

9

The cab door opened again. I heard an infant wail, so sad, so scared. My mouth was shut so it couldn't be me. The cries grew frantic as another child was crammed into the basket beside me. I let out a little wail myself and the other crying stopped in surprise. Then it started up again and I started too. We drew breath at the same time so we were crying in unison. Then I stopped and the other babe stopped too. It was as if we were talking to each other.

Hello! I'm here too. I'm just as anxious as you are.

Where are they taking us?

I don't know. I want them to take me back to my mother.

I want mine too!

Well, at least we have each other.

Our hands were trapped in our woollen shawls, but it was as if we were reaching out and clasping each other.

The cab jerked and the horses' hooves clacked and I remembered my own mother so painfully. Then we stopped and the door opened, and my fellow basket baby and I blinked in the sudden light. Someone took us up out of the cab, swinging us along into a vast, roaring, smoky hall. This brought back memories too. I now know that we were at a vast London station. Soon we were

10

stowed in our basket upon a seat and the train jerked into motion. The other baby and I cried lustily, but the steady chug and whir of the wheels beneath us grew soothing and soon we both slept.

I dreamed that I was back in my mother's arms, but when I woke I was still trussed up in the shawl and stuffed in the basket, and the baby next to me was wailing forlornly. I cried too because I was hungry and thirsty, my stomach empty and aching. The baby beside me set up a mournful descant.

When we lived in the huge bleak building we had always been fed every few hours and our napkins changed. I was now wet and sore, my shawl damp and reeking. So we cried and cried, and then slept some more out of sheer exhaustion – and then the train slowed and stopped. The door opened and we were swung out into the fresh air. Our carrier stamped his feet and marched forwards. There was a clamour of voices with a softer country burr. The basket rocked as hands reached in, lifting out my baby neighbour.

'This here is Master Gideon Smeed, fresh from the Foundling Hospital!'

I heard laughing and cooing and clapping. I was left in the basket by myself! I screamed – and more hands came back for me.

11

'No chance of forgetting this one. Miss Hetty Feather. I'm not sure you'll want her, missus. She might be little but she's a shocker for screaming. She's been squealing like a pig ever since we left London.'

'Oh well, it shows she's got spirit,' said a voice. 'Let's have a squint at her then.'

I was placed in strong arms, my face pressed against a very large soft chest. I snuffled against her. She smelled of strange new things, lard and cabbage and potatoes, but she also smelled of sweet milk. I opened my lips eagerly and I heard laughter all around.

'There! She's smiling at you, Mother! She's taken to you already!'

I was stunned. This was not my real mother. Was she a *new* mother? She held me in one arm, my basket baby brother in the other. Her large hands held us safe as she walked out of the station, children clamouring about her.

'I dare say you'll do a good job with them, missus. You bring on the scrawny ones something wonderful,' said the basket-carrier.

'It's a bit of challenge, two little ones together, but I dare say I'll manage,' she said. 'Let's take you home and get you fed, my poor little lambs,' she murmured in our ears.

We had a home. We had a mother. We were safe.

We never had to go back to the great chill baby hospital again.

Don't mock, I say! I was only a few weeks old. I didn't know any better.

My new home was a small thatched cottage with whitewashed walls, and roses and honeysuckle hanging around the front door. It was small and dark and crowded inside. It smelled of cooking all the time, plus strong yellow soap on a Monday, washday. That was *our* washday too. When the sheets and all our shirts and frocks and underwear were flapping on the line, our mother, Peg, popped all us children in the clothes tub. Gideon and I were tossed in first. Gideon always cried, but I bobbed up and down like a duckling and only wailed if Mother rubbed soap in my eyes.

Gideon was my foundling brother, my baby travelling companion in the basket. He was not much bigger than me, a pale, spindly baby with a thatch of black hair and large eyes that fixed you with a mournful stare.

'There's not enough meat on these two together to bake into a pie,' said our new father, John.

He poked both of us in our belly buttons. It was

a playful poke but we both shrieked. We weren't used to big, loud father people. All men were big and loud to us babies, but when we were older we saw that John was the tallest man in the village, with arms like tree trunks and a belly like a barrel. His voice was so loud his holler could carry clear across five acres. He was as strong as the huge shire horses he used to plough the land. No man dared argue with him because it was clear who would win – but Peg wasn't the slightest bit frightened of him.

'Get away from my new babies, you great fat lummox,' she said, slapping his hands away. 'You're scaring them silly. Don't cry, my lambkins, this is just your father, he don't mean you no harm.'

'Chickee-chickee-chickee, coochie-coochie-coochie,' said Father, tickling under our chins with his big blunt fingers. We screamed as if he was a storybook ogre about to snap our heads off our necks.

'Get out of it,' said Peg, flapping at him with a towel. She gathered Gideon and me up out of our improvised bathtub and wrapped us together in the towel, warm from the hearthside. She held us close against the vast pillow of her bosom and we stopped crying and snuffled close to our new mother.

'*My* muvver!' said Saul, swotting at us with his hard little fists.

He was just starting to walk, though he had a withered leg so that he limped. Father had fashioned him a little wooden crutch. Saul used it to prod Gideon and me. He hated us because he wanted Mother all to himself.

'There now, my little hoppy sparrow. You come and have a cuddle too,' said Peg, hauling him up into her arms alongside us.

'And me, and me!' said three-year-old Martha, burrowing in. Her eyes were weak, and one of them squinted sideways.

Jem held back, his chin held high.

'Don't you want to come and join in the cuddle, Jem dearie?' said Mother.

'Yes, but I'm not one of the babies,' said Jem stoutly. 'I'm five. Nearly.'

'Yes, my pet, you're my big boy – but you're not too big to say no to a cuddle with your old mum. Come here and meet your new brother and sister.'

I was wriggling and squirming, squashed by Saul.

'Here, Jem, you take little Hetty for me,' said Peg. 'Ain't she tiny? You were twice her size as a baby. She's had a bad start in life – both the babies have, bless them. Still, we'll soon fatten them up, just you wait and see.'

I nestled in Jem's arms. He might still be a little boy not yet five but he seemed as strong as our father to me – but nowhere near as frightening. Jem's hands cupped me gently.

'Hello, little Hetty. I'm your brother Jem,' he said softly, rubbing his face against mine.

I couldn't speak but my lips puckered and I gave him my first real smile.

Jem wasn't the eldest. He was the youngest child who really belonged to Peg and John. They also had Rosie and Nat and Eliza, and there were more still – Marcus, who'd gone off to be a soldier, and Bess and Nora, who were away in service.

All these children – so many that your head must be reeling trying to keep count of them all! *I* find it hard enough to sort them all out in my head. The older ones kept themselves separate from us younger fostered foundlings, though Eliza sometimes liked to play schools with us.

She lined us all up in a row by the front step and asked us to add two and two and recite the alphabet. At first Gideon and I couldn't even sit up by ourselves, so we clearly had no chance of coming top in Eliza's school. She lisped our answers for us, and answered for Saul and Martha too. She didn't have to invent replies for Jem. He knew simple sums and could read out of *The Good Child's ABC*.

'A is for Apple. B is for Bear. C is for Chair. D is for Daisy. E is for Elephant.'

I could chant my own way through by the time I was two. Eliza fancied herself a teacher and sat us in the corner if she felt we were stupid and caned us with a twig if we protested.

Jem was the true teacher. He showed me how to eat up my porridge and my mash-and-gravy and my tea-time slices of bread and jam. 'That's right, you're a baby bird. Open your beak,' he said.

I opened my mouth wide and then smacked my lips together, swallowing every morsel, though I was a picky eater and fussed and turned my head away when Mother tried to feed me.

We didn't have any toys. Mother would have thought them a waste of money. She didn't *have* any money anyway. However, Jem found a red rubber ball in a rubbish heap. He washed it well and polished it so it shone like an apple. He flung it high into the air and caught it nine times out of ten, and then kicked it from one end of the village to the other.

'Me, me, me!' I said, on my feet now, but still so little that I toppled over when I tried to kick too.

The others laughed at me, especially Saul, but Jem held me under my arms and aimed me at the ball until one of my flailing feet connected and gave it a feeble little kick.

'There, Hetty, you can kick the ball, just like me!' he said, hugging me.

He sat beside me on the front step and drew me pictures in the dust with his finger. His men and women were round blobs with stick arms and legs, his babies were little lozenges, his animals barely distinguishable one from the other, but I saw them through Jem's eyes and clapped and crowed delightedly.

He helped me toddle down the road to the stream and then held me tight while I splashed and squealed in the cold water. If I kept my legs still while he dangled me, the minnows would come and tickle my toes.

'Fishy fishy!' I'd shriek.

Sometimes Jem turned his hand into a fish and made it swim along beside me and nibble titbits while I laughed.

When I grew bigger, he pushed me in a little cart all the way to the woods and showed me red squirrels darting up the tree trunks.

'That's where they've got their houses, right up in the trees,' said Jem. 'Shall *we* have a squirrel house, Hetty?'

He knew an old oak that was completely hollow inside. He stood on one of the great spreading roots, lifted me up, deposited me inside the tree and squeezed in after me. There! We were in our very own squirrel house. We were only a foot or so from the ground but it felt as if we were right up in the treetops.

'There, little Miss Squirrel. Are you happy in your new house?' Jem asked, poking me gently on my button nose.

'Yes, Mr Squirrel, yes yes yes!' I said happily.

I loved our little treehouse so much I didn't want to go home for tea. I shook my head and protested, clinging to the bark with my fingertips. Jem had to carry me home kicking and screaming. I wouldn't be quiet until he promised we'd play there the very next day.

I went leaping onto the boys' bed at five o'clock in the morning, before Father and Mother were stirring, demanding that Jem keep his promise.

He stayed true to his word, even though I was behaving like an almighty pest. He carted me back to our house in the woods straight after breakfast. He patiently ate another pretend breakfast of acorns and grass, and he helped me care for my squirrel babies (lumps of mud wrapped in dock leaves). He even lined the floor of our house with moss and sprinkled it with wild flowers to make a pattern on our green carpet.

I stupidly babbled about our wondrous squirrel house that bedtime, and of course all the other children wanted to come and see it too, even

Rosie and Eliza. Nat sneered at Jem for playing a girly game of house with a baby, but Jem was unruffled.

'I *like* playing with Hetty, it's fun,' he said, and my heart thumped with love for him.

I wanted to keep the squirrel house just for us, but Jem was far too good-natured. 'Of course you can all come a-visiting,' he told everyone. But then he added, 'But you must remember, it's *Hetty's* house.'

I didn't mind Gideon coming. He was my special little basket brother and I loved him second best to Jem. I was a few days older than Gideon but he was a half a head taller than me now, though still ultra-spindly, his neck and wrists and ankles so thin they looked in danger of snapping. Mother took it to heart that he looked so frail and sneaked him extra strips of bacon and a bite of Father's chop, but the ribs still stuck out on his chest and his shoulder blades seemed about to slice straight through his skin.

Mother tried to encourage him to run about and play in the sunshine with us, but he preferred to cling to her skirts and climb on her lap whenever she sat down to shell peas or darn stockings.

I could sometimes tempt Gideon away to play, though he was incredibly tiresome when it came to my special picturing games.

'Listen, Gideon. Let's picture we're in the woods. We're lost and a huge huge huge howling wolf is going to eat us all up,' I'd say.

Gideon would start and tremble, and when I growled he ran screaming for Mother. She'd scoop him up in her arms and aim a swipe at me.

'Stop scaring the poor little mite senseless, Hetty. I'll paddle you with my ladle if you don't watch out.'

I'd been well and truly paddled several times and I didn't enjoy the experience. I didn't mean Gideon any *harm*. It wasn't *my* fault he was such a little milksop. But I smiled at him even so, and said he could come and visit my squirrel house. I let him squeeze into the cart with me while poor Jem puffed along pushing the two of us.

Gideon squirmed uneasily as I chatted about my house. 'Squirrels might bite,' he said fearfully.

'Oh, Gideon, *squirrels* don't bite! We'll bite *them*,' I said, giggling.

'Can't climb up the tree, Hetty,' Gideon wailed.

'It's easy, Gideon. I can climb. Jem can too,' I said.

'I might fall!' said Gideon, nearly in tears.

'Don't cry, Gideon. You won't fall. Just think, you're getting to see my squirrel house and Saul *isn't*.'

'Saul can come too,' said Jem quickly. 'And Martha.'

'No they can't – too much of a squash,' I said, wishing Jem wasn't always so kind. I just wanted him to be kind to *me*.

It was a waste of our kindness inviting Gideon. To help him appreciate the charm of the squirrel house I made us 'climb' in the air for several seconds before we hopped up into the hole in the tree. This was fatal. He clung to me desperately.

'*Whee* – we're right up in the treetops! See the birds flying!' I said.

'Have to get down! It's too high, too high!' Gideon said, peering down fearfully, though if he reached right out he could put his hand on the ground.

'It's not *really* high, Gideon, look,' said Jem, dangling his leg down.

'Hetty makes it high!' said Gideon.

Jem laughed. 'That's what she's best at, picturing. She's grand at it.'

'I wish she wasn't,' said Gideon, and he closed his eyes tight, as if he could shut out my picturing that way.

Gideon stayed in the cottage with Mother when Jem made me take Saul and Martha to the squirrel house. That was a waste of time too. I didn't mind Martha, but she was so near-sighted she had no idea what a squirrel *was*. She sat in the tree and blinked solemnly, waiting for something to happen. I served her tea in an acorn cup and gave her a slice of fairy bread on a leaf, and she tried to eat and drink politely, but she looked puzzled when there was nothing in her mouth. She started to eat the leaf itself and Jem had to prise it out quickly lest she was sick.

I'd have happily stuffed a whole *tree* of leaves down Saul's throat.

'This is a stupid place. It's not a *real* squirrel house. That's not a fine green rug, that's moss. That's not china, it's leaves. They're not babies. They look like pig poo. *Dirty* Hetty, playing with pig poo.'

I pushed him hard in the chest, because no mother can stand to have her babies insulted. I pushed a little too hard. Jem tried to catch him but he wasn't quite quick enough. Saul fell right out of my squirrel house. It truly wasn't far, and any other child would have jumped up again and laughed – but not Saul.

His eyes slid into slits and his mouth went square. 'You've hurt my poorly leg!' he bawled. 'I'm telling Mother!'

Oh dear. Gideon was clearly Mother's favourite, but she had a particular soft spot for Saul, Lord knows why. She fussed over his leg, rubbing it with different remedies – goose grease and witch hazel – and knitted him a special soft pair of stockings because his boot rubbed his twisted foot. Saul enjoyed this attention and exaggerated his limp in front of Mother for all he was worth.

She was outraged when Saul told tales on me. 'You pushed our Saul out of a *tree*, Hetty?' she said, horrified. She reached for her paddling ladle and I ran to hide behind Jem.

'It wasn't high up in the tree, Mother, and she didn't *mean* to,' said Jem, doing his best to defend me.

Oh, I did so love Jem. But it was no use: I was well and truly paddled, and Mother forbade all of us to play in the squirrel house.

Gideon looked mightily relieved, Martha was indifferent, Jem was clearly sad for me – but I was so aggravated I stamped and shouted and screamed at Mother. You can guess the result. I got paddled all over again, and sent to bed without any supper.

Mother came and sat beside me as I snuffled in the dark. 'Now, Hetty, are you sorry for being such a bad girl?'

'No, I am not sorry. *You* should be sorry for being a bad mother,' I mumbled beneath my blanket.

Mother had sharper ears than I'd reckoned. '*What* did you say, Hetty?' she said.

Oh no, was I about to get *another* paddling? My bed started shaking. Mother was making odd gasping sounds. Had I shocked her so much she was having a fit, like Ruben in the village after drinking too much ale?

I peeped above the blanket in terror. Mother was sitting on the edge of the bed, her hands over her mouth, splitting her sides with laughter. Oh, the relief!

'Don't you grin at me, girl!' she spluttered. 'I've never known such an imp as you. What am I going to do with you?'

'Paddle me and paddle me, even when I'm a big girl like Rosie,' I said, laughing too.

But Mother suddenly stopped. She put her arms round me and hugged me tight. 'Oh, I'm going to miss you so, little Hetty, even though you're such a bad, bad girl.'

I am absolutely certain that is what she whispered into my red hair. I didn't understand. I thought she meant when I had to attend the village school like Jem. I didn't dream I was only a temporary member of Mother's family.

Martha

3

I found it sorely trying when the blissful summer holidays ended and Jem had to spend all day long at his lessons. I didn't miss Rosie and Nat and Eliza one jot, but I missed Jem horrendously. I was left at home with Martha, who was no fun, and Saul, who was a sneaking toad, and Gideon, who was a milksop. They wouldn't play lovely games with me like my dear Jem. Mother didn't want us under her feet in the cottage, but neither did she want us toddling down the village lane and into the woods without Jem to keep an eye on us, so we were confined to the front step and our little patch of garden.

If I suggested spitting in the earth and making mud pies or drawing in the dust with a stick, then Martha would hang her head dejectedly because she couldn't see well enough. If I organized a game of Chase and held Martha's hand, she could run as fast as me – but then Saul would whine, because he always came last with his limpy leg. If I tried a picturing game and pretended a tall oak was a warty ogre and the grunting pig in the back yard a mythical monster, Gideon would play on gamely, but he'd wake screaming in the night. He'd refuse point blank when told to feed the pig our potato parings, and whimper to be held whenever Mother took us for a walk past the oak tree.

I'd hold my breath when Mother comforted then questioned him. Gideon did not wish to tell tales on me and get me into trouble. He would press his lips together when she asked what was ailing him – but Saul *delighted* in getting me into trouble and told all sorts of stories to Mother about me, and then of course I'd get paddled.

Sometimes I decided it was *worth* being paddled to plague sly Saul. I'd see him lick the jam from Martha's bread or drop a spider in Gideon's special mug of milk. I didn't tell stories on him – where was the fun in that? – but I'd creep up on him unawares and punish him. Once I spotted him leaning right over the gate to poke the poor pig with his wooden crutch, laughing when she squealed. I darted forward and gave him a shove. Oh, how *he* squealed when he fell face down in the pigsty. It was so soft with smelly mud he didn't hurt his poorly leg or his other leg either. He just hurt his dignity, lying there bawling, covered in potato peelings and pig poo.

I laughed and laughed and laughed. I even laughed while I was being paddled.

Jem laughed too when I told him, but he said I must take care not to be so bad when I went to school.

'Teacher has a big cane, Hetty, and she swishes it all day,' he said. 'She hurts much more than Mother.'

'She swishes *you*, Jem?'

'She swished my friend Janet for chalking her *b*s and *d*s the wrong way round, and when I said it wasn't fair, Janet had tried and tried to learn, she's just not very quick, Teacher swished me too and told me not to answer back.'

'I don't like Teacher,' I said.

I knew my *b*s from my *d*s already because Jem had taught me. But then I thought of Martha.

'Martha can't write any of her letters,' I said. 'Will Teacher swish *her*?'

'I won't let her,' said Jem stoutly.

But Martha didn't go to the village school when she was five. Mother boiled up a tub of water one evening and gave Martha her own special scrub, even though she'd had a washday bath on Monday. Mother gave her a special creamy mug of milk for her supper and held her on her lap while she drank it.

Father gave Martha a ride on his knees. *'This is the way the ladies ride,'* he sang, jiggling her up and down while she giggled.

Saul whined that it wasn't fair, *he* wanted a ride. Gideon said nothing, but he sucked his thumb and stared while Martha drank *his* milk. For once I didn't complain. I was too little to understand, but I saw the tears in Mother's eyes, heard the crack in Father's voice as he sang. I knew something was wrong – though Martha herself stayed blissfully unaware.

She went to sleep that night as soon as her head hit the pillow. I stayed awake, cuddling up to her, winding a lock of her brown hair round and round my finger as if I was binding us together.

Mother came and woke us very early.

'Is it time to get up?' I asked sleepily.

'Not for you, Hetty,' said Mother. 'Go back to sleep.'

It was still so dark I couldn't see her, but I could tell that she'd been crying again. She gently coaxed Martha up and led her out of the room. I turned over into Martha's warm patch and breathed in her faint bread-and-butter smell, wondering why Mother had woken her so early. I decided I should creep out of bed and go and see, but it still seemed like the middle of the night and I was so tired . . .

When I woke up again, the sun was shining through the window. I ran downstairs, calling out for Martha. She wasn't there. Mother wasn't there either. Rosie and Eliza were brewing the tea and stirring porridge.

'Where's Mother? Where's Martha?'

'They've had to go out,' said Rosie. 'Come and sit down like a good girl, Hetty.'

I didn't want to be a good girl. I wanted Mother and Martha. My heart was beating hard inside my chest. I was very frightened, though I didn't quite know why. I started screaming and couldn't stop, not even when Eliza bribed me with a dab of butter and sugar, not even when Rosie slapped my kicking legs. Jem eventually quietened me, lugging me up onto his lap and rocking me like a newborn baby, but he seemed almost as anxious as I was.

Rosie and Nat and Eliza knew something we didn't. They nudged each other and wouldn't look us in the eye over our breakfast. Jem questioned them persistently, I cried, Saul snivelled, and Gideon didn't get out to the privy in time and wet all down his legs. We couldn't manage without Mother. She was always there, as much a part of the cottage as the roof and the four walls. We were lost without her. And why had she taken Martha with her?

'You know where Mother's taken her,' said Jem, standing on the bench so he was eye to eye with Rosie. 'Tell us!'

'Stop pestering me, Jem. I've got more than enough to do without you and the babies fuss fuss

33

fussing. Hetty, if you start that screaming again, I'll paddle you with Mother's ladle.'

'Don't you dare paddle Hetty,' said Jem. 'She's not being bad, she's just fearful. She wants Mother.'

'Well, Mother will be back presently,' said Rosie evasively.

'Why did she go off without saying goodbye? Why did she take Martha with her?'

'Poor little Martha,' said Rosie, suddenly softening. Her lip puckered as if she was about to cry.

'Is Martha poorly?' Jem persisted, but Rosie wouldn't answer.

When Gideon had been poorly with the croup last winter, Mother had called in the doctor. He had looked grave and said Gideon might have to be sent to hospital.

'Is Martha so poorly she's had to go to *hospital*?' Jem asked.

He lowered his voice when he said the word. We'd heard the villagers talking. Hospitals were terrifying places where doctors cut you open and took out all your insides.

'She's had to go to the hospital, that's right,' said Rosie.

Nat sniggered, though even he looked troubled, his eyes watering as if he was near tears.

Perhaps Martha was very ill, about to die?

But this was all such nonsense. I had cuddled up to Martha all night long and she hadn't been poorly at all.

I clung to Jem and he rocked me again. He didn't go to school that day. He told Rosie he was staying home to look after us little ones. Rosie tried to make him go but she sounded half-hearted. She was glad enough to have him in charge while she scrubbed the cottage and set the cooking pot bubbling on the hearth.

Jem played patiently with Saul and Gideon and me. When the two little boys had a nap after their soup, Jem took me to the forbidden squirrel house, trying his best to distract me. I was deeply touched but it didn't work. No matter how hard I tried to picture, it stayed a grubby hole in a tree. My mind was too full picturing Mother and Martha.

Rosie had once won a Sunday school prize, a book called *Little Elsa's Last Good Deed*. It was a pretty book, bright blue with gold lettering, and I'd begged Jem to read it to me. He'd stumbled through the first few pages until we both got tired. It was a dull story and Little Elsa was tiresomely *good*. She didn't seem real at all. I leafed through the whole book, looking for pictures, but they weren't exciting like the Elephant and the Mandarin and the Pirate and the Zebra, my favourite pictures in *The Good Child's ABC*. I only liked the last picture, with Little Elsa lying in bed looking very pale and poorly, and an angel with curly hair and a shiny hat flying straight through the window to carry her up to Heaven.

But now I kept picturing Martha as the ailing child in some grim hospital, a doctor sawing at her stomach, an angel at one end, intent on stealing her away up to Heaven, and Mother down the other end, hanging onto Martha's ankles.

I sobbed this scenario to Jem and he did his best to reassure me.

'Mother and Martha will come home safe and sound, you'll see,' he said. 'In fact I reckon they're home already, and when Mother finds I've stayed off school she'll be right angry with me. And if you pipe up we've been to the squirrel house, we'll both get a paddling.'

We trailed back home. When we ran into the kitchen, there was Mother at the table, still stiff in her Sunday best, bolt upright because she was wearing her stays, though her head was bent. Martha was nowhere to be seen.

'Where's Martha, Mother?' Jem asked.

'Martha?' I echoed.

'Martha's . . . gone,' Mother said.

'The angels got her!' I said, starting to cry again.

'What? No, no, she's not dead, Hetty,' said Mother.

She took a deep breath. 'Where are the others, Saul and Gideon? Having a nap? Go and get them, Jem. I might as well tell all of you together. But Jem, wait – what are you doing at home, young man? Rosie, why didn't you make him go to school? Oh, never mind, make me a cup of tea, I'm parched.'

We gathered around Mother, staring at her. I nudged up close to Jem. Gideon clasped my hand tight. Saul started snivelling.

'There now, you needn't look so tragic,' said Mother, sipping her tea. 'Martha's very well. She's just not going to live with us any more.'

We stared at her, baffled.

'Where *is* she going to live, Mother?' Jem asked.

'She's gone back to the Foundling Hospital, dearie,' said Mother. 'You were too little to remember when she came to the family.'

'The hospital! They'll cut her into bits!' I wailed.

'No, Hetty. It's not that sort of hospital, my lamb. It's a . . . lovely big home for lots of children who don't have mothers,' said Mother.

'I remember you telling us about the hospital,' said Jem. 'That's how we got Martha, then Saul, and now Gideon and Hetty.' He put his arms round me, hugging me tightly. 'But why did Martha have to go back there? You're her mother now.'

Mother's face crumpled. 'I know, my dear. But

I was only her foster mother. I was simply looking after Martha until she was a big enough girl to go back to the Foundling Hospital.'

'So when will she come home to us?' Jem asked.

'The Foundling Hospital is her home now, my dear.'

'But Martha won't be able to manage without us! She can't see properly, and she's a little slow. She needs us to help her!' Jem cried.

'She will find some other good kind big child to help her,' said Mother. 'Now do stop your questioning, Jem. You're upsetting the little ones.'

She entreated him with her eyes, while Saul and Gideon and I sniffled by her side. We were too little and stupid and stunned to work out the obvious just yet.

4

We all mourned Martha – but within a few weeks we had almost forgotten her. I sometimes dreamed about her and reached out in my sleep for her hand or her hair, and then felt a pang. But Martha's place was soon taken by another little girl, a baby called Eliza.

'That's *my* name!' said our Eliza. 'Oh, let me hold her. She's such a little darling.'

Eliza and Mother fussed excessively over the baby. I thought her a plain, puny little thing, with a mewling wail that was most aggravating.

'Oh, Hetty, you should have heard yourself when you were a baby! You shrieked like a banshee,' said Jem, chuckling.

I was so relieved to see that Jem showed only a mild interest in my new little sister. He was fonder than ever of me, taking me everywhere with him. Father wanted Jem to help out on the farm when he wasn't at school, so Jem took me along too.

I helped with the harvest, I dug for potatoes, I milked the cows.

I thought at first that they were *our* crops, *our* cattle, and all the land was *ours*. It certainly felt that way, for all the other men treated our big father with respect. Some of the young lads even doffed their caps to him. But when Jem took me to the harvest supper in the barn beside the big farmhouse, I saw our father doff *his* cap to Farmer Woodrow.

His wife, Mrs Woodrow, was pouring cider and serving great plates of meat to everyone. She laughingly gave Jem half a tankard and said, 'Only give your sister a sip, young Jem.'

She was peering at me curiously. I stared back at her, and she laughed and pulled one of my red plaits. 'She looks a fiery one!' she said. 'So she's one of your mother's foundling children?'

Jem pulled me onto his lap protectively. 'Yes, ma'am. This is our Hetty.'

'Well, it looks as if your mother's doing a good job with her. How much does she get paid for looking after her?'

I craned round. Jem was red in the face.

'I don't rightly know, ma'am,' he said. 'But our Hetty's worth her weight in gold.'

'What did that lady say?' I asked when Mrs

42

Woodrow had passed along the bench to patronize another village child.

'Oh, take no notice,' said Jem, which of course made me notice more.

'Does Mother get paid for looking after us?' I asked.

'I'm big, not little like you. I don't *need* looking after,' said Jem, not really answering my question.

That Christmas Mother made me a doll – a rag baby with a sacking dress and a scrap of white muslin for a bonnet. She had little button eyes and a mouth that smiled. I thought her the most beautiful doll in the world and cradled her in my arms all the time, even while I ate my roast chicken. Gideon looked longingly at my soft, pretty rag baby, and begged to hold her just for a moment. Mine was the *only* doll. The new baby, Eliza, was too little for dolls, and big Eliza and Rosie great girls long past the doll stage.

Gideon's own present was a little horse carved out of wood by Father. It was an excellent horse with its own brown leather saddle. Saul had a horse with a saddle too, and made it gallop across the floor. Jem and Nat got pocket knives, and Rosie and Eliza bead necklaces, one blue and one green.

Marcus and Bess and Nora, the grown-up children, were not given leave to come home, but

Mother had sent them parcels. She said she'd sent another parcel too, a twin rag baby to mine, specially for Martha.

'Will Martha have a lovely Christmas day like us?' I asked.

'Oh yes, Hetty, she'll have a wonderful time with all her new sisters. I dare say they'll all get lots of presents and fancy food and they'll play games and have such larks,' said Mother. 'Don't you worry your little head about Martha, Hetty.'

I did still worry. Mother did too. When I trailed downstairs that night to trek out to the privy (I'd had two helpings of figgy pudding and had bad stomach ache), I found Mother weeping in a corner, holding Martha's old checked pinafore, clutching it to her chest as if it was her own rag baby.

Mother took me out to the privy and held my hand while I groaned – and then, when I was better, she carried me back indoors. It was chilly downstairs without a fire, but Mother wrapped me up tight in Father's huge smock and cradled me in her arms.

'There now, my lambkin,' she said. 'I have you safe. Don't fret.'

Her voice was hoarse and I felt a tear drop on my face. I wrenched a hand free from my tight wrappings and reached up and stroked her damp cheek.

'There now, Mother,' I said. 'Don't *you* fret.'

She laughed at that, but she was still crying too. She murmured something. I didn't quite catch what she said, but now I am absolutely certain it was: 'I shall miss you so, Hetty Feather.'

The enormity of what was to happen to me didn't dawn until late spring, when Saul went. For days Mother had been favouring him, pretending not to see when he poked me with his crutch, when he tripped Gideon, when he pinched Eliza in her cradle. Mother rubbed his poorly leg and encouraged him to stand up straight when he walked.

'That's it, my little man. Step out like a soldier – left, right, left, right.'

'Yes, I'm a soldier, like my brother Nat. I'm a soldier and I shoot people with my gun,' said Saul, aiming his crutch at me. 'Bang bang, you're dead, Hetty!'

He banged so enthusiastically he struck me sorely in the chest.

'No, *you're* dead, Saul,' I said, seizing the broomstick. 'I'm a soldier and I'm on my horse, gallopy gallopy, and I'm going to whack whack whack you!'

'Hetty, Hetty, stop that now! Stop plaguing us! I need a little time with your brother,' said Mother, pushing me away.

I flounced off in a temper. Jem was at school so I played with Gideon instead.

'We'll play whacking, Gideon,' I said.

'No! Don't want to!' Gideon whimpered.

'I'm not going to whack *you*, Gid. We'll whack Saul. Whack whack whack.'

'Not really?' said Gideon, looking horrified.

'Yes, really. We'll whack him and bash him and stamp on him,' I said.

'We'll hurt him!' said Gideon.

'He hurts us,' I said, pulling up my dress and examining the angry red mark where Saul had prodded me with his crutch.

'We must turn the other cheek.' Gideon was parroting the Bible in a sickening fashion. He always listened hard at Sunday school and absorbed the moral lesson. I listened when there were tales of lions and whales and animals walking two by two into a great ark, but I didn't pay attention otherwise.

I didn't feel like turning my other cheek to Saul, especially when Jem came home from school and *he* started making a fuss of Saul too. He gave him a piggyback ride all around the house and then let him play soldiers, taking pains to fall down dead every time Saul potted a shot at him.

When I tried to join in too, Saul screamed, 'No no no, this is *boys'* play, Hetty,' and Jem didn't dispute this.

46

I stomped off and murmured darkly to my rag baby, hating them all, even my Jem. I especially hated Saul. When Mother bade us kiss goodnight, I sucked my lips in tight and wouldn't kiss Saul. I did not relent, even when Mother shook me.

'You will be sorry, Hetty,' she said ominously.

'No I won't,' I said, but it came out 'Mm mi mn't' because my mouth was still shut into a slit.

'Please, Hetty, there's a dear,' Jem whispered into my ear, but I took no notice.

Saul didn't care in the slightest. He laughed at me triumphantly, eyes bright, cheeks scarlet with excitement, the centre of everyone's attention. He didn't have any idea what was going to happen either, not till Mother woke him at dawn.

I heard him getting cross, then crying . . . then screaming. I sat up, my heart thudding. I ran to him. Mother had him half dressed in his best Sunday clothes, but he was kicking hard with his good leg and pummelling with his arms. All the while he screamed, 'No, Mother, no, I won't, I won't, I *won't* go.'

Rosie and big Eliza were trying to help Mother get him dressed, while baby Eliza wailed miserably in her cradle.

'What are you doing? Why are you dressing Saul in his Sundays?' I asked.

'For pity's sake, Hetty, I can't be doing with your

questions, not now,' Mother gasped. 'Oh, Saul, my sweetheart, try to be a big brave boy.'

But Saul scrunched himself up small and sobbed. I stared at him. Suddenly I didn't care about all his proddings and pinchings. He was Saul, my brother, and I couldn't stand to see him so scared.

I plunged forward and threw myself at him, planting eager wet kisses on his cheek and neck and curly hair. Saul clung to me.

'Oh, Hetty, Mother's taking me away to the hospital and I can't never never come back!' he sobbed.

'No, you can't, Mother! You won't!' I shouted, and I started hitting and kicking her too.

Jem and Nat had to carry me away while Mother persisted with dressing Saul. I don't know whether he continued to cry. My own shrieks were too loud for me to hear anything else. Nat thumped me hard and shouted at me, Jem held me close and whispered soft words into my ear, but I didn't respond to either brother.

I was lost in the horror of losing Saul. I would never ever have the chance to be a good sister to him. I screamed until my throat was raw. I went on screaming until I slept. When I woke, I had no idea whether it was morning or afternoon. The house was horribly silent, though I could hear a little snuffling noise close by.

I reached out across the bed, but there was no one there. The snuffling continued, from *under* the bed. I leaned out, hung my head down, and saw Gideon curled up beneath me.

'Oh, Gid,' I croaked, barely able to talk. 'Come up into the bed.'

But he wouldn't, so I crawled underneath beside him, lying on the cold dusty floorboards.

'What are you doing, Gideon?' I asked. 'Are you pretending to be a chamber pot?'

I said it to make him laugh but he went on snuffling.

'You cry ever so quietly,' I observed. 'I scream and scream.'

'I know,' said Gideon thickly.

His face was so sodden with tears and snot he could scarcely breathe. I very kindly lifted up my nightgown hem and mopped him dry.

'Is Mother back?' I asked.

'Yes. But Saul isn't,' Gideon whispered.

I swallowed. My throat hurt so much I held it on the outside, clasping my neck with both hands. 'I was a bad sister to him,' I said wretchedly. I wriggled nearer to Gideon. 'I shall be a *lovely* sister to you now, Gid,' I said, putting my arms round him.

I was smaller than him, but he felt very little and spindly in my arms. I could feel him trembling.

'Hetty, will Mother take *us* to this hospital?'

'Hush!' I said sharply. It felt so much worse to have Gideon put it into words. I shook him a little and then felt bad. Hadn't I only just that minute promised to be a good sister?

'Of course Mother won't take us,' I said as firmly as I could. I patted Gideon encouragingly. 'You are her favourite. She wouldn't ever take you. And Jem wouldn't let her take me. Mother won't take us. Never never never. Say it, Gideon. *Never.*'

'Never never never,' we chanted.

I thought I would ask Mother, just to be certain sure, but somehow the words dried in my sore throat when I saw her. She was grey with grief, clutching little Eliza to her bosom, tears rolling down her cheeks.

I asked Jem instead.

'You won't let me go to that hospital, will you, Jem?'

'No, Hetty,' said Jem, hugging me tight.

I looked up at his face. His eyes were very red.

'Have you been crying, Jem?' I asked.

Jem *never* cried. He didn't even cry the day one of the horses bolted and knocked him to the ground. He got kicked in the head, so that one side of his poor face was black with bruises for weeks.

'I'm staying here for ever and ever, aren't I, Jem?' I said again. 'And Gideon is too.'

'Yes, Hetty. Of course you are,' Jem said again and again, but he still didn't seem quite sure enough.

I couldn't get to sleep that night, and when I eventually dozed off I dreamed of Saul. A large cruel nurse was picking him up and plunging him into the water butt, trying to drown him like a newborn kitten. I screamed at her and she seized me too, holding me fast by the scruff of the neck. I struggled in the butt and her hand pushed me down, down, down in the murky water. I woke with a start and found there was murky water in my own bed too.

I thought Mother would be cross with me for being such a baby, but she scarcely said a word. She moved slowly about the house, her head bowed. She fed and changed Eliza, and cooked bacon and cabbage for all of us, but most of the time she sat staring at the floor, wringing her big red hands.

Rosie ushered us out of the cottage to give Mother some peace. We were huddled miserably on the doorstep when Father came striding home.

'Hello, chickens.' He ruffled our heads and sighed. 'Oh dear. No cheeps from any of you,' he said, stepping over us with his great legs.

He said no more until he'd eaten his supper. Then he lit his pipe and called us to come and stand by his chair.

'Nat, go down to the Otter Inn and fetch me a tankard of ale. No spilling a drop, do you hear? Jem, you go with him. Eliza, go and see to your namesake sister. See if you can quieten her grizzling. Rosie, take Mother upstairs – she needs to lie down. Be off, all of you. I want to have a word with Hetty and Gideon.'

When they were all gone, he shook his head at us. 'Such long faces! Are you missing young Saul?'

'Most dreadfully, Father,' I said.

He blinked at me. 'Why, Hetty, you do surprise me,' he said. 'You two were always fighting! No doubt you're full of remorse now?'

I nodded. I wasn't yet sure what remorse meant, but the cold, sour, sick feeling in my stomach seemed to sum it up.

'Poor child,' said Father, patting me.

I climbed up onto his great lap and nuzzled my face against his chest. I could hear his heart going thump against my cheek.

'Mother won't take me away, will she, Father?' I said into the rough cotton of his smock. 'Nor Gideon?'

I waited. I felt Father take several deep breaths.

'Not till next year, my sweetheart, when you are both much bigger.'

'No! No, not then, not ever!' I shrieked, pummelling him with my fists.

'Stop that now, missy!' said Father, catching both my flailing hands in his large one. 'You've shrieked enough today, I'm told. There's no point wailing when it can't be helped. Now hush and listen. Mother and I love you, love Gideon, love little Eliza just like our own children. We still love Saul—'

'And Martha,' I said.

'And Martha,' said Father, seeming surprised I'd remembered her. 'But you're not our children, you're little waifs from the Foundling Hospital. You came to us as tiny babies. Mother has a knack with specially frail babies. She rears you up until you're fat and rosy-cheeked.' He gently poked me in the cheeks with his thumb and finger, but I wriggled free, a new thought having struck me.

I was remembering the pig out in the back yard. Mother had a piglet every year, pale and puny. She fed it and fattened it until it could barely sway on its trotters, and then Father came along, and although we weren't supposed to watch, we heard *squeal-squeal-squeal*, and the next day there was fresh pork on our plates.

'Is she fattening us up to *eat* us?' I said, gazing at Father as if he was an ogre.

He stared back at me, slack-mouthed, and

then he roared with laughter. 'Oh, Hetty, Hetty, you're a funny one,' he chortled. 'Of course no one's going to eat you! Mother will take you back to the Foundling Hospital when you're big enough, and you'll live with lots and lots of other girls. Martha will be there so you'll have one sister. And you'll be with the boys, Gideon, and Saul will be your brother.'

'I want to be with Hetty,' said Gideon, but Father paid him no heed.

'We need to be with *you*, Father. And Mother. And my Jem,' I said. 'Please can't we stay? I promise I'll be very, very, very good. I'll never shout or kick or cry ever again.'

'You're a caution, Hetty,' said Father. 'We would love you to stay here with us. We'd like to keep all our dear foster children, but you do not belong to us. You belong to the hospital. All foundlings must be returned by their sixth birthday. Don't look so worried. I'm sure they will be kind to you as long as you are a sensible girl, Hetty. They will school you properly and teach you to be a good Christian child.'

'Will we live there for ever?'

'No, no, they will train you up to be a servant girl and you will go away into service when you are fourteen,' said Father.

'Like Bess and Nora?' I said.

54

'Just like our Bess and Nora,' said Father. 'And then I dare say you can come home to us once a year just as they do.'

I pondered. Last Mothering Sunday I had admired my big sisters in their fancy print dresses and fine stockings when they'd travelled home on a visit. But they'd told Mother tales of cross cooks who beat them over the head with ladles and sly masters who tried to sneak kisses.

'I do not *want* to be a servant girl,' I said.

'Will I be a servant girl?' asked Gideon.

'Don't be dim-witted, lad!' said Father. 'No, no, I dare say you will be a sailor or a soldier boy like our Marcus.'

'*I* will be a sailor or a soldier and go adventuring,' I said.

'You are a very strange pair,' said Father, sighing. 'Now jump down and give me a little peace.'

'But you must tell us about the hospital, Father!' I demanded.

'Hetty, I don't know anything about the hospital. I've never even set foot inside it. I just know it's a good place for little children and you need never say you're ashamed to come from there,' said Father. 'Now stop plaguing me, girl. My head's aching.'

Father might never have been to this Foundling Hospital – but Mother had.

'Come with me, Gideon,' I whispered as Father sucked on his pipe and closed his eyes.

I tiptoed up the stairs, tugging Gideon behind me.

Rosie was guarding the door to Mother's bedroom, but I was bold.

'Father said we must talk to Mother,' I said.

I heard Gideon gasp at my outright lie. Rosie hesitated, but I pushed right past her determinedly. It was dark in Mother's room, the curtains drawn shut as if it was night-time. I could just make out the shape of Mother lying on her back. I wondered if she'd gone to sleep, but when I clambered carefully up onto the bed, her arm came out and held me tight. I hauled Gideon up too and he nestled on her other side.

'My lambs,' she murmured.

'Mother, Father has told us about the hospital. Is it truly a good place?' I asked.

I felt Mother stiffen. She swallowed hard. 'Of course it is a good place, Hetty,' she said.

I wondered if Mother could be a liar too. I lay thinking about it.

'Did Saul cry a lot when you said goodbye?' I asked.

Mother might be a brave liar, but she wasn't foolish. 'Yes, he cried,' she said.

'And did Martha cry too?'

'Yes, Martha cried too.'

'I shall cry,' Gideon whispered.

'I shall scream and kick and be so bad they won't let me stay, and then Mother can take me home,' I said.

5

I had loved Martha much more dearly than Saul but I had mostly forgotten her. However, I could not get Saul out of my head for months. I thought of him living in this huge hospital with so many other boys. I knew most boys weren't gentle and protective like my dear Jem. The village boys had often jeered and pointed at Saul, imitating the lopsided way he walked. One boy had pushed him hard and then laughed when he toppled over. I thought of all the foundling boys laughing and pointing and pushing Saul, and my eyes brimmed with tears.

Then I thought of all those boys mocking Gideon in turn. My fists clenched. I resolved to fight anyone who dared hurt my special brother. I was certain they would not dare hurt *me*. I was famous for my temper in the village. I might be the smallest but I was always the fiercest in any scrap. Mothers came and told tales to *my* mother about hair-pulling and kicking and sometimes outright punching. Poor

Mother was mortified. She tried reasoning with me but I reasoned back.

'They called me names, Mother. Half-pint and Ginger and Runt. I said my name was Hetty and they just laughed. So I hit them and they stopped.'

'Jesus said to turn the other cheek,' said Mother.

Maybe Jesus wasn't teased the way I was. I thought hard, trying to remember the Bible stories I heard at Sunday school.

'*God* said, an eye for an eye and a tooth for a tooth,' I declared, imitating the solemn holy tone of the Sunday school teacher. I hoped it would make Mother laugh. I knew I was in danger of yet another paddling.

This suddenly started up a new fear.

'Do they punish the children at the hospital, Mother?'

'Not if they're good girls and boys,' Mother said.

This was not reassuring. I thought hard.

'Is that why they're there? Because they're bad?'

'No, no, no. It's because their own mothers can't look after them,' said Mother.

'Why can't they?' I asked.

Mother sighed. 'There never was such a girl for questions. You make my head ache, Hetty.'

'Please tell, Mother!'

'Well, dear, some ladies have babies and they can't look after them,' said Mother.

'Why can't they?' I persisted.

'Perhaps they're very poorly. Or they haven't got a dear husband like Father to give them a proper home. The ladies don't want to go into the workhouse' – Mother whispered the word and shuddered – 'so they take their babes to the Foundling Hospital.'

'Do they cry when they say goodbye?'

'I'm sure they cry a good deal,' said Mother.

'Did my first mother cry?'

'I'm sure it fair broke her heart to part with you, Hetty,' said Mother.

'Why can't I go and live with that mother now, Mother, instead of being sent back to this hospital? I don't need looking after. *I* can earn money. I could sing and dance so that people throw pennies at me.'

'You can't carry a tune to save your life, Hetty, so maybe they'd throw tomatoes,' said Mother. 'No dear, you don't belong to your mother now. You belong to the Foundling Hospital.'

I did not want to belong to an institution. I wanted a mother. I crept off by myself, squeezing into the tiny space at the back of the pigsty and the privy. It was private because everyone else

61

was too big to squeeze through the gooseberry bushes and brambles to sit there. I wasn't comfortable because there were nettles and it smelled bad, but I didn't care. I pulled my skirts down over my bare legs, put my head on my knees and wept.

After a long time I heard them shouting for me. I stayed where I was. Then there were footsteps.

'Hetty? Hetty!' Jem called.

I did not reply to him, but I was sniffing hard.

'Oh, Hetty, I know you're in there,' said Jem. 'Come out. Please!'

I did not budge.

'I'm too big to come in and get you,' said Jem.

I heard the bushes rustling, then Jem swearing.

'That's a bad word!' I said.

'I know it's a bad word. Anyone would say it if they were scratched all over by brambles,' Jem panted. '*Do* come out, Hetty.'

I simply wouldn't.

'Then I will have to try to get in,' said Jem, sighing.

He forced his way forward, thrusting his arm through the bushes until his hand j-u-s-t reached my bare foot. He held it tight. I curled my grubby toes into his palm.

'There now,' Jem whispered.

'Oh, Jem,' I said, sobbing.

'I can't bear you fretting about the hospital,' he said.

'I'm not going,' I said.

There was a silence as we held hand and foot.

'I think you have to go, Hetty,' said Jem. 'But perhaps I could go too. We'll pretend *I* am a foundling boy. Yes, I can take Gideon's place and he can stay with Mother.'

'Dear Jem! I wish you could. But Mother and Father wouldn't let you,' I said.

There was another silence.

'I will be so sad,' I said. 'I will have to stay there soooo long.'

Jem had taught me how to count to ten. I tried to count on my fingers.

'I will be there one two three . . . lots and lots of years,' I said dolefully.

'I think it is nine years, Hetty. And then you will be fourteen and quite grown up. And do you know what will happen then?'

'I will have to be a servant, and cooks will hit me and masters will kiss me,' I said.

'Maybe for a short while. But then I will come to fetch you and look after you, and as soon as you are old enough I will make you my wife. I know I am your brother, but not by blood so we can marry! We will have our own cottage and work on the farm and you will keep house and look after our babies.

It will be just like our games in the squirrel house, but *real*, Hetty,' said Jem.

'*Really* real?'

'I promise,' said Jem.

I didn't always keep my promises, but Jem did. I seized his hand, kissed it passionately, and then crawled out of my hiding place to give him a proper hug.

Thoughts of the Foundling Hospital still loomed, but at least I had a wondrous future ahead of me. I just had to wait one two three four five six seven eight nine years, endure a couple more while I dodged blows and kisses as a servant, and *then* I would be sweet sixteen and Jem's bride.

I dressed up in Mother's best white Sunday petticoat, clutching a posy of buttercups and daisies, and tripped around on Jem's arm, picturing for all I was worth.

'You are my lovely big handsome husband, dear Jem,' I said.

'You are my very fine little wife, dear Hetty,' said Jem.

The others laughed at us, especially Nat, but we didn't care. Gideon didn't laugh but he looked wistful.

'I want to be your husband, Hetty,' he said.

'No, Gideon, Jem has to be my husband, but

64

you may come and live with us and be our big boy,' I said kindly.

I was out one day in the meadow playing Bride with my husband and big boy when I heard distant cheering and hurrahs, as if half the village were coming to applaud our marriage. I looked over the grass, squinting in the sunlight. I could see no one. They must be processing along the other side of the tall hedgerow.

Then I saw a gigantic grey head poking up above the hedge – a *huge* head with wrinkled skin and a tiny eye and the longest nose in all the world. I knew what it was!

'Oh my stars! E is for *Elephant*!' I gasped. 'There is an elephant walking along the lane.'

Jem was facing the wrong way. He did not take me seriously. 'Has it come to our wedding as a guest?'

'Don't picture T is for Tiger,' said Gideon. 'I don't like his teeth.'

'I'm not picturing! The elephant is *real*,' I said, tugging at them. 'Look!'

They turned and saw the head bobbing along above the hedgerow for themselves. Jem shouted, Gideon shrieked.

'Come on, let's see it properly,' I said, grabbing their hands.

'No, no, it will eat us!' Gideon cried.

'Don't be such a *baby*. Come *on*,' I commanded.

Jem and I hauled him along between us. We ran diagonally across the meadow towards the stile. The clapping and cheering grew louder, the vast head more wondrous the nearer we got.

When we reached the stile, Jem lifted me up, and then Gideon, and then we all jumped out into the lane. There was the elephant plodding along the path, a real true elephant with such wrinkled skin, such huge legs, such an immense belly! A man in a military coat and great black boots strode along beside the beast, leading him like a dog on a chain.

Another man capered about beside them, the oddest creature I had ever seen, with hair sticking up on end and a bright red nose, his feet in great black shoes that flapped comically. He was banging a drum and dancing. Two big boys danced along beside him, dressed in the oddest clothes – sparkly silver shirts and very short breeches and white *tights*. Jem's mouth hung open in shocked horror, but Gideon pointed in awe. These boys paused and suddenly went forward into a tumble, over and over and up in the air and over and over again.

'Oh my stars!' said Jem, overcoming his scorn at their girlish garb. He could go head over heels and stand on his hands, and frequently did so to amuse me, but he couldn't possibly caper like these boys.

Then came great wagons painted scarlet and emerald and canary yellow. There was a message written in curly writing on the sides of each one. I knew my alphabet but I couldn't figure words properly yet.

Jem read it for us:

'The Great Tanglefield Travelling Circus.

Observe Elijah, the largest elephant in the entire world.

See the exotic animals in our vast menagerie.

Gasp at Fair Flora dancing on the tightrope for your delight.

Chortle at the antics of Chino the Comic Clown.

Marvel at Madame Adeline and her star troupe of horses.

Hurrah for Tanglefield's Travelling Circus!'

Almost at the end of this magnificent procession rode a beautiful lady in sparkling pink – wearing no dress at all, just the merest stiff frill. Her long flame-red hair tumbled past her bare shoulders.

'Just look at that lady with scarcely any clothes!' said Jem.

'See her tiny shoes! Oh, I wish *I* had little shoes like that instead of big ugly boots,' said Gideon.

'Look at her hair!' I said in rapture. 'She has red hair just like mine! See, see!' I repeated, jumping up and down.

The wondrous woman raised her hand and waved to us, and we waved back wildly, honoured to be noticed.

Another comical man with a red nose and bizarrely big breeches came capering along at the very end, speaking into a large horn so that his voice boomed out above the hubbub.

'Come to Tanglefield's Travelling Circus tonight at seven, or Saturday at two. The show will be in Pennyman's Field: adults sixpence, children threepence – a total bargain, so come and see and wonder. Come to Tanglefield's Travelling Circus tonight . . .' He recited it again and again until the procession was out of sight and his voice a tinny whisper.

'Oh, Jem, Gideon, we must go to the circus!' I said, jumping up and down.

'We must, we must, we must!' said Gideon, jumping too, pink in the face.

'But we haven't got ninepence,' said sensible Jem. 'I have the two pennies that Mrs Blood gave me at the Otter Inn for collecting up all the tankards, but that is all.'

'We will ask Mother,' I said.

But Mother shook her head. 'Of course I haven't

any spare pennies for such a senseless thing as a circus. And even if I had, I wouldn't let you go. Rosie told me they were near naked in that procession!'

'They were so lovely, Mother, especially the lady all in pink spangles on a white horse. She had red hair, just like mine!'

'Yes, pink spangles!' said Mother, shuddering. 'A grown woman flaunting herself in front of decent folk, and men capering about foolishly, and a dreaded beast all set to run amok and trample everyone. It shouldn't be allowed. Of course I'm not spending precious money on such a wicked show.'

'Don't spend your money, Mother, spend mine!' I said.

'What do you mean, Hetty?' said Mother, frowning. 'You don't have any money, you silly little girl.'

'I do, I do! The Foundling Hospital gives you money for me.'

'Don't talk such nonsense, child. That money is to feed and clothe you, not send you to a heathen show like a circus.'

'Well, don't give me any food any more, and don't make me new frocks or buy me boots. I'd much sooner go to the circus,' I declared.

'I'll certainly send you to bed without any supper,' said Mother. 'Now hold your tongue, miss.'

I *couldn't* hold my tongue. I wanted to go to

the circus and see Elijah the performing elephant and all the other animals I'd heard grunting and growling inside the wagons. Maybe there were lions or tigers, wild wolves, even a white unicorn with a silver horn. I wanted to see Flora dancing on the tightrope, I wanted to see the comical clown, and oh oh oh, I so wanted to see Madame Adeline, the flame-haired lady in pink spangles.

I started to protest bitterly but Jem put his hand over my mouth. 'Be quiet, Hetty,' he said, tugging me away from Mother.

'But I don't want to be quiet! I want to go to the circus!' I persisted.

'Ssh! I might know a way,' said Jem. 'Just keep your mouth shut and wait till I tell you.'

I clamped my lips together and stomped off after him. Gideon stayed with Mother, climbing up onto her lap. He always hated it when I grew stormy. He was so fearful that I'd get paddled – far more fearful than me.

Jem pulled me out of the door and leaned me up against the side of the pigsty. 'I'll take you to the circus tomorrow, Hetty,' he said.

'Oh, Jem! You really will? But how will you get the money?'

'I think I know a way of getting in without needing any money,' he whispered, tickling my ear.

'But the comic man said sixpence for adults, threepence for children,' I said.

'I know, I know. But Nat told me a way to get in for nothing,' he hissed.

'Oh! Truly? Then let's go now!'

'No, no, we can't go now, Mother would know. This is a bad, secret way, Hetty. We will get into terrible trouble if we are caught,' Jem said, looking wretched. 'Perhaps we shouldn't try. I should set you a good example.'

'Oh no, we *must* go! I don't care if we do get into trouble. I want to go to the circus so badly, Jem.'

'I know. And so do I,' said Jem.

'And Gideon does too,' I said.

'Yes, I know, but I don't think we can risk taking Gideon. He will only start wailing or tell Mother,' said Jem. 'This has to be our secret, Hetty.'

'Our secret,' I repeated solemnly.

'What are you two up to?' said Mother, coming to the back door with a bucket of potato peelings for the pig.

'Oh, we – we were just playing circus, Mother,' said Jem. 'Hetty was pretending that our Polly Pig was the elephant.'

'Yes, yes, and I am the lady in pink spangles on her white horse,' I said, hitching up my skirts and galloping round and round.

Mother sniffed. 'No more talk of circuses, you

71

silly pair. Hetty, you feed that pig, and Jem, you run up to the top field to see if Father needs a hand with the horses.'

'Yes, Mother,' said Jem, rushing off.

'Yes, Mother,' I said too, taking the bucket of peelings. 'Here, Elijah Elephant, eat up – you need to grow a long wavy trunk,' I said, patting our pig on her snub nose.

'Oh, Hetty, you and your picturing,' said Mother. 'Still, at least you've stopped pestering. You can be a good little lass when you really try hard.'

I fidgeted under Mother's warm gaze because I was intent on being as *bad* a little lass as I possibly could. I held my tongue obediently that evening, though Gideon talked non-stop about the circus. He pranced about the table, twirling round and pointing his toes, till Father groaned and gave him a prod.

'Stop that silly flouncing nonsense, lad.'

Gideon's face crumpled and he crouched in a heap on the rag rug.

'He was only dancing, Father, like the circus folk,' I said.

'Boys don't *dance*,' Father said firmly.

I opened my mouth to tell him we'd seen the circus boys dance – *and* tumble head over heels and do handstands – but Jem gave me a nudge. It was never a good idea to contradict Father.

'Boys march like soldiers,' Father said. 'Show him, Jem.'

'Watch me, Gideon. Left, right, left, right,' said Jem, striding about and swinging his arms.

Gideon stumbled along limply, unable to tell his left from his right. 'I don't want to be a soldier,' he said miserably when we climbed into bed that night. 'I want to be a circus boy.'

'I want to be a circus girl, just like the lady in pink spangles,' I said.

'Oh, I wish wish wish we could go to the circus,' said Gideon.

I bit the thumb I was sucking. I badly wanted to take Gideon with me the next day – but I knew Jem was right. He would blurt everything out to Mother, to Father, to Rosie, to the whole family, even to the pig beside the privy. Whereas I knew how to keep my mouth shut when necessary.

6

I behaved in an exemplary fashion all Saturday morning. I even ate all my vegetable soup at dinner time, though I usually fussed and picked out the bobbles of barley and carrot, refusing to eat them because they looked as if they'd been eaten already.

Mother patted me on the shoulder. 'Good girl, Hetty!' she said proudly. 'Now I'm going to feed young Eliza and have forty winks. You children go and play and give me a bit of peace.'

Rosie and big Eliza went off arm in arm, talking big-girl chat of dresses and hairstyles and boys in the village. Nat ran off carelessly, kicking a stone, to meet up with his friends. That left Gideon, Jem and me.

Gideon looked at us happily. 'What shall we play?' he asked.

Jem and I looked at each other.

'Hetty and I were thinking we might play by ourselves right now, Gideon,' said Jem.

Gideon's face fell. 'Are you going to the squirrel house?' he whispered.

'Well, we might be,' I said uneasily.

'But you're not allowed,' said Gideon. 'Mother said.'

'Yes, so you'd better not come, Gideon, or you'll get into serious trouble,' I said.

'But I don't want *you* to get into trouble, Hetty. Or Jem. Please don't go,' Gideon wailed.

'Hush! We *have* to go. Now,' said Jem.

'But I haven't anyone to play with,' said Gideon, and his lip puckered.

'Picture someone, Gideon,' I said. 'Make them up. Here, I can see a little boy standing beside you, a kind, friendly boy. He likes dancing, just like you. You can dance together.'

Gideon looked round wonderingly, as if I'd actually conjured a child out of the ether – and Jem and I seized our moment and ran away.

There were children running from all over the village, courting couples, mothers, fathers, even old grandmothers and grandfathers hobbling along on sticks – all of them bound for Pennyman's Field to see the circus. We could hear the drums and see the top of a great striped tent, with all the red and green and yellow wagons parked in a semicircle behind.

I couldn't see the wondrous flame-haired Madame

Adeline or the tumbling boys in silver. I couldn't even spot enormous Elijah the elephant, but as we entered the field I saw the two clowns with red noses capering at the entrance to the tent. There was a stall selling sweetmeats and another selling little metal clockwork figures, comical cats and mice.

'Oh, Jem,' I said, tugging his hand – and he bought me a penny gingerbread heart hanging on a pink ribbon.

Now we only had one penny left. We needed a whole handful of pennies to get into the tent to see the circus performance. Everyone was standing in a line before the ticket booth, handing over their pennies and getting tickets in return. We watched two boys trying to run right past without paying, but a big man caught them both by the scruff of their necks and sent them flying with a kick to their backsides. I clutched Jem. I was used to being paddled, but I didn't want an ugly big man to kick *my* backside.

Jem squeezed my hand reassuringly. 'We'll go round the back,' he whispered. 'Nat says you can tunnel in under the tent, so long as you're speedy.'

I started trembling with excitement. We ran off, circling right round the tent. My eyes popped. There was Elijah, chained by his huge wrinkled leg to a stake, wearing a red and gold beaded cap with a matching saddle stretched over his vast back. He waved his trunk at us, then lifted his tail – and did an unmentionable thing! Huge dollops of unmentionable things!

I started spluttering with laughter, but Jem put his hand over my mouth.

'Ssh, Hetty,' he hissed.

He'd spotted Elijah's trainer sitting on an upturned tub, smoking a cigarette. Jem pulled me flat against the canvas of the tent so that he couldn't spot us. Three children suddenly came running past, squealing at the sight of Elijah in all his exotic splendour. The trainer man stood up, threw away his cigarette and whistled. Another man dressed in a red tailcoat came running from the nearest scarlet wagon. He held a long whip tight in his hand.

They moved in a flash, seizing the legs of the children as they wriggled underneath the canvas. All three were hauled out, shaken fiercely and shouted at. The redcoat man cracked his big whip and I shut my eyes tight, but I think he simply whipped the ground, not the boys. They were all crying now, even the biggest boy. He wore a blue cap stuck on his head at a jaunty angle. The redcoat man seized his cap and hurled it high across the field, and then all three were shoved and kicked on their way.

My heart hammered hard inside my bodice. What

if the men were to see Jem and me? I shook in my shoes, but Jem held me tight.

'It's all right, Hetty,' he whispered into my ear. 'We won't try while they're lurking here. We'll just have to wait patiently.'

We waited and waited and waited. We heard loud music inside the tent, shouts of excitement, roars of laughter. The circus performance had started. We were stuck outside, still intent on avoiding the eyes of the redcoat man, the trainer and Elijah the elephant. The great beast raised his head every now and then, trunk high in the air, as if he was sniffing us out. He strained against his stake. I held Jem's hand so hard my nails dug into his palm.

Then more men came, pushing a cage of howling hairy beasts. I saw their coarse dark coats, their long snouts, their great teeth – and I thought of grandmothers and little girls in red hooded cloaks. The redcoat man cracked his long whip and strode off after the wolves, all set to subdue them inside the tent.

We heard gasps and cries and sudden bursts of applause. I fidgeted from one foot to the other, desperate, till the caged beasts were eventually wheeled back and off to the side of the field. Elijah and his keeper stayed swaying and sitting, while the two silver-suited tumbling boys came dancing down the steps of another wagon. They paused to rub their hands and coat their sparkly slippers with some dusty stuff in a box.

'It's rosin, to stop them slipping,' Jem whispered.

Then they gave Elijah a fond poke, turned a couple of somersaults for practice, and ran into the ring. We heard more clapping and then a great *'Ooooh!'* as the two boys performed some special trick.

I quivered. I did badly want to see the two boys so I could try to copy their tricks for Gideon. I was tired of standing so still, so scared of these big men with their whips and hard boots, so sad that the circus was happening without me. Perhaps we should simply run away as fast as we could?

Jem felt me fidgeting and put his hands on my shoulders to steady me – just as Elijah's trainer stood up, stretching his arms in the air. I froze – but all his attention was on Elijah. He went up close to the great beast, lolling against the huge front legs. Elijah lowered his head, waved his trunk and opened his mouth. I held my breath, wondering if the beast was about to devour his master before my very eyes. But the elephant looked as if he was *smiling*. He slowly and tenderly wrapped his trunk around the trainer's neck and shoulders so that they stood in weird embrace.

Jem and I stood there, breathless. Then the man muttered something, Elijah unwound his trunk and stood majestically to attention, head up, trunk forward, ears alert. The trainer unhooked his chain from the stake and strode forward in his shiny boots. Elijah followed meekly, like a great grey wrinkly dog on a lead. They disappeared inside a flap in the tent, leaving only a mound of elephant dung on the grass.

'Quick, Hetty! This is our chance,' said Jem, pulling my arm.

We darted forward, praying that no more men would come out of their wagons and catch us. We could see one of the circus men standing by the tent flap – pitchfork in hand! We couldn't simply follow Elijah and his trainer or we'd be skewered. Jem ran round to the side and fell to his knees with a bump, as if in prayer. Then he stuck his head under the tent canvas. He pulled at me to do the same. I copied him obediently, though I was terrified my head would be prodded with a pitchfork on one side of the canvas, my backside kicked by a boot on the other. But I wriggled forward on my tummy into the hot, noisy tent, and at last we were both safe inside!

The ring was brilliantly lit but the spectators all around the tent were in darkness. We could just make out circles of seats, rising in tiers. Jem pulled me up and we edged our way round the back of the tallest tier until we reached an aisle.

Now we had a proper view of the circus ring, scattered with sawdust and edged with a little red wall. Elijah was in the middle of the ring *on his hind legs*, waving his trunk triumphantly while everyone clapped him.

The audience was so absorbed that no one noticed as we crept forward and slipped into two empty seats almost at the front. We watched Elijah perform his tricks, while the silly clowns with red noses darted in and out of the ring, pretending to be scared of him. Then Chino took a clockwork mouse out of his pocket and set it clacking and squeaking, and Elijah lumbered across to a big box and climbed right up on it, as if he was terrified in turn. The trainer pretended to be frightened too, so Elijah bent his head, took him in his trunk, and lifted him high in the air away from the scurrying mouse. Jem and I laughed heartily, loving their antics now that we were safe in our seats.

When Elijah eventually plodded out, the clowns stayed in the ring, capering with some of the children in the audience and playing with buckets of water.

'You can run down and join in, Hetty. I'll save your seat,' said Jem.

I shrank back shyly, not liking the funny clowns with their painted faces and clumsy clothes, scared they might throw their buckets of water over me.

'It's not like you to be bashful, Hetty!' said Jem, putting his arm round me. 'Are you pleased we got into the circus? I told you I'd find a way.'

'I'm very, very, very pleased,' I said.

The band struck up again, and a plump lady in a tight magenta costume came dancing into the ring. She ran over to a vast ladder at the side and started climbing up it, rung after rung, up and up and up, as nimble as a squirrel. She reached a little platform right at the top and clasped a long pole waiting there. We saw a taut rope stretching all the way across the tent, high in the air. She was Flora the tightrope walker!

The lady gave a flourish, seized her pole and stepped out onto the rope! She walked right along it, even pointing her feet and dancing, as if she was a magenta fairy flitting through the air. It hurt my neck to watch her and I could hardly breathe because I was so scared she'd fall. Jem had warned me so many times that I mustn't ever try to edge along the tree branches in our squirrel house. He nudged me purposefully now.

'You mustn't try this lark, Hetty, promise!' he whispered. 'My Lord, isn't she amazing?'

We watched as she skipped along, walked backwards, even *sat* upon the rope, arranging her deep-pink skirts around her and taking a book out of her pocket, pretending to read! These seemed marvels enough, but when she'd advanced all the way over to the other side, she took something from under a cloth on the other lofty platform. It was a little perambulator on two wheels with a baby doll sitting up inside. She took the vehicle, wobbling alarmingly, so that we all went *'Ooooh!'* Then she balanced it on the rope, with dolly still inside. Flora walked steadily back across the rope, as casually as any mother wheeling her baby. When at long last she reached the other platform and took her bow, she seized the doll and made *her* take a bow too.

Then Chino the clown came capering back with his silly friend, Beppo, plus two very little clowns in comical baby gowns with woollen booties on their feet. They had greasepaint on their faces and silly red noses. At first I thought they were simply child clowns, but then I spied a flash of silver beneath the baby gown and realized they were the two tumbling boys dressed up. They kept playing tricks on the clowns, leaping up into the air, landing on their hands and then walking upside down all round the ring. There was a lot of fun and games with bottles and napkins. Jem laughed so much he nearly fell off his seat. Then at last all four clowns took a bow and ran off. That seemed to be the end of the circus, because everyone clapped and then stood up, stretching.

'Oh!' I said. 'Oh dear, Jem.'

'What is it, Hetty? Aren't you enjoying the circus?' Jem asked.

'I think it's wonderful, but now it is ended and I didn't get to see her, the lady in pink spangles with red hair. *My* lady,' I said, nearly in tears.

'It's all right, silly. She'll be in the second half. This is only an interval, Hetty. There's lots more to come, I promise.'

'Really! And so we haven't missed her? We really will see her?'

'Yes, we will.'

'She's the one I like the best,' I said.

'But you haven't even seen her perform yet!'

'I still know.'

'I like the clowns, they are *so* funny,' said Jem, chuckling. 'I should so love to set folk laughing like that.'

'We could have our *own* circus!' I said. 'You could be a clown, Jem, and Gideon can be a boy tumbler, and *I* will wear a short pink skirt and ride on my horse. Let us run away and start our circus, you and me and Gideon, and then I won't have to go to the hospital,' I said earnestly.

'I wish we could, Hetty,' said Jem, looking wretched. 'We could maybe have a circus when we're married. Perhaps we could start a *farm* circus, and you could train the pig to stand on a tub and get the chickens to cluck in time and set all the goats dancing,' he went on, trying to humour me. 'Here now, Hetty. Eat your gingerbread.'

He was trying to distract me. I *did* have a very sweet tooth so I set about eating my biscuit, though it had cracked and crumbled rather when I wriggled under the tent flap. I insisted on sharing it with Jem. We ate every crumb until only the gold star was left. Jem stuck that on my forehead.

Then the band struck up and the clowns capered back into the ring. I fidgeted in my seat, breathless with anticipation. I saw a gentleman throwing daggers at a lady in sparkly drawers, a troupe of seals barking for fish, and a man eating fire as casually as we'd eaten our gingerbread, but I was still restless and unsatisfied. But then, oh, then, right at the end, the ringmaster cracked his whip and announced: 'Now, ladies and gentlemen, girls and boys. Tanglefield's Travelling Circus is proud to present Madame Adeline and her troupe of rosin-backed performing horses!'

I sat up straight as six sleek horses cantered into the ring. I was used to Dobbin and Rowley, the great shire horses in Father's care at the farm. These dancing, prancing horses seemed an elvish breed, so small and dainty. Two were spotted, two piebald and two grey, all with their manes and tails flowing, long and silky. Madame Adeline sat on the first grey, which was almost pure white but with a saucy black patch on one eye, so that he looked as wicked as a pirate. He arched his neck and stepped precisely in time with the music, clearly proud to have Madame Adeline on his back. She looked so beautiful in her pink spangles and short frilly skirt, her flame-coloured hair piled on her head, a black ribbon round her slim white neck.

She stood up on the back of the pirate horse, straight and proud, arms high in the air, never faltering. She smiled at our applause, and called something to the other grey horse. He galloped faster and faster. As he drew alongside Madame Adeline leaped from one horse's back to the other, landing with fairy lightness. She leaped on, from one eager horse to another, she swung herself down till her toes touched the sawdust, then up over the side of the horse, she even stood on her hands while he cantered.

I watched her open-mouthed, marvelling. Madame Adeline jumped through a hoop and landed lightly back on the pirate horse, as easily as if she was skipping down the village lane. I clapped until my hands were sore. She slowed to a trot, still standing, waving at all of us. I waved back wildly, desperate for her to see me.

'Hello, children,' she called.

I piped 'hello' back, standing up in my seat.

'Who would like to come and ride with me?' she said.

I didn't wait for a second. I hurtled out of my seat. Jem tried to catch hold of me by the hem of my dress, but I whisked it away and rushed frantically for the ring. There were already children right at the front, hopping eagerly over the little red wall into the circus ring. Madame Adeline was laughing and pointing, picking her rider.

'No, no, pick *me*!' I screamed, still running. I tried to jump down the steep wooden steps, lost my footing, and hurtled forward, tumbling head over heels.

'Oh my, here's a little acrobat!' said Madame Adeline as I lay with my face in the sawdust, totally dazed.

I felt her strong hands lifting me up. I stood there, trembling. She was even more beautiful close up. Her hair was bright red, her face powdery white though her cheeks were a delicate pink, and her lips thrillingly dark and shiny. I looked up at her and fell totally in love.

'Are you all right, little one?' she asked softly, as if we were alone together, not watched by an audience of hundreds.

'I am, oh yes, I definitely am,' I said, tossing my hair out of my eyes.

'You have lovely red hair, just like mine!' she said, laughing. 'What's your name, child?'

'I'm Hetty Feather, ma'am,' I whispered.

'How old are you, Hetty? You speak up very nicely, yet you can't be more than . . . four?'

'I'm five and three-quarters, ma'am, just small for my age,' I said.

'And you want to ride my horse with me, little Hetty?'

'More than anything!'

She laughed again, her teeth white and perfect, her lips gleaming. 'Then so be it, Little Star,' she said, touching the gingerbread star still stuck to my forehead.

She lifted me up up up and I found myself sitting on the smooth hot back of her horse. She swung herself up behind me, gave a little clucking sound, and the horse started trotting slowly round the ring.

I heard loud clapping all round the circus. Oh my word, they were clapping me! I stopped clutching the horse's beautiful white mane and waved one hand in the air in acknowledgement. Madame Adeline chuckled.

'You're a real showman! All right, Little Star, let's perform a few tricks for your audience.'

She clucked again and our horse started cantering. She held me tightly round the waist but I wasn't a bit scared. I dug in with my knees and arched my back to keep my balance. I heard Madame Adeline laughing approvingly.

'Faster?' she murmured.

'Yes, faster, faster!' I said.

She clucked and our pirate horse gathered speed, galloping now, overtaking all the other horses, round and round and round, so fast that all the seats within the tent seemed to be spinning. My breath bumped from my body. I felt as if I was truly flying, though all the time I was safe in Madame Adeline's grasp. I wasn't sure if the roaring in my ears was my own hot blood or the clapping of many hands.

At long last Madame Adeline shouted a command to the horse and he slowed obediently.

'Now, your star turn!' Madame Adeline murmured into my ear. 'Do you think you could stand up? I will hold you very safely, I promise.'

'Yes! Yes!' I said, scrabbling clumsily onto my knees.

'Steady! Just stretch upwards. I won't let you go,' said Madame Adeline.

I stood right up – but then my foot slipped as the horse cantered forward! I thought for a second I'd go tumbling down onto the sawdust, but Madame Adeline held me firm.

'There now, my Star,' she whispered. 'I told you I would hold you safely.'

I stood still, trying to get my balance, swaying to the left, the right, but after a half-circuit of the ring I started to get the knack of standing with my feet spread, my arms out, my back erect, my whole body moving with the rhythm of the horse. Madame Adeline still held me tight, but I'm absolutely certain I was almost balancing myself. The audience stood up in their seats and clapped, roaring their approval.

Then Madame Adeline clucked to the horse to slow right down. She slid off, taking me with her in her arms. Then she set me down gently.

'Take your bow, Little Star,' she said.

We held hands and bowed low, while the clapping sounded louder than twenty brass bands. Madame Adeline bent and gave me a kiss.

'Well done, my precious child,' she said, and then she patted me on the shoulder to send me back to my seat.

'Oh, Hetty! Oh my Lord, Hetty!' Jem cried when I found my way back to him. He thumped me on the back. 'You were *brilliant*, Hetty.'

'No I wasn't, Jem,' I said modestly, though I wanted to jump up and down and say, *YES, I AM BRILLIANT!*

People right along the rows of seats were turning round, craning forward, calling to me, while my neighbours patted me on the back and added their praises. I scarcely paid attention to them. Madame Adeline was standing on the pirate horse, circling the ring, leaping lightly from one horse to another, flying fairy-like across her steeds, waving and bowing – and then she was *going*, trotting right out of the ring, all five horses in step as they followed her.

'Oh! She's going!' I said, leaping to my feet again. 'It's over!'

'Wait, Hetty. The circus isn't over. Oh, look, it's the clowns again,' said Jem, pulling me back down beside him.

I didn't care for the clowns. I didn't want to watch the tumbling boys. I didn't even wish to see the great golden jungle lion baring its teeth and snapping sullenly at its trainer. I only wanted to see Madame Adeline and I fidgeted and fussed.

'Behave yourself, Hetty,' said Jem sternly, digging me in the ribs. 'Sit quietly. You'll see Madame Adeline again at the end.'

'Will I really?'

'If you are a good girl and sit as still as a mouse,' said Jem.

I tried my best, though I behaved like a very *agitated* mouse, quivering and sniffing. At last the band struck up and all the circus artistes trooped back into the ring. Even great Elijah plodded out, trunk waving in the air. My wondrous Madame Adeline came trotting in on the pirate horse. She waved and smiled at everyone, but her head was turning, glancing this way and that. She was looking for someone. Looking for *me*?

I stood right up on my seat and waved both arms in the air like a windmill, shouting, 'Madame Adeline! Madame Adeline!' Jem had to hang onto me hard by my dress hem.

'Goodbye, Little Star!' Madame Adeline called, kissing her hand and waving just to me.

I waved and waved back. Then everyone paraded out of the ring and the band stopped playing and the audience stopped clapping. Everyone started filing out. Jem pulled at me, but I clung to my seat, not moving until all that was left of the show was an empty tent and dirty sawdust. Then I burst into tears.

'Whatever is the matter *now*, Hetty?' asked Jem.

'I want the circus back!' I wept.

'You're the absolute limit! Aren't you ever satisfied? You've *seen* the circus. In fact you've *been* the circus, doing your double act with Madame Adeline.'

'I want to ride with her again. Oh, Jem, let us go and find her.'

'Don't be so silly, Hetty. She'll be in one of the wagons at the back of the tent, with those big bad men who will catch us and whip us.'

93

'I don't care. I want to see Madame Adeline. I *have* to see her. She will want to see me. I am her Little Star,' I bellowed, stamping my foot.

'You're a little whatsit,' said poor Jem, giving my arm a shake. 'Why won't you ever see reason, Hetty? I try so hard to please you but it's never *enough*.'

I felt bad then, but not enough to modify my behaviour. I pulled free from Jem when we got outside the circus tent, ready to run right round it to the back. I wasn't looking where I was going and fell headlong over a long rope snaking across the grass. I banged my head hard on a tent peg and it hurt so much I burst into fresh floods of tears.

'It hurts, oh, it hurts!' I wailed.

'It serves you right,' said Jem crossly, but he knelt down beside me and cuddled me close. It only made me cry harder.

'Is that our Hetty screaming?' It was Nat, jostling his way through the crowd. 'Did you get in to see the circus?' he said, sounding awed. 'I tried with some of the village lads, but we were all chased away. You two are so lucky! So why is Hetty bawling? My Lord, she's going to have something to cry for when we get home! Mother is beside herself and Father is furious. You're in for a right royal paddling, you three.'

'What do you mean, you *three*?' said Jem.

I scrambled to my feet, scrubbing at my eyes and

runny nose with the hem of my dress.

'Yes, you're really for it now!' Nat chuckled heartlessly. 'Mother's been searching for you for hours. Seems she wanted Giddy for some trifle, and then she couldn't find any of you. Eliza said you might have gone to the circus but Rosie pointed out you had no pennies. Mother's so demented she feared you'd all been *stolen* by the circus men.'

'I wish they *would* steal me,' I said, sniffing. 'I want to be with Madame Adeline.'

'Madame Addywho?' said Nat. 'Not the woman in the parade showing off all her legs as bold as brass? You should have heard what the lads said about her!'

'Don't you *dare* talk about her in that way!' I declared, flying at Nat, ready to reach up and pull his hair.

Jem hauled me back and shook me hard, shocking me into silence. 'Shut up, Hetty, or I shall slap you,' he said. He turned to Nat. 'You said *three*. Is Gideon missing too?'

'Yes, that's why Mother's in such a particular fret,' said Nat. 'We all told her he'd be fine so long as he was with you – but *isn't* he? Has he run off by himself?'

'He was never with us,' said Jem. 'It was just Hetty and me. Oh, Nat, Gideon is truly lost!'

7

We searched the field for Gideon in case he'd tried to follow us, but there was no sign of him. Jem bravely tried creeping round the back of the tent to see if he had strayed there. One of the circus men shouted at him, raising his fists in threat.

'Please, sir, I mean no harm. I'm looking for my little brother. He's lost!' said Jem.

'There ain't no little brother here. Now make yourself scarce before I give you a boot up the backside!'

'Madame Adeline!' I called, hoping she'd come running to rescue us, but she didn't hear me. Other men did though, and came hurrying out of their wagons.

'Clear off, you little varmints. The show's over!' one growled.

'Come on, you two,' said Nat. 'They're going to cut up rough any minute.'

We all had to run for it. We stopped at the edge of the field to catch our breath. I started crying again.

'We'd best take Hetty home, Jem,' said Nat. 'You never know, Gideon might be back home himself by now. I dare say he just hid himself somewhere in the yard. He's that timid he'd never go dashing off by himself.'

We hurried home, Nat and Jem holding me tight by the hands, but even so I kept tripping. I thought of Gideon, all alone, with no kind big brothers to help him along, and I felt truly dreadful.

I stopped thinking entirely of myself and Madame Adeline. Instead I said over and over again inside my head, *Please let Gideon be safe at home!* But when we ran up the path to our cottage and burst through the front door, Mother was weeping, Father was pacing the floor, Rosie and Eliza were wringing their hands, and even little Eliza was crying piteously in her cradle.

They looked at us, mouths gaping. Then Father and Rosie and Eliza gave great whoops of joy and relief, but Mother stared past Jem and me, her head turning left and right.

'Gideon?' she whispered.

We had to shake our heads.

'Oh, Mother, he's not with us,' I said.

'You have lost your little brother?' Mother gasped.

Gideon wasn't technically my *little* brother – he was born five days before me and was a head taller, though very spindly – but I knew it wasn't the right time to be pedantic.

'Hetty and I went off together,' said Jem, his face as pale as whey. 'Gideon was never with us.'

'You went off to that heathen circus, I'll be bound,' said Mother.

Jem hung his head.

'Shame on you, Jem! How dreadful to lead your sister astray,' said Father. 'You deserve a good thrashing.'

'Oh no!' I said. '*I* must be thrashed, Father, not Jem. *I* wanted to go to the circus to see Madame Adeline. Oh, Father, Mother, I rode with her on her horse and she said I was her Little Star!'

Mother and Father barely reacted. At least Father talked no more of thrashing.

'We must start up a proper search for Gideon. I thought you would all be fine *together* – but that little lad cannot cope on his own. He *must* be found. Do you think he tried to follow you to the circus?'

'He certainly seemed taken with the idea,' Mother wailed. She glared at me, as if it was all my fault . . . which perhaps it was.

Father and Nat went out together to look afresh for Gideon. Mother sent Jem and me upstairs to bed in abject disgrace. I cried and my dear brave brother cried too.

'It will be my fault if anything's happened to

Giddy,' he wept bitterly. 'Oh, Hetty, I should never have taken you to the wretched circus.'

'You only wanted to please me, Jem. Don't cry so. It's *my* fault, not yours,' I said, putting my arms round him, trying to comfort him the way he had comforted me so many times.

It was dark when at last we heard Father and Nat coming back. We jumped out of bed and ran to the top of the stairs – but they didn't have Gideon.

'There's no trace of the lad,' said Father. 'We've had half the village out searching. We've even tried the woods, but it's like looking for a needle in a haystack.'

The woods! I suddenly remembered what Gideon had said: *Are you going to the squirrel house?*

'I know where he might be!' I shouted, running downstairs. 'Oh, Father, Mother, he'll be at the squirrel house. He thought that's where Jem and I were going.'

'*What* squirrel house?' asked Father.

'Oh, Hetty, don't start your silly games. Go back to bed,' said Mother.

'No, Mother, Hetty's right,' said Jem. 'It's an old hollow tree. We used to play there. Gideon asked us if we were going there.'

'Put your jacket on over your nightshirt, boy, and show me,' said Father. 'You come too, Nat.'

I clamoured to come as well, but they wouldn't let me. I stayed shut up in the cottage with Mother and Rosie and Eliza and the baby – and one after another we all wept, longing for Father and the boys to come back, but terrified too, lest they didn't find Gideon.

'I am very wicked,' I wept, sidling up to Mother.

'Yes, you *are* wicked, Hetty,' said Rosie. 'Poor Mother, see what you've done to her.'

Mother had her head in her hands and was crying hard, her whole face wobbling in a distracting fashion.

'What shall I do if my little boy's dead?' she wailed. 'And what will the hospital say? They'll think I'm unfit to care for any more children. They'll take little Eliza away from me—'

'They shan't do that!' said Eliza, cradling her little namesake in her arms. 'Oh, Hetty, this is all your fault.'

I burst out crying afresh, because no one seemed to mind about *me*. I closed my eyes and pictured Madame Adeline.

'Come, my precious Little Star,' she said, holding her arms out. 'Come and live at the circus with me. We will perform every night. I will be the Big Star and you the Little Star. I will give you your own white pony. You will dance on its back and everyone will clap and clap. No one shall ever scold you, dearest Hetty. Jem will come and see us perform in the ring every night, and *he* will clap and clap and you will wave to him. He will tell people proudly that you are his little sister. Rosie and Eliza will beg you to wave at them too, but you won't take any notice of them. You don't want them to be your sisters any more. You don't want Nat to be your brother . . .' But then my vision of Madame Adeline faltered. She could not say the word Gideon. He was my brother for ever and ever, my fellow foundling, almost my twin. If he ceased to be my brother, if he had perished somewhere in the dark woods, then I would go demented with guilt and sorrow.

Madame Adeline faded until she was the merest glimmer of pink. I pictured Gideon instead, howling with terror in the great dark wood, calling for Jem and me until his voice cracked, running and stumbling and falling, lying there in the mud and the leaves, white and limp and broken. Wild creatures scuttled past him but he didn't blink his eyes. They were open for ever in his stark woodland grave . . .

I frightened myself so badly I started screaming. Rosie shook me hard.

'Stop that silly shrieking, Hetty! Shame on you! You just want to be the centre of attention. Stop it this instant.'

I couldn't stop. I managed to quell the noise, but

huge sobs still shook me every second, and tears rolled down my cheeks in a torrent. After a long, long while Mother held out her arms wearily. I crept forward and climbed on her lap. She held me close and whispered soothingly, but she was trembling too, her whole body tensed for the sound of footsteps.

Then at last we heard Father's big boots, the boys' scuffles. Father strode into the cottage and this time *he had Gideon in his arms*. He was holding him like a baby. Gideon's head lolled and his spindly arms and legs dangled lifelessly.

'Oh, he's dead, he's dead!' I cried.

'Hush, Hetty. The little lad's sleeping, but he's fair perished,' said Father.

Mother leaped up, brushing me blindly out of the way, and seized Gideon to her bosom. She wrapped her shawl around him, while Rosie ran for a blanket. Mother had kept the fire burning, so Eliza soon had a stone bottle filled with hot water and bound in a towel, to warm Gideon's icy limbs.

Father knelt beside Mother and spread his own jacket around them both, cradling Gideon's pale face with his big rough hands. Gideon's eyes were half open but he didn't seem to see us. His mouth was open too, but when Rosie tried to feed him a little warm gruel, it dribbled down his chin.

'He *is* dead!' I gasped.

'No, no, he's breathing, dear,' said Mother, bending

103

her head and putting her ear against Gideon's chest. 'We just need to warm him up a little.'

'He found his way to the squirrel house all by himself,' said Jem. 'But he couldn't hitch himself up into the tree. We found him lying underneath it, shivering and shaking. He cried out when Father picked him up but he's not said anything since. But you mustn't fear, Hetty. I dare say he'll be fine by morning.'

Mother and Father took Gideon to sleep in their own bed, circling him in their arms. I wanted to climb in with them, but they sent me away.

'They don't love me any more because I am so wicked,' I wept.

'Of course they love you, Hetty. You know *I* love you too,' said Jem, letting me scrabble under the covers with him. He wiped my eyes with the sleeve of his nightshirt and stroked my tangled hair. 'I'll always always love you, Hetty, no matter what,' he promised me.

When I went to sleep at last, I dreamed that Gideon never woke up. He lay stiff and white in a glass coffin like Snow White in the storybooks. Mother prayed at his head, Father prayed at his feet, and my brothers and sisters prayed on each side along the length of the coffin. When I tried to join them, they elbowed me out of the way, even Jem.

'Go away, Hetty. I don't love you any more. You are too wicked,' he said harshly.

I crept away by myself. No one noticed when I slunk out of the door. I wandered disconsolately down the lane until I heard the sound of distant drumming. I quickened my pace. By the time I could see the circus I was running fast. There, galloping towards me, was Madame Adeline on her fine white pirate horse. She wore her beautiful pink outfit, with pink roses twined in her flame-red hair. A long gossamer train flew out behind her like a flag.

'My Little Star!' she cried, and she leaned down and scooped me up beside her.

'Oh, Madame Adeline, may I come and live with you?' I said.

'Of course, my precious child!' she said, clasping me close, smelling wonderfully of sweetmeats and roses. She wrapped me tightly in her train. 'Indeed, you *are* my child, my own dear long-lost daughter, and now we will live together for ever. You are not really called Hetty Feather. I named you—'

'Hetty! *Hetty!*'

It was Jem, tugging me.

'Stop it, Jem,' I said furiously, struggling to stay in my wondrous dream.

'But you've wound all the bedclothes right round yourself! You must share them, Hetty.' He tugged hard.

'I'm *not* Hetty,' I said, tugging back because I needed them to be Madame Adeline's train. Then she could bind me close and keep me in the dream.

But it was no use, the dream was fading fast. I vanquished the blanket and lay there, my heart beating hard against my ribs. I relived each dream moment, whispering Madame Adeline's words.

You are my child, my own dear long-lost daughter.

Could it be true? There had been this instant connection between us, almost as if we had recognized each other. We both had flame red hair, pale faces, slender bodies. I had ridden the horse almost as fearlessly as she. Why hadn't I realized sooner? Madame Adeline was my own true mother!

She would not have wanted to be parted from me when I was a babe – but how could she look after me when she rode her horses every day? Folk looked down on beautiful ladies at the circus. I only had to think of Mother's reaction. Perhaps my dear real mother felt she was giving me a better chance in life sending me to the Foundling Hospital? But now I was absolutely certain she was missing me sorely. Perhaps right this moment she was lying awake, wondering if the little child with the red hair and the star on her forehead could possibly be her very own.

I sat upright in bed.

'What is it now, Hetty?' Jem murmured sleepily.

'I have to go to the circus,' I said.

'*What?*' Jem caught hold of me and pulled me back into bed. 'Are you truly demented? It's half past four in the morning. And I *took* you to the circus and look what happened!'

'You don't understand, Jem,' I said.

'I *know* I don't understand! You really are the limit, Hetty.'

'I *have* to go to the circus. Don't you see? Madame Adeline is my *mother*!'

'What did you say? Oh, Hetty, really!' He started laughing.

I pummelled him hard. 'Don't laugh at me! It's true. She told me in my dream.'

'Yes, in your *dream*, Hetty. Not really,' said Jem patiently, trying to catch my wrists. 'Stop hitting me!'

'But you have to believe me. It *is* real. We are so alike, Madame Adeline and me.'

'No you're not! Not the slightest little bit.'

'Look at our hair!'

'Hetty, I don't think Madame Adeline's hair is *really* red, not that bright colour. I think she maybe dyes it.'

'*My* hair is bright, and I do not dye mine. We are so totally alike. Take me to the circus and you will see for yourself.'

'I'm not taking you back to the circus.'

'Then I will go by myself.'

'If you try to do that you will get lost. You are too little to find the way. It will kill Mother if she loses another child. And Father will most likely kill *you* if he finds you – and me, into the bargain. Now lie down properly and go back to sleep like a good little girl.'

He forced me down on my pillow but I couldn't sleep, though I tried hard to seek refuge in my dreams. Eventually I heard Father getting up for work. I slid out of bed quickly and caught him as he went down the stairs.

'Why are you up so early, little minx?' he asked.

'I couldn't sleep, Father,' I said.

'I'm not surprised. I dare say this whole circus escapade was all down to you, Hetty. You have a knack for leading the others astray. Jem's a sensible lad but he's soft as butter where you're concerned.' Father shook his head at me. 'I don't know what to do with you, child. Perhaps it's just as well you won't be with us much longer.'

I felt as if Father's huge fist had punched me straight in the stomach.

'Yes, well might you hang your head,' he said. 'That little lad in my bed was a hair's breadth from death when we found him. He's still icy cold for all he's swaddled in shawls like a newborn babe.'

I dodged round Father and ran into his bedroom.

Mother was lying in bed, propped up on one elbow, crooning a lullaby. Gideon was in a little huddle beside her. I edged towards him, expecting to see a little Jack Frost brother, hair hoary white, icicles hanging from his nose and chin. But Gideon looked almost his usual self, though he was very pale.

I climbed up into bed beside him. Mother put her finger to her lips, frowning at me. She clearly wanted Gideon to sleep – but his dark eyes were wide open.

'Hello, dear Gideon,' I whispered. 'Are you better now?'

Gideon didn't seem able to tell me. His mouth opened and moved but no sound came out.

'I can't hear you,' I said, nuzzling closer, so that my ear was inches from his face.

'Hetty, Hetty, don't squash him! Go back to your own bed,' said Mother.

'But I—'

'I! I! Can't you think of anyone else but yourself, child?' said Mother sharply.

Gideon whimpered at her tone.

Mother glared at me. 'See, you're upsetting your brother. Go *away*!'

All right, I thought. I *will* go away. You don't want me. Father doesn't want me. Even Jem has had enough of me. You're all sending me to the hospital soon anyway. So I'll go away now and save you the trouble.

I stomped out of Mother's bedroom and then crouched at the top of the stairs, tucking my knees up under my nightgown and rubbing my cold feet. I longed for a warm jacket and my boots, but they were in my bedroom and I knew Jem would be suspicious if he saw me putting them on. I took Gideon's boots instead, lying on the landing, still caked with mud and grass from his trek into the forest. They were too big for me but it couldn't be helped. I had difficulty with the laces. I was used to Jem helping me tie neat bows, but I turned and twisted them until they held fast.

I waited, shivering, until I heard Father shut the front door on his way to the farm. I couldn't count beyond ten but I had some idea of time and waited several minutes until I judged it safe. Then I tiptoed downstairs as best I could in my ill-fitting boots. I grabbed a hunk of bread from the larder, and wound an old sack about my shoulders in lieu of a coat. I could not yet write, apart from my name, so I did not leave them a note. I felt a pang for not saying goodbye to Jem, but it couldn't be helped.

I went out the front door, and marched off to join the circus and my true mother.

Oh dear, I am shaking now as I write this. I did not get lost. I was only five then, but I was a very determined child. I hurried through the village, glad that most folk were still in their beds because I looked a queer sight in my sacking and borrowed boots. I could not wait for my own dear mother, Madame Adeline, to clothe me in some beautiful pink outfit so that I looked like a little fairy.

I found exactly the right hole in the hedge to scrabble through to get into the fields. I ran across one, the dewy grass soaking the hem of my night-gown. I stumbled several times, my boots rubbing my bare feet raw, but I was sure I would soon be shod in pink satin slippers. I reached the edge of the field. I fought my way through the second hedge.

There I was, in the circus field – but *where was the circus*? I opened my eyes wide, staring all around. Where was the big tent, the wagons, the horses, Elijah the elephant? Where, oh, where was Madame Adeline?

Had I come to the wrong field after all? Was it on through another hedge? Yes, I had simply miscalculated. But as I wearily started crossing the empty field, I saw the huge circle of crushed grass, scatterings of sawdust, the print of wagon wheels in the earth. Rubbish blew in the wind like gaudy flowers – all that was left of Tanglefield's Travelling Circus.

I had found my true mother – and lost her again.

I trudged all the way back home again. What else could I do? I didn't know when the circus had gone. If they'd packed up and travelled all night after the show, they could now be many miles north, south, east or west. And I was too small and scared to run any further. I was freezing cold in spite of my sack, my nightgown was soaked through and stained all over with mud where I'd stumbled, and Gideon's boots seemed intent on paring every inch of flesh from my feet.

I trailed all the way back to the cottage, and as I hobbled homewards I did think with satisfaction that they'd maybe make a fuss of me now. I must have been missing for hours. I thought of the to-do when Father returned with Gideon in his arms. I hoped for just such rejoicing when I limped through the front door. Mother would cast Gideon aside and swoop me up into her arms, Nat would clap his hands, Rosie and Eliza would kiss my pinched cheeks, and Jem . . .

I gave a genuine little groan as I thought of dear Jem. How could I have left him without saying a single word of farewell? He would be heartbroken. He might be running crazily round the village this very minute calling for me, striding through the woods, wading through mud and mire, calling my name until his voice cracked. I could picture him so vividly . . .

But I cannot always picture the banal truth. Jem wasn't out searching for me frantically. Jem was fast asleep in his bed, not having missed me for one moment. *None* of the family were aware that I had run away to join the circus. They were all still in their beds, snoring. Even baby Eliza was fast asleep in her cot, though it was past her feeding time.

I thought I'd changed the world but no one had noticed. I got into trouble with Mother later because of the state of my nightgown, but she was too distracted with Gideon to concentrate on giving me a paddling.

Gideon did not get properly better. He warmed up, he ate and drank, he walked around in his uncomfortable boots, he did his few chores – but he seemed like a ghost child now. He was more nervous and timid than ever. If I jumped out at him and went *'Booo!'* he would cower away from me and cry, even though he could see it was only me. He could still laugh, just about, though I laboured long and hard at this. I pulled faces, I tickled him, I said silly rude things, I stood on my hands and waved my legs in the air so he could see my drawers – and yes, Gideon's nose might wrinkle, his mouth twitch into a tiny smile. But he didn't talk any more. He'd always been a quiet child – well, *any* child living with me would seem silent by comparison – but now he didn't talk at *all*.

Mother coaxed him, Father badgered him, the big girls petted him, Nat and Jem tried tricking him and I certainly plagued him, but he stayed resolutely silent.

I could offer him some trinket that I knew he really coveted, perhaps a glass bead as blue as the sky. I'd put it on the table in front of him and say, 'Do you like this bead I found, Gideon?'

He'd nod.

'Would *you* like it?'

He'd nod more eagerly.

'Well, all you have to do is say, "Please may I have the bead, Hetty?" and it is yours.'

Gideon's head drooped.

'Come on, Gid, it's *easy*. You can say it, you know you can. You don't even have to say please. "Can I have the bead?" That's all you have to say.'

Gideon's head drooped further. I took hold of his

jaw and tried to make his lips mouth the words. No sound came out, though tears started to roll down his cheeks.

'Are you *hurting* Gideon, Hetty?' said Mother, bustling into the room.

'No, no, Mother, I'm simply encouraging him to speak,' I said.

Mother paused, diverted by my quaint speech. 'You're a caution, Hetty. I've never known a child like you. I don't know what's to become of you – or Gideon either.' She suddenly sank to her knees and opened her arms wide, hugging both of us to her bosom.

I cuddled up close to Mother. She might not have the starry glamour of Madame Adeline, she might be rough with her tongue, she might paddle me hard for my naughtiness, but she was the only mother I'd known and I still loved her dearly.

'Don't send us to the hospital, Mother!' I begged.

She started, as if I'd read her mind. 'I wish I could keep you, Hetty,' she said, looking straight into my eyes. 'I can't bear to let you go – and it breaks my heart to think of little Gideon there, especially not when . . . when he's not quite himself.'

I wriggled guiltily.

'You will look after your brother when you're at the hospital, Hetty?' Mother said earnestly. 'He can't really look after himself. He'll need you to speak up for him. Will you promise you'll do that, dear?'

'I promise,' I said, though I was shivering so I could hardly speak.

'It's not as if *all* the children will be strangers,' said Mother, perhaps trying to convince herself as well as Gideon and me. 'Saul will be there, and dear little Martha. They will look out for both of you.'

I didn't have Mother's faith in my sister and brother. Besides, the only brother I wanted looking out for me was my own dear Jem.

I started following him like a little shadow, tucking my arm in his, huddling close to him at the table, sitting on his lap. He was so patient with me, playing endless games of picturing: we were pirates, we were polar bears, we were soldiers, we were water babies, we were explorers in Africa – and the simplest and most favourite game of all, we were Hetty and Jem grown up and living together in our own real house, happily ever after.

I was used to dear Jem indulging me, but Gideon was the family favourite. They treated him now like a very special frail baby, dandling him on their knees and ruffling his dark locks. Even Father stopped trying to turn him into a little man. He hoisted him onto his huge shoulders and ran around with him, pretending to be one of his own shire horses.

Gideon squealed in fear and joy, though he still didn't speak.

But suddenly I seemed to be the pet of the family too. Father took me out in the fields with him and held me tight while I rode on the shire's back. The horse was too big to be a comfortable ride and was a simple Goliath plodder compared to Madame Adeline's elegant performing pirate horse – but even so I kicked my heels and held my arms out, pretending I was dressed in pink spangles in the circus ring.

Nat had started whittling simple toys from pieces of wood. He fashioned me a horse and Gideon an elephant. To be truthful, the only way we could distinguish them was by size, but it was kind of my big brother all the same.

Rosie and Eliza were surprisingly sweet to me too, letting me play grown-up ladies in their best dresses, even tying my hair up high and fastening it with pins. We played we were three big girls together and they sprayed me with their precious lavender perfume and told me special big-girl secrets.

Even little Eliza seemed extra fond of me and smiled and waved her tiny fists in glee whenever I picked her up.

'You're like a real little mother, Hetty,' said Mother, sounding truly proud.

I basked in all this praise and attention. For

a child considered ultra-sharp, my wits weren't working at all. It wasn't till the last night that it actually dawned on me. Rosie and Eliza sang baby songs to Gideon and gave us great kisses all over our cheeks until even my pale brother turned rosy as an apple. Nat gave us a bear hug. Father sat us both on his big knees and jiggled us up and down, playing, *This is the way the ladies ride*. Mother made us each a cup of cocoa brimming with cream, a rare treat. Just two cups, one for Gideon and one for me. I looked over at Jem. I knew he loved cream too.

'Can't Jem have cocoa too, Mother?' I asked.

'No, dear, it's just for you two little ones,' said Mother. 'Now drink it all up like a good girl before I get you both ready for bed.'

I went to sit beside Jem, who had been very quiet all evening. 'Take a sip, Jem,' I whispered.

Jem shook his head quietly. He kept his head bent but I saw he had tears in his eyes. My stomach squeezed tight. Why was Jem so sad?

I saw Mother boiling up a great pan of water on the stove: hot washing water, though it wasn't bath night. Then at last it dawned on me. She was going to take Gideon and me to the hospital *tomorrow*!

I'd known for years that I had to go back to the Foundling Hospital. For the past few months folk had referred to it openly and often – I had myself. But it had still seemed distant, long in the future, not anything to worry about right this minute. But now suddenly it had sprung upon me. This was *it* – my last night in the cottage.

The sweet cocoa soured in my mouth. I crept so near Jem I was practically in his lap. He saw I'd realized, and put a finger to his lips, nodding at Gideon. My little brother was smiling as he sipped his cocoa. Mother pulled off his shirt and said, 'Skin a rabbit,' and Gideon made a bunny face, twitching his nose. He was almost his old self again, though he still wasn't talking. I knew if I cried out that we were going to the hospital the very next day, Gideon would be frightened into fits. So I closed my mouth, pressing my hands over my lips to make certain I would not talk.

Jem hugged me tight. 'What a dear brave girl you are, Hetty,' he whispered in my ear.

I didn't want to be brave. I wanted to scream and make a huge despairing fuss, but I could see that would spoil everything for Gideon – and for me too. So I held my tongue and choked down my cocoa, though I couldn't stop my tears brimming as I gazed around the little room that had been my home for the last five years. I could not bear to think I would never see it again. I could not bear to think I would not see Mother, Father and my brothers and sisters, my family. I especially could not bear to think I would never see my dear Jem again.

The tears rolled down my face and I hid my head in my hands.

'Look at Hetty, she's tired herself out!' said Eliza.

'A quick bath in the tub and then you'll be tucked up in bed, Hetty dear,' said Rosie.

I let my sisters undress me and lift me up into the soapy water. Mother washed me all over and rubbed the soapsuds into my hair so hard I thought the red might run away with the water. Then I was towelled vigorously, a nightgown thrust over my head, and I was carried upstairs. I kept my eyes closed all the time, even when everyone gave me a goodnight kiss. I was tucked up beside Gideon, who was already genuinely asleep. I lay there, waiting.

Then Jem crept upstairs. He got into bed beside me and put his arms around me. I buried my head in his chest and wept.

'There, Hetty. There, there, dear Hetty,' he murmured.

'I don't want to go!' I sobbed. 'I shall run away. Yes, I shall run away right now.'

'Where will you run to, Hetty?'

'I shall find the circus. I shall live with Madame Adeline,' I said. 'Perhaps she really is my mother.'

'How will you find the circus? It could be right up in Scotland or way down in Cornwall. The circus is *gone*, Hetty.'

'I'll still run away,' I said.

'But what will you eat? Where will you live? Who will look after you?'

'I will eat berries and nuts, and I will sleep curled up in trees and haystacks and barns.' I paused, trying to work it out in my head. 'And – and if you will run away too, Jem, then *you* can look after me.'

'Oh, Hetty. I wish I could. I've tried to plot it out. I could maybe get farm work far away where they don't know me – though I'm not really big or strong enough yet. And you can't work for years and years, Hetty.'

'You could do the work for me.'

'Yes, but they wouldn't let you tag along too. They would say you needed to be cared for. They would seize you and put you in the workhouse, and that would be much worse than the hospital. So don't you see, Hetty, we *can't* run away, though I wish we could with all my heart.'

'Oh, Jem, please please please don't let them take me away,' I wept, past reasoning.

He held me close and murmured stories in my ear about my time at the hospital. 'Everyone will like you – how could they not? – and you will make good friends there. You will learn lots at school and the years will go by in a blink, and *then*, when you are all grown up, I will come and find you, remember?'

'We will truly have our own house?' I snuffled.

'Yes, our own dear house, and we will live there together. And when I am an old old man with a grey beard and you are an old old lady, hopefully *not* with a beard—'

I giggled in spite of everything.

'Then we will scarcely remember we were ever separated. I promise we will be together and live happily ever after, just like the fairy tales.'

He told me this over and over until I went to sleep in a soggy little heap on his chest – and whenever I woke in the night he whispered it all over again.

Then suddenly Mother was shaking me, easing me out of bed. I clung frantically to Jem.

'There now, Hetty,' he said. 'Let me dress her, Mother. You go and get Gideon ready.'

Jem did his best to dress me in my best clothes, though I did not make it easy for him, keeping my arms pinned to my sides and curling my feet so they couldn't be stuffed into my boots.

'Stop being so difficult, Hetty dear,' he said wearily. 'I will dress too and come with you as far as I can. Try to be a big brave girl.'

I didn't feel big and brave. I felt very very small and very very scared, but I did not make a fuss as Jem fastened my Sunday frock, tied the ribbons of my starched pinafore and buttoned my boots. I washed my face and Jem brushed my hair for me, running his hands through the silky newly-washed strands.

'At least I'll be able to pick you out from a crowd of hundreds, Hetty,' he said. 'No one could ever have as red hair as you. There! You look lovely now.'

I gave him a fierce hug.

'Careful! You'll crease your pinafore,' said Jem.

'I hate silly pinafores,' I said.

Oh, how I longed to be barefoot in my old flower-sprigged cotton dress, ready for a day's larking with my dear brother. I clutched him harder and he held me fast.

'Ready, children?' Mother called.

She had Gideon dressed now, but he was still half asleep, his eyes drooping. We went downstairs and Mother cut us bread and poured us milk. I was too fearful to eat and Gideon too tired. I sat on Jem's lap and Gideon sat on Mother's. It was as if we'd regressed five years and were back to being little babies.

'It's time to go,' said Mother.

Gideon wriggled a little, looking puzzled.

'Come on, my pet. Let Mother carry you,' she said, hoisting him up in her arms.

He held his wooden elephant tight by the trunk. I had my dear old rag baby *and* my new horse, but

I wished Jem had made it for me and not Nat. But Jem had another gift for me, a tiny present in a twist of rag. I opened it up carefully and found a silver sixpence, polished until it shone. I stared at it in awe.

'I earned it running errands. I'll earn you many more sixpences,' Jem whispered earnestly. 'Then, when you're bigger, I can take you to the circus in style.'

'Oh, Jem!' I said. 'Dear, dear Jem.'

'Keep it safe in your pinafore pocket. You can spend it on anything you like.'

I held the sixpence tight in my hand. I knew I would never be tempted to spend a penny of it. I would do my level best to hang onto it for ever.

Father was already out at the farm and Nat and the girls were still asleep. Even baby Eliza was quiet in her cradle. I could not say goodbye to them, so instead I whispered goodbye to my little stool and the scrubbed table and the coloured pictures on the walls. They were mostly scenes from the Bible – baby Jesus in the stable, Joseph in his coloured coat and Daniel in the lions' den. The picture I liked best hung halfway up the stairs: two chubby children in nightgowns with a tall white guardian angel spreading his wings over them protectively.

I ran up to the angel picture and said goodbye.

As I turned back to Jem and Mother and Gideon, I fancied I heard a beat of big wings, a sudden breeze in the thick air of the cottage, as if the angel had stepped right out of the picture and was arching his wings over me.

I tried hard to picture him above us as we trudged down the lane towards the village. We got to the crossroads – and there was Sam waiting with his horse and cart. Gideon clapped his hands, totally misunderstanding. He thought this was a special shopping day. Sam was taking us to town to buy new clothes or new boots, a new kettle or a set of china plates or a washstand, and perhaps a toffee apple or a sugar cane for us children if we were very good.

'Well, the little lad doesn't seem too down-hearted,' Sam said, chucking him under the chin. 'The little missy looks mournful though, bless her.'

'Say goodbye to Jem now, Hetty,' said Mother, lifting Gideon up into the cart.

'No! No!' I said, tears spilling.

'I'll come on the cart with you,' said Jem. 'Hush, Hetty, I'm coming too.'

'You'll miss a morning's school,' said Mother.

'What's school, when I can be with Hetty an hour longer?' said Jem.

'You can't come, Jem. Sam has business in town and won't be able to take you back in the cart.'

'Then I'll walk back,' said Jem. He said it as if

seven miles was a short stroll. He sounded so firm that Mother didn't argue with him further.

Jem lifted me into the cart and jumped up after me. Mother settled herself with Gideon on her lap. He reached out to me and touched my wet cheeks, looking anxious now. Then he looked up at Mother.

'Hush, my pet,' she said, as if he'd spoken.

Then Sam clicked his teeth at his old brown nag and she started trotting along the road and up the hill. Jem held me tight. I craned my neck to see the village for as long as possible. As we got higher up the hill, I could just make out our own cottage on the edge of the village, like a little grey face with thatched hair on top. Then it blurred into a grey dot. I was starting to feel sick from twisting backwards, so I wriggled round and faced forward, my head on Jem's shoulder.

9

Jem and I were both numb with misery and so tired from our broken night that both our heads nodded in spite of ourselves. Every now and then I woke with a start and Jem murmured, 'There now, Hetty, I'm here.' Once I woke first, and when Jem twitched and started awake with a cry, I said quietly, 'There now, Jem, I'm here,' reaching up to put my arms round him.

Then we saw smoke in the distance, and houses started to line the road, and we were almost at the town. On those rare shopping days in the past we'd wriggle around excitedly and start to sing. This time we were silent.

'I meant to tell you a story all the way to comfort you, but the words wouldn't come,' Jem whispered.

'Never mind, never mind,' I whispered back. 'I do love you so, Jem.'

'I love you too, my Hetty. You have your sixpence safe?'

'In my pocket, look. Oh, Jem, I've nothing to give you!'

'Give me a kiss, Hetty, that's all I want.'

I leaned even closer and carefully blew a big kiss into his ear.

'There, my kiss is inside you now,' I said, imagining it flying around like a little caged bird.

Sam drove his cart through the crowded streets of the town towards the big station. It loomed above us, its great steel archway a gaping maw. I'd always loved peeping inside at the huge trains blowing out steam with a roar like gleaming dragons – but now I shrank back. We clung to the sides of the cart, shivering. Then Mother saw the great clock and gasped.

'Look at the time! Oh Lordy, we'll miss the train if we're not hasty. Set us down, Sam.'

She jumped from the cart, taking Gideon in her arms. He moaned at the noise and hid his head under her shawl.

'Come, Hetty. Jem, you have to go home.'

'Let me go on the train too, Mother, I beg you.'

'No, son. I haven't got the fare for you. The hospital sent the exact amount, one third-class seat and two children.'

'I can hide from the ticket man, Mother,' said Jem. 'I can run right through the barrier and—'

'Nonsense! Do you want to get us all into

trouble? Now we're late, the train is due to leave any minute. Get *down*, Hetty!' She pulled me from the cart, twisting my arm in her haste, so that I started bawling.

'Stop that noise!' said Mother. 'We must go to find our carriage.' She looked anxiously at Jem. 'Take care going home, for goodness' sake. If you lose your way, find a kindly-looking lady to set you on the right path. Promise me you'll be a sensible lad and go straight back. I can't take any more worries.'

'But, Mother, I *have* to come too,' said Jem, jumping down from the cart and putting his arms round me. 'Hetty needs me so. I have to look after her.'

'You *can't* look after her. You're only a silly little boy,' Mother snapped in her distress and frustration.

It was as if her words were some dreadful antidote to our magic spell. Jem had always towered like a giant, but now he shrivelled into a small boy scarcely bigger than me – a boy who started sobbing.

'Say goodbye *now*, Jem,' Mother commanded.

Jem reached up to Gideon in her arms and kissed his white cheek. Then he bent and kissed me too, on both my cheeks and then my lips.

'Goodbye, Hetty. I love you so,' he mumbled.

'I love you too, Jem. I love you, I love you, I love you.'

131

'You won't forget me, will you, Hetty?'

'Never ever ever ever ever ever . . .' I still chanted it as Mother tore our hands apart and bustled Gideon and me past the barrier and the ticket man, urging us towards the train. I craned my neck and saw Jem waving and waving. I sawed my own free arm wildly in the air until Mother found the third-class carriages at last and tugged us up into the train as the whistle went.

I sat on the seat by the door, my legs sticking out. I fingered the leather strap to open the window. As we started chugging slowly out of the station, I wondered if I dared leap right out. I could jump onto the platform, rejoin Jem, and then we could run away together . . .

Mother slapped my hands away from the strap. 'Stop that, Hetty! Do you want to fall out to your death?'

'Yes!' I declared, deciding I did indeed want to die if I couldn't be with Jem.

As the train gathered speed and hastened through the town and out into the countryside, I pictured myself leaping out of the window. My guardian angel would scurry down and snatch me up in his strong arms. We would fly up and up to Heaven. I would wear a snowy nightgown and build castles in the clouds and jump from star to star . . .

'I definitely want to die,' I declared.

'That's a dreadful thing to say, child,' said Mother, shocked. 'You can't mean it.'

'Yes, I do. I'd like to go to Heaven right this minute.'

'If you choose to kill yourself, you'll go straight to the Other Place, Hetty,' Mother reminded me.

I thought about H-e-l-l. I remembered the time a hot coal fell out of the fire and glanced against my leg. It had hurt so badly I screamed and screamed – and then I'd had to stump around with a rag bandage for a week or more. I pictured burning my whole body, cooking for all eternity.

I decided I didn't want to die just yet. I stopped fiddling with the carriage door and slumped in my seat, my chin on my chest. Gideon reached out and clutched my hand. His eyes were wide with fear now. He burrowed hard against Mother.

'There now, my lambkin, Mother's here,' she said automatically.

Gideon kept quiet, but he started crying, tears seeping down his cheeks. I cried too, clutching my rag baby, using her soft legs as a handkerchief when I got too damp and soggy. Mother pulled me closer, her arms round both of us now.

The train started slowing down. I peered out of the window in agitation. Were we there already?

Mother saw my expression. 'It's a long

journey, Hetty. A couple of hours until we get to London town.'

Gideon wailed fearfully, understanding properly now. The train stopped at a little country station and a large woman in a purple gown squeezed herself into our carriage. She smelled very sweet and her cheeks were very red. I thought she must have been running hard to catch the train, but Mother sniffed slightly and edged away from her.

The purple lady beamed at all three of us. 'Hello, my dearies. Why the tears and long faces?' She peered at Gideon's pale face and dark-circled eyes. 'Oh dear, is he not well, the little lad?'

'He's been poorly,' Mother said shortly. She stuck out her shoulder, trying to protect Gideon from the purple woman's glance.

She looked at me instead. 'And what about this little mite?' she asked. 'Why are you crying so, my dearie?'

I sniffed, not knowing what to say. 'I don't want to go to Hell,' I mumbled – though I wanted to go to the hospital even less.

'Hetty!' Mother hissed.

The purple women shook with laughter. We could hear her stays creaking. She threw back her head, her chins wobbling. Then she reached into her reticule for a lace handkerchief and dabbed at her streaming eyes. 'Children!' she said to Mother. 'Oh my Lord, the things they say!' She looked at me, pinching my cheek with her fat fingers. 'Cheer up, little girlie. Have you been a bad girl plaguing your mother, is that it? Here, I know what will cheer you up.' She ferreted around at the bottom of her bag and came up with a fruit drop as red as a ruby. 'Aha, what have we here? Pop it in your mouth quick!'

'Thank you kindly, but Hetty's not allowed—' Mother started, but the drop was in my mouth before she could finish her sentence.

'There, that worked a treat, didn't it?' said the purple woman triumphantly. 'Shall we find one for your brother now?' She discovered an emerald-green fruit drop and offered it to Gideon.

Mother sighed. 'Oh, very well.'

She stoppered Gideon's mouth with the sweet.

'Say thank you, children,' said Mother.

I thanked the purple woman and Gideon nodded his head.

'Think nothing of it, my dears,' she said. 'How old are you, missy?' she asked me.

'I'm five going on six, ma'am,' I said.

'And what about you, little boy?'

Gideon said nothing. Mother didn't seem inclined to answer for him.

'He's five too,' I piped up.

The purple woman seemed surprised. She peered at Gideon, she peered at me. Then she looked at

Mother. 'They're never twins! They don't look a jot alike.'

'They're not twins,' Mother said uncomfortably.

'Oh my. But they *are* brother and sister?' She pulled one of my red plaits. Then she lowered her voice. 'Do they perhaps have different *fathers*? Neither child favours you, my dear.'

Mother snorted down her nose. 'I don't care to discuss it. Particularly not in front of the children.' She couldn't have been plainer if she'd said *Mind your own business* – but the purple woman would not be put off.

'No need to be so humpty-tumpty, missus,' she said, chuckling. '*My* two kiddies have two fathers, and neither father was my husband, but we've managed just fine and dandy – and I've a real husband now to support us all.'

She showed off the gold ring on her fat finger. She was talking in riddles as far as I was concerned, but Mother was outraged.

'I'm a respectable married woman,' she said. 'These two dear lambs happen to be my *foster* children.'

'Really, my dear? Well, there's a thing! Foster children, eh? That's a fine idea. So are their real mothers dead then?'

'*No!*' I said.

Mother usually told me off when I used that tone,

but she patted my shoulder now. 'They've never known their mothers. These are children from the Foundling Hospital.' She said it with her head held high, as if it was something to be proud of.

The purple woman certainly seemed impressed. 'The Foundling Hospital, hmm? I dare say they pay you royally then. How much do you get for their keep, if you don't mind me asking?'

Mother clearly *did* mind, but she murmured, 'Eighteen pence a week.'

'For the two of them?'

'Per child.'

'My Lordy, that's a fortune, especially as these two are the size of sparrows, hardly likely to eat you out of house and home.'

'I look after my children for love, not money,' said Mother. Then her voice broke. 'And now I have to take them back to the Foundling Hospital and my heart is breaking.' She started sobbing. Her arms were still stretched round us so she couldn't hide her face. She wept openly, tears dripping down her dear big face.

The purple women seemed taken aback. 'Don't upset yourself so, dearie. I'm sure they'll be well cared for. It's not as if you're putting them in the workhouse, now, is it? They'll do very well back at the hospital, and you can always get yourself another baby or two to keep your income steady.'

'You don't understand,' Mother sobbed. '*I* didn't understand. These children seem like *mine*.'

We understood, Gideon and I. She was our mother. She'd been Martha's mother too, and Saul's.

I threw myself against her chest, winding my arms round her neck. Gideon was fairly suffocating but did not protest. We three hugged each other hard. All thoughts of Madame Adeline rode right out of my head on that white pony. At that moment I was hugging the only mother I wanted.

The purple woman was at last subdued. She stopped talking until a new woman joined our carriage at the next station. Then they set up a conversation together, their voices low so we could scarcely hear them. It seemed they were talking about us.

We clung tightly to Mother the entire journey. At long last the train hissed and puffed into a vast echoing station with steel buttresses arching overhead, like a smoky cathedral. Doors opened and slammed, and there was a scurrying and clamour that unnerved all three of us. We stood still while people pushed us and jostled us and complained in harsh, high voices.

'Let's go back home, Mother!' I begged.

Mother looked at us. Her hands tightened on our shoulders. She bit her lip. For a moment I thought she was actually going to bundle us back on the train. But then she took a deep breath.

'We *can't* go back home, Hetty,' she said very sadly. 'You are my dear children, but you are not allowed to stay with me. You have to go to the Foundling Hospital now.'

She led us across the station forecourt to a public lavatory. This was such a novelty to us that in spite of our misery we marvelled at the white porcelain and brass chain and the proper paper for wiping ourselves. When we had relieved ourselves, Mother washed the train soot from our hands and faces and then fumbled in her purse. She brought out two bone lockets, each hanging on a silk ribbon.

'These are for you,' she said, tying one round my neck.

'Is Gideon having a necklace too, Mother?' I said, surprised.

I picked up my locket and peered at it. There was a long number engraved on one side. I read it out with difficulty: I didn't know my numbers yet the way I knew the alphabet.

'This is your number at the hospital, Hetty. You are foundling number 25629 and Gideon is number 25621.'

'So are there thousands and thousands of children at the hospital, Mother?'

'No, no, the hospital has been open a very long time. All the first foundlings have grown up and maybe had children and grandchildren of their own, and now they are in their graves. So many children,' said Mother. She bent closer to us. 'And you two – and Saul and Martha – are the best foundling children ever. Take no notice if folk spurn you or cast aspersions because your real mothers could not care for you. You hold your heads up high and let me be proud of you.'

We stared back at her earnestly, tipping our chins up and stretching our necks. She gave us each a warm kiss on the lips and then took us by the hand.

'Come then, my children.'

We emerged into the loud, hissing bustle of the station. Mother led us outside, where the hansom cabs were waiting.

'Please take us to Guilford Street,' said Mother, fingering her fat purse to show she could pay the fare.

'The Foundling Hospital?' said the cab driver. He sucked his teeth and shook his head at us. 'Poor little mites.'

We clambered inside his cab and peered out in awe and terror at the crowded London streets. Mother might have been a country woman, but she proudly showed us St Paul's Cathedral as we passed slowly over Waterloo Bridge. We could not believe the traffic everywhere. We were used to seeing one cart at a time in the village lanes. There seemed to be

140

hundreds of cabs and carriages and carts and huge omnibuses crowded with city folk. Men in smart dark suits marched on foot over the bridge. I wondered if they could be some strangely garbed army, but Mother said they were simply businessmen on their way to and from work. There were ladies too, their skirts drawn up in comical bustles at the back, trit-trotting in their tiny shoes. They had to hold up their skirts and tread warily when they crossed the streets, which were covered in horse dung.

We were country children and used to horse dung – *and* clearing out the pigsty – but we'd never smelled it so strongly before. The river smelled sour and strange too, with a greasy slick shining in the water. What sort of city was this where you couldn't stroll along the streets or swim in the river?

Once we were over the bridge, the cab travelled through such a muddle of streets, some very broad and big, some narrow twisting alleyways, so that I was hopelessly muddled and confused. My heart thudded whenever I spotted any great grey building in case it was the hospital. At last the cab slowed and came to a stop outside great iron gates enclosing a plain wide building with many arched windows.

Mother drew in her breath and clutched our hands tight. She didn't need to tell us. We were at the Foundling Hospital.

10

Gideon and I huddled in the cab. Mother had to pull us out.

'Please be so good as to wait,' she said to the cabman, and approached the porter. 'If you please, sir, I'm bringing my two foster children back to the hospital,' she said.

He nodded and let us through the forbidding gates.

Mother walked us along the long gravel path towards the doorway. We stared up at all the windows but we couldn't see inside. There were no children peeping out at us, no children playing on the grass, no children anywhere. I strained my ears but could hear no chatter, no singing, no laughter.

Mother rang the doorbell, and a tall woman in a dark dress and white apron opened the door. She had a white cap tied on her head and a long grim face. She did not smile.

'Foundlings 25621 and 25629?' she said.

'Yes, ma'am,' said Mother huskily. 'This is Gideon Smeed and Hetty Feather. They are such dear children. Hetty is very bright indeed, and Gideon is very good and loving, though he doesn't speak just at present. He needs a little extra cosseting—'

'We treat all our foundlings in exactly the same manner. We have no favourites here,' said the nurse. 'Come along, children.'

She held out her hands. We shrank backwards, clutching Mother.

'Say goodbye,' the nurse said firmly.

I was struck as dumb as Gideon. I couldn't believe it was actually happening. Not now, not so coldly and quickly.

Mother gathered us together and kissed us, first me, then Gideon. 'Goodbye, my dear lambs. Try to be good and make me proud of you,' she whispered. 'Hetty, look after your brother.'

She straightened up and took a step backwards. Then she turned and ran down the path, her hand over her eyes.

'Mother!' I called.

Before she could look back the nurse shut the door, trapping us inside the hospital. She clasped our hands determinedly. Her own hands were icy cold and startlingly smooth – we were used to Mother's big work-roughened hands.

'I am Nurse Beaufort. Come with me,' she said, setting off at a quick march.

We had to scurry fast to keep up with her. Gideon

tripped once and she jerked his arm impatiently, hurting him. He started crying then, big tears splashing down his cheeks.

'Don't cry so, Gideon. I am here. I will look after you,' I said desperately.

'Ssh, child. You are not allowed to talk until outdoor playtime,' said the nurse, yanking my arm too.

She pulled us up a long flight of stairs. There was another nurse standing there, waiting. She was dressed in an identical dark frock and white starched apron, but she was smaller and very squat. Her dress strained at the seams and her white cap seemed too small for her dark-pink face. She had little eyes, prominent nostrils and several chins, looking for all the world like a pig in a bonnet. I gave a little snort, half laughing, half crying.

'Be quiet, child,' she snapped. She seized me by the shoulders and propelled me to the right. My head jerked round. Tall, grim Nurse Beaufort was propelling Gideon *the other way*.

'Oh no, if you please, Nurse, Gideon and me, we have to stay together!' I said, struggling.

'I am not a nurse! I am Matron Peters. Now come *along*, child. You cannot go with your brother. The small girls' wing is *this* way,' said Pigface Peters.

'But you don't understand! He's only little. He can't manage without me.'

'Nonsense.'

145

'It is *not* nonsense!' I shouted, stopping in my tracks. 'I have to look after Gideon. I promised Mother.'

'You must forget all about your foster mother now. You are a foundling child and you will obey *our* rules. Our boys and girls live separately – and so will you.'

'Then let me say goodbye to Gideon! Let me explain to him. Oh *please*!'

'Stop this ridiculous fuss this instant, Hetty Feather!'

'I *won't* stop! You are very cruel and wicked and I hate you!' I cried.

I twisted my wrist out of her grasp and ran the other way, after Gideon.

'Gideon! Oh, Gideon!' I shouted.

He was dragging his feet and drooping, his boots barely supporting him. He looked round, his eyes wide, his mouth a great O of terror.

Then fat pig-trotter fingers seized me by the shoulders. She hauled me along, kicking and screaming, marching me to the right, away from my poor brother.

'How *dare* you behave so atrociously! You will be sorry, my girl, very sorry.'

She pushed me into a strange cold room with small bathtubs in orderly rows.

'Right, missy, take your clothes off instantly. You need a bath.'

I stared at her. 'But I've *had* a bath. I'm clean as clean, look!'

'*Country* clean,' she said scornfully. 'You need a good scrubbing to get rid of all those nasty bugs and beasties. Get those clothes off while I fill the tub.'

I took off my coat and then sat down to start unlacing my boots. The matron crumpled my good coat up into a little ball and dropped it into a basket. I gave her one boot and she threw it on top of my coat, careless of the muddy soles. She saw my shocked expression.

'You won't need these any more,' she said, giving the basket a contemptuous shake.

I blinked at her. Were the foundling children required to run around *naked*?

'You will wear our uniform now,' she said.

'Can I wear my best clothes on Sundays, miss?'

'You must call me *Matron*. No, you wear your white tippets and aprons on the Sabbath, with bands around your cuffs, specially snowy white. And woe betide you if you get them dirty. Now hurry *up*, child. Get the rest of your clothes off and step into the bath this instant.'

While she was topping up the bath, her back turned, I took Jem's precious sixpence out of my pinafore pocket. I stuck it inside my mouth for want of a better place to hide it. The coin tasted unpleasantly metallic and felt as big as a dinner plate against my cheek, but it couldn't be helped.

I was right to be so cautious. Once I had my pinafore and dress and drawers off, standing shivering in my shift and stockings, the matron darted at me, snatched my rag baby and threw her in the basket too.

'She's not clothes! She's my baby!' I protested, though it was hard to talk distinctly with the sixpence wedged in my cheek.

'It's nasty and dirty. And you're not allowed dollies here.'

'But I can't sleep without her!'

'Then you will have to stay awake,' said the matron.

She pulled the shift over my head, plucked my stockings from my feet, lifted me up and plunged me into the bath. Then she took a cake of red carbolic soap and started scrubbing me viciously. I wriggled and squirmed at the indignity, especially when she started washing my long hair, digging her fat fingers into my scalp and kneading it as if my head was a ball of dough. I put my hands up, trying to protect my poor head. My fingers scratched her wrists and she dug harder, furious.

'Keep still, you fiery little imp,' she said, lathering me into a foam. She fetched another jug to rinse the suds away. 'This will quench that fire!' she said, pouring icy cold water over me.

148

I gasped in shock and would have screamed at her, but I had to keep my mouth stoppered because of the sixpence. Then she hauled me out onto the cold floor and wrapped a thin towel round me.

'Well, dry yourself, child, hurry up, hurry up!'

When I was halfway dry she sat me on a stool and picked up a pair of scissors. I started trembling. What did she intend to do now? Cut off my fingernails? Cut off my *fingers*?

She attacked my head with a hairbrush, smoothing out all the tangles so that my hair fell in a silky curtain past my shoulders – and then she started snip-snip-snipping, cutting my hair off right up to my ears.

'Oh, *please* don't cut my hair!' I begged, but she paid no heed. She snipped until my hair was shorter than a boy's and I was covered in damp red tendrils. She brushed them off me with the towel and then fetched another basket, the clothes inside this one neatly folded.

'This will be your clothes basket, Hetty Feather. You are to keep your clothes in it at night, and woe betide you if you rumple them.'

She pulled out boots and stockings and bade me put them on. The stockings were stiff and bunched at the toes with repeated darning, and the boots were much too big for my small feet. I told Matron, but she didn't appear to care.

'Put your dress on now – the *right* way round, you silly child. I will tie your apron for you.'

I hesitated. Where were my new undergarments? I saw something white in my basket, but it was simply a strange old-fashioned cap. There was no shift, no drawers, nothing!

I sidled over to my old clothes.

'Leave them alone! They're going to be disposed of straight away.'

'But, miss – Matron – I have no drawers!' I said, agonized.

The matron's pig face went even pinker. 'You do not wear such garments here,' she said. 'Now put that dress on at once.'

I stuck my poor shorn head through the stiff brown serge. It felt hard and scratchy against my scrubbed skin. She did up my buttons at the back for me, tied on the apron, and then stuck the cap upon me.

'There!' Matron marched me over to a speckled mirror above the stone slab sinks. 'Respectable at last!'

I stared at the forlorn figure in the mirror. Was that weird little creature in the cap really *me*? I shook my head violently, but the girl in the mirror shook her head back at me.

'Now you will join the other infant girls. Come with me.'

I hung back, fidgeting. 'Please, miss – Matron – I need the privy,' I blurted.

She consulted the watch pinned to her chest. 'The infant relief break is not for another hour. You will have to wait.'

'But I need to go *now*! Please, I'm nearly wetting myself!'

She sighed impatiently. 'The privies are outside in the yard. I'm not trailing you all the way there. You will have to use a chamber pot. Go in that little room and be quick about it. You must learn to control your bladder as well as your temper, Hetty Feather.'

I ran into the room, selected an ugly pot and sat on it, trembling. What sort of a madhouse was this? I put my fingers up under my cap and felt the shorn ends of my hair. I gave a little sob. Even if I managed to run away back to Jem, maybe he wouldn't love me any more because I looked such a fright.

'Hurry up, child!' Pigface grunted outside.

Safe behind the door, I took the sixpence out of my mouth, stuck out my tongue and waggled it at her. Then I hid the sixpence in my new tight cuff and jumped up from the pot.

'Now wash your hands!' she said as I came out of the little room. 'Dear goodness, do you know nothing of hygiene?'

I didn't think it at all hygienic to run around without underwear. I wondered if the matron wore drawers herself. I imagined her big piggy-pink bare bottom.

'What are you smirking at?' she said suspiciously.

I lowered my eyes and shook my head. 'Nothing, Matron.'

'Then come along with me. You will join your class at their afternoon tasks.'

She took hold of me by the wrist. I looked back at the little basket of my Sunday clothes, so lovingly washed and pressed by Mother. They were all in a muddy jumble now, my poor rag baby sprawling on top, arms and legs akimbo.

'Come on! You've no need of those nasty old clothes any more, I've told you that already,' said Matron Pigface.

'Mayn't I just kiss my baby goodbye?' I begged.

'I've never heard such nonsense. It's only a bundle of rags!' she said, and she would not let me.

I pictured my poor baby so forlorn without her mother. I heard her wailing, abandoned in the basket. I wished she was little enough to hide about my person, like the sixpence. But there was nothing I could do. I had to leave her there, tumbled about in my clothes. I never saw her again.

As Matron Pigface marched me along to my class, I thought at least I would meet up with Gideon again – but there was no sign of him. I was thrust into a room of some forty or fifty girls of five or six or seven, but there was not a single little boy. The girls were sitting at small wooden desks, all startlingly similar in their white caps and mud-hued dresses. They all stared hard at me and then whispered. I shifted from one sorely-shod foot to the other, feeling so shy and strange.

'This is Hetty Feather,' said Pigface.

Several of the little girls giggled. My hands clenched into fists.

'Thank you, Matron Peters,' said a starch-aproned nurse at the front of the class. She wasn't pink and pig-faced, she wasn't grim and pale. *This* nurse had rosy cheeks and dimples and wisps of curly hair escaping from her cap. She was as sweet and fresh-faced as Rosie or Eliza or any of the village girls. She smiled at me.

'I would watch this one. She's got a *very* contrary way with her. Redheads are always little vixens,' said Matron Pigface Peters. 'She needs that temper quelled. Spare the rod and spoil the child, remember!' She shorted, and then waddled out of the room, her stays creaking loudly.

'Hello, Hetty dear,' said this new nurse, beckoning to me.

I crept up to her desk. I saw a leather strap lying across it. Oh Lordy, was she about to punish me already?

No, she leaned towards me and said gently, 'Do not look so fearful, child. It must seem very strange your first day here, but I promise you will soon get used to life at the hospital. You seem very small. Are you turned five yet?'

'I am almost six,' I said.

'Excellent! Then I think you are old enough to learn how to darn, Hetty.' She brought out a stocking and a needle and wool from her desk. 'Did your foster mother teach you how to sew, Hetty?' she asked.

The word Mother made my eyes well up. I shook my head wordlessly.

'Then I will show you.'

She threaded the big needle, squeezing the end of the wool over with practised skill, and then put her hand inside the stocking. She started looping the wool across the hole in neat lines.

'There, do you see?'

Then she started weaving the wool the other way, making the neatest, smoothest patch. I watched, fascinated in spite of my misery. My head was itching horribly after my haircut and I put up my hand to scratch, knocking my cap sideways.

'Try not to scratch, dear, it's not very ladylike,' said the nurse. She put down the beautifully darned stocking and took my cap off. She smoothed my poor shorn hair, drying now, and sticking straight up in the air.

'My goodness, I think I remember you!' she said. 'You were the smallest baby I'd ever seen – and you had the reddest hair!'

She was the nurse who had cradled me when I was newborn and wouldn't suck properly! She was dear kind Winnie, though now she told me to call her Nurse Winterson. She bade me sit on a stool beside her while I struggled to darn a stocking myself. I badly wanted to impress this gentle nurse and show her I could act like a big girl, even though I was so small – but I couldn't get the hang of darning at all.

I pulled the needle too hard so that it came right off the wool, and then I had no end of bother re-threading it. Nurse Winterson kept threading it for me, and patiently guided my hands, but I could barely do a single stitch. I was in such a state I came near to flinging the stocking upon the floor.

I heard whispers and giggles from the other girls. Every now and then I looked up from my wretched task and glared at them. They all seemed identical at first, but when I peered harder I saw some had rosy cheeks and some had pale; some had snub noses and some had freckles; some had blue eyes and some had brown. There was one girl with a pair of spectacles on her nose who had her head bent right over her stocking, examining her stitches. There was something familiar about the bend of her head, the little frown lines above her nose . . .

'Martha!' I cried out. I jumped to my feet in my excitement, my stocking rolling to the floor. 'Oh, Martha, it's truly you!'

I ran down the line of desks and threw my arms around her neck. The other little girls squealed and squawked at my behaviour. Martha herself edged away from me, looking alarmed.

'Hetty, Hetty!' Nurse Winterson came speeding after me. 'You must not be so passionate, child! And you have to learn to stay still in your seat like a good little girl.'

'But it's *Martha*, my sister Martha!' I cried. Martha still looked dazed. 'Tell them, Martha! I am your sister Hetty.'

Martha blinked her poor squinting eyes. 'Hetty?' she said. 'Did I have a sister Hetty?'

'Oh, Martha, you can't have *forgotten* me!' This was such a terrifying thought that I burst into floods of tears.

'Oh yes,' said Martha, nodding now. 'You were the little one who cried a lot.'

She really seemed to have no other clear recollection of me. The girls on either side of her giggled, and Martha blushed and wriggled further away from me, clearly embarrassed.

I let Nurse Winterson lead me back to my chair. I picked up my stocking and applied myself to darning, but tears kept brimming and the stocking blurred in my hand. I was so shocked that Martha had barely remembered me, her own sister. Did she not remember any of us – Rosie, Eliza, Nat, Jem?

Surely she must remember Saul. I wondered when we were to meet up with all the boy foundlings.

A bell rang at four and all the other girls stuffed their stockings into workbaskets in their desks. Nurse Winterson took my poor cobbled stocking and held it up, examining my enormous stitches.

'Oh, Hetty, you've sewn the sides together! How could anyone get their foot into this stocking?' she said, wafting it gently in front of me.

The other girls giggled and grinned. I felt my cheeks turn fiery red.

'We will try again tomorrow,' said Nurse Winterson. 'Cheer up, Hetty. We will make an expert seamstress of you yet. Now, run and play outside with the other girls.'

I followed them forlornly. I did not want to play with any of them and I was sure they did not want to play with me. They scurried along the corridor and down the stairs, calling to each other, though they subsided abruptly when another nurse appeared on the stairs. She clapped her hands crossly.

'*Quietly*, girls! No talking at all until you get outside,' she said. She noticed me skulking at the top of the stairs. 'Come along, child, don't loiter. The girls' playground is down the stairs and through the big door.'

'Please, miss – Nurse – mayn't I go to play with the boys?' I asked.

She drew herself up, hands on her hips. 'Of course not, you bold little girl!'

'But I need to see my brother Gideon. He will be so wretched without me. Please, Nurse, I need to see my brother so badly,' I begged.

Nurse Winterson came and stood beside me, her hand on my shoulder. 'Perhaps it will help Hetty settle down if we let her see her foster brother for a few minutes,' she suggested.

But the other nurse shook her head firmly. 'Really, Winnie! Will you never learn? You can't afford to be so soft-hearted with the children. If we change a rule for just one child, they will all be clamouring for special privileges.' The fierce nurse turned to me. 'Now run away and play or you shall be whipped!'

I ran because I certainly did not want to be whipped. The other girls were playing games of tag, or strolling around together arm in arm, or sitting in little circles telling secrets. I did not have anyone to play with.

I peered around desperately for Martha. She was walking with a girl on either side, all of them singing a song. I sidled nearer until I was walking two steps behind. One of the girls craned round.

'Stop following us!' she said.

'I'm not following *you*, I'm following my sister,' I said fiercely. I ran round them and stood right in front of Martha. Her eyes blinked anxiously behind her spectacles.

'I am so happy to find you, Martha. I have so much news to tell about Mother and Father and dear Jem, and did you know that Gideon is here too, we travelled together in a big steam train, and there is a new little baby Eliza, and do you ever see Saul, and that horrid matron took all my best clothes and my rag baby, and I've been to a real circus and ridden on a white horse . . .' I was babbling now, trying to get some kind of reaction from poor Martha. She looked bewildered.

'I don't really remember,' she said. 'That was long ago. I only remember *now*.'

'But now is so horrid!' I said, starting to cry again.

'Don't cry!' said Martha. 'Please don't. It hurts my head. All right, Hetty, you can walk with us. This is Elizabeth and this is Marjorie.'

They both sighed, but let me trail after them. When they resumed their silly song, all tra-la-la's and tootle-tootles, I did my best to imitate them.

Nurse Winterson rang the bell at the end of playtime. She smiled at me. 'There, Hetty, you've made friends already,' she murmured to me.

She didn't understand that Martha was simply trying to be kind because of our dimly remembered kinship – and Elizabeth and Marjorie certainly did not wish to be friends.

We were all marched to the privies, where we took

it in turns to relieve ourselves, ten girls at a time. We then washed our hands with the horrible carbolic soap. I could barely reach up to the basin and got water right up my arms, wetting the uncomfortable cuffs on my sleeves. My hidden sixpence was rubbing a bruise on my skin, but I bore the pain proudly.

Then we were marched again – one two, one two, one two – into a large echoing dining room set with very long tables. The little girls scrambled onto benches. I stood bewildered in the crush and lost my chance of sitting next to Martha. I had to squash right on the end of a bench next to a fierce-looking fair girl with a high forehead, who dug me hard with her elbow when I took a bite of the bread on my plate.

'You're not *allowed*, not yet!' she hissed.

We had to wait as endless lines of big girls filed in too, until the whole hall was filled with girls girls girls, all scarily alike in their brown dresses and white caps.

My stomach was rumbling because I'd missed having any dinner on this most terrible day, but I still had to wait until Matron Pigface said, 'Let us say grace, girls.'

I did not understand and mumbled, 'Grace.' The fierce girl snorted derisively.

'For what we are about to receive may we be truly grateful, amen,' she chanted with all the others.

We'd never said grace at home, we'd just grabbed our bowls from Mother and started spooning, but I *was* truly grateful for my slice of bread and my wedge of cheese. I wolfed them down in four bites and waited. And waited. There didn't seem to be anything *else*, apart from a mug of watered-down milk.

I was a country child. We might have been poor but Mother believed in giving us big platefuls and our milk was always creamy rich. I wondered if my helping was minute because I was the smallest girl here, but when I peered around, I saw that even the very big girls with chests filling out their tippets had the same size slices.

I wondered how I was going to bear the enormous emptiness inside my stomach. I didn't realize that it wasn't simply hunger, though that was a small part of it. An entire loaf of bread and a round of cheese could not have eased the ache of my loneliness.

I wondered how Gideon was faring in the boys' wing, unable even to ask for what he wanted, and my tears brimmed again. The fierce girl beside me took no notice, but a big girl with long plaits came over to our table.

'You can go and play for a little, you babies,' she said. She stopped in front of me. 'Oh dear! Are you feeling monk?'

'She's new today,' said the fierce girl. 'They're *always* monk when they're new.'

I didn't know what monk meant exactly, but I certainly felt it.

'Don't cry, baby,' said the big girl, and she lifted her own apron and dabbed at my eyes. 'You're so *weeny*. Don't worry, I'll look out for you. My name's Harriet.'

'My name's Hetty.'

'My, they're very similar. Some of the girls call me Hatty.'

'I had long hair like yours,' I said, taking hold of her long silky plaits. 'But that nasty horrid matron with a pig face cut it all off.'

Harriet giggled but put her hand over her mouth. 'You mustn't talk like that about the matron! She wasn't being deliberately nasty or horrid, all the new girls have their hair cut off, it's the rule, in case of lice. But don't fret, yours will be as long as mine in two or three years.'

Two or three *years*! I'd been in the Foundling Hospital for less than a day and yet it already felt like a lifetime.

'Do you know your way around all this great big building, Harriet?' I asked.

'Of course I do. Don't worry, you'll learn your way around soon too.'

'Do you know where all the boys are?'

'Yes, they are in the west wing.'

'Do you know how to get there?'

162

'Yes, but I have never been. It's not allowed.'

'Have you never seen the boys?'

'Oh, yes, yes, sometimes we see them across the yard at play, and we watch their sports day once a year. We see them in chapel too, though we're not supposed to peer round.'

'Couldn't we go together now, just to have a peep at them?'

'Of course not, Hetty. We would be seen and then we would get into fearsome trouble.'

'I don't care. I need to see my brother,' I said.

'Ah.' Harriet was silent for a moment. 'I had a brother. Two brothers. They are here too. Michael and John.'

She said their names uncertainly, as if she wasn't sure. I felt my throat tighten. She didn't seem to remember them properly, and yet she was a big girl, not a small girl who was easily muddled, like Martha. I resolved even more strongly that I would never never never forget my dear brothers (especially Jem) or my sisters, and that *somehow* I would find the boys' wing and seek out Gideon.

Harriet wouldn't take me to the boys' wing but she *did* take me to the big girls' room. There was no nurse keeping order so the girls chatted as they mended clothes, sewing up split seams in the ugly brown dresses and hemming torn aprons.

'Come here, Hetty, let me show you something,' said Harriet.

I feared I was in for another sewing lesson and I'd already proved myself spectacularly untalented at darning – but Harriet pulled off a long length of cotton thread, tied it together, and then placed it round her outstretched hands.

'Watch carefully! I will teach you how to play cat's cradle.'

I watched, though I didn't see a cat or a cradle, just strange patterns forming as Harriet fiddled the cotton with her fingers. She tried her best to show me what to do, and praised me extravagantly when I managed to flip the thread into the right zigzag pattern.

'*Clever* baby!' she said.

I felt a little indignant – she seemed all too ready to treat me like a two-year-old – but I didn't protest. It was wonderful to have found a friend in this huge and horrifying hospital, *two* friends, if I counted kind Nurse Winterson.

But at night-time I was utterly friendless. All the little girls were lined up and washed by a big girl. She had long plaits like my Harriet, but she was nowhere near as kind. She scrubbed at our hands and faces with the horrid carbolic soap, not caring in the slightest if it went in our eyes.

Then we were led to the infant dormitory, a vast room of fifty iron bedsteads. I was taken to a bed right beside the door and my clothes pulled off me by another big girl. She stuck a nightgown over my head. It was so long it trailed on the floor. My shorn hair stuck out wildly in all directions. Some of the other girls laughed and pointed. I licked my fingers and tried to make the tufts stick to my scalp.

'Stop doing that, you look so silly!' said the big girl. 'Fold your clothes up neatly – *neatly*, I said – and put them in your basket at the end of the bed.'

I did as I was told. I hid my lucky sixpence in my basket too, resolving to find a safer hiding place when no one was watching.

'Now say your prayers. Don't take too long about it, mind. Then get into bed.'

I knelt down, put my hands together and shut my eyes. 'Dear God, please get me *out* of this horrid, hateful place,' I prayed. 'Please don't let the matron and the nurses and the other boys be plaguing Gideon. I know it is all my fault he cannot speak any more and I am such a sorry girl. Please bless my dear family at home and don't let me ever forget them. Please especially bless Jem. Please—'

But the big girl was tugging me impatiently. 'That's enough. Into bed. Now!'

I opened my eyes and saw that all the other girls were already under their covers. I hurried into bed myself. The big girl dimmed the light and said, 'Goodnight! No talking now.'

She went out of the door and closed it tight. Immediately a whispering started. The girls called each other, chatting about their day. They started talking about me as if I wasn't there!

'What about the new girl, Hetty Feather?'

'She looks a sight. That hair!'

'She's so small and scrawny.'

'I saw her sucking up to Harriet.'

'She's so stupid at darning.'

'She went down on her knees to pray, pretending she's so holy.'

'She's just acting monk to make people sorry for her.'

'I don't like her at all.'

I jumped out of bed and ran to the nearest girl. 'Well, I don't like *you*!' I cried, and I pulled her ear hard. She screamed and I ran to the next bed. 'And I don't like you!' I pulled another ear, then ran on. 'Or *you* – or *you*!'

They all set about shrieking, and then the door burst open and someone stood there, an oil lamp held high, illuminating her ugly features. It was Matron Pigface!

'What is this terrible noise? How *dare* you behave so badly! And who is this child *out of bed*?'

She seized me, shining the lamp in my face. 'Hetty Feather! Behaving like a child of Satan on your very first night here! Get back into bed this instant, and if you put so much as a foot on the floor all night you will be whipped severely.'

She smacked at me as I dodged past her and dived into my bed.

'Now you are all to go to sleep *this instant*!' Pigface commanded.

After she'd waddled out of the room there were several muttered remonstrances, but soon every girl was breathing heavily. Some murmured as they dreamed, some snored. I was the only one awake.

I lay on my back, feeling so wretchedly lonely in my narrow bed. I longed to snuggle up beside Jem or Gideon. My arms ached for my dear rag baby. I lay trembling hour after hour. I felt so small in this huge room of spiteful girls. I seemed to grow smaller and smaller as I lay there. I clutched myself in fear that I was actually shrinking. I did not seem myself any more. I gripped my elbows tightly and gritted my teeth. I had to hang onto myself. I was not going to become just another foundling girl in hideous apparel. I might have to wear the dress, cap, apron and tippet, I might have to obey all their dreadful rules, but inside my head I still had to stay Hetty Feather.

11

I woke to the clamour of a bell. A new big girl strode up and down the dormitory, shouting at us to get up. It was cold and my bladder was bursting, but I had to strip my bed, roll up my mattress and put on my hateful uniform before I could shuffle to the privy. A big girl – yet another, so *many*, how would I ever learn who was who? – washed our hands, inspected our necks and brushed our hair. Then we had to line up and walk two by two to the dining room. I did not have anyone to walk with. I decided I did not care. I pictured to myself another Hetty, and we held hands and walked downstairs together, whispering to each other. Several times the other girls tried to elbow me out of the way, but Hetty and I elbowed back. We had small arms but *very* sharp elbows.

'Stop pushing and poking each other!' a nurse called. 'Who is that girl there, the little one?'

'Hetty Feather,' the other girls chorused, triumphant that I was in trouble again.

'You must learn patience and decorum, Hetty

Feather. We expect little girls to queue up quietly for their food at the hospital, not trample and grunt like little pigs in a sty.'

She said it humorously but she nearly set me off crying again, because I thought of our pig in the sty, and Jem and Mother, and a wave of homesickness washed over me.

'So you're a new little girl,' said the kitchen maid at the end of the table, serving out bowls of porridge. She was small and slight – if it wasn't for her careworn face I might have mistaken her for one of the big girl foundlings. Her maid's uniform hung about her, her skirts trailing past her boots. 'I'm new here too. It feels very strange, don't it?'

I nodded forlornly.

'I'm sure we'll both settle down soon,' she said. 'Here, specially for you!' She took a twist of paper out of her apron pocket and sprinkled the contents on the top of my porridge. 'Sugar!' she whispered.

All the other girls had entirely plain portions.

'Get on with it, Ida! There isn't time to *talk* to the children,' the fat cook called from the serving hatch.

Ida winked at me. I did my best to wink back, though I hadn't quite mastered the art and I fear I squinted dreadfully. Ida's unexpected kindness cheered me even more than the sprinkle of sugar.

I still had to face the ordeal of morning school. We had a proper mistress, not a nurse, an elderly lady called Miss Newman. She did indeed resemble a new kind of man: she was tall and square-shouldered, with a severe bun scraped back from her wrinkled forehead. She could control her hair, but her eyebrows wriggled in unruly fashion above her small spectacles. She was plainly dressed in a grey blouse with a white collar and a dark grey skirt, with just a silver clasp on her belt to break the monotony – but she looked exotically glamorous in comparison with the dull uniform of all the nurses.

She stood at the front of our classroom and peered hard at all us girls. She saw me and raised her formidable eyebrows. 'What is your name, little girl?'

'Hetty Feather, Nurse – miss.'

'You will address me as Miss Newman, if you please.'

'Yes, Miss Newman.'

'Did you attend school in your foster home?'

'No, Miss Newman.'

She sighed. 'Well, you are going to have to concentrate very hard, Hetty Feather.'

She held up a large placard with four pictures. There was a round rosy fruit, a big brown furry creature, a yellow piece of furniture, and a black and white animal waving its tail. Each picture had writing underneath it.

'A is for Apple, B is for Bear, C is for Chair and D is for Dog!' I declared.

Miss Newman stared at me. 'I thought you said you had never attended school, Hetty Feather.'

'I haven't, Miss Newman.'

'So how have you learned to read?'

'My big brother Jem read to me,' I said proudly. 'So I learned all my letters.'

Miss Newman nodded approvingly. 'Then he was a kind brother to you, child.'

'Oh, he *is*, the kindest brother in the whole world,' I said fervently.

Miss Newman led all of us through the alphabet with her coloured placards – and then we progressed to the much duller but still interesting spelling out of little words. It was not long before I could stutter 'The c-a-t is on the m-a-t', and in the second half of the long morning's lesson I grasped a scratchy pen and wrote line after line of shaky *a*s and *b*s and *c*s. Then I wrote my first sprawling word – *c a b* – and drew a picture of the London cab that had taken me away to this grim new life.

Miss Newman liked my picture, she liked my word, and when she had showed me how to sign my artwork *H e t t y*, she embellished it with a gold star.

I was pleased and proud, but the star made me think of the wondrous night of the circus and Madame Adeline and then the awfulness of Gideon going missing, and I had to fight to stop my tears brimming all over again.

'She thinks she's so clever just because she can read and write, but look, she's nothing but a crybaby,' Sheila hissed to her friend, Monica. Sheila was the fierce fair girl with the high forehead and I already detested her.

However, Martha came and peered very closely at my picture, running her finger along the lines as if it helped her to see. 'Very good, Hetty. And you have a gold star! I've never had a gold star yet. I won't either. I am a total dunce.' She sighed, though she said it cheerily enough.

'Well, *I* think you're very clever,' I said loyally. Even if Martha did not remember me properly, I remembered *her*. We were still sisters, no matter what.

Martha was truly very good at our singing lesson. We had to stand in lines and sing long dreary hymns. I did not know the words yet so I could only hum uncertainly to the piano music, but Martha's voice soared high above the others, making me shiver with its sweetness.

Wait till I tell Mother! She will be so proud that Martha can sing like an angel, I thought. Then I realized I would never be able to tell Mother. I had to fight the tears this time, knowing that if I cried again the other girls would torment me. I screwed up my face desperately.

'*Look at Hetty Feather!*' sang Sheila, keeping in time to the hymn. '*She looks like she's about to w-e-t herself!*'

I *did* actually need to go to the privy. I couldn't get used to the idea of only being able to go when the nurses commanded. My bladder and bowels had a will of their own and I prayed I would not have an accident. One girl was wriggling and jiggling towards the end of the line and Miss Newman spoke to her sharply.

'Stop fidgeting, Sarah Barnes!'

Sarah jumped – and then water started trickling down her legs, spreading in a pool about her boots. The girls on either side of her sprang away, and everyone stared and pointed. Miss Newman sent Sarah out of the room in disgrace. She shuffled soggily away, her head bowed, her face scarlet with shame.

I had a desperate private conversation with my own bladder. I had seen a pig's bladder at home so I had some idea of what mine looked like. I pictured tying the end up tightly with string, making many knots. It worked so well that when we were eventually allowed a trip to the privy, I sat there for several minutes before I could squeeze out a single drop.

'Come *along*, Hetty Feather. For goodness' sake, child, you must be finished now! You're just being contrary.'

A nurse came and dragged me off while I was still weeing. A little splashed down my legs, but not enough to make a puddle. I thanked the Lord for my long skirts, though it wasn't comfortable.

We had our dinner in the great dining hall. I saw Harriet and tried to go and sit with her, but I was hauled back to sit on a bench with the other girls my age.

We had a different kitchen maid to dole out a few morsels of boiled mutton and carrots and potatoes. I received a standard portion, but when the other kind kitchen maid passed behind my bench, taking her great dish back to the kitchen, she slipped one more potato onto my plate. It had a little dab of butter on top and tasted especially delicious. She watched me eat it up, smiling at me.

'Did that new kitchen maid give you an extra potato, Hetty Feather?' Sheila demanded crossly.

'She had one left so she gave it to me. Because I'm little and I look sweet,' I said. 'Not like *you*.'

Sheila had a very high frowny forehead and a fierce expression, her mouth drooping like a dog. I pulled my own features into a Sheila-face, and the two girls opposite laughed. Even Monica sniggered, though she was Sheila's best friend.

It was a stupid mistake to ridicule Sheila, especially as she was much bigger than me. She cornered me out in the playground when there wasn't a nurse in sight.

'I'll teach you, Hetty Feather,' she said, and she punched me in the stomach, so that I doubled over.

Then she ran behind me and pushed hard. I toppled down onto my chin. I grazed my hands painfully, tore the knees out of both my stockings, and sliced my poor chin right open.

Monica squatted down beside me, looking aghast. 'Oh, Sheila, you've hurt her! She's bleeding frightfully, look!'

'Only a little bit,' said Sheila, but she looked worried too.

'What if she tells Matron?' said Monica. 'You will be whipped, Sheila!'

'Good!' I said, struggling to my feet. I wiped my stinging chin with my hand. I was startled when I saw the bright red on my fingers but I decided to be brave. I'd played soldiers often enough with Jem at home. I knew you had to show courage when you were wounded. I marched off, swinging my arms, my dripping chin held high.

Matron Pigface came into the playground just then, bell in hand, ready to ring for us to go indoors for our needlework session. She took one look at me and gasped. 'Hetty Feather! Whatever have you done to yourself, you wretched child?'

Every girl in the playground stood still, staring at me. Out of the corner of my eye I saw Sheila and Monica clasping hands.

'*Answer* me, Hetty Feather!' Pigface bellowed.

I did not want to answer her. I did not want to admit to all the infant foundlings that Sheila had knocked me down and I had failed to punch her back. It was too shaming.

Matron Pigface was peering closely at my chin, inspecting my hands, lifting my skirt to see my torn stockings and oozing knees. 'Have you been in a *fight*?'

I shook my head, because I hadn't had the wit or strength to fight Sheila back.

'So did some girl here *attack* you?' Pigface demanded.

I opened my mouth at last. I looked at Sheila. I didn't want to give her the satisfaction of everyone knowing she had triumphed over me. 'No, miss . . . Matron. No one attacked me. I fell over because these blooming boots are too big.'

Pigface shook me by the shoulders for impertinence until my head waggled. Then she seized me by the wrist and hurried me off to the washroom. She scrubbed at my chin and hands and knees with carbolic soap. It stung horribly but I stood still and stiff, because I was a wounded soldier and would not show weakness to any enemy. Then she painted my chin with strange purple liquid from a medicine bottle. This stung even worse than the soap and I wriggled just a little.

'Keep *still*, Hetty Feather,' Pigface said, but when she'd finished applying the violet medicine and replaced my blood-splattered tippet with a fresh one, she gave me a nod that was almost approving. 'Run along to join the other girls at needlework, Hetty – and watch where you're going this time!'

She did not accompany me. I was supposed to know my own way around the building after twenty-four hours' residence. I darted off, but I was concentrating on the pain of my chin. I darted in the wrong direction, to the left instead of the right. I blundered down a long echoing corridor, turned a corner – and seemed to find the washroom all over again.

I stared at the big white room, my hands over my sore chin, wondering how I could possibly have come full circle – when a small snivelling *boy* came rushing in, with ink all over his hands.

We stood staring at each other, equally taken back.

'What are you doing in the boys' wing, little girl?'

'I – I got lost,' I said honestly, then sighed in irritation. Why, oh, why could he not be Gideon?

'You will get whipped if they find you,' he said.

'I know. I don't care. I'll go in a minute, but please could you tell me first, do you know my brother Gideon? Is he all right?'

'Gideon?' said the little boy, sneering. 'You mean the idiot boy?'

'He is not an idiot!' I shouted fiercely. 'I shall hit you if you say he is!'

His hands went to his mouth, smearing ink all over his face.

'Now you're all black and it serves you right,' I said.

I ran out of the washroom, right along the corridor until I saw a whole troop of boys bustling out of a big room. I peered hard at this army of brown, but I couldn't spot Gideon at all. However, all the boys could see me. They let up a whoop and a shout.

'Girl! Girl! Girl!'

A nurse came running, shouting at me furiously. I knew I had to make a quick escape. I flew back back back along the corridors, back to the safety of the girls' wing, where I slowed down and walked sedately, trying to look innocent. I joined my class at their darning.

'Where have you been, Hetty Feather?' asked Nurse Winterson. 'Oh dear, your poor chin! What happened to you?'

All the girls looked up expectantly, Sheila clearly anxious. I wanted to get her into trouble with Nurse Winterson. But I still did not want it made plain to all that she had got the better of me. I held my tongue a second time.

'I tripped and Matron took me off to put this purple stinging stuff on my chin,' I said.

'It is gentian violet, Hetty. I dare say it hurt a great deal. You have been very brave, dear.'

I thought the girls might groan to see me singled out so favourably, but they nodded at me, almost in a friendly fashion. I did not know then that I had avoided the worst sin of all at the Foundling Hospital.

No matter how a child is teased or tortured, they must never ever ever tell a nurse or matron. If they do, the others will torment them until their last day at the hospital.

I had unwittingly kept to this rule and won everyone's respect. I sat and stitched demurely, while Nurse Winterson read us a story. I loved stories, and this was a splendid fairy tale – but for once I could not concentrate.

My mind was whirling. I knew how to reach the boys' wing, but I would be spotted immediately if I went back there, unless . . . Unless I could find some way of disguising myself.

I did not see how this was possible, until later in the day, when Harriet sought me out.

'Poor Hetty! Look at your sore chin. Oh dear, oh dear,' she said, making a great fuss of me.

I rather enjoyed this, and even managed to squeeze out a few tears so she could pet me. She took me to the big girls' room and sat me close by her side while she started sewing. She took a pair of boys' trousers from the big basket and started patching a knee. I stared at the trousers on her lap – and smiled. I knew how to obtain the perfect disguise!

I waited until Harriet had to go to a cupboard for more thread, peered round quickly, then seized another pair of trousers from the brimming basket. I could not be seen carrying them so I thrust them up my skirts, wedging them in a bunch as best I could.

I positively waddled on my way back to my dormitory, but I managed to deposit the trousers safely in my mattress.

The next day I purloined a jacket – and I was ready! I decided my best chance of reaching the boys' wing undetected was during the playtime after dinner. There were fewer nurses on duty, many of them dining themselves. I stood in the playground awaiting my opportunity. The other girls took no notice of me. Sheila seemed disconcerted that I had not told tales on her, and left me alone.

I hesitated, standing near the girls' entrance, suddenly in a funk, frightened of being caught and whipped. I made myself think hard of Gideon. I pictured him so clearly that he seemed to be standing before me, white and trembling, tears running down his face, his mouth opening and shutting soundlessly. It was such a sad image, it galvanized me into action.

I gave one last glance to check I was unobserved, and then I ran into the entrance and up the stairs, all the way to the dormitory. I tore off my cap and tippet and apron. I struggled out of my scratchy brown dress. Then I pulled my stolen jacket and trousers out of my mattress and put them on. The trousers were too large and much too long, but I rolled each leg up at the hem until they rested on my boots. The jacket was too big too, but it was easy enough to shrug it up on my shoulders. My shorn hair suited my purpose well. I had no mirror, but looking down I could see I appeared a convincing boy, though I was on the short side. I clenched my fists and tapped myself on the chest.

'Courage, Hetty,' I whispered.

I hastened out of the dormitory, hating the heaviness of the jacket on my shoulders, the chafing of the trousers on my skinny legs. I sped along the corridor, but then heard the squeak of a nurse's boots marching along the polished floor.

If she caught me in boys' apparel, all would be lost. I darted into the girls' washrooms and hid behind the door, trembling. *Squeak squeak squeak* came the boots, louder now. They paused at the door of the washrooms. A head poked in and peered, but I was crammed right back into the corner and she didn't see me. She went marching on her way, while I breathed out at last. Once she was out of earshot I peeped anxiously out of the doorway, and then resumed my journey.

I turned to the right until I found the boys' washrooms, and then I carried on down the corridor until I reached the stairs. I ran down them, but there at the bottom, right by the door, stood a nurse watching the boys playing outside. I stopped still, pressing back into the shadows. I could not bear to be thwarted now, when I was so nearly there. I waited, willing her to move, and eventually she yawned and stretched and sauntered off.

I hurtled out into the playground, blinking at the sight of so many small boys in brown. They were so lively too. We girls wandered aimlessly up and down, or talked in tiny groups, or played decorous clapping games. These boys were all running and capering and kicking stones and shouting – all but one. A spindly boy with a stark haircut stood all by himself, his head bowed, his hands weirdly splayed as if he were searching for something that wasn't there.

'*Gideon!*' I called.

He looked up and I ran over to him. He cowered away as if I was going to hit him.

'It's me, Gideon! It's Hetty, your own sister!' I cried.

He peered at my shorn hair and breeches, looking doubtful.

'It's really me. Oh, Gideon, I've missed you so!'

I embraced him, my arms tight around his neck. I felt him crumple, his head on my shoulders, and then he started sobbing.

'Oh, Gid, it's so hateful hateful hateful, isn't it? If only we could be together it wouldn't be too bad.'

He straightened up and looked at me imploringly.

'I can't stay, Gideon. The nurses would see I'm

183

not a real boy – especially when I went to the privy!' I giggled – and Gideon smiled through his tears. 'How has it been for you, Gid? Have they been horrid to you, the other boys?'

Gideon hung his head.

'What about Saul? He's here, isn't he? Does he look out for you, stand up for you?'

Gideon hunched up further. Saul was clearly not a protector.

'Well, you must fight back. If you cry, it will only make them worse. The other girls are hateful to me, but I punch them and pull their hair and stamp on their feet until they scream,' I said, exaggerating fiercely. 'You must do the same.'

Gideon stared at me. We both knew this was a ridiculous suggestion.

'*Try*, Gideon. And you must *say* things. They will think you are stupid if you won't talk. They will call you bad names like Idiot Boy.'

Gideon flinched.

'But you're not an idiot, you're clever, just like me. You can talk perfectly, you just *won't*. Please say something to me now, Gid.'

Gideon shook his head helplessly.

'For my sake – because you stopped talking when you got lost in the woods that night I went to the circus, remember?'

It was clear from Gideon's eyes that he did.

'I've felt so bad since, knowing it was all my fault. It would make me feel *so* much better if you said something. Anything. You can call me names if you like. You can say, "Hetty Feather is a mean, nasty, pigface, smellybottom sister!" Go on, say it!'

Gideon resisted, but he smiled again.

'Well, say it in your head if you won't say it out loud. Talk to yourself every day. Talk about *home*. We mustn't forget, Gideon. It's the most important thing of all. Martha can barely remember anything, not even me! But if we talk to ourselves and picture home again and again and again, it will stay true in our heads. We must picture Mother—'

Gideon moaned softly.

'Yes, remember Mother, her dear red face, her lovely warm smell, her big chest, our mother. And great Father, remember him galloping around with you on his shoulders. And Nat with his jokes and his whittling. Did they take your wooden elephant, Gid? They took my dear rag baby. But I've still got Jem's sixpence safe. Oh, Gideon, picture Jem, remember our dearest brother, and listen to me, listen hard: Jem is going to come for me when I'm older, and he'll come for you too, and we'll all live together and be happy again – and you will be free to dance, Gid. You can even wear a silver suit if you like. Remember the tumbling boys and their dance?'

Gideon's face suddenly lit up. He pointed his foot in its clumsy boot and then twirled round, while I clapped. But the other boys were watching. They started pointing and jeering.

'See the idiot boy dancing!'

'He is *not* an idiot,' I said, clenching my fists. 'I will punch any boy who calls him that.'

They laughed harder, because they all towered over me.

'Who *is* this little red-haired runty lad?'

'Is he new? I've never seen him before.'

They were gathering round us, which made me nervous.

'He's a rum little fellow! Where's his waistcoat and cap? He's only half dressed!'

'What's your name, boy?'

'I'll tell you his name – it's Hetty Feather!' someone said.

I spun round – and there was Saul, grown thinner and taller, his face pinched. His bad leg bent sideways and he clutched a cane for support.

The other boys roared at my name. 'The cripple's talking such rot! Hetty Feather! That's a girl's name.'

'She *is* a girl. She is my foster sister,' said Saul. He looked at me, his cheeks flushed. 'Remember, remember, remember, Hetty Feather. You tell Gideon to remember – but you forgot *me*!'

'He's a *girl*?' said the biggest boy. He seized

hold of me and thrust his hand down my breeches, though I struggled and shrieked. 'He *is* a girl!' he yelled triumphantly.

'There's a girl over here!'

'A girl, a girl, a girl in breeches!'

'Come and see the girl, the red-haired girl!'

They were all running towards me. I saw a nurse in the distance raise her head and stare over at the hubbub.

'I have to go, Gid, or I shall be in terrible trouble. But you remember, promise? Remember everyone at home. Remember *me*, your Hetty.'

I gave him a quick kiss on his cheek. I might have tried to kiss Saul too, but he spat at me. So I spat back, then dodged round him and ran.

The boys shouted after me, some of them running in pursuit. I heard a wail. I turned. Gideon was waving wildly at me. His mouth was open.

'My Hetty!' he called, his voice cracking.

There was uproar as they all heard him speak, but I could not stay to congratulate or comfort him. I shot inside the entrance and ran like a rat, desperate for cover. I heard bells clanging and knew it was the end of playtime. I made it undetected all the way back to the girls' dormitory. I tore off the jacket and breeches, tugged on my dress and apron and tippet and thrust my cap upon my head. I was a girl again. I had got away with it!

12

Each day was so alike: up in the morning as the bell rang; dressing, washing, eating, even going to the lavatory at the allotted hour. We learned the same lessons every day, reading and writing and singing and scripture, then the wretched darning every afternoon. We ate the same meals – porridge for breakfast, boiled beef or mutton for dinner, bread and cheese for supper every Monday, Tuesday, Wednesday, Thursday, Friday and Saturday, all identical – so *Sundays* came as a total surprise.

We were handed special snowy-white Sunday tippets and aprons, and given a severe warning by Matron Pigface Peters to keep them spotless. Woe betide any girl who dribbled her porridge down her front at breakfast! Then we all trooped off to chapel, marching in a crocodile. I still did not have a friend in my own class so I had to trudge along beside Matron Pigface herself, while Sheila and Monica walked directly behind and kept kicking the backs of my legs and treading on my boot-heels.

I turned to try to kick them back, but Matron Pigface tugged my arm and glared at me.

'Behave yourself, Hetty Feather! Pray to the Lord above to make you a good meek little maid, not the total varmint that you are.'

I wasn't sure what a varmint was, but I decided I wanted to stay one if I possibly could. I didn't want to be good or meek. I certainly didn't want to stay little so that all the others could squash me flat. I didn't much care to be a maid either. If I had to be a foundling, then the boys seemed to have far more fun.

The Sunday service in the chapel wasn't fun for any of us, girls or boys. We had to sit as still as statues on the hard pews. If we so much as swung our legs, Matron frowned and tapped us. If any small foundling fidgeted or fell asleep during the long, long sermon, a big girl would poke her hard in the back – and doubtless the little boys over on the other side of the chapel were being subjected to similar nips and knocks.

The foundlings who formed the choir were the only children who could mingle, girls and boys together. I was surprised to see my own sister, Martha, up there at the front, the smallest child in the whole choir, looking especially earnest with her spectacles on the end of her snub nose. She had a very short solo and sang like an angel, hands folded, head high, mouth wide open. I felt true sisterly pride, goose pimples on my arms at the sweetness of her voice. If only Mother could have been present to hear her!

I blotted out my pew of foundling girls sitting hip to hip in their ugly brown frocks. I pictured my entire family, Jem beside me, whispering loyally that he was sure I could sing every bit as sweetly as Martha, Nat surreptitiously whittling a piece of wood, Rosie and Eliza in their Sunday print frocks with their hair specially curled, Father large and lumbering, holding his neck awkwardly because the collar of his starched Sunday shirt was rubbing, and Mother rocking the sleeping baby, her eyes shining to see us all together. Gideon would be with us of course, sitting bolt upright, dancing his toes in time to the music. I suppose Saul would have to be here too – but right at the other end of the pew, away from me.

I peered round to see if I could possibly spot the real Gideon and Saul in the distant sea of brown boys – and got poked hard in the back for my trouble. I had to sit still, and pray and sing and listen while the vicar preached endlessly about miserable sinners. I was *very* miserable and I knew I was a sinner, so I decided I had better pray hard inside my head so that I wouldn't tumble straight down to the fiery flames of Hell.

'Dear Lord, please make me a better girl,' I prayed earnestly, over and over – but as the sermon droned on and on, I switched the prayer to 'Please God, let this service finish *soon*.'

When it was finally over, I had pins and needles from the tips of my toes right up to my bottom and I stumbled when I stood up. We filed out of the chapel, row after row, while the rest of the congregation gawped at us. I wondered who all these strange ladies and gentlemen were. They certainly weren't hospital staff. I had a sudden wild fancy that they were parents come to seek out their lost children. Perhaps my real mother was there, looking for her lost babe. Perhaps she really *was* Madame Adeline. I peered at all the ladies, trying to spot a flame of red hair under all the Sunday bonnets, a flare of pink lace at the throat of a stark Sunday dress.

'Stop staring, Hetty Feather!' Matron Pigface snapped.

'But they're staring at me!' I muttered, but not quite loudly enough for her to hear.

Harriet was one of the big girls supervising our privy visit when we got back.

'Who *are* all the ladies and gentlemen?' I asked her.

'They are the Sunday visitors,' said Harriet.

'Why are they here?'

'They like to look at us,' said Harriet. 'They will watch us at our Sunday dinner too. So mind your manners, little Hetty!'

I was not sure whether she was serious or not, but when we marched into the dining room, one two, one two, there they were, the ladies and gentlemen all lined up expectantly. We stood behind our benches while a big girl said grace in a very loud sing-song, making her voice extra holy because it was Sunday, and everyone was staring at her. Then we clambered onto our benches and the kitchen maids started serving.

It was roast beef, one slice each, with roast potatoes and carrots and cabbage from the garden. My special kind maid pushed her way quickly down to my table and gave me the biggest slice of beef and the largest, crispiest potato. She winked at me as she did so.

The ladies and gentlemen surrounding us were making such a noise I dared to speak myself.

'Thank you!' I whispered, smiling at her. 'You're very kind to me. What is your name?'

'I'm Ida Battersea.'

'Do I call you Matron or Miss?'

'You can call me Ida. What is your name, dear?'

'I'm Hetty Feather.' I wrinkled my nose. 'It's a silly name.'

'I think it is a very distinctive name,' she said.

'Oh, I do *like* you, Ida!' I said. I forgot to whisper, and a nurse came bustling up, glaring at me.

'Were you *talking*, child?' she demanded.

'Oh no, ma'am, it was me. I'm very sorry, ma'am,' said Ida.

'You must learn to hold your tongue,' said the nurse, as if Ida was one of us girls.

She flushed and bowed her head, but when the nurse moved away, Ida pulled a comical face at her back. I laughed and choked on my hot potato.

Ida had to serve the next table, and as soon as she was gone, three fine ladies stepped right up to our table and watched us eat.

'My, they're so neat and dainty! See how they spoon their gravy so carefully!' said one.

Of course we were neat and dainty. We knew that if we spilled anything down our Sunday tippets we'd get our knuckles rapped.

'Aren't the little ones sweet! Do you see that one with the high forehead? That's a clear sign of intelligence,' said another, singling out Sheila, who smirked at her in sickening fashion.

'I'm rather taken with the very little one. She's not much more than a baby,' said the third. 'Poor little scrap, I doubt she'll survive the winter.'

I scowled at her, which was a mistake.

'Oh dear, look at that expression! She's a surly little thing. No, no, *my* one's smiling prettily,' said the second lady, fumbling in her purse. 'Here, my dear, a little treat for you.'

She put a wrapped sweet beside Sheila's plate. Sheila popped the sweet down the front of her tippet before anyone else could see. Aha! So *that* was why she'd smiled so.

I knew how to play this game now. The three

ladies trotted further down the dining hall, and their place was taken by a gentleman and a lady, arm in arm.

'Oh, I do like the little ones,' said the lady.

I sat up, opened my eyes wide, and smiled.

'That's a dear little love, the one at the end. Look, she's smiling!'

'Bless the child, she's taken a shine to us!'

I grinned and gurned deliberately while they oohed and cooed – but they sauntered off without giving me anything. Sheila saw my face and laughed at me. She patted the tiny bulge in her tippet where her sweet was and licked her lips.

But then another lady and gentleman came nearer, both so fat that his waistcoat buttons were a-popping and her corsets were strained to bursting point. They were exclaiming over the meagreness of our portions, though this Sunday fare was practically a feast to us.

'I'm sure the children are half starving!'

I sucked in my cheeks and looked mournful.

'See the little one at the end! What a shame, she needs feeding up. Here, my dear, this is for you.' The gentleman pressed a slab of toffee in my hand. I gave him the greatest grin of my life and tucked it into my tippet immediately, with a triumphant little nod at Sheila.

Dear Ida came back with a second course for us, a

milk pudding with a splash of red jam. Ida served out the pudding *and* the preserve, so I got a whole spoonful of raspberry jam. My spirits lifted considerably. I hoped Gideon was faring equally well in the boys' dining room. Ladies often made a pet of him so I thought he might get singled out and given sweetmeats.

I collected four more boiled sweets myself, so that I was growing quite a chest under my tippet. I planned to eat my feast in bed, but as soon as we got outside after our Sunday meal, the big girls pounced on us little ones.

'Come on, give us your sweets, fair dos!' they said, feeling up our cuffs and down our tippets, practically turning us upside down and shaking us in their search for our sweets.

One girl snatched my precious slab of toffee, another gathered up my boiled sweets. I cried and tried to fight them off but there were too many of them.

'Poor little Hetty! Leave her alone, she's my baby!' Harriet shrieked, rushing to my rescue.

She managed to save one last sweet, a barley sugar. 'There you are, my pet. Eat it up quickly before someone grabs it. Shame on you, girls, descending on the babes like a swarm of locusts!'

She swept me off with her. I cuddled up close and sucked my barley sugar while she petted me.

I learned to be more wily the next Sunday, stowing my sweets under my cap. They made my shorn hair a little sticky but I didn't care. It had a good scrubbing on bath night. Meanwhile sucking my sweets helped the long nights seem less lonely.

I dreamed of home when I eventually fell asleep. It was so sad to wake and find myself imprisoned in the bleak hospital dormitory. I wondered how they were managing at home without me – especially Jem. I knew he would be fretting, frantic to know if I was all right. It gave me an added incentive in my writing class with Miss Newman. As soon as we could master our pens sufficiently, we were allowed to write home.

It was a long letter and it made my hand ache terribly. Miss Newman wrote it on a board and we copied it out laboriously:

Dear Mother

> *I now have the greatest pleasure in writing these few lines to you, hoping to find you quite well and happy, as it leaves me at present. Please give my love to all the family.*

> *I remain*
> *Your affectionate girl*
> *Hetty*

197

We were told to copy it exactly, neither adding nor deleting anything. Older girls who were fluent enough occasionally tried to add a few more personal lines, but Miss Newman had to approve them before they could be sent.

I was exhausted by the time I reached 'affectionate' and didn't concentrate hard enough. If I didn't insert enough *f*s and *t*s, or got my *i* and *o* the wrong way round, Miss Newman put a line through it and I had to start all over again. I longed to add my own personal message:

I detest it here and I miss you so and Sheila is mean and I hate Matron Peters and she stole my rag baby and I don't wear drawers nowadays.

However, I'd seen other girls have their letters confiscated if they so much as commented on the monotonous food or complained about being stared at on Sundays. I simply inserted two words after *Please give my love to all the family – especially Jem*.

After I'd signed my name, I filled the rest of the page with kisses.

Now that I could write, more or less, I tried hard to copy some of my picturings down on paper so that my stories were preserved. It was very hard to *find* any paper. I dared to steal a sheet from Miss Newman's special supply in the stationery cupboard, but it was mostly kept under lock and key. Harriet once obligingly tore a couple of pages from her exercise book, but my steadiest supplier was dear Ida. She slipped me paper bags and greaseproof paper from the kitchen. I stuffed them down my tippet and went around crackling all day until I could hide them in my mattress.

It was hard to find a place to write privately. Sometimes I sat up in the middle of the night and scribbled in the dark with a stolen stick of charcoal, though in the morning I saw my lines of writing wobbled up and down and sometimes crossed right over each other.

It wasn't enough to write *my* stories. I wanted to read new stories too. I had the Bible, and some of the stories were exciting, but the words were very hard to decipher. Miss Winterson lent me her book of fairy tales, and I read them over and over again. I went to the ball with Cinderella in my glass slippers, I let down my long hair like Rapunzel, I swam in and out of underwater coral palaces with the little mermaid.

Ida spotted me reading on my lap during dinner time. 'Watch out or one of them nurses will be after you, Hetty,' she hissed.

'I just love reading, Ida. I don't know what I shall do when I have to give the fairy-tale book back to Miss Winterson.'

She chewed her lip. 'I'll see if I can find you some

stories, Hetty. It's a wonder a tiny girl like you can read so well. You need encouragement.'

'What's that you're saying?' Matron Pigface came waddling up, snout quivering.

I quickly sat on my book, not wanting to get Nurse Winterson into trouble for lending it to me. I thought Ida would mumble something and move on, but she stood her ground.

'I said she needs encouraging, Matron,' she said.

'And why's that, pray? Matron Pigface enquired.

'Because she's clever,' said Ida.

'Clever as a cartload of monkeys, I'll grant you that,' said Matron. 'She needs watching all the time, that one. She doesn't need encouraging, she needs *suppressing*.'

Ida still didn't give up. 'She learns so fast. I think she could become a real scholar.'

Matron Pigface snorted with laughter. 'A foundling? Don't be ridiculous, girl. She'll be a servant, like all the others. That's all she's fit for and don't ever think otherwise. Now get back to the kitchen and stop wasting time! You're here to serve the food, not give your impertinent opinions. And don't let me see you favouring Hetty Feather or I shall make sure you lose your position.'

Ida swallowed. 'Beg pardon, Matron,' she said, and scurried off.

I sat uncomfortably atop the book of fairy

tales, fearing that I'd got Ida into serious trouble.

Ida didn't serve my table at supper. She stayed up at the end where the big girls sat. Matron Pigface bustled past me. She said nothing, but the look on her face said it all. *There! You've lost your friend now. You've been put in your place, Hetty Feather. I'm mistress here.*

But the next morning at breakfast Ida hovered at my table. I looked round anxiously for Matron Pigface but couldn't see her.

'It's her day off,' Ida whispered. 'I wish she'd stay off for ever. I can't abide her.'

'I call her Pigface,' I said.

'Well, you're very bad,' said Ida, but she grinned. 'Here, Hetty, shove this down your tippet.' She pulled a paper out from under her apron. 'It's Cook's, her special *Police Gazette*. She's read it now. She says there's lots and lots of stories in it.'

'Oh, Ida, thank you!'

I don't think Ida was a keen reader herself. She can't have read the *Gazette* stories or she wouldn't have passed them on to me. They weren't remotely suitable for small girls: tales of grisly murders and violent passion. I read them in a rush of excitement, my eyes popping.

I became a remarkably fast reader because it was so hard to find a private place where I could read in secret. I had to hide in cupboards and crannies and lurk at the back of buildings, with maybe five minutes to read in peace before the wretched bell started ringing. My eyes flew down each page. It was as if I had a minute to eat a whole meal. I bolted down each story in a great undigested lump – and it frequently kept me awake half the night.

When the matron put the light out and the whispering started, I stoppered my ears with my fingers and told myself the stories inside my head, but the other girls would not leave me alone. Sheila was especially tormenting, continually making reference to my red hair and temper.

'Oh, sew your lips up with a darning needle!' I responded. 'You'd better mind I *don't* lose my temper like mad Flora Jackson. She was a maid in a big house in the country and her mistress scolded her all the time, so one dark night Flora took leave of her senses and seized a ball of string and the sharpest carving knife in the kitchen. She trussed up her nagging mistress in her nightclothes and cut off her tongue, so she could not scold her any more. So be warned, Sheila Mayhew. I know where the knives are kept in the kitchen!'

There were stifled shrieks up and down the dormitory.

'How silly you are, Hetty. You certainly don't frighten me,' and Sheila – but her voice was high and squeaky and she certainly *sounded* frightened.

'What happened to Flora's mistress, Hetty? Did she *die*?'

'Oh no, she was left with her poor tongue cut in half so she couldn't speak any more – she just *gurgled*, oogle-oogle-oogle!'

'Ooooh!' the girls shrieked, so loudly that Matron Pigface came stomping back to give us all a severe scolding.

'Matron Peters had better watch out too,' I murmured darkly when she'd gone at last.

The next night the girls all begged for more stories of mad Flora and her mistress, and I recited the whole story again: there had been three whole pages devoted to this grisly tale in the *Police Gazette*. The next night I told them a new story, the night after that another, and when I had used up all the *Police Gazette* horror tales, I found it easy enough to make up my own.

Everyone begged for more, even Sheila and Monica, though half the girls woke up shrieking with terrible nightmares. Several took to wetting their beds and suffered horrible public humiliation, trailing their smelly wet sheets behind them – but these were the very girls who cried, 'Tell us a story, Hetty, a really bloody one,' the moment the lights went out.

I carried on like Scheherazade (Nurse Winnie was reading us *Tales of the Arabian Nights* during our darning sessions now), but one night I woke up to hear desperate sobbing coming from the bed opposite.

I was used to hearing the other girls cry – I sometimes cried myself – but this was different. I climbed out of bed and pattered over. It was the new girl, Polly. I seemed to have frightened her into fits.

I wasn't the new girl any more. There had been three new girls since me – Jane, Matilda and Maria – and each time my heart beat faster in the hope I might make a new friend. I tried to be kind and reassuring, I guided them to the privies, the dining hall, the classroom and the playground. I protected them when Sheila and Monica and the others starting their teasing, I helped them learn their letters, I even showed them how to darn, though I still found it a struggle myself.

But somehow my attempts didn't work. Jane was a dull, dull, dull girl who stared blankly with her mouth open when I tried to get her to picture things. She was shocked by my night-time stories.

'You're a very bad girl, Hetty Feather, telling about them things,' she declared, and would have nothing to do with me.

Matilda was more fun and I liked her big brown eyes and ready smile. She was a little slow at picturing herself, but marvelled when I turned the grey wastes of the playground into the hot sandy desert or the salty ocean as we played explorers or pirates. She begged for more when I told her my gory *Gazette* stories. Oh, Matilda seemed a perfect friend, and for a week or two I was actually happy at the hospital – but then Maria came.

Her bed was beside Matilda's and she sat next to her in class, so Matilda looked after her a little, which I thought only kind and fair, but soon Matilda and Maria were going round arm in arm, whispering secrets. *They* were friends now and I was the girl who was allowed to trail round after them on sufferance.

I resolved to give up my search for a friend. It was too painful. I made up my own companions in my head and we got along well enough. My imaginary friends all adored me, and begged to link their shadowy arms through mine, and listened spellbound while I told them stories.

Polly had appeared at midday, a plump girl with watery blue eyes. She had arrived with long white-blonde hair to her waist, but after a session with Matron Pigface and her dreaded scissors, she now looked like a dandelion puffball under her cap. She cried on and off in a dreary way throughout the day, but none of us took much notice. It was standard new-girl behaviour. She made not a peep of protest when I told my stories in the darkness of the dormitory. When we were settling down to sleep, I did call out, 'Goodnight, Polly,' but she did not reply, so I thought she must be sleeping already.

She was clearly not asleep now, though she still didn't answer when I whispered her name. She tried to lie still, her face in her pillow, but she could not stop sobbing.

'Don't cry so,' I said softly, patting her heaving shoulder. 'I know it's horrid here, but you will get used to it.'

Polly went on sobbing.

'I'm so sorry I told the story. I did not mean to frighten you so. I won't ever tell about the Meat-axe Murderer again, I promise. And he's all locked up in prison, so he can't hurt you.'

'It's not the Meat-axe Murderer man,' Polly sobbed. 'I want to go *home*.'

I sighed. 'So do I,' I said. The longing for Jem and Mother and everyone overwhelmed me again. I bit my lip hard to stop myself crying too. 'Oh, Polly, so do I.'

I reached out to pat her shoulder. She jumped at my touch.

'What is it? I didn't hurt you!'

'You're so cold.'

'It *is* cold. Here. Move up.' I burrowed under her covers, getting right into bed with her. 'Oh, your pillow's soaking wet! You must have been crying for hours.'

I moved her head and turned the pillow over. 'There, that's better, isn't it?'

She put her hands up over her head. 'I look so ugly now,' she wept.

'It does look a little strange, but it will grow soon. I quite like mine now. I look like a boy.'

'I don't *want* to look like a boy!' Polly sobbed.

'Oh, I do. They have much more fun. I have a wonderful big brother, Jem. He is going to come and fetch me home when I am old enough, and I have another even bigger brother, Nat. I have two more brothers here, in the boys' wing, and a sister, Martha, who sings in the choir very beautifully. I was very worried about my brother Gideon, so I dressed up in boys' clothes and went and found him, and I shall go again soon to check on him. I have another brother, Saul, but I don't think much of him at all. Don't you have brothers? I have yet another brother who's a soldier – his name is—'

And then I was stuck. I held myself rigid, hands over my mouth. I couldn't remember! I was forgetting my family already. I had never known this big brother, but we had talked of him often. Mother had always sighed when she said his name and kept his letters tied up with blue ribbon.

I started trying to say each member of the family, mumbling their names under my breath.

'Are you praying, Hetty?' Polly asked.

'Marcus! Oh, I have remembered!' I said, hugging Polly hard in my relief. 'I must never ever forget them. I shall say them over and over again each night. You must remember all your brothers and sisters, Polly.'

'I have none,' she said. 'My foster mother is Miss Morrison, who used to keep the school, Miss Morrison's Seminary for Young Ladies. She took a fancy to bringing up a foundling babe when she retired. She is my foster mother and I miss her sooooo.' Polly started wailing again. 'Every night I sat on my bed with its lovely rose quilt and she brushed my hair one hundred times.' She clasped her shorn head despairingly. 'There's nothing left to brush now!'

'We will picture it together,' I said. I started running my fingers through her sad, feathery tufts. 'There, this is the brush, and your hair is growing again, feel, growing and growing, it's past your ears now. I'll keep brushing, my goodness, how it's growing! There, feel it resting on your shoulders now?'

I felt Polly put her hands up in the dark and I braced myself, thinking she was going to be another Jane. But no, she felt the thin air and then whispered, 'Oh, it's back, and so long, and *this* time it's curly.'

'Oh, Polly, you can picture! Will you be my special friend?'

'I should like to be your friend more than anything, Hetty,' said Polly.

I stayed cuddled up with her until dawn, then I hurtled back to my own bed only a few moments before the big girl monitor burst into the room.

I helped Polly smooth her apron and tippet into place when we got dressed. When I placed her cap upon her head, I whispered, 'There, all your new curls are tumbling down past your shoulders.'

When Ida smiled at me at breakfast, I said, 'This is my new friend, Polly.'

Ida nodded at Polly in a kindly way.

'Ida is quite the nicest maid in the whole hospital,' I told Polly.

Ida blushed deeply, the pink in her cheeks making her look almost pretty. 'Hetty is quite the most *artful* girl in the whole hospital,' she said sprinkling sugar on my porridge. She sprinkled a little on Polly's plate too.

I made sure Polly sat next to me in lesson time, and I resolved to help her with her ABC very patiently. But I didn't need to! Polly's schoolmistress foster mother had taught her charge well. Polly could read as fluently as me, though I was now top reader of the entire infants class. She could write neatly too, in a curly copperplate that sent Miss Newman into raptures.

'Look, girls, mark this penmanship! See with

what style Polly writes her lesson, and not a single mistake!' she said, showing us all Polly's page.

If Polly had not been my true friend, I would have been a little irritated. Half the girls groaned jealously. Sheila and Monica started making up a vulgar verse together about Polly Penmanship. I quelled them with a terrifying look. No one should be allowed to tease my friend!

Polly proved gifted at darning too, sewing neatly and smoothly, an accomplishment that proved more popular. Our clothes were not marked in any way. We were handed out our clean clothes randomly on Sunday. If you were given badly darned stockings, the toes all cobbled together, you knew you'd be driven mad by the irritation, forever forced to take your boot off to ease the stocking this way and that.

Polly and I pictured together every playtime. We'd spread our arms and pretend we could fly. We might look as if we were simply running up and down the playground with our arms outstretched, but we knew we were swooping high above the sooty rooftops of London town. One day we'd fly to visit Polly's foster mother and sit at Miss Morrison's skirts and eat seedcake for our tea; the next day we'd fly to my village and sit with Jem in my squirrel house and eat gingerbread.

I told Polly about Madame Adeline and Tanglefield's Travelling Circus. I invited her to take part, though privately I was a little unsure about her as a circus performer. Although she got no more food than the rest of us, she remained a very sturdy child, flat-footed in her institution boots. But I need not have worried. Polly had as much imagination as me.

'There was a parrot at Miss Morrison's. He was called Polly too, though I think he was a boy. He used to squawk dreadfully and nip everyone, but he was very good with me. It was my special job to feed him, and he'd say, "Good girlie, good girlie." So I'll be a bird trainer at the circus and teach parrots to sing songs, and great hawks and eagles and albatrosses will fly about my head and do such tricks,' she said. She waved her hand and I *saw* her performing birds and marvelled.

I shared my purloined *Police Gazettes* with Polly, and we gasped and giggled together at their grisly stories. I wondered if Polly would wish to terrify the dormitory with her own version at night, but she was a tactful girl and left the public tale-telling to me.

She did still cry at times, long after the other girls slept, but I always slipped into her bed and cuddled her close and comforted her.

13

Polly and I even got ill together that winter. I'm not sure which of us started sniffing and sneezing first, but within a day we both had red and running noses and hacking coughs. Matron Pigface Peters gave us a rag each to wipe our noses, but they were made of harsh, hard cloth and rubbed us raw. Our heads were aching and our arms and legs hurt. All we wanted to do was lie down, but we were forced up into our everyday routine. It was especially cold and we stood shivering at playtime, barely able to stand.

'Run around, children! You need plenty of fresh air to blow those horrid colds away. Don't pull those long faces at me!' said Matron Pigface.

'But we're so cold, Matron. Mayn't we stay indoors just this once?' I snuffled.

'Cold? Of course you're cold if you loll around like that! Do some skipping! Take some exercise, you lazy little girls. And stop that shivering! You've got your good thick coats.'

We had our coats, but we had no woollen scarves or mittens. We had no underwear, so the icy wind blew straight up our skirts. We staggered miserably up and down, our faces grey, snot running freely. By bedtime we were both wheezing and dizzy with fever. I could not croak out a story for everyone. I could barely breathe. I lay there, head throbbing, while my bed seemed to rise up and down, voyaging to the ceiling and back. I lifted my head and was violently sick all over my pillow and coverlet. I crouched, shivering and sniffing, desperate to know what to do. I was sure I'd be punished for making such a terrible stinking mess. I had to try to clear it up, but I didn't know *how*.

'Oh, Hetty Feather, have you been *sick*?' Sheila called. 'I can smell it from here. How disgusting you are!'

'She couldn't help it,' said Polly. 'I feel sick too. Oh no—!' She vomited as well.

'Stop it! You're *both* disgusting,' said Sheila.

Some of the other girls woke too and groaned and complained.

'Ssh! I hear footsteps. It's Matron!' Monica hissed.

I started crying then, unable to lie down in my bed, terrified I might be whipped for being out of it. But it wasn't the dreaded Matron Pigface Peters. Lovely Nurse Winnie was on night duty. She came in with her lamp.

'Oh dear, oh dear, who's been sick?' she said. 'Is it you, Hetty? And poor Polly too!' She came up to me and felt my forehead. 'You have a fever, dear. You need proper nursing – and you too, Polly. Come along with me, girls.'

She ushered us out of the dormitory and down the corridor, into a room we'd never been in before, like a small dormitory with twelve beds.

'This is the infirmary, girls. Let's strip off those soiled nightgowns and get you washed and clean again, poor lambs.' She was so gentle with us that we both started crying, unused to such tenderness. When we were in our clean nightgowns, we were tucked into bed in the infirmary with new softer rags to blow our noses and bowls beside us in case we were sick again.

'There now. Try to get some sleep. I'll go and check the other girls and strip your soiled beds. Don't cry so. You'll feel better soon.'

'We're not going to be punished?' I said.

'Goodness, Hetty, you're both ill with the influenza. Of course you're not going to be punished.' Nurse Winnie sounded shocked. 'Dear goodness, what must you think of us!'

'I think *you're* lovely, Nurse Winterson,' I said.

She was truly angelic to both of us: she held the bowls when we were sick again; she lifted us onto the chamber pot; she wound wet towels round us to bring down our fever; she gave us sips of sugared water; she read aloud to us when we were restless; she clasped our hands when the doctor came to examine us. By this time the infirmary was full of sneezing sick girls, with further beds lining the corridor.

'Half the hospital has gone down with this wretched virulent influenza,' he said as he listened to Polly's chest. 'However, you're a sturdy child with excellent lungs. You'll be running around in a day or so, as right as ninepence.'

He looked graver when he undid my nightgown to listen to my chest. He bent closer, till his pomaded hair was right under my nostrils. He kept prodding me with the cold end of his stethoscope, shaking his head. 'This child is nowhere near as robust,' he declared. 'Severely undernourished. She has a sparrow's bones, no meat on them at all. She needs feeding up!'

'I eat the same as Polly, sir,' I said, but he took no notice.

'Give her black beer in the mornings, and full cream milk and plenty of porridge – or you'll lose her,' he said bluntly.

I shivered, with excitement as much as fear, because I could not help delighting in the fact that *I* was the child so sorely ill. I hated it when Polly was sent back to the dormitory the next day, almost fully recovered. I was so worried she might

216

form a friendship with another girl in my absence – but I could not help basking in the attention of dear Nurse Winnie at nights. Mercifully Matron Pigface Peters went down with the influenza herself and kept to her room. Several of the nurses were also ill, so during the day we were looked after by anyone available. Sometimes it was a big girl. One glorious day Ida came with a specially ordered bowl of creamy porridge for me. She sat beside my bed and insisted on feeding me, spooning porridge into my mouth as if I was a little baby. I was still feeling sick and kept shaking my head, but Ida tapped my mouth gently with the spoon, coaxing me.

'There's a good girl, Hetty. Another few spoonfuls just for me, eh? And look what I have for you here – a little slab of my own home-made toffee. You may suck on a square when you've finished your porridge.'

I cried a little then.

'Don't cry, dearie. Does your chest hurt bad? Perhaps you need a piece of flannel at your throat?'

'No, no, it's just you're being so kind to me. It's almost as if I was at home,' I wept. 'I miss Jem so much – and Mother.'

'What was your foster mother like, Hetty?' Ida asked.

'She was just . . . Mother.'

'She was kind to you?'

'She was very kind. Though she paddled me when I was a bad girl.'

'I'm sure you could never be truly bad,' said Ida. She lifted me up off the pillow to drink my milk. She had her arm round my shoulders, and I leaned against her gratefully.

I decided I was in no hurry to get better when Ida and Nurse Winnie were making such a fuss of me, especially when Nurse Winnie smuggled me a reassuring note from Polly.

Dear Hetty,

    I do hope you are not too ill. I miss you so dreadfully, it is HORRID without you.

    From your very loving friend, Polly.

Dear Polly I replied,

    It is ENORMOUSLY horrid not being with you, but I am trying hard to bear it. I will get better soon, I promise. Nurse Winnie is my friend and Ida is my friend too, but you are my most very SPECIAL friend in all the world and I am very affectionately

    Your Hetty

I was still not very strong and I had to labour long and hard over my letter. I asked Ida how to spell the great big words like *enormously* and *affectionately*, but she blushed and looked wretched.

'I'm not very good at writing, Hetty. I can't rightly say,' she said.

'Well, never mind, I'll ask Nurse Winterson,' I said, sad that I'd embarrassed her.

'I never had much schooling, see,' Ida said. She looked at me earnestly. 'That's the good thing about the hospital. You girls get a proper education. You're brought up almost like young ladies.'

'Yes, but we're *not* young ladies. We have to be servants,' I said, wrinkling my nose. 'I don't want to be a servant.'

Then it was my turn to blush because I realized I'd been tactless. 'I am sorry, Ida,' I said, taking her hand.

'There are worse positions in life,' she said flatly. 'And you're very bright, Hetty. Perhaps – perhaps you'll get a position as a lady's maid and wear a fine uniform and never have to do any hard work. Should you like that?'

I considered. 'Perhaps I should like it if she was a very *kind* lady, and let me dress up in her silks and velvets and gave me cake at tea time,' I said.

Ida laughed. 'You have wheedling ways, but I doubt any lady will let you do that.'

'Then I won't be a servant at all. I shall run away to the circus.'

'Oh yes?' said Ida. 'And what will you be there? A performing monkey?'

'I shall be a fine lady on a white horse,' I declared.

'With rings on your fingers and bells on your toes?' said Ida, not taking me seriously.

'No, I shall join my real mother, Madame Adeline, and she will give me a costume of pink spangles and we will ride our horses together in the circus ring,' I said.

'Whatever makes you fancy your mother is a circus lady?' said Ida.

'Oh, I am absolutely certain of it,' I said. 'Madame Adeline told me herself. More or less. And when I am big enough I shall go and find her, just you wait and see.'

'Well, you're not big enough yet, Hetty. You're still the smallest girl in the whole hospital. You must eat up all the milk puddings I bring you, every last morsel, and then you will get better.'

I *did* get better, though I think it was due to the love and attention of Ida and Nurse Winnie, not their milk puddings and medicine. But one of our sick girls, Sarah Barnes, grew worse. The nurses wrapped her in soaking sheets, but she was still burning hot when I touched her and she could barely sip her sugared water. She was so weak they had to lift her onto a chamber pot like a baby. And all the time, morning, evening, all through the night, she coughed and coughed.

I slipped out of bed and went to stand beside her, shivering. 'Poor Sarah,' I whispered. 'Is your throat very sore?'

'Yes!' she mumbled. 'Yes, it hurts.'

'Shall I get Nurse?'

'No. No, I want—'

'Who?'

'I want my *mother*,' Sarah sobbed.

I told Nurse Winnie and she looked stricken.

'Poor lamb! I wish she *could* see her foster mother, but it's strictly against the rules.'

'But she's so ill.'

'I know, Hetty, I know,' she said wearily, and she covered her face with her hands.

'Nurse Winterson . . . is Sarah *dying*?' I whispered.

'I hope not. But she is very, very poorly,' said Nurse Winnie.

Sarah started crying again that night, calling for her mother. She wouldn't quieten, no matter how Nurse Winnie tried to soothe her.

I got out of bed and crept nearer. I had the fanciful idea that I could picture Sarah's mother for her, tell her that she was coming very soon, that she loved her little daughter – but Nurse Winnie took hold of me and forced me back to bed.

'I know you mean well, Hetty, but you must not get too near poor Sarah, especially while she is coughing so. You must not risk re-infecting yourself. You're still quite a sick girl. Now go back to sleep, there's a good child.'

I tried to do as I was told, pulling my blanket high over my head to cut out the sound of Sarah. When I woke up in the morning the room was strangely quiet. I sat up. Sarah's bed was empty, her sheets pulled off, her mattress bare.

'Where's Sarah? Is she in the washroom?' I called anxiously.

'No, Hetty.' Nurse Winnie came over to me, her face very white, purple shadows under her eyes. 'No, Hetty, Sarah's gone to Heaven. She's with the angels now.'

I sat still, stunned. I'd asked if Sarah was dying, but I hadn't really meant it. Sarah was such a *real* girl, with her cough and her running nose and a tendency not to reach the privy in time. Yet now she was an angel in a long white dress, with wings sprouting out of her small shoulder blades? I was accomplished at picturing, but it was very hard imagining Sarah lolling on heavenly clouds, a halo over her lank brown hair.

'Don't be sad, Hetty. Sarah is happy now, and her poor cough is better,' said Nurse Winterson – but she didn't sound at all sure.

I lay down again, my heart beating fast. They said I was getting better, but might *I* die too? A new nurse came to take over from Nurse Winnie, a little sharp-faced woman I'd not seen before. It seemed she usually worked in the boys' wing, but was now working a shift with us because three of our nurses were ill themselves.

Nurse Winterson told her the news about Sarah. She was whispering but I could still hear her.

'Let's hope she is the only one we lose,' said Nurse Winnie.

'One of our boys is failing fast,' said the new nurse. 'A sad little lad, much troubled. Calling for his mother, and his father, and all his brothers and his sisters—'

'That's maybe my brother! I must go to him!' I said, getting out of bed.

'No, Hetty, don't fret, it won't be *your* brother,' said Nurse Winnie – but the sharp-faced nurse seemed taken aback.

'He *has* a sister Hetty!' she said.

'I have to see him. He's calling for me! I have to see him before he goes to the angels like Sarah,' I said frantically.

'Hush, child, it's not allowed,' said the sharp-faced nurse.

'*I* will allow it,' said Nurse Winnie.

She wrapped my blanket around me and lifted

223

me in her arms. She must have been exhausted after a long traumatic night, but luckily I was very light.

'You can't take her!' said the other nurse.

'Yes, I can,' said Nurse Winnie.

She carried me out of the infirmary, along the corridor, all the way to the boys' wing.

'Oh, Nurse Winterson, I love you dearly! Thank you so much. I need to see my brother Gideon so badly,' I said.

'I know you do, Hetty. I will make sure you see him.'

She pushed open a door with her hip and we entered a room with the familiar smell of carbolic and sickness. There were boys in the beds, sniffing and coughing, and a nurse bending over a boy at the end, looking grave. She was startled at the sight of us.

'Don't be alarmed. I have brought Hetty to see her brother,' said Nurse Winnie.

'Gideon! Oh, Gideon, I'm here!' I cried.

But it wasn't Gideon lying in the bed.

'Oh goodness! It's *Saul*! But . . . is Gideon all right?' I begged the nurse. 'My brother Gideon? He's very frail, with a weak chest. Where is he? Oh please, he hasn't died and gone to join the angels?'

'Hush, child, keep your voice down. Saul is very

sick. But Gideon is perfectly healthy. He has not caught the influenza,' said the nurse.

'You promise that's true?' I said, not certain I could trust her.

'Hetty!' said Nurse Winnie. 'Now, dear, do you have some words of comfort for your brother Saul?'

He was the *wrong* brother. I really wanted to rush out of the infirmary and find Gideon so I could see for myself that he was truly well – but I knew that in the circumstances this would not be looked on favourably. So I took a deep breath and stared down at Saul.

He was lying wretchedly in bed, his curls damp with sweat, his cheeks flushed with fever.

'Hello, Saul,' I said softly. 'It's me, Hetty.'

'I'm not sure he'll know you, child. He's very fevered,' said the nurse.

But Saul's brown eyes were open, staring straight at me. He knew me all right. He'd heard me burble about Gideon. He knew I'd never have begged to come and visit him. I suddenly felt terrible.

'Oh, Saul,' I said, wishing I could cry to look truly sorry. 'Oh, poor Saul, you look so ill. I've been ill too, but not as much as you. It must hurt so much. Here, let me hold your hand.'

I tried to take it, but he pulled away from me.

'I know you don't like me, but never mind, because I like *you*,' I said. I was lying now, but it

225

seemed only right and fair. 'You are my dear brother and I wish I could comfort you. I wish Mother could come.'

Saul's eyes filled with tears. I tried desperately hard to think what it must be like to be him.

'I think Mother loved you best,' I whispered, bending down beside him. I started stroking his damp hair. This time he didn't try to push me away. 'Yes, you were her special baby, her little lamb, but then Gideon and I came along and she had to attend to us. You got pushed out of the way. No wonder you did not like us. But Mother still loved you best. When she took you to the hospital she was so sad. She could barely speak for days after, she just moped in a corner, missing her special boy.'

'Hetty, Hetty, try to *cheer* your little brother,' said Nurse Winterson.

But Saul was smiling a little and I knew my words were cheering him immensely. I stayed crouched by his side, whispering to him about Mother, and he stopped tossing restlessly and curled closer. His hand was near mine, and this time when I took it he clasped me back.

His eyelids starting drooping. When they closed, I started uneasily, fearful that he might be dead – but I could hear his laboured breaths and the wheezing of his chest.

'Come, Hetty. He is sleeping peacefully now. I must take you back,' said Nurse Winnie.

I staggered to my feet, stumbling over something on the floor. It was Saul's crutch.

'He'll not be needing that any more,' said the sharp-faced nurse ominously, tidying it into a cupboard.

I burst out crying then. It was almost as if she'd taken Saul himself and stowed him in the cupboard. I cried all the way back to the girls' wing, though Nurse Winnie did her best to console me. She was sorry for me, and doubtless frightened lest any other nurse asked why I was crying so. I tried to stop, because I didn't want to get her into trouble, but I felt too sad. For all I prided myself on my picturing skills, I'd never before imagined what it was like to be Saul. I had pitied myself often enough, and fretted about dear Gideon, but I'd never cared a jot for Saul.

I resolved to be a true sister to him if by some miracle he made a full recovery. I'd disguise myself in breeches again and slip along to the boys' wing on a regular basis. I'd make a great fuss of *both* my brothers. I'd wheedle sweets out of the Sunday visitors and hide them away from the thieving big girls. I'd keep every one for Saul and Gideon, and take pleasure in seeing them suck them. They'd give me sticky embraces, telling me I was their dear sister Hetty.

But the next morning I heard the boys' nurse whispering to Nurse Winnie. I heard Saul's name – and I knew he was dead. I started crying anew.

'Oh, Hetty, you have such sharp ears! You poor lamb, I am so sorry. Still, at least you were able to say goodbye to him,' said Nurse Winnie.

'I can't bear it if he's really dead,' I sobbed. 'I haven't had time to make him like me!'

'Of course he liked you, Hetty. You were a lovely sister to him. You must try not to grieve so. He will be happy now in Heaven. He will be there with our dear Sarah.'

I tried to imagine Saul and Sarah playing together in white angel nightgowns. I did not think Saul would care for Sarah. Her nose would run and she would start wailing. He would provoke her and prod her with his crutch.

'Nurse Winterson, will Saul be lame in Heaven?'

'No, that is the joyous thing. God will cure him. Saul will be able to run around on two strong legs. Isn't that wonderful?'

'Why couldn't God cure him *here*?' I said.

'Oh, Hetty, you're such a child for questions, even when you're ill,' said Nurse Winterson, sighing hard.

They let me out of the infirmary the next day. Polly greeted me with a great hug.

'I thought you might die and then I couldn't bear it,' she said fervently.

'I think I *nearly* died. Sarah did – and my brother Saul.'

'Will you go to their funerals?' Polly asked in awe.

I rather hoped I *would* go. I had never been to a funeral, but it seemed to be a very grand and sombre occasion – and anything was better than the monotony of the hospital routine. I think they must have *had* funerals, but I wasn't invited. We sang a special hymn in chapel on Sunday – and that was the last time their names were ever mentioned.

14

Christmas was coming but I didn't know whether to get excited. I asked Harriet how it was celebrated at the hospital.

'Christmas is rather like a special Sunday,' she said, which depressed me utterly.

I hated the long cold hours in chapel. I'd started to hate Sunday dinner too. I still simpered so that the ladies and gentlemen would give me sweets, but the big girls were wise to me now, and stole them all from me the moment I stepped outside the dining room.

I tried looking to Harriet for protection, but she had developed a ridiculous passion for one of the younger gentlemen visitors and hung back, blushing and smiling, frequently the very last foundling out of the dining room.

He wore a gold tie-pin in the shape of a P, so Harriet spent entire *hours* wondering if he was a Philip, a Peter or a Paul.

'I think I heard his wife calling him *Peregrine*,'

I fibbed, making up the silliest name I could think of.

'Nonsense, Hetty! And that lady isn't his *wife*, she's far too old, years and years older than him. She might even be his mother, though I rather think she is his older spinster sister.'

She was a very plain, pale, serious-seeming lady who always wore plain charcoal-grey dresses with no adornments – so perhaps Harriet was right.

She certainly seemed convinced he was fancy-free and conducting a full-scale flirtation with her, though as far as I could see he didn't so much as glance in her direction. But she was happy to dream.

'Will all the ladies and gentlemen gawp at us when we eat our Christmas dinner too?' I said.

'Oh yes!' said Harriet happily. 'And they will be in the chapel for the Christmas service with the choir and the *tableau vivant*.'

'What's a *tableau vivant*?' I asked.

'Oh, it's very pretty, a representation of the Nativity. I hope each year that I might get picked as Mary. I would so love to play the virgin mother in all her holiness with everyone gazing – especially *him*.'

I knew all about the Nativity. Every Christmas time Mother hung up a big picture of baby Jesus in the manger, with all his visitors adoring him.

'So is this *tableau vivant* like a play?'

'There are no words, Hetty, and you have to keep very still. It's like a living picture.'

This wasn't such good news. It didn't sound as if anything *happened*. I longed for drama, angels proclaiming at the tops of their voices, innkeepers turning away the holy couple, wise men processing with their exotic gifts.

'How do we know who is who if no one moves or says anything?' I said.

'Don't be so silly! They wear special costumes. Mary has a beautiful dress of brilliant blue and a long white veil,' said Harriet, sighing wistfully. 'Imagine!'

Oh, I could imagine. I suddenly understood. Harriet had been wearing an ugly brown dress and a ridiculous cap since she was five years old.

'I do hope you get to be Mary,' I said. 'Or if not, perhaps *I* could be Mary?'

My heart beat fast at the thought. I pictured myself in that blue dress, felt the soft bright silk on my arms, the long veil brushing past my shoulders.

'Oh, Hetty!' said Harriet, and I saw she was trying not to laugh. 'You are much too little. And you have red hair.'

I was rather put out by this. Harriet was meant to be my friend.

'I could stand on a box. And my hair wouldn't show much underneath my veil,' I said, a little sulkily. However, I had another idea. 'Or as I am really little, perhaps I could be baby Jesus? I could crouch inside a box, and be like baby Jesus in the manger.'

This time Harriet couldn't help laughing heartily. 'You are so comical, Hetty! You couldn't possibly pass as Jesus! No, they have a *real* baby, one of the new foundling babes from the nurseries. Last year it cried so loudly that it almost drowned out the singing of the choir.'

'I could do that. I am very good at crying,' I said. 'Who chooses the children for the *tableau vivant*?'

'I'm not sure,' said Harriet. 'Perhaps the matrons and the nurses?'

I had no chance at all if Matron Pigface Peters had any say. But dear Nurse Winnie would surely put in a good word for me.

'Or maybe it's the teachers,' said Harriet.

Aha! Miss Newman was too strict a teacher to have obvious favourites, but we all knew she favoured Polly and me because we were the cleverest. Perhaps she would pick both of us? I thought hard about costumes. I did not wish to be a shepherd or a guest at the inn. Their costumes would be very commonplace. But the wise men would surely wear fine gowns of velvet and brocade – and if they were kings, they should have golden crowns on their heads!

'Oh, Harriet, we could be the three wise men!' I said. 'You could be the big one and you could be first to bow down to baby Jesus and give him a big present. And then Polly could be the middle-sized wise man and give a middle-sized present. Then I could come last and be a teeny tiny wise man with a very teeny tiny present.'

Harriet laughed so hard that tears rolled down her cheeks. 'It's not *Goldilocks and the Three Bears*, Hetty! You are so funny! And besides, we are girls, so we only play the lady parts. The boys always play the wise men.'

'But that isn't fair!' I reckoned it up, counting on my fingers. 'There are heaps and heaps of men parts. There are only two lady parts, Mary and the innkeeper's wife. Unless – is an angel a man or a lady?'

Harriet did not look sure. 'I think an angel can be either,' she said.

'Then I could be an angel and wear a long white nightgown. Oh, and I could have *wings*, great feathery wings. Do you think I could have wings that really fly?'

'*Pigs* might fly before they let you be an angel, Hetty,' said Harriet. 'Everyone says how fierce and bad you are. And you fidget so. You could never be part of a *tableau vivant* where you have to stand still as still throughout the entire service. Now stop plaguing me about the *tableau vivant*. Tell me, did you happen to notice the exquisite cravat my gentleman was wearing this morning?'

But I was in a sulk and did not want to discuss Philip-Peter-Paul-Peregrine. I didn't care if he was choked by his own exquisite cravat. I just wanted to be in the *tableau vivant*.

I told Polly all about it that night.

'We could both be angels, Polly. Well, perhaps not the big special angel who tells the wise men about Jesus.'

'Gabriel,' said Polly.

'Yes, that one. But there are lots of *other* angels – the hymn says, *A host of heavenly angels*, and I'm sure a host means a great deal. So we could be small angels, baby ones—'

'Cherubs,' said Polly.

'Yes, cherubs!' I thought back to the Nativity picture at home. 'There were definitely cherubs at the Nativity. They were up at the corners, flying above the stable, but they didn't have any clothes on, just little wisps.'

'We would have to wear clothes, Hetty,' Polly said firmly.

But we weren't chosen to be angels, wisps or no wisps. *Monica* was picked to be a small angel. We were astonished. She was such a thin, colourless girl with very little personality. She just echoed everything Sheila said. Sheila seemed equally taken aback, convinced that she would make a far superior angel. She started to tease and torment Monica – but Monica didn't retaliate. She had become irritatingly holy since being chosen.

'You're making Jesus very unhappy calling me silly names and pinching me, Sheila,' she declared. 'I shan't play with you any more until you say sorry.'

'I'm not a bit sorry,' said Sheila, marching off. 'I'd far sooner play by myself.'

She stood stamping her feet and glowering in a corner of the playground while Monica smiled in a maddening saintly way and struck angelic poses. I walked arm in arm with Polly past Sheila and felt almost sorry for her. A truly kind child would have invited Sheila to walk with us – but I am afraid I am only kind when I want to be.

I definitely tried to be kind to my real friends. I decided I wanted to give a Christmas present to Polly, to Harriet, to Nurse Winterson, and to Ida. I did not have any money apart from Jem's precious sixpence, safely hidden inside the knob of my bedhead. I did not have an opportunity to go shopping in any case. I had not been outside the grounds of the hospital since arriving.

This meant I had to make my presents. I certainly wasn't a competent needlewoman. Besides, I had no materials. But I was an opportunistic thief. I was sent in disgrace to Matron Peters's room for cheeking one of the nurses. While standing there being seriously scolded, I saw she had a Chinese bowl of dried lavender and rose petals on her little table. This gave me a wonderful idea. I edged nearer and nearer the bowl, my hands behind my back.

When Matron Pigface consulted her punishment book to check just how many times I had been in trouble, I grabbed a big handful of dried flowers and stuffed them up my sleeve.

I worried a little when I said my prayers at night, in case thieves went straight to Hell, so I told God I was very sorry. But it didn't stop me snatching a torn apron from the mending basket the next day, and hanging onto my needle and thread instead of handing them in to Nurse Winterson after our darning session.

I made four little lavender sachets with my stolen snippets. I tried to fashion them into hearts, but they were woefully lumpy and lopsided. I wanted to sew long loving messages on each, but I didn't have the skill or the time, so I simply stitched each name. Ida was mercifully short, and Polly was simple enough. I had to write Harriet in very tiny stitches, but even so her name had to wind round the edge of her heart. I could not possibly attempt Nurse Winterson in its entirety, and I was fast running out of time, so she had to make do with a hastily stitched NW. She seemed delighted all the same, and kissed me on the cheek. Harriet kissed me too, and gave me her own presents. She had fashioned me a very little dolly out of scraps of wool. She was too small to cuddle close so was no real substitute for my rag baby, but I was still very grateful and gave Harriet many kisses back.

Polly had a present for me too – a pen! She had found a jay's feather in the playground and fashioned the end into a proper quill.

'I can't quite figure how to get any ink,' she said, a little anxiously. 'It would spill if I tried to smuggle some from the classroom inkwells.'

'Never mind, Polly. I can write secret stories in *invisible* ink, or perhaps I could prick my finger and write in blood, though it would have to be a very *short* story. But I *love* my quill pen.'

'And I love my scented heart,' said Polly, and we gave each other a fierce hug.

Ida gave me a present too. I was rather hoping for one, but I thought it would be some delicious titbit, maybe another slab of toffee or a little iced cake.

'Here, Hetty,' she whispered at Christmas Eve supper. 'Don't open it until tomorrow morning, now!' She dropped a little square parcel in my lap.

Definitely a cake, I thought, my mouth watering. I hoped it would have extra-thick icing, and maybe yellow marzipan too, and a surplus of cherries. I was in such a greedy daze of anticipation I almost forgot I had a present to give to Ida too. I fumbled up my sleeve where I had hidden it.

'Are you looking for a handkerchief, Hetty?'

'No, no. Where's it *gone*?' I said, wriggling and scrabbling.

Ida's present had gone right up my sleeve and down inside my dress. I tapped my front. There it was, a little lump above my own real heart. I edged it up towards the neck of my dress.

'Is it moving? Oh dear Lord, have you got a mouse down your dress?' Ida squealed, backing away from me.

'No, silly Ida! It's *your* present.'

'You have a Christmas present for me?' said Ida.

'Yes. Ssh!' I said, peering round to make sure we weren't being observed. I scrabbled down my dress. 'I haven't got any fancy paper to wrap it with, so

240

you will see what it is right this instant. Perhaps you can wrap it up yourself and try to forget what it is, and then when you open it on Christmas day it will come as a splendid surprise. Ah!'

I fished the lavender heart right out into the open. It had got squashed out of shape during its journey up and down my frock and my stitches seemed very big and uneven. I offered it shyly, hoping Ida wouldn't laugh at my efforts.

Ida didn't laugh; she *cried*. She stared at the crumpled heart in her hand and tears welled in her eyes, spilling down her cheeks.

'Oh, Ida, don't cry. I'm sorry it's such a small and shabby present. I will try harder next year,' I said earnestly.

'It's a *wonderful* present – so kind of you, Hetty – oh, bless you, child,' Ida mumbled, and then hurried away to the kitchen, forgetting her serving tray in her haste.

Sheila glared at me. 'What have you done to make Ida cry, Hetty Feather?'

'I have made her *happy*,' I said stoutly, though I wasn't quite sure if this was true.

I couldn't wait till Christmas morning to open my present from Ida. I got up in the middle of the night, clutching my precious small parcel. I tiptoed the length of the dormitory to the washroom. I knew where the nurses kept a candle and matches, in case a child was taken poorly in the night. I took the candle into a corner and lit it with a match. Then I sat down cross-legged and opened my parcel.

It wasn't cake. It wasn't anything to eat at all. It was a tiny book, bound in red, with gilt lettering: *The Story of Thumbelina*. I opened it up with trembling fingers. The story was about a very, very small girl called Thumbelina, and there were *coloured illustrations*! I saw Thumbelina with pink cheeks and very yellow hair, tucked up neatly in a brown walnut-shell bed. I stroked her hair and patted her tiny quilt and then read the first few pages, though I had to squint in the candlelight and it was fearfully cold in the dank washroom.

Dear Ida! She had chosen the smallest book she could find so I could hide it easily about my person. Thumbelina was even smaller than me, yet she was the heroine of her fairy tale, and when I peeked at the ending I saw she lived happily ever after.

I was frozen solid when I eventually stole back to bed, but glowing inside, warmed by Ida's loving generosity. At breakfast I waited until she came to serve us our porridge and then I grabbed hold of her hand tightly.

'Thank you, Ida!' I said passionately. 'I do love you so.'

The other girls giggled, thinking I was simply thanking Ida for my porridge. But Ida understood.

She gave my bowlful an extra sprinkling of brown sugar and patted my shoulder, smiling all the while.

I marched off to chapel feeling very happy. For once I sat through the long, long service without fidgeting, because I had the wondrous Nativity *tableau vivant* to gaze at. The participating children kept still as statues. Even the newborn babe in the cardboard manger slept peacefully throughout. Mary was one of the big girls in Harriet's class, thin and dark and a little gawky, but strangely graceful now. She knelt before the baby, hands clasped in awe, her beautiful bright-blue dress draped decorously about her.

Joseph was one of the big lads, tall as a man, splendid in his orange striped robe. The shepherds were arranged artistically on the left, some standing, some kneeling. There was even a stuffed sheep, and the smallest shepherd clutched a toy lamb. The three wise men paraded on the right, wearing large gold crowns studded with glass jewels. Each boy sported a long false beard to show they were very old and very wise. Oh, how I longed to have a beard too!

Best of all, there were the angels, an entire flock of them, standing aloft upon the stable roof, in gauzy white with great feathery wings, Monica amongst them, pink and pious, her eyes raised upwards.

There was one angel who seemed to be truly flying, dangling on a rope from the chapel rafters, his bare feet on the points of a silver star; the most wondrous angel, with a halo illuminating his dark curls. You will never guess who it was! My own little brother, suspended in mid-air, his arms gesturing gracefully, his toes pointed, dancing down from Heaven.

'It's Gideon!' I whispered proudly to Polly. 'My brother Gideon.'

I felt I could sit there in the chapel for ever. I was so happy for Gideon, and so relieved that he was well and making such a grand job of this angel acting. I glowed with pride when I heard the ladies and gentlemen talking as we ate our Christmas dinner afterwards.

'Bless the children, they looked so splendid in the *tableau vivant*.'

'They kept so still, even the tiny ones.'

'The little boy angel was by far the best.'

'Oh, I agree! A true little angel up there in mid-air!'

I nudged Polly, and happily munched my way through my roast goose and my plum pudding. We each had an orange too. Some of us little ones were inexperienced orange eaters and tried to bite into the bright dimpled skin. I might have done the same because we never had oranges at the cottage, but I watched Polly and copied her as she peeled the skin away and divided her orange into segments.

We had no official presents as such, but when we lifted our mugs to take a drink, we discovered a brand-new polished penny. I hid mine later on top of Jem's silver sixpence. I went to sleep that night with Polly's pen under my pillow, Harriet's doll tucked in beside me, and my tiny book clutched to my chest.

15

We were given an orange and a new penny the next Christmas – and the next and the next and the next. That was the worst thing of all about the hospital: the sheer sameness of every single day.

If things *did* change, it always seemed to be for the worse. Harriet left the hospital to go into service as a nursery maid. She cried when she said goodbye, telling me she'd never care for any of her new nursery charges the way she cared for me. I missed her dreadfully. She had been so kind to me, and I'd loved sitting on her lap and being babied. Thank goodness I still had Polly!

We moved into the upper school, into a different dormitory. Of course I remembered to transfer Jem's sixpence to my new bedpost. I had to say farewell to dear Nurse Winnie and Miss Newman. Thank goodness Ida could still serve me every day in the dining room, giving me illicit gifts of raisins and jam and knobs of butter when no one was watching.

'How are you doing, Hetty?' she'd always ask.

'I'm doing very well, Ida,' I mostly said.

I wasn't doing well, I was doing very badly. I didn't care for my new teacher, Miss Morley, and she certainly didn't care for me – or Polly either. Miss Newman had been strict but she liked both of us. When we answered correctly or asked an interesting question, her eyes lit up behind her spectacles and she seemed delighted to teach us.

Miss Morley stopped asking us to answer questions, because she knew we'd get them right, and this seemed to irritate her.

'Don't sit there with that smug expression on your face, Hetty Feather. We all know *you* know the answer,' she'd say, and she'd give a false yawn and encourage all the others to laugh at me.

I couldn't *help* knowing the answers because our lessons didn't progress. We could mostly all read and write by now, and do the simplest sums – and there we stuck, not working our way forward at all, going over the same dull facts again and again.

There were maps all round our classroom wall and I'd stare at all the different countries and picture a flea-sized Hetty sailing across the blue sea and landing on each pink and yellow and green land.

'Stop daydreaming, Hetty Feather, and attend to your dictation,' Miss Morley snapped.

'Can't you tell us a little about the countries on the map, Miss Morley? I wonder what it is like in great big Africa or India or Japan? Do the children do dictation there? Do they wear long dresses and caps, or do they wear short clothes – or maybe if it's very very hot, no clothes at all?'

The others sniggered and Miss Morley flushed, though I hadn't meant to be impertinent.

'Stop these ridiculous questions, Hetty Feather. You don't need to know the answers. It's not as if *you're* ever going to voyage to foreign parts. You're going to be a servant like all the other girls. You only need to write a decent hand, read a recipe and add up your groceries correctly.'

I felt I needed to do so much more! I still hated the idea of being a servant. I feared I would be a very bad one. We were taught how to wash clothes and scrub floors now, helping out with all the household chores in the hospital. I hated getting hot and wet. I was so bored I distracted myself by telling stories in my head, not concentrating on the tedious housework.

'Use some more elbow-grease, Hetty Feather!' they'd scream at me. 'Watch what you're doing!' they'd yell when I started and knocked over my pail of water.

Polly was as bored as I was, particularly in lessons. She could not bear our arithmetic sessions because Miss Morley frequently made mistakes. Polly pointed out a simple subtraction error on the blackboard early on, waving her arm earnestly.

'What *is* it, Polly Renfrew? I haven't finished the sum yet.'

'I know, Miss Morley, and I'm sorry to interrupt, but I don't think you've noticed that you've subtracted an eight from a three and put the answer as five, and yet you haven't borrowed ten from the next line so that nine is incorrect,' she said helpfully.

She wasn't being impertinent. At this stage she didn't realize that Miss Morley's grasp of arithmetic was extremely shaky. She thought she'd simply made a silly slip and would be grateful for her intervention.

Grateful! Miss Morley flushed an ugly scarlet and rubbed the entire sum from the blackboard. 'How *dare* you admonish me, Polly Renfrew! Come out here.'

Polly stepped forward uncertainly.

'Hold out your hand.'

Polly held it out politely, as if Miss Morley was going to shake it. But she seized her long ruler instead and went *whack whack whack* across Polly's soft white hands.

We all jumped. Our eyes stung. We'd been threatened with whippings and beatings many times in the infant school, but the only actual physical punishment any of us had received was an impatient tug on the ear or a light tap on the backs of our legs. This was a cruel assault. We could see the painful red weals on Polly's palms. Polly's face crumpled and she started crying.

I was beside myself. 'How dare you hit her when she's done nothing wrong at all, you cruel, wicked woman!' I cried, and I seized her ruler and hurled it into a corner of the classroom. The whole class gasped. I was a little shocked myself. I hadn't quite meant to say those words, they just spurted out of my mouth in a torrent.

'Come here, Hetty Feather!' Miss Morley said. 'I will not stand for this behaviour!'

I thought she would retrieve her ruler and beat me to within an inch of my life. I decided I would not cry like poor Polly. I would hold my head up high and be a brave, unflinching martyr. She could beat me three times, six times, even a dozen; she could beat my hands into a bloody pulp but I would not murmur or shed a tear. I would stare back at her like a basilisk, wishing her dead.

But she didn't beat me even once. She seized hold of me by the wrist, digging her nails in hard, and tugged me right out of the classroom. I thought she was simply standing me in the corridor and decided I didn't mind in the least. I could just stand and picture the past in my own private daydream. But Miss Morley marched me right along the corridor. I realized she was taking me to Matron.

My heart started thudding then. The senior school matron made Pigface Peters seem sweet as sugar. Matron Bottomly was thin and pinched, with a permanent pucker in her forehead. She had a big hooked nose like a beak and always looked as if she'd like to peck you very hard. Matron Bottomly had already told me off several times for talking in corridors, she had chastised me for tearing my dress when I fell over playing tag, she had made me scrub a whole floor twice over because I'd left one or two slimy soap smears. (Oh, how I wished Matron Bottomly had slipped on them and landed on her bony stinking bottom!) What might she do when she knew I'd shouted at a teacher, taken her ruler and thrown it away?

I felt I *might* cry now, but I stared hard, scarcely daring to blink in case the tears started spilling. I was pushed unceremoniously into Matron Bottomly's room and forced to stand there in front of her while Miss Morley gave a highly exaggerated account of my rebellion.

'It was total insubordination, actual physical violence!' Miss Morley declared dramatically, drops of spittle on her chapped lips.

Matron Bottomly rose from her desk and looked me up and down. I started trembling but I looked her up and down back, my fists clenched.

I will not cry, I said inside my head. *I will not cry,*

no matter what they do to me. I can bear it, whatever it is. They cannot kill *me. I will be brave.*

'You are a child of Satan, Hetty Feather,' said Matron Bottomly. 'You have his Hell-red hair and his flaming temper. We must quench this devilish fire. You must be taught a severe lesson.'

I was so crazed with fear I thought she meant a literal lesson. I dared to breathe out, because I knew I was always quick to learn. But this punishment had nothing to do with books.

'Take hold of her, Miss Morley,' said Matron Bottomly.

They each seized a wrist and pulled me to the door. They dragged me down the corridor. I thought they were taking me to the boys' wing. We'd heard fearful rumours that the baddest big boys were beaten with a cat-o'-nine-tails. Perhaps they were now going to whip me with this dreadful instrument! I gritted my teeth, though they were chattering now.

But when we reached the grand staircase, they dragged me up one flight of stairs and then another, right to the very top of the building, to a little attic room in the tower.

They opened a door at the end. It was empty apart from an old blanket and a chamber pot.

'No!' I cried. 'No, please – you can't put me in there!'

'Oh yes we can, Hetty Feather. You stay here and

253

pray to be a better girl,' said Matron, and she thrust me inside. The door slammed shut and I heard the sound of a key turning. I was locked in! I heard their footsteps retreating. Perhaps they were simply trying to frighten me. They would come back any minute. They couldn't leave me locked in here!

There was only one very small window, set high up in the wall. It had bars across, as if this was truly a prison. I tried jumping up but could only catch a glimpse of sky. I was very small, but there was no way I could ever wriggle through those bars – and it was a sheer drop anyway.

I tried hurling myself against the door, knocking all the breath out of my body. It held fast. I was truly a prisoner.

'Well, what do I care?' I said aloud. 'I will show them. It is not so very dreadful to be locked in for an hour or two. They will have to come back soon because it is nearly dinner time. Meanwhile I shall amuse myself. I shall pretend I am a princess locked up by two evil wicked witches in a tall tower.'

I pictured this determinedly, inventing a magnificent Prince Jem who climbed the tower and rescued me. We lived happily ever after in his wondrous kingdom – while the two witches were locked up in their own tower for ever.

I amused myself with this story for quite a while, but my stomach started rumbling. I could not hear the clock chiming from my isolated prison but I was certain it was long past dinner time now. So they intended to starve me, did they? Were they going to keep me locked up right until supper time?

I kept staring at the chamber pot. It was clearly there to be used, so perhaps I truly was to be left for hours yet. I decided I would not sit on the pot, no matter what. It would be too humiliating for the contents to be inspected by Matron and Miss Morley.

The hours went by, and I fidgeted on my blanket, trying to divert myself. In the end I simply had to squat on the pot in an undignified fashion or have an accident. I waited further hours, and after a long, long while all my picturing skills faded. I could think of nothing to divert myself. Surely it would be supper time soon?

They *had* to let me out for supper. They couldn't leave me locked up in this tiny room until I starved to death. I listened desperately for the sound of approaching footsteps, but there was just endless silence. I tried singing to make a sound in the room, but my voice sounded too high, too weird, as if I was a crazy girl.

I tried to lie down on the blanket, but the floorboards were hard and the blanket smelled stale and musty when I nuzzled into it for comfort. I remembered my long-ago rag baby, and started weeping. Once I'd started I couldn't stop. I sobbed frantically, but still no one came.

'I'm sorry!' I shouted. 'Please come back, Matron! I've learned my lesson now!'

But she didn't come. It seemed to be getting darker in the small room. Oh my Lord, was it evening now? Were they going to keep me locked up all night long?

I shouted until my voice cracked, but still nobody came. I threw myself about the attic, kicking and screaming. I tore off my stupid cap and pulled my own hair. It was long again now, in two tight plaits, but I undid them and shook my head in despair, my hair wild about my shoulders.

I was so thirsty from crying I could barely swallow. How could they leave me without even a few sips of water? They *had* to come back soon or I would surely die. Was that what they really *wanted*? Oh dear Lord, what if they never came back? What if I mouldered up here in my dark prison for ever? What if they waited until I was a grisly skeleton in scraps of brown, crumbling to dust?

Then, at long, long last, when it was getting really dark, I heard footsteps coming along the corridor, and the sound of a key in the lock.

'Oh, at last!' I said. 'I'm so sorry. You will let me out now, won't you?'

It was Nurse Macclesfield, one of the senior school staff. She was carrying a bucket and a plate and a mug. 'Of course you are sorry, Hetty Feather – and you'll be sorrier still by morning!'

'What! You're not going to keep me locked up here all night!' I said in horror.

'You must learn the error of your ways, you wicked girl.' She seized my pot, pulling a face of disgust, and emptied it into her bucket. Then she put the plate and mug down on the floor and went to close the door on me again.

'No! Oh, Nurse Macclesfield, have pity on me! Let me out!'

I tried to cling to her, but she pushed me away.

'Don't you dare try to attack me the way you attacked poor Miss Morley. She said you were like a wild beast. It's time you were tamed!'

She slammed the door shut on me, rattled the key in the lock and marched off.

'Please come back, please, please!' I screamed, though I knew she would not relent.

At last I drank the water down in three great gulps, and ate the single slice of dry bread. It was almost pitch dark now, and I hunched up on my blanket. I could not think up a single new story, but old tales from the *Police Gazette* started swirling in my mind. Mad Flora crouched beside me, knife clutched at the ready. The Meat-axe Murderer slavered at the door, dripping with blood.

I pulled the blanket right over my head, but

they crept underneath too. I put my hands over my ears because they were whispering menacingly, threatening me.

'Oh, Hetty, are you in there?'

Wait! Was this a real voice, outside my attic prison? I heard knocking at my door.

'Hetty? Have they locked you in there?'

I knew that husky voice.

'Is it really you, Ida?'

'Oh dear God, they've really locked you up inside.'

'Ida, please, turn the key and let me out!'

'I can't, my love, those witches have taken away the key,' she said. She sounded as if she was crying herself.

'How long are they going to keep me here?' I asked desperately.

'I don't know. I think maybe all night long. I'm so very sorry, Hetty. I only just found out. I didn't see you at dinner but I thought I'd simply missed you. When I did not see you at supper either, I asked Polly and she said they'd taken you away to punish you. She was in tears too, poor girl, saying it was all her fault, that you were trying to protect her from Miss Morley. What did you *do* to her, Hetty?'

'I snatched her ruler away when she'd struck Polly. Oh, how I wish I'd struck her with it. I hate her. I hate them all.'

258

'I hate them too. You must try to be brave, dear Hetty. They will have to let you out tomorrow. If they don't, I will go to a governor's house and report them for wicked cruelty,' Ida said wildly.

'I'm not sure I can manage a whole night,' I wept. 'It's so dreadfully dark and I'm so scared all by myself.'

I thought of little Gideon then, all by himself in the squirrel house the night we went to the circus. No wonder he'd been so traumatized. Was I going to be shocked senseless too?

'You're not alone, Hetty,' said Ida. 'I will stay. I cannot get in, but I am only the other side of your door. I will wait until you go to sleep.'

'But you will get into trouble if they catch you.'

'They won't catch me. If I hear anyone coming, I'll run along the corridor and hide, and then creep back afterwards. I'm not leaving you here so frightened.'

'You're so good to me, Ida.'

'I'd give anything to look after you properly, Hetty. For two pins I'd slap those evil witches until they gave me the key, and then I'd let you out and have you sleep in my own bed – but I have to keep my position. I'd never get any other work without a good reference, and I'm not going to end up in the workhouse. I'll tell you a secret, Hetty. I spent three years there, and it was a dreadful, dreadful place.

No, I'm doing well for myself now and saving up my wages. I've the future to think of.' She paused for a long moment. 'Shall I tell you . . .?'

'Tell me what, Ida?'

'No, no, maybe not now, not yet.' She was silent.

'Are you still there, Ida?' I asked anxiously.

'Yes, of course I am. You curl up, my dear, and try to go to sleep. Did they give you a mattress?'

'I've got a blanket, but it smells so horrid.'

'Put your cap over your nose – that will smell of fresh laundering and hair oil, good smells. Now, you're the girl for picturing. Picture you're lying on a soft scented pillow, so fresh and dainty, and you have a feather mattress and a beautiful warm quilt. Oh, you are getting so cosy now, aren't you, dear?'

'I didn't think *you* could picture, Ida!'

'I can do lots of things, Hetty. Now nestle under your splendid quilt. Shut your eyes, dear. You're getting very sleepy. You're going to go fast asleep and have happy dreams, *such* happy dreams. One day all your dreams will come true, Hetty. All my dreams too . . .' Ida's voice murmured on and on, and somehow the stout door splintered away and we were together, both of us in our soft feather bed, lying on fresh pillows . . .

Then I woke up with a start, my neck twisted, my whole body aching, locked in the dark all alone. But somehow it wasn't quite as bad as before because Ida's voice echoed in my head, helping me picture the bed, and after a long time I fell asleep again.

Then I heard the key in the lock. The door opened and I was blinking in daylight.

'Well, well, well, Hetty Feather!' Matron Bottomly peered in at me, a look of triumph on her ugly face. 'You look suitably chastened, child. Are you truly sorry, or do you need another twenty-four hours to teach you your lesson?'

'I am very sorry, Matron,' I said meekly, my head bowed, because I could not stand the thought of further imprisonment.

'I am glad to see you truly penitent at last,' said Matron Bottomly, smiling grimly. 'I'm pleased that vicious spirit of yours is broken at last. Now perhaps you will show suitable respect to your elders and betters.'

Oh, how I hated her, talking about me as if I was a tamed wild beast. Of course I wasn't the slightest bit sorry I'd stuck up for poor Polly. I had no respect whatsoever for Matron Bottomly or Miss Morley. They were undisputedly my elders but they certainly *weren't* my betters. They were cruel, wicked women, not fit to look after children. How dare they beat us and lock us up like criminals and act as if it was for our benefit!

16

I resolved to run away.

'Oh, Hetty, I will run away too,' Polly said, hugging me.

Her hands were still scored with red weals from Miss Morley's ruler, and her eyes were red too, because she'd cried bitterly the entire time I'd been incarcerated.

We tried to concoct a sensible plan of action. We fancied ourselves the cleverest girls but we lacked inventive ideas. We knew so little of the world outside the hospital. We only knew our foster homes – and so we thought of our lost foster mothers.

'If Miss Morrison knew the way we are treated here, I'm sure she'd take me back into her care. She'd take you too, Hetty, because you are so bright and clever.'

'If Mother knew they'd kept me locked up in an attic all night, she'd *definitely* take me back – and my goodness, Jem would rise up and seize Matron Bottomly and kick her up her stinking bottom,'

I declared. 'And of course you could stay with *us*, Polly. You might care for my brother Nat, who is almost as dear as Jem, and then you can marry him when we are older and we can live in adjoining cottages.'

We alternated futures, flying between one household and another, the way we'd pictured our pretend visits as little children. It had been so easy when we were small girls, but now it seemed incredibly difficult. We could fly there in an instant in our imagination, but it was a far harder task working out each step in reality. We had no clear idea how to get to our foster homes. I knew we had to go on a long journey by train, but I did not even know the names of the stations – and though I had a little money (Jem's sixpence and my Christmas pennies), I knew they would not be nearly enough to pay the fare.

'How will we actually get out of the hospital?' said Polly.

We rarely set foot outside the grounds. We had been taken to tea at a governor's house several times, and once some girls had been picked to go on an outing to Hampton Court – but not us. We were always carefully guarded, and the grounds were regularly patrolled by staff. Surely if we simply started running, they would seize us and bring us back? I could not stand the thought of further incarceration in the attic room.

'We have to make firm plans,' I said, though I did not have any idea how to do this. I'd lived in the hospital so long that the outside world had faded like a dream. I had pictured home often enough, but I'd added so many details that now I wasn't sure what was real.

The mother and father in my mind were now like good guardian angels. Yet contrariwise I could also remember Mother paddling me, Father shouting angrily. My brothers and sisters seemed like siblings in a storybook, not really connected to *me*. Martha was now simply the girl in spectacles who sang sweetly in the chapel on Sundays.

I even felt I'd lost contact with Gideon. I'd dared my dressing-as-a-boy trick twice more in the infants school, and last year at the boys' sports day I'd looked hard for him. He eventually spotted me and risked edging close to say hello. I did not recognize him till he did so. He was so tall now, and had filled out a little, seeming less sad and spindly.

'Hello, Hetty,' he said softly.

'Oh, Gideon, it's really you!' I said.

I did not care about hospital rules. I threw my arms around him. However, it felt odd, as if I was embracing a stranger. We asked each other politely if we were all right, but then stood smiling shyly, at a loss for further conversation. I was so glad he was still talking properly, but I did not like to point this out in case it embarrassed him. Eventually I asked him if he ever thought of Mother and home. I wished I'd held my tongue because his brown eyes grew misty. He shook his head, though I was sure he was lying. Then one of the boys' teachers looked our way and Gideon ran off hastily.

I had glimpsed him since, going in and out of the chapel, but was not even sure it was really him – there were so many tall thin boys with brown eyes.

I decided I could not include him in my escape plans. We had been parted too long. It was almost as if he wasn't my brother any more. There was only one brother I was sure of. My vision of Jem shone like a lantern in my head. I was sure I still knew every freckle on his dear face, every curl of his hair, every curve of his ear. I knew the sound of his sneeze, his yawn, his merry laughter. I felt I could instantly pick him out from fifty thousand other boys. He would be almost a man now, able to find work. He could look after me – and Polly too. She was dearer to me now than any of my sisters.

She did not give answers now in Miss Morley's class. She wrote down her sums silently from the board, and if Miss Morley made mistakes, she copied them without comment – though she bit her lip. Alone with me, she talked as usual, but she was quiet with everyone else, her head bent as if to escape notice.

But someone was quite definitely noticing her. A large woman dressed all in black, with a very pale face and dark shadows under her eyes, started coming regularly on Sundays, leaning heavily on the arm of her husband. She wore an enamelled hair locket around her neck and had a habit of rubbing it with her plump white fingers, as if it was a tiny lamp and she was trying to summon a genie.

She didn't seem interested in the tiny girls who usually attracted the most attention. She didn't glance at the capable big girls, almost ready for work. We were used to strange women eyeing them up and down, on the lookout for a useful servant. No, this large lady in black always paused at our table of ten-year-olds and hovered there, blinking her shadowed eyes and fingering her locket. She watched our every mouthful, she strained to hear our whispered remarks, she peered with her large head at an angle, as if she was Matron checking the neatness of our plaits and the cleanliness of our necks.

The large lady kept looking in our direction. Not at me, but at Polly.

'That lady in black is really starting to annoy me,' I grumbled. 'She will not stop staring. Poke your tongue out at her, Polly!'

'Don't be unkind about her, Hetty. She looks so *sad*,' said Polly. 'Who do you think she can be?'

'Maybe she's your long-lost mother, come back to claim you after all this time. She's rich and respectable now and can afford to buy you back from the governors,' I said.

'I think her husband *is* a governor,' said Polly. 'I saw him on Friday when the mothers were petitioning. I remember his whiskers and his fat watch-chain.'

'Look at the buttons on his waistcoat, all set to pop off! Have you ever seen such a stomach!' I said.

'But he looks a kindly man,' said Polly.

Perhaps he read her lips, because just then he nodded at her and smiled. Polly smiled back demurely. The lady in black gripped her husband's arm and swayed a little, as if she felt faint.

'There! She's recognizing you, her little lost Polly,' I said, carried away with my story.

I started elaborating on my romance, but Polly wasn't listening. She was looking at the couple and they were looking at her. It was almost as if they were alone in the vast dining room. The hundreds of other foundling girls did not seem to exist – even me.

I felt my stomach tighten, so much so that I could not finish my Sunday dinner. I was immensely relieved when the table was tapped and it was time to file out. I hurried Polly away from the couple, suggesting we find a quiet corner to read – but Matron Bottomly stood in the doorway.

'There you are, Polly Renfrew! Come with me to my room, child.'

Polly gasped. There was only one reason for going to Matron Bottomly's room. It meant that you were going to be severely punished.

'But Polly hasn't *done* anything,' I said, taking her hand.

'Did I ask for *your* comments, Hetty Feather?' said Matron. 'Hurry along now, if you please.'

I had to slink away while Polly marched off after Matron Bottomly. She peered back at me anxiously and I gave her a cheery wave of encouragement, though inside I was in turmoil.

I went off to the dormitory and waited by her bed. I waited and waited and waited. Normally Matron Bottomly was brisk with her punishments. She'd give you a severe talking to. If you had been exceptionally bad, you were whacked with a stick. I was the only girl so far who'd been locked up in the attic. She surely wouldn't dream of shutting *Polly* up there. Polly was so scared of the dark. If she woke in the night, she always needed to wake me up too so I could hold her hand. If she was shut up alone in the attic all night, she'd go demented. I was sure she hadn't done anything wrong at all – though we were all used to being

269

seized indiscriminately and punished for some insignificant or imagined offence.

I cast myself down on Polly's bed, beating it with my fist in my frustration. 'I hate it here, I hate it here, I hate it here,' I muttered into Polly's pillow.

I shut my eyes tight, picturing myself marching to Matron Bottomly's room and rescuing Polly – but I so dreaded the punishment attic myself, I didn't quite have the courage. I lay there, hating myself as well as the hospital.

At long last I heard Polly's footsteps. I sat up and stared at her. She wasn't flushed and tear-stained. There were no cruel red marks on her hands. Yet she looked immeasurably different. She was walking slowly, as if treading water, and her eyes were dazed. She blinked when she saw me.

'Oh, Hetty,' she said, and her hand went to her mouth. 'Oh, Hetty, I hardly know how to tell you.'

I stood up and faced her. 'What *is* it, Polly?'

'I – I am leaving the hospital,' Polly whispered.

'What?' I said, shaking my head.

'I know. I can scarcely take it in myself, but it's true. I've to gather up my things and go now. I am to live with Mr and Mrs McCartney – she is the lady in black.'

'Oh my Lord! Is she *really* your mother?' I said.

'No, no. She had a daughter our age, Lucy, but

she died of the influenza last winter and now she wants to adopt me to take Lucy's place.'

'But people aren't allowed to adopt us! We belong to the hospital.'

'I know, but Mr McCartney is a governor and a very generous benefactor. They will do whatever he wants,' said Polly.

'And – and is it what *you* want?' I asked hoarsely.

'Oh, Hetty, I don't know!' said Polly, tears suddenly rolling down her cheeks. 'I can't bear the thought of not seeing you any more – but of course I want to leave the hospital.'

'Do you *like* them, the McCartneys?'

'I think so. They seem very kind, though still very sad. I am to have Lucy's room and all her clothes and even all her toys. She has five large china dolls, and a doll's house with an entire family of very little dolls – a mother, a father, a grandmother with little spectacles, a grandfather with a grey beard, and five children, one a tiny baby doll in a crocheted shawl. It was Mrs McCartney's when she was a child and she described it very carefully. She gave it to Lucy and now it is to be mine.'

'You are too old for dolls and doll's houses,' I said sourly.

'I know, but I don't mind,' Polly said.

'*I* mind,' I cried. 'I mind it all. Oh, Polly, don't

go and be their child. Please stay here with me. You are my only friend. I can't bear it at the hospital without you.'

'I'm so sorry,' said Polly, hugging me. 'I haven't any choice. Matron Bottomly says I have to go now. But I will beg my new mama and papa to bring me back here to visit you – and I will write to you lots and lots. Then, when we are fourteen, we can meet up properly because you will be out of the hospital too.'

'Yes, but I will be a servant then,' I said. 'You will be a lady.'

'We will still be *us*, Hetty,' said Polly.

But we knew there was already a divide between us. I could not be mean enough to rebuke Polly further. I knew I would have jumped at the chance of escaping the hospital. I would not have sacrificed that chance for anyone, not even my dearest friend. But the McCartneys had not chosen me as their new daughter. They had chosen Polly, and I could understand why.

She was fair and neat and placid, while I was small and fiery with flame-red hair. She had the table manners of her spinster schoolteacher foster mother: she cut up her food daintily, nibbled slowly and drank from her cup with her little finger stuck out at an elegant angle. I had the manners of a rough country child: I still bolted my food and talked with my mouth full and slurped my milk. Polly's voice was gentle and she enunciated every word carefully, while I spoke in a wild torrent. Of *course* they picked Polly.

I swallowed hard, trying to compose myself. I kissed her wet cheeks. 'I will miss you sorely, Polly, but I am also truly happy for you,' I said.

'I'm sorry I've been so lucky,' said Polly, still crying.

'I think those McCartneys are lucky having you for their new daughter,' I declared.

We hugged again, and then I helped her gather her few possessions. She insisted on taking every present I'd ever given her, even the little squashed heart with huge stitching. Matron Bottomly came marching into the dormitory, rubbing her hands.

'Are you ready, Polly dear?' she said, so sickly sweet now that Polly was leaving. 'Mr McCartney's carriage is waiting. *What* a fortunate girl you are!'

'I do hope you get to be fortunate too, Hetty,' said Polly earnestly, squeezing my hand.

'Ha! I doubt anyone will ever come wanting to adopt an imp of Satan like Hetty Feather,' said Matron Bottomly. 'Come along now, Polly. You have got a clean cap and tippet on? Still, you'll probably be taking them off the moment you get to your new home. Fancy!' She giggled unpleasantly, smoothing her apron. 'You'll tell them how happy you've been here in the hospital, won't you, dear?'

'Oh yes, she's been deliriously happy,' I snorted.

Matron Bottomly glared at me. 'You always have to have the last laugh, miss. But the laugh's on you this time, Hetty Feather. You'll miss your friend badly, I can tell.'

'We will stay friends, Matron Bottomly,' said Polly.

I wasn't so sure. And I was right. I waited week after week, desperately hoping that Polly and the McCartneys would attend chapel and then come to observe the grisly public Sunday dinner. But they never once put in an appearance.

I had one letter from Polly. It was formal and restrained, because she knew Matron Bottomly would have a good rummage through it before handing it over to me.

My dear Hetty,

I miss you very much, but in every other respect I am truly happy. Mama and Papa are so very kind and my new life is incredibly comfortable and luxurious. I wish you could come and visit me here. Mama does not wish me to go to the hospital to see you as she feels it will bring back too many memories. I am not even called by my own name

any more. I am Lucy now – but to you, dear Hetty, I
will always remain
  Your very affectionate friend,
  Polly

I reread her letter many times, but then one Sunday, in a fit of despair, I tore it into tiny shreds. I felt Polly might have tried just a little harder to persuade her new parents to visit the hospital. Could they not take pity on me? It was so dreadful having to live my life without Polly when she had been my dearest friend and constant companion for years.

'You must try to make a new friend, Hetty,' Ida said, patting my shoulder sympathetically as she served our dinner.

She was trying to be kind, but her advice was useless. How *could* I make a new friend? All the girls in my year were comfortably settled in their friendships. I could trail round after this group or that group but no one really *wanted* me.

Now that I was on my own, Sheila and Monica were especially tormenting. They mocked and mimicked me a dozen times a day. I affected a lofty indifference to their silliness – but I often cried bitterly into my pillow at night.

It did not help that I was at such an in-between age. I was not yet one of the big girls, with their new chests and their secrets and their infectious giggles. I was not old enough to be a maid to any of the mistresses or nurses, or given any extra responsibilities about the hospital. My life was a dreary routine of the schoolroom and repetitive domestic chores, day after day after day.

I did take my turn caring for the newly arrived foundlings, washing the hands and faces of all the little five-year-olds bawling for their mothers. You would think *I* would try to be a little mother to them, maybe making one my special baby the way Harriet had long ago cared for me. But I was in such low spirits I couldn't really feel a fig for any of these puny little girls. I washed them and carted them to the privy and lined them up two by two to walk to the infants playground without even bothering to learn their names ... until one day a brand-new foundling girl arrived. She wasn't particularly distinguishable from any of the other girls: brown eyes, shorn head, scrawny body, with a lamentable habit of bursting into floods of tears whenever she thought of home.

'Do stop crying so, Alicia,' I said, wiping her running nose.

'I cannot help it. And I'm *Eliza*, not Alicia,' she said.

I didn't react at all. My brain was sleeping. Her name meant nothing to me. But *she* was much more alert.

'Haven't you got those infants ready for bed *yet*, Hetty Feather?' Matron Pigface Peters snapped as she bustled past.

Eliza blinked. She rubbed her eyes and then stared at me, suddenly smiling, though her face was still damp with tears and snot. 'It is *you*, Hetty! I have found you!'

I stared at her blankly.

'You are my sister!' she declared.

The hospital suddenly vanished. I was back in the cottage with Jem, and Mother was there in the corner, nursing a baby in her arms – baby Eliza!

I clasped her fiercely, and she smiled and squirmed within my embrace.

'Oh, Eliza, it's so wonderful to find you!'

'Jem said I had brothers and sisters already here, but I was to look most particularly for you, Hetty,' said Eliza.

'Yes, yes, dearest Jem! We have a sister Martha – you will be so proud of her when you hear her sing in chapel, but she does not quite remember home the way we do. And we have one lovely brother here, Gideon, but sadly we will not see him often as the boys are so separate from us.'

'And Saul?' Eliza said. 'Jem taught me: *Martha who has poorly eyes, Saul who has a poorly leg, Gideon who cannot talk – and Hetty who isn't one bit poorly and talks all the time!*'

'Oh, Jem is so wonderful,' I declared fervently. 'Eliza, you must tell me every single thing you can about home, especially everything about Jem.'

'Jem *is* wonderful,' said Eliza. 'He knows everything.'

'Yes, he does – but he doesn't yet know about Saul. I'm afraid he died several years ago, Eliza. He caught the influenza.'

'Will I catch it?' Eliza asked, looking alarmed.

'Oh no, no, you seem a very strong, healthy little girl – and it's summer now, anyway.'

'Hetty Feather, get that child into bed this *instant*!' Matron Pigface bellowed.

Eliza whimpered at her harsh tone.

'Don't let her bother you – she's silly old meanie matron,' I whispered into Eliza's ear as I hurried her into bed. 'Don't cry! I'll come and find you later. I shall creep back after lights out.'

I tucked her up carefully and gave her a quick kiss on her sad little wisps of hair. The other infant foundlings stared, and Matron Peters tutted and tossed her head. I went back to my own dormitory feeling light-headed with sudden joy. I whirled round and round, dancing a little jig, flinging out my arms and stamping my boots.

'Look at Hetty Feather, she's gone totally loopy,' said Sheila, tapping her forehead significantly.

'She's *always* been loopy,' said Monica. 'My

Lord, Hetty, I hope you don't fancy you're *dancing*.'

She started up a stupid imitation. Another time I'd have slapped her, but now I couldn't be bothered. I undressed quickly and got into bed, pulling the covers over my head.

I lay in the dark, thinking of my newly-found sister. I remembered how scared and lonely I had been when I came to the hospital at her age – and how baffled to find that Martha scarcely remembered me. I would be *such* a different sister to little Eliza. I would watch out for her every day, and woe betide anyone who taunted her or stole her Sunday sweets. I would help her with her reading and writing until she was the star of the infants class. I could even help her with her darning because endless practice over the last five years had made me an accomplished needlewoman.

I would tell Ida that Eliza was my sister. I was sure Ida would give her little treats of butter and sugar too. I would make up stories to entertain her – *not* lurid adaptations from the *Police Gazette*! No, I'd tell beautiful stories of princes and palaces, tales where good fairies waved their magic wands and little foundling girls wore white silk gowns and silver slippers, and went to the ball, and lived happily ever after.

I would tell Eliza such a story tonight, I decided.

I would be her good fairy sister, waving my wand to make her warm and happy. Perhaps Eliza and I could even run away back home together? Jem had clearly remained constant. He had told Eliza to look out particularly for me. He was still my own dear Jem and I loved him with all my heart.

I had so many questions for Eliza. How tall was Jem now? How broad were his shoulders? Had his voice broken? Did he still whistle while doing his chores? Did he speak of me often? Had he told Eliza of our plans? I rather wanted him to have kept them secret, but I decided I would not mind too much if he had confided in Eliza. She was such a sweet child she could come and live with us eventually. I would be like a second mother to her.

I waited in a happy fever until all the girls in my dormitory were asleep and then crept out of bed and tiptoed along to the door. It was so black and eerie out in the corridor that I almost lost heart and scampered back to bed, but I felt ashamed of myself. Great girls of nearly eleven should not be scared of the dark.

I forced myself to picture little Eliza sobbing piteously in her infant cot, waiting in vain for me. I could not let her down. I took a deep breath, clenched my fists and stumbled on in the darkness until I reached the infant dormitory at last. I held my breath as I passed Matron Pigface Peters's room, but I could hear her ugly snorting snores through the door. I pictured her flat on her back, snout quivering, big mouth pursed, and had to clamp my hand over my mouth to stop myself laughing.

I crept past her door, down into the infants dormitory. It was still so dark I could scarcely make out the little iron beds, let alone their occupants, but I knew the newest foundlings slept nearest the door. I listened – and heard muffled sobbing.

'Eliza?' I whispered.

'Oh, Hetty, you've come at last! I'm over here!'

I felt my way towards her and then hugged her tight. 'There now! I told you I would come. Budge over and make room for me. I am freezing to death!'

I clambered in beside her. She was very cold herself, but I put my arms right round her and rubbed her little shivery shoulders and arms, and after a minute or so we both started to warm up.

'There now, is that better?' I whispered.

'Oh yes, Hetty, much!'

'Do you know something, Eliza? When I was even smaller than you, I used to jump into our brother Jem's bed and cuddle up close to get warm,' I said.

'Oh, I did too!'

I paused. I was astonished, to be truthful. Jem had never cuddled Martha or Saul or Gideon – only *me*.

'Well, Jem is very kindly,' I said, a little stiffly. 'And I'm sure he wanted to take care of you, Eliza. You must miss him dreadfully. I know I still do. Please tell me all about him, and Mother and Father, and Rosie and big Eliza and Nat.'

'Oh, they are all very well,' said Eliza. 'Mother's hands are sore with the rheumatics, and Father gets fierce sometimes, and my big sister Eliza stays at home to help Mother, and my brother Nat is courting and very silly. I saw him kissing Sally from the village and she's *horrid*, with a big fat floppy chest.'

'Ssh! *Whisper*, Eliza – we don't want the others to hear us. Now, tell about Jem.' I swallowed. 'Is *he* courting?'

'Oh no, not Jem,' said Eliza. 'He says he's waiting.'

'He's waiting, is he?' I whispered, my heart pounding under my nightgown. Oh, dear, sweet, faithful Jem, I thought. 'I wonder who he's waiting for?' I asked.

'Oh, I *know*!' said Eliza.

'Tell me then,' I said, scarcely able to speak for excitement.

Eliza took a deep breath. '*Me!*' she said, and collapsed into further giggles.

'Hush!' I said fiercely. 'Don't be so silly, Eliza. Tell me who Jem is really waiting for.'

'Me, me, me, me!' Eliza chanted.

'Yes, but you are only a little girl and Jem is nearly a man,' I said, trying to put her in her place.

'I am still his sweetheart,' Eliza declared. 'Jem says when I am quite grown up and can leave this horrid hospital, he will come and marry me.'

'*What?*'

'Yes, and I am to wear a long dress and Jem will wear a fancy gentleman's suit – and guess where we will live, Hetty!'

I did not answer her. I could not speak. I felt as if my heart was being torn in two.

'We will live in our squirrel house!' Eliza said triumphantly.

'No!' I mumbled.

'Yes yes yes! We have this squirrel house, Jem and me. It is deep in the woods. It's our secret place and we have such lovely games there.'

Eliza prattled on and on. I could scarcely bear it. I put my hands up and covered my ears, but her little mouse squeak echoed inside my head.

Jem had shared all *our* most secret special plans with this silly little child. He had repeated all his promises to her. He had duplicated everything. He had not even bothered to invent new games for her.

I bit my lip hard, but I could not stop myself sobbing.

'Are you crying, Hetty?' Eliza asked. 'Don't be

sad. We have each other now. And when we leave here I will ask Jem if he would mind very much you coming to live with us too, as you are family.'

She was doing her best to comfort me – but I had to fight hard not to push the poor little thing out of her own bed. I could not endure it. My dear Jem had betrayed me utterly. No, he wasn't *my* Jem. He had parroted all his special promises to Eliza – and she innocently triumphed in his attention. He clearly had no intention of keeping his word to her any more than he had to me. He'd just been playing with us, saying sweet things to keep us little girls happy. Oh, how it hurt now to find out he'd been mouthing meaningless nonsense.

I crept back to my own bed as soon as Eliza started dozing, but I couldn't sleep. I lay there, crying, my fists clenched. I felt so stupid. I'd believed every word Jem had said. I'd loved him with all my heart. I'd trusted him. I'd been so sure that he really would wait for me.

'Oh, Jem, how could you repeat everything to *her*?' I whispered into my pillow. 'You're wicked, wicked, wicked.'

But as the night wore on, I started to feel I was being ridiculous. Jem hadn't been *deliberately* unkind. I knew he wasn't really a wicked boy. He was a sweet, kindly soul who simply wanted to comfort his silly little sisters. I could see it was ludicrous for my five-year-old sister Eliza to talk of Jem as her sweetheart and future husband. It was equally ludicrous for me to think Jem truly wanted to marry me. We'd both been little children. Jem was telling us a fairy story to try to kid us we'd live happily ever after. Of course he wouldn't marry either of us.

He'd remember us both fondly, if a little sadly. Then, in the fullness of time, he'd fall in love with some village lass like Nat's Sally and marry her. His future was plain to me now. And my future was plain too. I was Hetty Feather, a foundling, imprisoned in the hospital. When I was fourteen, I'd leave to be a servant. That was all I had to look forward to. I would be a drudge for the rest of my days.

17

The hospital cook scalded her hands badly with boiling water, and could not work for weeks. Ida was asked to take over her duties until Cook recovered. She was allowed to choose one of us girls to help her in the kitchen. Ida selected the great fourteen-year-old girls at first, as expected – but then announced she'd like to give some of the younger girls a chance.

'I'd like to try out Hetty Feather for a day,' she said.

Matron Bottomly snorted derisively. 'You'll regret *that* decision,' she said, but she let Ida have her way.

All the other girls moaned and grumbled and said it wasn't the slightest bit fair. I said nothing at all. I stayed silent when Ida set me to peeling the vegetables, freshly picked from the hospital garden. She told me to have a little nibble at the carrots and pod a few peas for myself, but I didn't bother. I even shook my head listlessly when she offered me a spoonful of syrup from her larder.

'You're always hungry, Hetty! Aren't you feeling well?' Ida said, putting her hand to my forehead.

'I'm all right. Leave me alone,' I said, shrugging her hand away.

'Oh, Hetty, please, dear, tell me what's wrong,' said Ida.

'*Nothing!*' I snapped. 'Stop pestering me.'

If I'd spoken like that to Miss Morley or Matron Bottomly, they'd have slapped me for impertinence, but Ida just looked wounded. Her big blue eyes blinked at me reproachfully. I felt bad because she had always been so very kind to me – but I was *tired* of being kind back. I'd spent weeks making a fuss of Eliza and listening to her endless prattle about Jem when every word was a torment. I couldn't tell her to shut up and keep out of my way. She was my little sister after all. I knew just how sad and lonely she was feeling, how very bleak the hospital seemed after our cosy cottage.

When I'd first come here, it had meant so much to me that Harriet had made a special pet of me. I felt duty bound to do the same for Eliza, even though the sound of her squeaky little voice made me wince, and her habit of quoting Jem in each and every sentence drove me to distraction.

I *had* to stop myself hurting her – but I didn't

see why I had to take such care with silly old Ida. I wished she wasn't so stupidly sensitive. She had spirit enough with the others. I'd seen her put Sheila in her place often enough, and she was wonderfully sharp with the nurses, even though forced to toady to Matron Stinking Bottomly. Why did she have to care what I said?

I sighed at her set shoulders and wounded expression. She was making pastry, thumping her rolling pin with unnecessary pressure. Ida had introduced pies into our diet while Cook recovered, and they were much appreciated by everyone. I idly picked up all the cut-off ribbons of pastry. I started to fashion them into a big fat dough lady. I turned her into a matron with a silly cap and a grim expression.

Ida stopped making her endless huge pies and stared at my creation. She smiled, forgetting she was offended. 'That's so good, Hetty!'

'No, it's not,' I said, and I suddenly squashed the figure flat.

'Oh, look what you've done! I wanted to bake it to keep her. My, you're in a bad mood today, aren't you?'

I shrugged and made patterns in the spilled flour on the kitchen flags with the toe of my boot.

'Don't do that, you're just treading it in,' said Ida. She took a deep breath, still unaccountably intent on humouring me. 'How about your taking a turn with the pastry rolling?'

'I don't want to.'

'It's a skill to be proud of, making good pastry. I've picked up a lot of knowledge working in the kitchen. I could teach you all sorts, Hetty. Maybe you could eventually get a position as a cook-general if you learned a few recipes.'

'I don't *want* to be a cook-general,' I declared.

'It's far better than being a kitchen maid or a tweeny.'

'I don't want to be any kind of stupid servant,' I said. '*Especially* in a kitchen.'

This time I'd really gone too far. Ida flushed. She thumped the pastry with her rolling pin. She looked as if she'd like to give me a good thumping too.

'Oh, I'm all too well aware that you look down your nose at servants,' said Ida. 'So pray tell me, Hetty, what exactly *are* you going to do with your life?'

I could not answer her. I had clung to the idea of marrying Jem for so long. Now I could see how painfully silly I had been.

'What was it again?' said Ida angrily, putting her floury hand to her ear as if I'd spoken. 'Run away to the circus to join your real mother?'

It was my turn to flush. I'd forgotten I'd once told Ida about Madame Adeline. She was another childish dream. I remembered the roar of the crowd as we cantered around the ring, the sound of all those many pairs of hands clapping me . . .

I stuck my head in the air. 'I might just do that very thing,' I said.

'Oh, Hetty, as if that circus lady could *possibly* be your mother!'

'She could be. She practically said so,' I said fiercely. I did not really believe it now, but I could not bear to let my last dream fade away.

'You're getting a big girl now,' said Ida, shaking her head. She'd rubbed a floury sprinkle over her cheeks and her cap was awry, making her look foolish. 'You're far too old for these silly daydreams. You've got to be practical, know your place, work hard, make something of yourself.'

'Like you, you mean?' I said spitefully.

'You might not think much of my position, Miss High and Mighty, but it suits me perfectly,' said Ida. 'I work hard and I keep respectable and I save my wages.'

'Yes, but what *for*? You do the same thing day after day, week after week, year after year. You must be mad, Ida. You don't have to stay here. *You're* not a foundling. You could walk out and get a better job anywhere.'

'I've got a good job *here* and I was very lucky to get it too, coming from the workhouse,' said Ida.

'You're talking nonsense, Hetty. I know you must be missing Polly sorely but there's no need to take it out on me. I've tried my best to cheer you up.'

'I shall never be cheerful here, never never never,' I declared.

I simply could not stop myself. Ida was my only true friend left in the hospital and yet I seemed determined to alienate her. I stayed rude and sulking all day, doing the barest minimum of work.

'Judging by today, I doubt you can even be a servant when you leave here, Miss Hetty Head-in-the-Air,' Ida sniffed. 'No one in their right mind would ever take you on as a skivvy, let alone a cook. Now, are you going to snap out of it and be a good sweet girl tomorrow?'

I snapped my fingers and then presented her with my own glum face. 'Does it look like it?' I said.

'Well, go away and stew, you stupid girl. I'll pick someone else to come and help me.'

'As if I care,' I said, and marched out of the kitchen.

I cared dreadfully when Ida picked *Sheila*. I knew she'd done it deliberately to annoy me. Ida didn't like Sheila any more than I did. She just wanted to pay me back. It was bitterly painful to peep through the kitchen hatch and see Ida and Sheila stirring a vat of rice pudding together, laughing away. When Ida saw me looking, she popped a handful of raisins into Sheila's grinning mouth. She gave a little nod, as if to say, *That will show you, Hetty Feather*.

It showed me all right. It looked as if I'd lost my last friend at the hospital through my own stupid behaviour. I should have gone to Ida privately and apologized, but I was too proud. I stalked around by myself, dutifully keeping an eye on little Eliza but otherwise taking no notice of anyone.

I sat listlessly in the classroom, never bothering to answer a single question now. I felt so dull and slow I could scarcely lift my pen to write any words. I found my grades slipping. I had been first equal with Polly at everything, but now I was sliding down almost to the bottom of the class, along with Mad Jenny and Slow Freda and Stutter Mary, the three sad girls who could barely read and write.

I tried even *less* with my household tasks. Every Sunday I daydreamed in chapel and ate my dinner stony-faced, staring down all the chattering ladies and gentlemen. There seemed no point in smiling. They would never pick *me* to be their new little adopted daughter. I was small, sour, red-haired Hetty Feather.

I could not even get interested when everyone started talking about the Queen's Golden Jubilee in June. What did I care for our fat little monarch? Miss Morley's lessons became very focused on the Royal Personage. At long last she used the coloured maps on the classroom wall, showing us all the different lands the Queen ruled over.

When she told us the Queen was also Empress of India, half the class assumed she *lived* in that huge hot sub-continent. Miss Morley laughed at such ignorance. She said the Queen mostly lived here in London, at Buckingham Palace – and she would quite definitely be in London on 23 June, the day of the Golden Jubilee.

Miss Morley seemed utterly obsessed with Queen Victoria. She gave us dictation about our Loyal Sovereign, she told us the history of her fifty-year reign, she even had us calculating how many seconds would tick by during the Royal Procession if it started at eleven and ended at two. I assumed this was a specific obsession peculiar to Miss Morley – but it seemed to be shared by all the staff. Even little Eliza started babbling about our Great Queen and showed me a picture that she'd drawn in the infant class. I admired it wearily, though her Queen Victoria looked very like a fat stag beetle with a crown upon its head.

We even prayed for Queen Victoria in chapel on Sunday, which seemed to me a little bizarre. Why should all us foundlings, born in shame and destined to live our lives as servants, pray for such a fabulously rich and fortunate old woman who owned whole continents? She should surely be on her padded knees, praying for God's mercy for us.

At the end of the service Matron Bottomly marched to the front of the chapel and ascended the pulpit, her beaky nose pecking the air. She was smaller than the vicar, so only her head was in view, sticking up comically like a coconut on a shy. I had such an urge to aim my hymn book at her!

'I have a very important announcement to make, children,' she said. 'As you all know, our dear Queen has ruled over us for fifty wonderful years. Next Thursday is the day of the Golden Jubilee, when the whole country will celebrate her glorious reign. We are going to celebrate too! You have all been invited to a festive gathering at Hyde Park in London. You will be given a splendid meal at this venue and join in all kinds of fun and games, and then Her Majesty the Queen herself will come and greet you!'

There was a great '*Ooooh*' of excitement and astonishment, though perhaps we were more thrilled at the sound of the splendid meal and the fun and games than the prospect of seeing the Queen.

I was excited too, I could not help it. We were going to escape the dreary hospital for a whole day! Oh glory!

'Settle down now, children. You must be especially well behaved. Any child who is seriously surly or disobedient will *not* be included in the trip to see the Queen,' said Matron Bottomly – and her ridiculous coconut head turned so that she was looking straight at me.

Oh, I understand you very *well, Matron Stinking Bottomly*, I thought. *It would give you such huge delight to be able to deny me my rights. How it would please you to declare before everyone that Hetty Feather was too wicked to attend the Jubilee Celebrations.*

I smiled demurely back at Matron Bottomly. For once in my life I wasn't stupidly going to cut off my nose to spite my face. My behaviour over the next few days was exemplary. I tried hard in lessons on Monday, Tuesday and Wednesday, but not *so* hard that my knowledge irritated Miss Morley. I meekly wrote down her exact words during dictation. I figured out each silly sum, finding how many days it would take Queen Victoria to sail to India if her mighty ship steamed along at a certain terrific rate of knots. I wrote a neat, unimaginative essay on 'What I should say should I meet Her Majesty the Queen'.

I had myself performing copious curtsies, simpering 'If you please, ma'am,' repeatedly. Miss Morley gave me a big red tick and wrote *Excellent* at the bottom of my page. She actually wrote *Excellant*, but I decided not to point this out. I sewed aprons exquisitely, using tiny stitches and turning each corner with a perfectly sewn double hem, as if I was making the finest robes for the Royal Household. I dusted every corridor and corner of the hospital, my feather duster reaching *up* to the picture rails and *down* to the wainscoting. I practically lined up every infant foundling and gave them a good dusting too.

Oh, how irritated Matron Bottomly must have been when Thursday morning dawned bright and sunny, and there I was, smiling, as good as gold. She was probably tempted to give me a slap for sheer cussedness. She did not have the imagination to invent some wicked misdemeanour on the spot. She simply gave me a hard poke in the back and said, 'Mind your manners while you're out, Hetty Feather. All of London will be looking at us.'

We were all issued with clean clothes from top to bottom that Thursday, breaking with all known custom. Our caps and aprons and tippets were laundered and starched so snowy white they looked brand new. Matron had had every big girl ironing all day Wednesday, when we'd all shuffled round in our stockinged feet while every big boy polished our boots. We were given bread and butter for our breakfast because the nurses were so fearful the little ones might spill their porridge down their crisp white chests. Every child had mouth and hands dabbed at with a damp cloth after breakfast, and all the infants were forced into the privies and frightened into copious evacuation so that none would disgrace the hospital during our long outing.

We were lined up in the playground like a miniature brown army, boys one side, girls the other, in serried ranks of six, from the littlest five-year-old fresh from foster care to the biggest, blowsiest girls about to leave to go into service.

Matron Peters positioned herself at the front with the infants, Matron Bottomly brought up the rear with the big ones, while all the nurses and teachers patrolled up and down the lines.

'Right! Let us all step out and look lively. Remember, the entire reputation of the Foundling Hospital rests on *you*,' Matron Bottomly bawled.

We set off at a quick march – one two, one two, one two. It felt so extraordinary to go out of those iron gates and walk down the road. The very air smelled different, so clean and fresh and invigorating.

London would have looked wondrous to us in a thick fog, but this sparkling, sunny June morning made every great grey building gleam palatially. Every window ledge was decked with bunting, every lamppost embellished with bouquets, every flag flapping in the light breeze. We were told not to break step or loiter even for a second, though I craned my neck and stared when we were marched along Oxford Street, marvelling at the vast emporiums, their windows a wonder of patriotic red, white and blue decoration.

I couldn't get used to the crowds – such

huge numbers of people, all shouting, laughing, screaming. Some of our little children started crying in sheer shock, and even I felt frightened, especially when we had to cross a vast road. There were policemen who held up the traffic for us, but they were only puny men. I did not see how they could control so many cabs and carriages and enormous omnibuses. But somehow we all crossed safely, hanging onto each other, our palms sweating.

It was a long, long walk and the little ones in front started dragging their feet and limping in their hard boots, but our spirits picked up as we passed the great Marble Arch and entered the park.

There were ten enormous marquees and many other smaller tents as far as you could see. There were merry-go-rounds and helter-skelters and whirling chairs and swingboats. Children ran around freely everywhere, climbing on the painted horses, sliding down the helter-skelter, squealing with fearful joy in the chairs and boats high above our heads. There were thousands and thousands of children, from tiny tots in pinafores to great girls and boys much taller than me. They were all wearing such wonderful clothes! Many of the girls were dressed in white or soft flower colours, bluebell, primrose, lilac or pale rose-pink, skipping around in soft shoes. The boys wore jolly blue and white sailor suits with

299

jaunty straw hats. They stared at all of us in our ugly brown frocks and breeches, our silly caps and aprons, our red-robin waistcoats and cumbersome jackets, our stiff stout boots. Some openly pointed and commented:

'Look, look, it's the children from the institution!'

'Are they all orphans from the workhouse?'

'No, no, they're foundlings from the hospital. Don't they look quaint!'

We stared back, still in our marching rows, red in the face from the heat and our humiliation. But then Matron Bottomly addressed us through a megaphone.

'This is a message for the senior school! You are allowed to play in the fairground for an hour, so long as you stay within close proximity. All the rides are free. But everyone must report back to marquee number ten at one o'clock sharp for our festive luncheon. Do you all understand?'

We gazed at her, barely able to take it in. Did she really mean we were free to roam as we wished? A few of the big boys made a dash for it before she could change her mind, but a lot of us wavered uncertainly. We were so used to having every minute accounted for. We did not know how to *cope* with an hour of freedom.

Well, *I* could cope. I ran to the merry-go-round,

circling it twice to select the finest horse. They all had names painted on their arched necks. I looked in vain for a Hetty, but I did find a Polly, a black-and-white stead with a red saddle. I had to lift my skirts in an unladylike fashion to clamber onto her, but I didn't care. Some of the girl riders were sitting demurely sidesaddle, but that looked so silly and lopsided. I had ridden bareback with Madame Adeline. I knew what I was doing.

The organ music struck up and the merry-go-round started turning. I clasped the gold rail and urged Polly forward. We went round and round until all the children blurred and the great green park seemed to be spinning on its axis like a giant globe.

As I stepped off dizzily, I spotted Eliza looking a little dazed amongst a cluster of infants. They were being shepherded around by dear Nurse Winnie. I dashed over to her.

'Can I take Eliza on the merry-go-round, Nurse Winterson? I promise I'll look after her most carefully,' I said.

'Yes, of course you can, Hetty,' she said. She looked longingly at it. 'For two pins I'd have a ride myself!'

I lifted Eliza onto a black horse with a white patch on his face. He was called Star. 'You shall be a little star, Eliza,' I told her.

I thought she would be in ecstasy, but she shrieked when the merry-go-round started going faster.

'Don't like it, don't like it!' she cried, squirming around. 'Let me get *off*, Hetty!'

'You can't get off, silly, you've only just got *on*. Don't be scared, Eliza, it's *lovely*.'

'No it's not!' Eliza said, shutting her eyes tight and clinging to me like a little monkey.

When at last the merry-go-round slowed down, Eliza shot off to Nurse Winterson without a backward glance. I shrugged my shoulders, telling myself I was glad to be free of her. I saw my other sister, Martha, near the helter-skelter and I went rushing over to her, worried that she'd fall trying to get up the steep steps inside. However, she had her two friends, Elizabeth and Marjorie, with her, and they elbowed me out of the way impatiently.

'Martha's got *us*, Hetty,' said Elizabeth.

'She doesn't need *you* to help her. She says you fuss far too much,' said Marjorie.

Martha herself simply smiled at all of us, blinking behind her thick glasses.

'Very well, suit yourselves. That's perfectly fine with me,' I said, sticking my nose in the air. I pretended to recognize someone in the great crowd and waved heartily. 'There's my friend! I must go,' I said, running off.

I ran and ran, circling round all the fairground rides, not quite sure which to select. It felt so odd being all by myself when everyone else seemed to be surrounded by friends.

'Oh, Polly, if only you were here,' I whispered.

I knuckled my eyes because they were unaccountably wet – and then opened them wide, because right in front of me was a tall dark boy in foundling uniform, nodding at me shyly.

'Gideon!' I said.

'I came looking for you, Hetty,' he said.

I was overwhelmed that he had taken the trouble to seek me out. In the past I had always been the one to run after him.

'How are you, Gideon?'

'I suppose I am very well,' he said solemnly. He spoke perfectly clearly and coherently, but with a hesitant, mannered air, as if he rarely opened his mouth.

'Oh, Gideon, do you hate it at the hospital too?' I asked, clutching his arm.

He blinked in alarm at my forward gesture, but nodded at me. 'I dislike it very much, but I dread leaving it too. I do not want to be a soldier.'

'It's much, much better than being a servant, you silly boy! Think of the excitement and foreign lands and great battles!'

'Think of the fear and the blood and the

hardship,' said Gideon, shuddering. 'I dream about it sometimes. I know I will not be able to bear it. I do not want to live my days in barracks and army camps. The other boys torment me here, but I'm sure it will be far worse living amongst men.'

'Then let us run away together, Gideon, and escape our fate!'

'You're still dreaming, Hetty. Don't tell me you're still planning to run back home to live with Jem so that he can take care of you!'

'No,' I said shortly. 'Not now. I will make my own way.'

'Well, that is good,' he said, clearly humouring me.

'We will make our way together. We are still special sister and brother,' I declared. I spun him round and then focused on the fair. 'Oh, Gideon, come on the swingboats with me!'

'They're swinging so rapidly. I think I shall be sick,' said Gideon, but he came with me obligingly.

We crouched on either side of the boat, tugging hard on the ropes so that we swung up and then sharply down, as if we were riding a stormy sea. I pictured the waves and the screaming seagulls and the wild wind as we tossed our way over the ocean to a distant promised land, gabbling this breathlessly to Gideon while he laughed at me.

'You're still the same old Hetty,' he said. 'Oh, stop pulling so – we're going too high!'

'Let's go higher and higher and higher!' I said, tugging with all my might.

Gideon groaned and shut his eyes as the whole park heaved this way and that beneath us, but I stared out, seeing right over the huge marquees and the milling throng of children. Way over to the south of the park, beside the silver stream of the Serpentine, I saw another big striped tent, a cluster of wagons – and a great grey creature with a long waving trunk.

'Oh my Lord! It's Elijah! It's the circus! Oh, Gideon, stop pulling, we must slow *down*.'

'Don't fret, I *want* to slow down,' said Gideon weakly, his face greenish-white.

'It's so wonderful! The circus!' I babbled, clutching the edges of the swingboat to try to make it stop.

'Hetty, you'll tip us both out,' Gideon groaned.

'Oh, stop your moaning, boy! Come on, we can jump out now. *Wheee!*' I made a leap for the ground and landed lightly. Gideon jumped after me and landed on his hands and knees.

'Ouch! Oh goodness, have I torn my breeches?'

'Of course you haven't,' I lied, pulling him up by the hands. 'Come on, Gideon. I'm going to the circus, and *this* time I'm taking you with me!'

'**W**e *can't* go to the circus, Hetty!' said Gideon. 'It's not within close proximity! It couldn't possibly be further away.'

'Oh, for Heaven's sake, who cares!' I said gaily.

'But it's nearly one o'clock. We have to be back at marquee number ten. Didn't you listen to what the matron said?'

'As if I care what Matron Stinking Bottomly says!' I said. 'Come on, Gideon! Here's your chance to see the circus for yourself at long last. Don't you want to see Elijah close up – and wondrous Madame Adeline and her horses? And remember the boy acrobats in their sparkly silver clothes, don't you want to see *them*?'

Gideon did waver then, looking longingly in the direction of the circus, though we couldn't even see the tip of the tent or the top of Elijah's trunk now that we were down on the ground.

'And it won't cost a penny this time. Everything is free today because of the Jubilee. Come *on*, Gideon.'

'We will miss our meal in the tent,' said Gideon.

'Never mind. Maybe we'll be back in time to snatch at something.'

'But we'll get into such trouble.'

'There are so many of us I don't think anyone will notice there are two foundlings too few. And even if they do find out, what will we care? We will have seen the circus!'

'You would care if you were a boy, Hetty. If we are very bad, we get whipped.'

'Listen, I have been so fearfully bad I got locked up without food or water in a bleak attic for days and days,' I said, exaggerating slightly. 'I'm going to go to the circus now even if they lock me in the attic for the rest of my life. And so are you, Gideon.'

I tugged at his arm but he pulled away.

'I *can't*, Hetty. I simply daren't. You go, if you must, but I do so hope you won't get into trouble.'

I stared at his pale, obstinate face and knew there was no way I could persuade him.

'All right, I shall go by myself,' I said. I gave him a kiss on his white cheek. 'You will kick yourself for not coming with me!'

I ran off in what I hoped was the right direction. I looked over my shoulder to see if Gideon might just be wavering, but he'd already been swallowed up by the crowd.

'Oh, Gid,' I said, and even though I was sure he couldn't see me, I waved to him.

Then I ran off to find the circus by myself, though it was hard to work out which way to go. The crowd was so thick. I had to dodge and weave and dart between folk wherever I could. Troops of children were gathering and marching towards the marquees for their festive meal. My stomach was rumbling. I couldn't help wondering just how festive the meal would be. Perhaps cake? Jellies? But I couldn't lose my huge chance out of sheer greed!

People were peering at me strangely, laughing at my bizarre uniform. I quickly took my cap off and stuffed it down my tippet, but I had no way of hiding the rest of my clothes.

A formidable woman with an official badge pinned to her bosom seized hold of me. 'Aren't you one of the foundlings from the hospital? No, no, my child, you're going entirely the wrong way.' She consulted a list. 'You're due in marquee number ten – *that* way!'

'Yes, ma'am,' I said, spinning round and walking the way she pointed – but within seconds she was out of sight, so I could turn and fight my way back in the direction of the circus.

It took me a good half-hour before I was even near. I was so hot my frock was sticking to my back and some small child had smeared his hokey-pokey ice all over my skirts. My cap had edged its way out of my tippet and was now lost, ground underheel by hundreds of feet. But when I spied the red and purple tip of the striped circus tent, I forgot all about my bedraggled appearance. I pushed forward determinedly, so eager now I was nearly running.

I saw Elijah, standing tethered to a pole, wearing a head-dress of gold in honour of the Queen. He was smaller than I remembered, but of course *I'd* been much smaller when I last saw him.

The crowd was even thicker now that I was near the circus, and many small boys pushed and shoved. When I pushed and shoved back, one little monster kicked me hard on the shins. I kicked back harder though, for once in my life thankful for my stout institution boots, though my feet were hot as Hell inside them.

I got nearer and saw a tower of acrobats standing on each other's heads, but they weren't dressed in silver, they were all in red. Of course those tumbling boys in silver spangles would have new costumes now, and perhaps their younger brothers had joined their act. I pushed my way through the entrance, into the tent. It was boiling like a cauldron, packed with children keen to see the free show. I barged my way along the front row to claim the only empty seat.

There were clowns running backwards and forwards throwing buckets of water around. It all seemed a familiar routine and I laughed hysterically even though I did not really find them funny.

Then I heard a neigh and a thud of hooves, and I tingled all over and cried out in joy. But where was Pirate, the pale grey with the black patch? These horses were all a glossy chestnut brown, with purple plumes in their manes. And who was this? *Two* women, with big chests and fat thighs, in tight violet spangled dresses, with huge floppy purple bows stuck in their hair, one blonde, one dark.

Where was Madame Adeline? These two dumpy imposters rode round and round the ring. Their act was a travesty compared to Madame Adeline's. Surely they could not have taken her place? I knew every turn she'd taken, every trick, every toss of her beautiful red hair. I had pictured it so many hundreds of times inside my head. These two purple fools galloped round monotonously, waving their hands for applause. I could not bear to clap them. I clasped my hands in agony. When they cantered out of the ring at last, I pushed my way back along the row and elbowed my way to the entrance, taking no notice of the mutters in my wake.

I clutched hold of a circus hand giving out flyers for the circus.

311

'Where is Madame Adeline?' I demanded. 'When will she be performing?'

'Madame who?' said the man. 'Never heard of her.'

'Madame Adeline and her troupe of horses,' I said. 'She's the star of this circus!'

'No she ain't! The only horse act we've got is Miss Molly and Miss Polly, the Equestrian Twins. You've just missed them,' he said impatiently. 'Now leave me alone, girlie, I've got a job to do.'

He gave me one of his flyers and turned away from me. I stared down at the strip of paper in my hand.

Mr Geoffrey's Wondrous Whirligig Circus it said in big bold italics at the top of the page.

I blinked at it, even rubbing the words with my finger as if I could reassemble them into any order that made sense. Who was this Mr Geoffrey? This was Tanglefield's Travelling Circus! I was sure that was the right name. But I wavered as I slid my eyes down the list of performers. Miss Lizzie's troupe of *baboons*? Mr Lionel Luck, contortionist? The Zebidee Family of Tumblers? I had not heard of any of them. And then, in bold lettering: *Archibald, the Infant Elephant!* What were they talking about? I *knew* the elephant was called Elijah. I could not have remembered it *all* so inaccurately.

'Why has the circus changed so?' I asked the

circus hand desperately, shaking his striped sleeve. 'Why isn't it called Tanglefield's Travelling Circus any more? Why are there all these new people? Why has Elijah's name been changed? And *where* is Madame Adeline? You *must* have heard of her!'

'Will you stop pestering me? I've got a job to do. Can't you read, child?' He tapped his wad of flyers impatiently. 'It's there, plain as the nose on your face. Does it say Tanglefield's Travelling Circus? No, it does not. This is Mr Geoffrey's gaff – and he'll have my guts for garters if he catches me chatting. He's a sharp man, Mr Geoffrey, never one to miss an opportunity. This is better than a ten-foot advertisement on a hoarding. Now, on your way. Ain't all you kids meant to be having a free nosh? Little girlie . . .? Oh my Lord, don't start crying on me. I can't abide it when kiddies cry.'

I was weeping in sheer frustration, still too stunned to understand.

The circus hand sighed. 'I reckon Tanglefield's will be up on the heath. I hear they've got all the rag-tag-and-bobtail circuses up there.'

I stared at him. 'You mean there are *different* circuses?'

'There must be thousands, if you count all over Europe – and America too. I was once part of the Great Fernando's Travelling Circus in the States. Now *that* was a gaff and a half. We'd start our procession with twenty elephants – *twenty*, I tell you – and two miles later you'd come to the very last animal wagon, how about that? I'll wager this Tanglefield's Travelling Circus you hold so dear couldn't hold a candle to *that*.'

'Do you really think they'll be on this heath?' I asked.

'Without a doubt,' he said. 'Hampstead Heath, that's the one.'

'Where is that, sir?'

'Oh, for goodness' sake, what do you want of me now – a map? You hop off home and get your pa to take you.'

I hopped off. I didn't have a home and I didn't have a pa. I would have to find Hampstead Heath by myself. I'd never have another chance to find Madame Adeline.

It took me a very long time to fight my way out of the heaving park. I didn't battle back towards the big marquees just in case someone from the hospital spotted my brown dress amid the froth of fancy frocks. I followed the shimmer of the Serpentine instead. I marvelled at all the boats on the water, longing to have a go at rowing myself up and down, but I had a more pressing purpose.

I caught hold of a kindly-looking lady in charge of a bunch of small children. 'If you please, ma'am, can you tell me the way to Hampstead Heath?'

'Well, let me see now. I believe it's over in that direction.' She gestured vaguely. 'But it's a very long way off, too far for a little girl. Where is your school party, child? Are you lost?'

'Oh no, ma'am, they're over there,' I said quickly, and edged away before she could question me further.

My heart sank a little at her words. *A very long way off.* I was so very hot and starving hungry now, and my boots were pinching dreadfully – but I was still resolved. I would get to Tanglefield's Travelling Circus and find Madame Adeline even if I had to crawl there on my knees.

It was scarcely any easier making my way when I was out of the park gates. The streets were so crowded that I had to scurry along in the gutter, though I trembled every time a cab or carriage drove close, terrified of the iron-shod hooves of the horses.

I walked along the wide, grand road of Piccadilly. The crowds were thicker than ever. Then there was a clamour and a cheer, and everyone surged forward, teetering at the edge of the pavement, nearly tumbling on top of me.

'Up you come, little 'un!' said a perfectly strange man, picking me up before I could protest and perching me on his shoulder. 'There now, you're safe with me. See them coming? My, you'll be able to tell your grandchildren one day that you had a grand view of Queen Victoria's Golden Jubilee Procession!'

I saw many red-coated soldiers with white-plumed helmets riding horses – and then a black open carriage drawn by six grey horses – very fine, but not a patch on Madame Adeline's. A small fat woman sat in the carriage looking dazed, waving her plump little hand mechanically.

'There now, you've seen the Queen!' said the gentleman.

'Thank you very much, sir,' I said – though I wanted to see Madame Adeline so much more! 'Would you say I am nearly at Hampstead Heath now?'

'What's that? You're nowhere near, silly child. There now, don't look so disappointed. You've seen the Queen, God bless her!'

'Yes, sir, thank you, sir, could you set me down now, please, sir?' I said.

I started walking as soon as he put me down. It was hard to progress with the crowd thick as treacle, still cheering, chanting, singing songs, some of the younger ladies even lifting their skirts and dancing. I struggled on, asking every kind face if I was going the right way to the heath, but they either did not know or told me it was too far a journey for a little girl like me.

I was so tired and out of breath I could barely speak, but when I tugged the sleeve of maybe the fiftieth lady and asked if she could tell me the way to Hampstead Heath, she smiled at me merrily.

'Yes indeed, dearie. Don't she look like a sparrow in her brown stuff frock, Desmond?' She nudged her companion, a red-faced young man with ridiculous whiskers. 'Yes, little sparrow, Desmond and I are going there too. There's a big funfair and a circus.'

'Oh! Pray tell me, is it Tanglefield's Travelling Circus?' I asked desperately.

'I don't rightly know, my dear. I fancy there are all sorts up on the heath. You're a quaintly spoken child. Isn't she sweet, Desmond?' The lady nudged him and he nodded obligingly.

'She's a dear little thing, Rebecca. Though you are even dearer,' said Desmond.

Rebecca nudged him and laughed again. They seemed so taken with me that I dared ask: 'If you are going to Hampstead Heath, might I possibly walk with you?'

'We're not *walking*, child!' she said, bursting into peals of laughter. 'Especially not when I'm wearing these heels! We're taking the omnibus at Tottenham Court Road. You can come with us by all means.'

I went with them, though I thought Rebecca very silly and simpering, and I did not care for whiskery

Desmond either. I knew omnibuses cost money and I had none, but as I'd hoped, Desmond paid the pennies for my fare, scarcely seeming to give it a thought.

'Thank you kindly, sir,' I said. 'Do you think we might go upstairs?'

'Of course we can, little sparrow,' said Rebecca. 'Desmond, get them to make way for us.'

The omnibus was already so crowded we were all squashed hip to hip, but Rebecca managed to manoeuvre me right to the front so that I could peer out. It was wondrous to have a bird's-eye view of everything, almost as if I truly *was* a sparrow. I stared down at all the hats and bonnets below me, and then in the distance saw a long line of little white caps.

Oh my lord, surely it couldn't be the foundlings on their long march back to the hospital? I asked Rebecca the time and she got Desmond to produce his big gold watch from his waistcoat pocket. A quarter to four! I felt faint. I had lost all sense of time. I had thought I might somehow manage to rush back to Hyde Park and join up with all the others for the march back. But now it was clearly much too late. Had they counted every foundling at marquee number ten? Did Matron Bottomly realize I was missing? She would be so angry. I thought of the punishment attic and shuddered. I could not go back to the hospital now. Without quite meaning to, I had run away at last!

The omnibus took us northwards, and I clutched the rail of the bus, my heart beating hard. Rebecca addressed me every now and then, and I said, 'Yes, ma'am,' and 'No, ma'am,' scarcely taking in what she was saying. My eyes were open but I'd stopped focusing on the sights of London. I was praying fervently inside my head: *Please let me find Tanglefield's Travelling Circus. Please let me find Madame Adeline. Oh, please please please let her somehow really be my mother so that I can live with her.*

The air grew fresher and the streets less crowded. I glimpsed green fields and many trees. I was reminded of the only real home I had ever known. 'Is this the countryside?' I said wonderingly.

'This is the start of the heath, little sparrow. And look, there's the funfair, right over there!'

I saw it spread out across the heath, more merry-go-rounds and helter-skelters, coconut shies and shooting games and all kinds of swings, but I scarcely gave them a glance. I saw several big striped circus tents!

'Thank you so much,' I said as we all tumbled down off the omnibus.

'Don't you want to come on the rides with us,

little sparrow? You shouldn't wander around by yourself, there's all sorts here today,' said Rebecca.

'Oh no, thank you. I'll be all right. I'm meeting someone here,' I said. 'Someone very special.'

'Ah, isn't she lovely, Desmond? Who is it, little sparrow? You're surely too young to have a sweetheart already?'

'It's my mother,' I blurted out – and then I rushed away from them.

I ran towards the nearest tent, so agitated that I tripped and nearly went sprawling.

Please please please let it be Tanglefield's – and please please please let me find her!

I gabbled it out loud this time, not caring if folk stared at me. I saw some words on a big placard:

THIS WAY TO THE GREAT
TANGLEFIELD'S TRAVELLING CIRCUS!

Perhaps I was imagining the words because I wanted to see them so badly. I knew all along that there was only a *chance* that Tanglefield's would be here on the heath. They could be at any town or village in the whole of Britain.

I blinked to get the words properly in focus. Oh glory, it really *did* say Tanglefield!

'Oh thank you, thank you, thank you,' I gabbled, nearly sick with excitement.

I ran nearer. I saw Elijah tethered behind the tent, the real Elijah, truly vast and more weirdly wrinkled than ever, his great ears in the air, trunk waving. I had found my circus! And now I just had to find Madame Adeline and all my dreams would come true.

The flap on the circus tent was closed. A notice declared: *Next performance at five thirty.*

I couldn't wait that long. I dodged round the tent, nervously skirted Elijah, and timidly knocked on the nearest wagon. An old man came to the door in just his undershirt and trousers, his braces flapping.

'What do you want, missy?' he said, frowning at me. There were traces of red on his nose and around his mouth.

'You're Chino the clown!' I said.

'No I'm not, not when I'm taking my break! Now be off with you. I need my forty winks.'

'I'm sorry to disturb you, Mr Chino. It's just I must see Madame Adeline. It's very urgent. Oh, please tell me she's still with the circus, Madame Adeline and her six ponies?'

'Well, she can barely run to two now. She's a bit down on her luck, our Addie. Past it, if you ask me. But the circus is in her blood, you know how it is.'

'The circus is in my blood too,' I said grandly. 'I'll thank you not to talk disparagingly of Madame Adeline. I am related to her.'

321

'*Are* you now?' he said, peering at me doubtfully. 'Well, she's over in the wagon at the end, the green one with the stars on the door. But she'll likely be taking a nap and won't be too happy to be disturbed.'

'She'll want to see me,' I said.

I had to believe it. I had no other dreams left. I said it so passionately that the clown believed me too.

'Go and knock at her door then,' he said, squinting at me. 'Mm, maybe I *can* see a likeness.'

I walked over to the green wagon, trembling now. I reached up and knocked timidly on the door. It was painted all over with silver stars. *My Little Star!* I waited. Perhaps I'd been *too* timid? I knocked harder, *rat-tat-tat*. I heard a murmur inside. Someone shouted crossly, 'For pity's sake, who *is* it?'

My throat was so dry I could barely call out. 'It's me, Hetty Feather,' I mumbled.

The door opened and an old lady with sparse grey hair peered out at me. She was wearing a pale-green silk dressing gown, rather grubby and stained, and scuffed slippers on her splayed feet. Oh dear Lord, I'd gone to the wrong wagon!

'Who did you say? Hetty Feather? What do you want, child?' she asked, rubbing her eyes irritably. Her hair was all awry at the back, and she combed it with her fingers when she saw me looking.

322

'I'm so sorry, ma'am. I did not mean to disturb you. I'm looking for Madame Adeline,' I whispered.

'And why is that?' she demanded. She held the door, looking as if she might slam it in my face.

It was time to be blunt. 'Because I think I might be her daughter,' I said.

The old woman blinked at me. *'What?'*

I licked my lips and repeated it. She stood staring at me, shaking her head in astonishment.

'Well, you'd better come inside,' she said at last, beckoning to me.

I climbed the steps to her wagon and walked in through the starry door. It was like a real little room inside. There was a green velvet upholstered chair with a lace antimacassar and a little table covered with a fringed chenille cloth. A cabinet crammed with china ornaments stood in a corner, though she must have had to wrap and store every one of her treasures while travelling. I spotted a little bed with rumpled covers let down like a shelf from the wagon wall. I peered at it, thinking Madame Adeline must indeed be taking a nap – but there was no head on the pillow, no body beneath the sheets.

'Sit down child,' said the old woman, indicating a padded footstool beside the chair. She set a silver kettle on top of a spirit stove and fetched two willow-pattern china cups and saucers. She then produced a slab of cake, checkered pink and yellow sponge

coated with thick marzipan. My mouth watered. I
had had no lunch at all and I was starving hungry.
The old woman looked at my face and cut a large
slice of cake.

'You look as if you need it!' she said.

'Oh, I do, and it's such lovely cake too! But mayn't
I meet Madame Adeline first?'

The old woman smiled strangely. There was
something familiar about her smile. Could she be
Madame Adeline's mother – and therefore my very
own grandmother?

'Are you perhaps recognizing me now?' she said.

I shifted uncertainly.

'Maybe this will help you?' she said, shuffling in
her down-at-heel slippers over to a wooden cabinet.
She opened the doors to display a little dressing
table with a large mirror. There was also a bright-
red head of hair balanced on a stand.

'My wig,' she said, and she picked it up and
carefully positioned it over her own grey locks. *'Tra-
la!'* she said, raising her arms in an ironic flourish.
'Madame Adeline herself!'

I stared at her. She still looked like an old woman
in spite of her bright hair.

'You will have to imagine the greasepaint and the
costume for now. I'm not getting ready for the show
just yet,' she said.

'You are really Madame Adeline?' I gasped.

'Your obvious astonishment is not very flattering, child,' she said, yawning. 'Strange that you didn't recognize your own mother!' She laughed a little.

I felt my face flaming. She bent down beside me, suddenly gentle.

'Whatever put such a strange fancy into your head?' she asked.

'You said I was your Little Star,' I said.

'Did I?'

'You came to our village and picked me out from all the other children and I rode on Pirate with you,' I whispered.

'Oh, my dear Pirate,' she said, sighing. 'He broke his leg three years ago. He had to be destroyed and it nearly broke my heart. I've never had another horse like him. So I came to your village long ago?'

'Five years.'

'You must have been very young then, and yet you remember it so vividly. How old are you now, about eight?'

'I'm nearly eleven, ma'am.'

'So why did you fancy I was your mother? Don't you have a mother of your own?'

'No I don't. I'm a foundling. I've never known who she is. But I just thought, as you were so kind to me, and we look a little alike, and we both have such red hair . . . well, so I thought . . . I just so *hoped* . . .' I was crying now, gulping with great ugly sobs.

'Oh dear, Hetty, you poor little creature!' She bent down and put her arms round me. I smelled her own sweet powdery smell and howled. She held me close, rocking me as if I was a baby – her baby. I cried all over her green silk dressing gown, but she didn't seem to mind.

'There now, you poor love,' she said when at last my sobs slowed.

She lifted me up and sat me in her own armchair, then poured me a cup of tea and gave me the big slab of cake. I ate and drank with gusto in spite of my sadness. As I munched my excellent cake (she cut me another slice as soon as the first vanished), she coaxed me to tell my story. She laughed with me when I described my antics with Jem back in the village; she looked as if she might cry herself when I told her about the miseries and humiliations at the hospital.

'You poor little pet, no wonder you had such a strange fancy! But I'm still bewildered that I made such a strong impression on you that you remembered me all this time.'

'Of course I remember!' I looked at her imploringly. 'Don't you remember me, your Little Star?'

I saw her hesitate. I realized in that moment that I must have been one of many many many 'Little

Stars'. Perhaps she picked a likely child for every performance. How could she possibly remember me among so many?

'Of course I remember you,' she said quickly, but I knew she was lying to save my feelings. 'The very little girl with the flame-red hair. Yes, you were indeed a Little Star. And yes, in the ring, we must have looked like a real mother and daughter.'

'But – but you're absolutely certain that I'm *not* your daughter?' I blurted out.

'Oh dear, Hetty! I wish I could pretend, but no, I am absolutely certain you are not my daughter. Though rest assured, if you *were*, I should never have given you to this Foundling Hospital, no matter what my circumstances. I would have dearly loved a baby.' She bent her head, biting her thin lips. 'I cannot have children. There was an accident when I was a child myself. I fell while training one day, and one of the horses galloped over me and kicked me violently in the stomach. I was told it was my own fault – I should have remembered to curl up to protect myself. My womb was ruptured and I could not ride again for more than a year.' She held her stomach now as if it still hurt her.

'Can't we pretend, Madame Adeline? Can't we make out to everyone that I really *am* your daughter? Chino the clown believed me, I'm certain. You could train me up and I could ride with you and – and I'd take care of the horses and look after you – I could sew your costumes – *anything*.'

'Dear Hetty, I've never had such a dear, kind, tempting offer! But the circus is no life for a child. There's such hardship, such struggle, such pain. I've seen tiny children of three and four screaming as they're bent in two, their limbs twisted this way and that by their own parents to crick them into the right kind of bendiness for an acrobat act. It's especially no life for girls, with all the men leering at their brief costumes in the ring. Terrible things happen, Hetty, terrible things. No, you must go back to your hospital and try to be a good girl so you don't get punished any more!'

'I *can't* go back! Oh, please, please let me stay with you!'

'Dear child, I wouldn't be allowed to keep you. Folk would say I had abducted you. They would fear for your moral welfare here in the circus – and rightly so. No, after the show I will accompany you back to the hospital myself.' She looked at a brass clock ticking on a shelf. 'I must start getting ready now. Do you want to watch me one more time?'

'Yes, of course!'

I thought she might send me out of the wagon while she got ready, but she let me stay to watch her transforming herself. She sat before her mirror, placed the great red wig back on its stand, and tied her own ruffled wisps back under a kerchief. Then she applied greasepaint to her pale face, a thick white, with bright pink on her cheeks. She put blue on her lids and outlined her eyes with black kohl, and then set her lips in a strange thin smile so she could fill them in with carmine paint.

She went behind a screen, took off her dressing gown and put on her pink spangled dress and white tights. I heard her sighing and groaning as she struggled into the tight costume and squeezed her swollen feet into little pink ballet shoes. Then she emerged self-consciously and carefully put the red wig back on her head.

She stood before me, my Madame Adeline, ready to pass muster in the circus ring, though now, close up, I could still see the lines on her face under the thick make-up, the sadness of her eyes beneath her blue lids, the sag of her ageing body in the unforgiving costume. I felt a fierce protective love for her, as if she was truly my mother.

'You look beautiful, Madame Adeline,' I lied.

She gave me a kiss on the cheek and then went to wipe the smudge of carmine away, but I protected it with my hand, wanting to wear the marks of my kiss with pride. She slipped her green dressing gown round her shoulders and took me to the entrance of the tent, open now, with people pouring in to see the show.

'Make sure this child gets a good seat,' she said to one of the circus hands. 'I will come and collect her after the show to take her back home.'

She went off with one last wave to me. I sat in the front, waiting tensely, while the audience chatted and chewed food and started calling out impatiently for the show to start.

Then Chino came capering into the ring, followed by his clown friend, Beppo. Everyone laughed at their foolish antics, but now that I knew Chino was just a sad old man doing his job I could not find him funny. I did not even enjoy it when he ran rings round Elijah the elephant and performed the clockwork-mouse trick. I could not marvel at Elijah either as he wearily performed each plodding trick, his skin sagging, his tiny eyes half blinded by the bright flare of gaslight.

I watched the lady walking the tightrope, grown very plump, though she was still as nimble dancing up in the air. I saw the silver-suited tumbling boys, three of them now, one as small as me. I wished Gideon was with me to see them leap and cartwheel. I saw the gentleman throwing daggers at the lady, the seals clapping their flippers, the man eating fire. It was as if they were all phantoms in a dream. I had pictured them vividly so many times, glorifying everything, so that now their real acts seemed a dull disappointment.

'Now, ladies and gentlemen, girls and boys, Tanglewood's Travelling Circus is proud to present Madame Adeline and her rosin-backed performing horses!'

I sat up straight, fists clenched, scarcely able to bear the tension. Madame Adeline came cantering in on a piebald pony, another following close behind. The two horses stepped in time to the music, sometimes hesitating and missing the beat. They were old now, their manes yellow-grey, their flanks sunken.

Madame Adeline stood up on the back of the lead horse, straight and proud as ever, smiling with her carmine lips. I watched her perform every trick, leaping precariously from one horse to another, swinging her legs, standing on her hands, jumping through hoops – my heart in my mouth in case she slipped.

'Hello, children,' she called. 'Who would like to come and ride with me?'

She looked straight at me and beckoned. I had to go to her. I felt foolishly conspicuous in my ugly brown frock. Small though I was, I was clearly the eldest child scrambling into the ring.

Madame Adeline smiled at me and helped me up onto the first piebald horse, swinging herself up after me. We trotted round the ring while everyone clapped.

'Shall we perform properly for them, Hetty?' Madame Adeline murmured into my hair.

'Yes, yes!'

Madame Adeline clucked and our horse gathered speed, galloping round and round the ring while I grabbed his mane and dug my knees in hard to keep my balance.

'Your star turn now!' said Madame Adeline. 'Time to stand up.'

It was much harder now that I was taller and Madame Adeline not so strong. I wobbled precariously, trying desperately to keep my boots connected with the horse's back. I could only manage a split second before I collapsed back onto the horse with a bump – though everyone still clapped.

We slowed down and I scrambled off inelegantly, terrified that folk would see I wore no drawers. Madame Adeline held my hand and we took our bow together.

'Well done, dear Hetty,' she whispered. 'Watch the rest of the show and then I will come for you to take you back.'

I smiled and nodded at her – but after she'd left the ring I stood up and sidled my way along the row to the end. I slipped out of the tent.

'Goodbye, dear Madame Adeline!' I whispered, blowing a kiss in the direction of her wagon.

I could not return to the hospital and the terrible punishment attic. I had run away for ever. I had to fend for myself now.

19

I stepped out purposefully, though I had no idea where in the world I was going. The fairground smell of onions and fried potatoes made my mouth water. I had no money – but I watched a finicky lady nibble at a cone of fried potatoes, pull a face and toss them to the ground. I darted forward and snatched them up. I wolfed them down hurriedly. That was supper taken care of.

It was starting to get dark, so now I needed a bed for the night. I wandered past the noise and glare of the fairground onto the wild heath. At first there were still couples all around me, strolling through the trees, rustling and giggling in the bushes, but after five or ten minutes' walking I seemed to be all alone. I knew the heath wasn't proper countryside, but it had the same good fresh earthy smell.

I stared up at the stars and moon, marvelling in spite of my desolation. I had not seen the night sky properly since I was five. I held my arms up as if I was trying to embrace the constellations. I remembered

Jem naming some of the stars for me, and my eyes filled with tears. I knuckled them fiercely. I had done enough crying for today. I had to be practical and find a safe place to sleep.

In the dark I could not find a hollow tree to turn into a squirrel house, so I found a large bush instead. The ground felt dry and sandy underneath. I crawled under the thick branches and curled up in a ball, cradling my head with my hands.

'This is *better* than a squirrel house,' I told myself. 'This is a cosy little burrow, and if I shut my eyes I shall picture it properly.'

I pictured a sweet bedchamber with a patchwork quilt of buttercups and daisies and clover. It was very similar to the illustration of the field-mouse's burrow beneath the cornfield in my *Thumbelina* storybook. Oh, how I wished I had my precious gift from Ida with me now. However, I'd read it so many times I knew the story almost by heart. I repeated it to myself – and by the time Thumbelina flew off with her swallow I was fast asleep.

I woke with a start in the middle of the night, cold and stiff and terrified. I could not make my picturing work now. I felt utterly alone, like the last child left on earth. I could not stop myself weeping then. I went back to sleep wondering if I might not even be better incarcerated in the punishment attic of the hospital.

I felt more cheerful when I woke in the soft summer daylight. I rolled out from under my bush, stretched heartily and strolled about. I had no privy but it was easy enough to squat behind a tree. Now I needed a washroom. To my delight I found a series of ponds, gleaming silver-grey in the early sunshine. I had no idea how to swim, but I took off my boots and stockings and dress and had a quick splash in the shallows.

I had no towel to dry myself so I ran madly all the way round the pond, and when I came back to my clothes I was nearly dry. I smoothed the creases from my dress as best I could, and polished the dust from my boots with a clump of leaves. I let my hair loose, combed it with my fingers, and then replaited it as neatly as I could.

Now I needed breakfast! This was more of a problem. I wandered around looking for nuts or berries but I could not find any at all. Perhaps if I found my way back to the fair I'd be able to forage for thrown-away scraps? But I'd wandered so far now I had no sense of direction. I simply walked *on*, not sure whether I was heading north or south, or simply going round in circles.

I saw a blue wisp of smoke coming from a small copse, and as I drew nearer I smelled a wonderful savoury cooking smell. I crept closer and came upon a group of dark gypsies in strange bright clothes

337

frying some kind of meat. I wondered if they might share their meal with me. For a few seconds I even had a fantasy of becoming a gypsy girl and travelling in their caravan and selling clothes pegs and telling fortunes, but their dog barked at me furiously and a ragged child started hurling stones at me.

They were clearly not making me welcome so I wandered on, hungrier than ever. I reached the edge of the heath at last and walked out onto the pavement, feeling strangely disorientated to be back in the town so rapidly. I kept my eyes peeled for dainty ladies throwing away half-eaten food, but there were mostly gentlemen in the streets, walking quickly, glancing at their watches, running to catch omnibuses, obviously off to work.

I walked on and on, peering in at the windows of all the big grand houses. I could sometimes see right down into the basement kitchens, with servants scurrying around.

'I am *never* going to be a servant,' I said to myself, trying to lift my spirits. 'I am Hetty Feather and I am not taking orders from anyone. I am as free as the air. I can go anywhere. I can do anything. I can totally please myself.'

But my spirits still seeped right down into my hard boots, and I was snivelling as I walked, unable to control myself. I was so tired and light-headed I sank to the ground, leaning against someone's wall. I covered my face with my hands so that folk passing by would not see I was crying. Then footsteps paused in front of me. Something landed in my lap. Oh Lord, was this another child throwing stones? I took my hands away from my eyes – and stared at a big bright penny shining on the brown stuff of my dress. I looked up and a kindly-looking lady nodded at me.

'There, dearie,' she said, and went on her way.

She thought I was a beggar child! My face flamed red – but my hand grasped the penny.

'Thank you so much, ma'am,' I called after her.

Perhaps her gesture inspired the other passers-by. Maybe they hadn't even noticed me before. But now my tear-stained face attracted attention, and another penny soon landed in my lap, a farthing, and then a halfpenny, soon a whole jingle of copper coins.

Oh my Lord, this was easy! I could sit here at my leisure and look mournful and folk would pay me! But then I saw a dark-uniformed man in the distance, a helmet on his head. I was pretty sure he was a policeman. I was also pretty sure that begging was against the law.

I gathered my coins into my fist, scrambled up and ran off as fast as I could. I careered down long, long roads of houses, my throat aching, my heart jumping in my chest, not even daring to look round in case he caught me. I feared the police had prisons and I did not want to end up in a cell.

Then I came to a parade of shops and dared to pause at last. The policeman was nowhere in sight. I loitered in front of every shop window, and then came to a stop outside a baker's shop. The smell of freshly baked bread brought a flood of water to my mouth and I felt faint.

I stared at the cakes and buns on display in the window. There were slabs of the pink and yellow cake, Madame Adeline's favourite, and white-iced fancy cakes, and red and green and yellow jam tarts, and all manner of golden latticed pies and glazed buns, shiny and soft and curranty.

I had no idea how much such wonders would cost. They could be sixpence each, even a sovereign for all I knew. Perhaps the woman in the white apron inside the shop would scoff at my impertinence if I proffered my small handful of coins. But I was so hungry I decided to risk it.

I opened the door and stepped inside. 'If you please, ma'am . . .' I started shyly.

'Yes?'

'I – I'd like to purchase a little cake – or maybe a bun?'

'Well, make your mind up, dear,' she said, but she didn't sound too impatient.

'Perhaps a cake, the pink and yellow one – *and* a

bun?' I suggested, and then I anxiously showed her my coins. 'Do I have enough money?'

'More than enough, dear.'

She put my cake and bun into a white paper bag, twirled it round so that the corners were twisted fast, took twopence halfpenny from my hand, and gave the bag to me.

'Thank you kindly, ma'am,' I said.

She laughed a little then. 'You've got the best manners of any street child I've ever come across before!' she said. 'Goodbye, dear. Take care of yourself.'

I *could* take care of myself! I had found a place to sleep, a place to wash, I had earned lots of money, and now I could breakfast like a queen! I ate my cake and bun, and when I came to a tea stall I bought myself a large mugful for another penny. Then I went marching on, refreshed and renewed, peering all about me.

I found myself wandering in more huge parkland. For a moment I thought I was back in Hyde Park because I heard an elephant trumpeting – but I discovered I was near the Zoological Gardens. I peered through the railings and saw an elephant even larger than Elijah with a curved seat on his back. Ten or twelve children were strapped onto the seat, while another boy rode bareback on his neck, his boots nudging the beast's great ears.

I had a desperate desire to ride an elephant too! I paid sixpence to get into the zoo, and another twopence for a ride. This was the last of my money so I very much hoped the ride would be worth it. I queued impatiently at the landing stage amongst a great crowd of girls and boys, waiting until at last it was my turn to be hoisted onto the great grey creature.

'I am very good at riding. Please may I sit on the elephant's neck?' I begged the keeper.

'Don't be silly, missy – you're a young lady,' said the keeper, and he put one of the boys on the elephant's neck.

The boy nodded at me triumphantly, pulling a silly face. Other boys shrieked and squirmed beside me, jostling for the best position on the seat – but I was adept at elbowing my way when I wanted. One of the other girls was hopelessly squashed, however, with two rude boys practically sitting on top of her.

'Move next to me,' I said.

She smiled at me timidly. She was beautiful, just like a fairy-tale princess, with big blue eyes, rosy cheeks and long golden curls. She wore a cream silk hat and a matching silk dress, with white stockings and white kid boots with tiny blue buttons.

'Come on, wriggle past those silly boys,' I said, reaching out and grabbing her.

She squeezed past them and I pulled her

safely down next to me. I could feel her trembling violently.

'What's the matter?' I asked in astonishment.

'I'm frightened!' she said.

I didn't know if she was frightened of the elephant, frightened of heights, frightened of the rude boys, or simply frightened of getting her pretty pale clothes dirty. I reached out and held her hand.

'There now, no need to be frightened. I will look after you,' I said. 'My name's Hetty. What's yours?'

'I'm Rosabel,' she said.

I sighed. Trust her to have a beautiful name too!

The elephant was fully loaded now, so the keeper gave him a little tap and we set off, plodding down the path. The boys shrieked loudly and Rosabel clutched me as if she would never let me go.

'Oh dear, it's so scary! I wish the beast wouldn't *roll* so,' she gasped. She peered down desperately. 'I've lost sight of my mama and papa. Can you see yours?'

I would have a hard job seeing either!

'I am here on my own,' I said proudly.

'Without even your nurse?' said Rosabel.

'I don't have a nurse any more,' I said. 'I am too big.'

'No you're not, you're little, much smaller than me,' said Rosabel. 'Oh, *there* is Mama. I see her lilac parasol!' She risked letting go for a second, attempting a little wave.

I stared at her mother. 'She is very young and beautiful,' I said wistfully.

Her papa was waving too. He looked a kindly, jolly man, with a pink face.

'Papa is pleased with me for taking the elephant ride. He feels I am too timid,' said Rosabel. 'But Mama says all girls are naturally timid.'

'I'm a girl and I'm not the *slightest* bit timid,' I said.

'Perhaps we could be friends and then you could teach me how to be bold and independent,' said Rosabel.

My heart leaped. Maybe Rosabel's family would take me under their wing? I could be a devoted companion to their little daughter! They might even adopt me like Polly. I wasn't sure I should be happy wearing cream silk dresses and fancy hats and white boots. I knew how dirty they would be by the end of the day. Maybe they would let me choose a darker colour for my clothes, red or blue or purple – *any* colour so long as it wasn't sludge-brown. I didn't hunger after dolls and toys but I was sure a cosseted child like Rosabel would have a whole shelf of storybooks – and I could share them.

I was still eagerly picturing my future with Rosabel as the elephant plodded back up the path to the landing stage. I kept hold of Rosabel's hand and helped her down carefully.

'Rosabel! Over here, my dear!' both parents called.

I trotted over with her, but the mama suddenly looked horrified and even the papa appeared grave.

'Say goodbye to the little girl, dearest,' said the mama, very firmly.

'She is my new friend Hetty,' said Rosabel.

'Don't be ridiculous, Rosabel. She is just a dirty street child. Leave go of her hand. You should never have let her get so near to you!' said the mama.

The papa turned on me. 'Be off with you,' he said, swotting at me.

If they thought I was a street child, I would act like one. I stuck out my tongue and waggled it hard before running away. My feelings were hurt nevertheless, but I diverted myself by inspecting all the creatures in their cages: the scampering monkeys, the pacing lions, the savage bear in his pit. I felt sorry for all these poor caged animals. I wanted to set them free so that the monkeys could snatch up all the flimsy parasols, the lions could leap at all the scornful parents and the bear maul them to pieces.

I was starting to feel sorry for myself too, walking around alone in my hideous brown frock and boots, while all the well-dressed families stared and sniggered at me. Even the rude boys were here with mamas and papas, big happy families, many of them picnicking on the grass. I stared at their checked tablecloths spread with pork pies and whole chickens and egg-and-bacon tarts, and wondered about darting in like a dog and snatching something. But then what would the woman in the baker's shop say about my manners! I might be a beggar now but I was *not* going to be a thief.

I sat myself down on the grass and looked mournful, hoping that strangers would start flinging pennies at me again, but it seemed to be the wrong sort of place. People had come to the Zoological Gardens to observe the animals, not a small stray child. Folk passed me by without giving me a second glance.

I decided I'd have to move further afield if I wanted to earn enough for my supper. Most of my generous donors had been gentlemen. I needed to get away from this family environment. I figured that there would be more gentlemen in the centre of town, so I left the gardens, walked out of the park and continued on my way.

I wandered back towards Oxford Street and Regent Street, my empty stomach clamouring now, and both boots rubbing my feet sore and bloody. Finally I had to stop and take my boots off altogether. I was sitting on the kerb airing my dirty toes, my boots neatly beside me, stockings tucked inside, when two boys came dashing up. One hollered something unintelligible right in my face. I shouted back furiously. He punched me in the chest and I aimed a kick at him with my bare foot. He pushed me hard so that I fell – and he and his friend scurried off. I sat up gingerly, cursing them. I cursed even more when I went to put on my boots again. They had vanished, stolen by the two scheming boys!

I cried a little then, because I knew how much I needed those boots even though they hurt me. My genuine tears brought me a little consolation – two more gentlemen gave me pennies – but when I got to my feet to look for another baker's shop I realized I was in trouble. The pavements were hard, with sharp stones, whereas my feet were soft and blistered raw. I could not walk far now.

I bought myself a meat pie from a street stall and wolfed it down, though the meat was all fat and gristle and the pastry limp. I thought of Ida and her delicious pies. She had been such a true friend to me yet I'd been so very unkind to her. She would hate me now – if she ever thought of me. She'd have Sheila for her pet. She'd give her tiny culinary treats and save up to buy her a special Christmas present . . .

I felt miserably sick at the thought (or perhaps it was the meat pie). My bladder was also bursting. I wandered up a dark alley off Regent Street to find somewhere private so I could relieve myself.

I found myself in a wide square with a garden full of city men, smoking and larking and taking the air. There were girls too, some ragged and barefoot like me, offering posies to the gentlemen, begging them to buy their flowers. There were a couple of older girls too, their lips painted carmine like Madame Adeline's, wearing lurid dresses and showing a lot of petticoat. They kept approaching the gentlemen, seeming to be begging too.

I hesitated, wondering if I should try too.

'Clear off, you, ginger nob. This is *our* patch!' one girl yelled at me.

Another girl gave me a hard push. 'You're too young! Give way for your elders and betters!' she said, cackling with laughter.

These weren't girls I dared tangle with. They were bigger and rougher than the street boys who had stolen my boots. There was a sharpness about their pinched, painted faces that frightened me. I ran away, up another darker alley, then lifted my skirts and used the gutter, jumping when a rat leaped out at me.

A girl and a gentleman came blundering down the alleyway, arm in arm, whispering together. Their words made me feel sicker than ever. I dodged round them and scurried back to the square, desperate to reach the wide public street once more.

'Are you all right, little 'un?' said one of the

flower-sellers, a softer-looking girl in a shabby blue print dress, carrying a big basket of flowers.

'Yes, thank you, I am perfectly fine,' I said, though I knew I must look wretched and tear-stained.

'You don't *look* fine. I wouldn't stay round here. It's not a good place for a little girl like you,' she said. 'Here, do you want a posy?'

She picked out a tiny bunch of three rosebuds, their stems carefully wrapped round with ribbon so that their thorns were covered.

'It's beautiful, but I'm afraid I have no pennies,' I said.

'I don't want no pennies! It's a gift to cheer you up,' she said.

'Thank you very much! You're very kind,' I said, sniffing the sweet roses.

'Off you hop,' she said. 'I wouldn't even loiter round here. Go straight home. You're too little to be out on the streets.'

I nodded and smiled at her and turned on my way, comforted. I went back down the alley towards Regent Street, but a gentleman stepped out of the shadows right in front of me, making me jump. He was a very grand gentleman, with a fine hat and coat and a fancy silver brocade waistcoat. He could surely mean me no harm . . .

'Hello, my dear,' he said softly. 'What a lovely nosegay! May I buy it?'

'If you please, sir, it's not really for sale,' I said.

'No? But I will pay you a lot of money. A shilling? Two? Maybe half a crown?'

I stared at him. He did not seem a foolish man at all, quite the opposite, so why was he willing to pay a fortune for three little wilting roses? I wanted to keep them for myself because the flower-seller was so kind to me – but I could feed myself for days and days on half a crown.

He saw me hesitating. 'You're clearly very fond of your flowers, child. Never mind, you keep them. I'll tell you what. I have a house nearby with a very pretty garden. I will take you there and you can pick a whole armful of roses.'

'It's very kind of you, sir, but—'

'No buts, my dear. You must come with me. You're trembling! I had better find you a soft shawl to keep you warm – and stockings and shoes for those poor little bare feet. Oh dear, they do look sore.'

He bent down and stroked my feet, fondling my toes. I did not like this one jot and stepped backwards, but he had hold of my ankle. I stumbled and he caught me, lifting me right up in his arms.

'No, please! Put me down, sir!' I said, struggling, but his arms were strong and his hand clamped over my mouth.

'Ssh now, little girl. No crying. You will be fine with me,' he said, walking rapidly.

I tried to bite the hand over my mouth but he held me so tight I couldn't move my teeth, I couldn't even draw breath to scream. But then something went *bang* right on his head, someone kicked him hard between his legs, and he groaned and dropped me. A hand snatched mine.

'Quick, run!'

I ran for my life, hanging onto her hand. It was my kind flower-seller! She had hammered the man with her basket and then kicked him with swift expertise. She tugged me up even darker alleys, and then pushed me into a shadowy doorway. We flattened ourselves in the recess, listening hard – but could hear no footsteps.

'There! I didn't think he'd follow us, but you never know,' she said. 'What was you *doing*, going off with the likes of him? Couldn't you tell he was up to no good?'

'Yes, but I didn't know how to get away.'

'Yell out and give them a good kicking, that's what you do. You don't want to go *near* gentlemen like that.'

'It was so kind of you to rescue me – and you've dropped half your flowers!'

'We'll retrace our steps in a little while and see if we can find any. Don't you worry. What's your name, little 'un?'

'Hetty Feather.'

'I'm Sissy, dear. I'm fourteen.' She said it as if she was quite grown up. She did indeed look years older than the big girls at the hospital, with their prim frocks and plaits. 'How old are you, Hetty?'

'Ten, nearly eleven.'

She didn't seem surprised. 'Our Lil's ten too. She's about your size, bless her. She usually sells flowers along with me, but she's poorly just now. She's got a way of looking all big-eyed so that the gentlemen melt.'

'Can *I* help you sell flowers today?'

Sissy looked me up and down. 'I don't see why not. You need someone to look after you. There's gentlemen and gentlemen. You need to work out which is which. Not that *I* can always tell.' She sniffed. 'Still, I might work on the street, but I like to think me and Lil keep ourselves respectable. If ever I'm tempted otherwise, I just think of Mother.'

'Is your mother . . .?' I hesitated delicately.

'She died two years ago, and the last baby died with her. She were wore out, poor love.'

'Do you have a father?'

'Yes, we do, but we'd be better off without him,' Sissy said bitterly. 'What about you, Hetty?'

I shook my head. 'I haven't got a father or a mother,' I said.

Sissy plucked at the stuff of my dress. 'So is this some kind of orphan uniform?'

I felt I could trust her. 'I used to live at the Foundling Hospital, but I've run away.'

'Ah!' said Sissy, nodding. 'Were they cruel to you there?'

'Ever so cruel,' I said firmly.

'Well, you stick with me, girl, and I'll learn you some tricks. Let's have a look at you now.' She scrutinized me carefully, then wet her finger, rubbed it across the grimy wall, and marked under my eyes with soot. 'That's better. If you look really ill, the gentlemen will feel sorry for you. Can you look really sad, Hetty?'

'I'm brilliant at it,' I said, lowering my head and letting my mouth droop.

'Yes, you're a natural, almost as good as our Lil.'

'I can cry too if you like.'

'No, no, you'll smudge the soot and end up looking like a chimney sweep. Right, my dear, let us see if we can gather up those posies.' She held my hand tight. 'Don't worry about that gentleman, Hetty, or any others of that ilk. I'll be looking out for you now.'

We found the spot where Sissy had valiantly attacked the vile foot-stroker, and gathered up as many fallen flowers as we could, though some had already been trampled underfoot.

'We'll soon sort them out,' said Sissy, kneeling down and arranging them deftly. 'Lovely moss roses, these are, and gentlemen will pay a penny for a little posy. They make a sweet little surprise for a lady, my posies do. That's how me and our Lil do better than most of the other girls. We don't just sell flowers, we make 'em look special. When we sell our violets in the spring, we bind them with green leaves and a tiny piece of lace or ribbon. We beg them from this milliner who used to know our mother. Then we make such a pretty nosegay, some gentlemen might even pay threepence to show their ladies it's spring at last.'

'How pretty,' I said, trying to copy Sissy, prinking the drooping little roses and arranging them just so.

'That's right, Hetty, you're getting the hang of it already. Come with me then, girl. We'll go down St Martin's way. The gentlemen won't pay so much but it's safer there. Don't want no nasty men making off with you again, do we, Hetty?'

I trotted along beside Sissy and sat with her on the steps of a great church by a huge square with fountains and vast lion statues. It was so crowded I wondered if the Queen was returning on another Jubilee procession, but Sissy said it was simply folk coming out to go to the theatre and the halls. Most of them ignored us, though I looked extra mournful and Sissy accosted them energetically.

'Come on, sir, buy a lovely posy for the missus. Beautiful moss roses freshly picked! Make a girl

354

happy, sir. Only tuppence – what a bargain!'

It was a novelty at first and I enjoyed myself, but then it started raining and everyone hurried by under umbrellas, not even glancing in our direction. I hoped Sissy might give up, but she sorted the few coins in her pocket anxiously and said we had to stay.

'We need at least another shilling, Hetty, hopefully twice that,' she said worriedly.

'But you could buy a big meat pie and buns for you and your Lil with the money you've got,' I said, hoping she'd share a few pennies with me too.

'Bless you, Hetty, it's not just a question of money for our food. I have to make the wherewithal tonight to buy fresh flowers from the market in the morning – these will all be withered by then. And then there's Father to consider. He'll start fretting for his drinking money. If I don't get home with enough for his beer, he'll take it out on me *and* our Lil.' She took a deep breath. 'Maybe I'd be better going back to where I was. I reckon I could earn a couple of quick sixpences there. You could stay here, Hetty, and I'll come and collect you, I promise.'

I wasn't quite sure what she meant, but I clung to her nevertheless. 'No, Sissy, stay. We'll get the money here.' I cast my eyes around. I was used to weighing up the hospital visitors on Sunday, working out who might be generous with sweets. I saw a portly middle-aged couple and took a chance.

I snatched a posy and ran up to them in the pouring rain. 'Oh please, ma'am, sir, would you care to buy one of my pretty posies?'

They seemed taken aback.

'What are you doing in the rain, child? And barefoot too! Why don't you run along home?' said the lady.

'Oh, I daren't, ma'am, for my father will beat me viciously if I don't take him money for his drink. And then there's our Lil too, she's poorly.' I decided to embellish things a little. 'And then there's my sister Sheila, she's got the smallpox and is hideously disfigured, and my sister Monica, who's been kicked by a horse and is very dim-witted now.' I started going through half the dormitory at the hospital, inventing ailments and misfortunes galore. I took care to keep my tone tragic and my face a mask of mournfulness – but to my astonishment the lady and gentleman started *laughing*.

'Be off with you, you naughty minx. You should not tell such stories!' said the lady.

'Yes, it's very bad of you to try and con us – but here's a little something for your cheek,' said the gentleman. He fished in his pocket and handed me a couple of coins.

'Oh thank you kindly, sir,' I said, bobbing him a curtsy.

I thought he'd handed me a couple of pennies, but when I opened my fist I saw it was *two shillings*!

'Oh, Hetty, you're a marvel!' said Sissy, giving me a hug. 'There, you've brought us luck! We can indeed go home now.'

I stood still. 'But . . . I have no home,' I said.

'You come along with me,' said Sissy. 'You can stay with Lil and me for now.'

'Won't your father mind?' I asked anxiously.

'So long as he's got enough to drink he don't mind anything,' said Sissy. 'Come on, little Hetty. Come home and meet our Lil. She'll take a shine to you, I'm sure.'

20

Sissy led me through a maze of dark alleyways to her home. They were so dark that I kept stumbling on the uneven cobblestones, and when I tried walking in the gutter I stepped in something unspeakable in my bare feet. I hoped I might be able to have a proper wash at Sissy's house – but when we got there at last, it came as a rude shock.

I was not a fool. I knew Sissy was very poor. I hadn't pictured her in a palace. I'd thought she would live in a very modest house, rather like the country cottage where I'd lived with my foster family.

But Sissy's family didn't have their own house. They had one room in a large, bleak, five-storey tenement building, the bricks black with grime, the window glass mostly missing, the roof partly collapsed.

I stared up at it in horror. 'Is it falling down?' I asked.

'It soon will. It's been condemned a while now so the rent's cheap. Do you want to pee first? We're up four flights of stairs, so it's a good idea to go now if you want to.'

There was no proper privy, just a stinking hole in a tumbledown shed in the back yard. Judging from the smell and the slime on the walls, folk simply tipped their chamber pots out of the window. There was a tap over a drain. Sissy turned it on for me so I could sluice my feet – but only a dribble of water came out.

'That tap's no use. Never mind,' said Sissy. 'I'll go up to the pump at the end of the street later on and bring a jug back.'

There were cockroaches crawling along the dark corridor of the fourth floor. Sissy stamped on them with her boots, while I walked on tiptoe, agonized. She opened the door of the room right at the end. It was very dark, but I could see it was pitifully small and barely furnished. There were two thin mattresses on the floor, and a rickety chair and a stool. Someone had hung sacking curtains at the narrow window and worked a rag rug for the floor, but these were the only homely touches. A big slovenly man sprawled on one mattress while a little girl huddled on the other, coughing and coughing.

'Lil? Oh, dearie, ssh now. Here, darling, take a drink,' said Sissy, hurrying to her side.

She helped Lil sit up and held an old tin cup

to her lips. 'There now, my lovey, this will help,' she said.

'Cough, cough, cough! It drives me mad,' said the father, scratching his head. 'She only does it to annoy, I'm sure. A man can't even have a little nap for that cough, cough, cough. Clear your throat, Lil, and then shut up.'

He rubbed his eyes and then blinked at me. 'Who's this? Clear off out of here, this ain't your room!'

'Hush, Father, this is my new little friend Hetty. She's brought me luck. She's a dab hand at flower-selling, almost as good as our Lil. Look what she's earned for us!' She held out one of the silver shillings.

He snatched it, bit it hard and then shoved it in his pocket. 'Well, I'll be off for a little constitutional,' he said, not giving me a second glance now. 'I'll just stretch my legs and maybe take a drink to ease my parched throat. I'll be back within the hour.'

He stuck his feet in his old broken boots, clapped a greasy bowler hat on his tousled hair and made his way over to the door.

'Within the hour!' Sissy muttered. 'We won't see him till midnight – and good riddance. There now, Lil, take another sip, that's my good girl. Give Hetty a smile, dearie, and show her that *someone* in our family has good manners.'

Lil tried valiantly to master her cough. She was a tiny scrap of a girl, her eyes very large in her peaky face. Her hair was limp and bedraggled, but tied up jauntily with a bright red ribbon, which sadly emphasized her eerie pallor. Her eyes popped as she coughed, her whole face contorting alarmingly – but as soon as she could draw breath she grinned at me.

'Hello, Hetty! Oh my Lord, look at your red hair! That's a queer dress – do you like it? How old are you? Do you have a mother? How much did you get for one posy? I got threepence one day 'cos the gentleman took a shine to me!'

'Now, Lil, give Hetty a chance to answer!' said Sissy, laughing. 'She don't see many folk now, Hetty, so that's why she's so excited to see you. You have a little chat with her while I run out for more water and some supper.' She jingled the coins in her pocket. 'We'll have a treat tonight, girls!'

I sat on the edge of Lil's mattress and let her question me relentlessly. I told her all about the Golden Jubilee, and Madame Adeline at the circus, and my night on Hampstead Heath, and the Zoological Gardens, and the horrid gentleman who seized me before Sissy rescued me.

Lil listened, wide-eyed. 'Dear Sissy! She's always looked out for me and she'll look out for you too,

Hetty,' she said. 'When I die, perhaps you can be a comfort to her.'

Her words came as a total shock. I blinked at her anxiously, not knowing what to say. 'I'm sure you'll get better, Lil,' I mumbled.

'No, no, I'm coughing blood. That means you're dying. Can't fool me!' said Lil. 'I'll miss Sissy so when I'm dead.'

'And she will miss you too, Lil, terribly. But at least you'll be with your mother then,' I said, trying to be comforting.

'I'll be with Mother?' Lil echoed. 'Oh, I should like that very much! Are you sure, Hetty?'

'Certain,' I said, trying to sound convincing. 'Your mother is up in Heaven, and when you die you will be an angel with her.'

'An angel with wings? Will I be able to fly?' Lil asked.

'Oh yes, you'll have great white feathery wings and be able to fly all over Heaven. Sometimes you might swoop down to earth and see Sissy and make sure she's all right,' I said, warming to this theme.

'Oh, I'd love that! Will she be able to see me or are angels invisible?'

'She might just catch a glimpse of you, or hear you whispering her name,' I said.

I'd never glimpsed my brother Saul or heard him

calling me – but I *had* sometimes felt a poke in my ribs, as if he'd prodded me with his old crutch.

Lil spread her arms and flapped them like wings, but the effort made her start coughing again.

'Oh, Lil, don't cough so,' I begged, frightened that she might die then and there in front of me.

I tried to give her the murky water in her cup, but she just choked and spluttered. I patted her helplessly on her back, feeling her sharp little shoulder blades under the thin stuff of her nightgown – almost as if she was already sprouting small wings.

'There now,' said Sissy, bursting into the room, bringing with her a warm savoury smell. 'Oh dear, Lil! Here's some fresh water. Clever girl, Hetty, it helps to rub her back. Now, Lil, see what a feast I've got – *and* some more of that nice medicine. Oh, how it will soothe your poor chest. We're going to get you better and running about in no time.'

It was clear that Sissy wouldn't have any truck with talk of dying and angels. She held the medicine bottle to Lil's lips and made her swig a mouthful between coughs – and it did seem to help a little. Then Sissy unwrapped a waxed-paper parcel to show us three large potatoes and a quantity of fried onions. We seized a potato each and munched ravenously.

They tasted very good, though they were not quite the great treat I had expected.

'What did they feed you at this hospital place, bread and water?' asked Sissy.

'Yes, they did give me bread and water,' I said, remembering my night in the punishment attic.

'Was they really cruel to you, Hetty?' asked Lil.

'Really, really cruel,' I said.

'Did they beat you with a big stick?'

'Well . . . they had whips,' I said.

'Whips!' said Lil, her eyes round. 'Did they whip you till you bled?'

'They were always *threatening* to whip me,' I said. It sounded a little lame. 'They once locked me up in a little attic room all day and all night, and that was far worse than being whipped. Imagine, Lil, being shut up in a tiny room, a total prisoner . . .' My voice trailed away, because Lil could imagine it all too well.

'Did they go out and get sodden drunk and then come back and beat you in a fearsome rage?' asked Lil.

I pictured Matron Bottomly and Matron Peters glugging from a gin bottle. It was such a bizarre idea I couldn't help laughing – and dear Lil laughed too.

'No, they didn't drink, but they frequently got into fearsome rages, especially with me.'

'Did they all hate you, Hetty?'

'Yes! Well, both matrons did. Some of the nurses were all right. Nurse Winnie was very kind, but the teachers were very cruel. Miss Morley once beat my friend Polly with a ruler and I snatched it away and beat her back,' I said, getting a little carried away.

'You had *teachers*?' said Sissy. 'Did they learn you to read and write, Hetty? Could you teach our Lil? She's very bright, I know she is. If she could only read, it would pass the day for her.'

They had no books or paper but I improvised, 'writing' on the bare floorboards with a sooty stick. Sissy squashed up beside us on the mattress. I taught them *a* and *b* and *c*, making them sound out each letter. When Lil succeeded in spelling out *cab*, we clapped her. She got so excited she jumped about, and that started her coughing again, very badly this time, as if she would never stop. Sissy held her close and gently laid her down when she stopped at last.

'There now, my little Lil. No more excitement for today. You go to sleep, dearie. You should try and sleep too, Hetty.'

I lay down beside Lil on the mattress, fully clothed. I had no nightgown and I could not take off my frock as I would reveal I had no underwear.

'Have you read lots of books, Hetty?' said Sissy. 'How about telling Lil one of the stories to help her get off to sleep?'

'Once upon a time there was a very little girl no bigger than my thumb,' I started. 'She was so tiny she curled up every night in a walnut shell . . .'

We all curled up too and went sound asleep until the girls' father came stumbling into the dark room. I felt Sissy tense and Lil gave a little frightened whimper as he staggered over to our mattress. He bent over us, smelling horribly of beer.

'All tucked up like birds in a nest,' he mumbled, slurring his words. 'Goodnight, my chicks. Cheep-cheep!' He laughed at his own joke and then crawled on his hands and knees to his own mattress. He fell on top of it and was snoring heavily in seconds.

'Thank the Lord he's happy-drunk rather than roaring for a fight,' Sissy whispered. 'We never know how it will take him.'

'Does he get drunk *every* night?' I said.

'If he has the money. He's been so much worse since Mother died,' said Sissy. She sounded much younger now – and despairing. 'He used to work at the docks, but he can't hold down a job, the state he's in. I have to earn to keep us all. I never make quite *enough*.'

'I'll help you, Sissy. I'll look proper mournful tomorrow and we'll make a fortune, you'll see,' I said.

Sissy got up before dawn, moving slowly and softly so as not to wake Lil.

'Sissy?' I whispered.

'I'm off to market to buy my flowers,' she murmured.

'I'll come with you,' I said, though I was dizzy from lack of sleep.

I was already dressed and I seemed to have given up on washing, so I was ready in an instant. It was raining, which made my lack of boots particularly uncomfortable. My feet were numb from walking across the slippery cobblestones. It was a struggle keeping up with Sissy.

We walked to the huge market at Covent Garden, abuzz with activity though it was still dark. Even though I was exhausted, I paused to marvel at all the wagon-loads of peas and potatoes, the barrows and carts piled high with tomatoes and lettuces, the great baskets scarlet with cherries and strawberries.

There were people fresh from the country, tall men in smocks like Father, round red-faced women like Mother, reminding me painfully of long-ago times. Sissy tapped me gently and we walked on to the flower market. Again I was dazzled, my eyes stinging with the shock of such bright colours, sunny yellow asters, hot orange pokers, fat pink peonies, blue and deep-purple lupins, my nose wrinkling with the overpowering smell of roses and great white lilies.

Sissy sprang into action, bargaining with last night's money until she had a huge basketful of flowers. Then we sat beneath the big arcade, fashioning the flowers into bright bouquets and tiny posies. I tried to help her, though I still felt light-headed and my hands were clumsy. When at last we were done, she spent her last penny at the coffee stall, sharing the hot drink with me. We had no more money for buns or rolls, but Sissy kept a sharp eye on the floor of the fruit market and snatched up a discarded withered apple and a bruised pear, providing us with a meagre breakfast.

We went to the steps of St Martin's, but another older flower-seller was there already, and she wouldn't let us stay too. Sissy tried Charing Cross Station, but again we were too late. We had to go to the square off Regent Street, though Sissy made me sit close beside her, and whenever any weird-seeming gentleman paused, she put her arm round me protectively. There weren't too many gentlemen, weird or otherwise, because the rain was relentless. I wasn't really *cold* because it was summer, but I felt chilled right to the bone, and by afternoon my stomach was rumbling pathetically.

'Aren't you hungry, Sissy?' I asked.

'I'm always hungry,' she said. 'But you get used to it.'

I wasn't sure I would ever get used to this. Selling flowers had been a novelty yesterday, but now it was so tiring and tedious.

'Buy my sweet flowers, sir. A posy for your lady, only a penny. Go on, sir, there's a gent,' I'd gabble, but nearly always they walked straight past, ignoring me. I didn't have to rub soot under my eyes or adopt a mournful expression – I am sure I looked genuinely ill and exhausted.

'Please, oh, please buy my flowers,' I begged, but I could have been a sparrow cheeping for all the attention I attracted. Then a plain lady in charcoal grey paused nearby. She watched while Sissy and I accosted each passing gentleman. I wondered why she was lingering. Did she want a nosegay to brighten her severe outfit? I smiled in her direction.

'Would you care to buy a posy, ma'am?' I asked.

She shook her head and I drooped a little more.

'Are you a regular flower-seller, child? I do not recollect seeing you here before.' She was looking at me strangely. 'What are you doing here?'

'She's with me, missus. She's all right,' said Sissy protectively.

'She looks a little tired,' said the lady.

'I am, ma'am,' I said. 'If you buy some flowers, we will be able to buy a bite to eat. We have had no breakfast today, nor dinner.'

'Are you both very hungry?' she said. 'I have an idea. Perhaps you would like to accompany me to a nearby teashop?'

My heart jumped. A teashop! Oh, how I longed for

a cup of tea and a bite to eat! But Sissy was looking dubious.

'We ain't got the wherewithal to go in no teashop,' she said.

'I will happily pay for you,' said the lady.

'Oh, Sissy, please, do say yes!' I begged.

She still seemed reluctant. 'What's the catch, eh?' she asked.

The lady smiled. 'Yes, you're right, Sissy, there *is* a catch. I would like to ask you a few questions.'

'What about?' Sissy looked alarmed. 'Look, missus, we bought our flowers fair and square from Covent Garden Market. I've got a regular pitch. We don't get no hassle from no one, not even the police. We're totally honest and respectable. We never go off with no gentlemen.'

'I'm sure you're right. I'm not here on any official business, I promise you. I'll be frank. I'm a writer. My books are published by the Religious Tract Society. They are stories of street children very much like you.'

'What's your name then?'

'Sarah Smith.'

Sissy looked at me. 'You read books, Hetty. Have you ever heard of her?'

The only children's writers I knew of were Mr Andersen and the two Mr Grimms. I'd had no idea that ladies could write storybooks. I looked at

Sarah Smith with great interest. She was staring back at me.

'So you can read, Hetty?' she said. 'Who taught you?'

Ah. I had to be a little careful now. I could not breathe a word about the hospital or she'd act like Madame Adeline, and want to take me straight back.

'My brother Jem taught me, ma'am,' I said, truthfully enough.

'And where is he now?'

'I lost him long ago,' I said sadly.

'So what is your name, child?'

'Hetty Feather, ma'am.'

She nodded as if she approved of my name. 'Then do please come with me, Hetty. And you too, Sissy. I simply wish to ask you a few questions to use as background for a new story of mine. I'm thinking of calling it *A Penny for a Posy*. Do you like the title? It will be all about little flower-sellers like you.'

'Could you put us *in* your story, ma'am?' I asked excitedly. 'Could you use our names? Oh, I should so like to be in a real storybook.'

'I don't want *my* name in no storybook,' said Sissy.

She made it clear she was only accompanying me on sufferance. We made our way out to the busy

thoroughfare of Regent Street. I thought we would
go to a humble teashop full of working folk, but Miss
Smith made for the door of a grand restaurant, all
great glass windows and gilt decoration.

'We can't go in there. We'll get chased away,' said
Sissy. 'It's much too grand for the likes of us.'

Certainly the waiter at the door was looking
us up and down and glaring. Sissy was neat
enough in her print dress, but her hair was
straggly and she wore men's boots with their soles
flapping. I looked even worse by now, my hair
a-tangle, my brown dress dirty and crumpled, my
bare feet filthy.

'We are too shabby, miss,' I said.

'Nonsense,' said Miss Smith, taking our hands.
She led us into the restaurant, giving the waiter
haughty directions. 'We would like a table for three,
please. Could we have the menu brought straight
away? My companions are very hungry.'

The waiter bowed reluctantly and ushered us to
a table right in the corner. He held the chair out for
Miss Smith and then hesitated. Miss Smith coughed
reprovingly. The waiter sat Sissy and me down too,
though he grimaced, as if he'd been asked to seat
two monkeys at the zoo.

He made a particular to-do over Sissy's flower
basket, trying to take it from her. Sissy hung onto it
determinedly.

'I'll put these in the cloakroom for you, miss,' he said.

'No, you don't! I want them where I can see them. Anyone could help themselves in the cloakroom,' said Sissy.

'Yes, that basket will be fine at our feet, under the table. The flowers smell heavenly,' said Miss Smith.

The waiter did as he was told, though he raised his eyebrows and sighed. Sissy jutted her chin out and glared back at him, but she was biting her lip and fiddling with a lock of her lank hair. She stared at the gleaming knives and forks on the white tablecloth before us, clearly unused to copious cutlery.

The waiter handed us three large menus. Sissy stared at hers, blinking rapidly.

'What would you like?' said Miss Smith. 'You can have anything on the menu. What's your favourite food, Sissy?'

Sissy shrugged her shoulders, seeming ungracious because she simply did not know what to say. I glanced down the long list of items, utterly astonished at the choice. I'd had no idea you could select whatever you wanted in a restaurant. I would have liked to linger over my choices, picturing each dish, but I knew I had to help Sissy as tactfully as possible. The words on the menu were just elegant squiggles to her.

'If you please, I would like the steak-and-kidney pudding,' I said. 'Would you like that too, Sissy?'

Sissy nodded dumbly.

Miss Smith summoned the waiter back and ordered two meat puddings for us, and a little fish for herself. Then she poured us a glass of water each from a crystal carafe. Sissy and I drank thirstily while Miss Smith sipped. She started asking Sissy questions, perhaps trying to put her at her ease.

'How long have you been selling flowers, Sissy?'

'Since I was little.'

'And what do you do in winter, when fresh flowers are in short supply?'

'Sell oranges.'

'Is your mother a flower-seller too?'

'No, miss, she sewed stuff.'

'What sort of a seamstress was she?'

'I dunno.'

'And what about your father?'

Sissy sniffed, not bothering to reply. Miss Smith persisted gently, but Sissy's answers became more and more monosyllabic.

Then our dinners arrived and all our attention was taken by the steak-and-kidney pudding, a great soft suet mound stuffed with choice meat and oozing with gravy. There were potatoes too, and carrots and peas, a big plateful.

I waited cautiously in case Miss Smith wanted to say grace, but Sissy simply sat, stunned.

'You may begin, girls,' said Miss Smith.

I picked up my knife and fork and Sissy copied me, though she held the knife in her left hand and the fork in her right. I did not like to tell her in case I embarrassed her. She struggled with her cutlery but still managed to eat with gusto. I was surprised to see the inroads she'd made on her pudding almost immediately. Then I realized she'd transferred half of it to the napkin on her lap. I guessed she wanted to take it home for Lil. I hoped it wouldn't ooze gravy too soggily.

'Now, Hetty, it's your turn to sing for your supper,' said Miss Smith. 'Tell me about your life. How did you come to be a flower-seller? What did you do before that? Start right from the beginning.'

Sissy looked anxious, but I smiled serenely. I felt Miss Smith had been short-changed by Sissy, who hadn't provided her with any telling details for her *Penny for a Posy* story. I decided to do my best. I could not tell the truth of course, and relate my *own* story. I could picture a much more colourful tale.

'I was born in the country, but my dear mother died when I was born,' I began. 'Father went to pieces and started drinking. It wasn't so bad when he came home merry, but he could get into fearsome tempers sometimes and we all trembled in our beds.'

Sissy stared at me, astonished that I was appropriating *her* father. I carried on determinedly, picturing for all I was worth, inventing a cruel stepmother who sent me off to work in a loathsome factory when I was only eight, and a grasping landlord who cast us out into the streets. I told of two evil women, Miss Peters and Miss Bottomly, gin-soaked old harridans, who harassed us most dreadfully. To give my story a little variety I had a magical episode when I joined a circus and performed nightly in a magnificent equestrian act.

I continued this alternative life history throughout my steak-and-kidney pudding, and talked non-stop through a plum tart and custard, and then a cup of real coffee and a little dish of chocolates.

Sissy stayed silent and open-mouthed, only fidgeting when I told Miss Smith the prices of flowers and my favourite Covent Garden supplier, because I was clearly getting a few of my facts wrong. I was not deterred, however. So long as I spoke fluently, filling in many little details, I was absolutely certain I was convincing.

Miss Smith seemed to think so anyway. She took copious notes in her black notebook.

'There!' I said eventually, feeling that I had certainly earned our splendid dinner. 'Will you put some of my story in your book, Miss Smith?'

'I am very tempted,' she said, closing her notebook

and smiling at me. 'However, I think *you* should write your story, Hetty. You are far more inventive than I am. I rather suspect your story is pure fiction from beginning to end, but twice as interesting for that very reason.'

I blinked at her. 'What – what do you mean?' I said.

'She means she knows you're telling whopping great lies, Hetty,' said Sissy, standing up. She had her napkin of suet pudding carefully tucked under her shawl. She reached for her flower basket. 'Come on, little 'un. Time to scarper.'

'No, wait, Sissy! I haven't paid you for your time,' said Miss Smith. She fumbled in her reticule and brought out two silver half-crowns and a little card.

'This card has my name and an address on it. It is an office off The Strand where we are setting up a rescue society for young girls on the street. If you show anyone the address, they will be able to direct you there. You will always be sure of a warm welcome – and if you ever find yourself in need of new accommodation or an alternative occupation, we will do our best to help you. Now off you go, my dear. Thank you so very much for taking care of Hetty, but she is in my charge now. I will take her back to the Foundling Hospital.'

I stared at her. How did she *know*? I hadn't

breathed a word to her about the hospital. I looked at Sissy. 'You didn't tell her, did you?'

'Of course I didn't,' said Sissy. She looked at Miss Smith. 'She can't go back there, miss. They're dreadful cruel to her there – they whip her and lock her up in attics.'

'Do they, Hetty?' said Miss Smith. 'Answer truthfully now.'

'They will quite *definitely* lock me up if you take me back there now!' I said.

'We will see about that,' said Miss Smith. 'Don't worry about Hetty, Sissy. I promise I will make sure she's all right. You have clearly been very kind to her and looked after her well, but I don't think she could survive on the streets without you.'

'I'll say!' said Sissy. She pocketed Miss Smith's coins, eyes gleaming at the thought of what they could buy in the way of treats for Lil.

'Take the card too, please. And do not hesitate to use it,' said Miss Smith.

'Thank you kindly, miss.' Sissy took the card and then lugged her flower basket off the floor. 'Have a posy, do. And you truly won't be too hard on Hetty? She was only romancing. She tells lovely stories – she can't seem to help it.'

She handed Miss Smith her biggest bunch of roses, gave me a quick peck on the cheek, and then lumbered out of the restaurant with her basket, taking care to bump into the supercilious waiter on her way out.

I could not bear to see her go. I got up to run after her, but Miss Smith had hold of me.

'No, Hetty.'

I started crying. 'Poor Sissy truly does have a dreadful father, and they don't have enough food, and there's a little sister, Lil, but she is very ill and I think she is dying,' I wept. 'I swear I'm not picturing now, Miss Smith.'

'I know. Sissy seems a brave, resilient girl, but she certainly has a very hard life. But tell me, Hetty, do you really want that life for yourself? You know you don't belong on the streets.'

'Perhaps that's true – but I *don't* want to belong to the hospital,' I said. 'I still don't understand how you knew I came from there.'

'Your distinctive name has been on many people's lips since your disappearance on the trip to Hyde Park. You have even been mentioned in the newspapers,' said Miss Smith.

'Really!' I said, rather thrilled. 'But how did you know *I* was Hetty the foundling when you saw me selling flowers?'

'Oh, come now! The foundling uniform is very distinctive, even without your cap and tippet. And, oh dear, what happened to your boots?'

'Two horrid boys stole them.'

'There, you see, you're not safe to be on the streets. You need to be properly cared for in the hospital.'

'They *don't* care for me there,' I sniffed. 'You don't know what it's *like*, Miss Smith.'

'Yes I do. At least, I have an outsider's view. I used to visit on Sundays with my brother, Peter, though I always felt uncomfortable staring at all of you while you ate your Sunday dinners.'

I stared at her: her pale, serious face, her plain charcoal-grey dress. I remembered Harriet's beloved, the man with the tie-pin in the shape of a P . . .

'Oh, I remember you now!'

'Yes, and I remember you, the cross little red-haired girl with the big friend who fluttered her eyelashes at my foolish fop of a brother,' said Miss Smith, laughing. 'Don't look abashed, Hetty. I think you had every right to be sulky in those particular circumstances. But I *am* concerned that you hate the hospital so. I have recently been invited onto the board of governors because of my rescue work with children and my books for the Religious Tract society. I thought the Foundling Hospital an excellent institution in most respects. The children all seem well-nourished and healthy, their food is fresh and simple, and I'm particularly impressed that everyone receives a decent education and proper training.'

'But all the girls are trained to be *servants*,' I said.

'There is nothing wrong with being a skilled servant, Hetty,' said Miss Smith, shaking her head at me.

I sniffed again, lolling back in my chair. '*You* wouldn't care to be a servant, Miss Smith,' I said impatiently.

'I agree I would sooner be a writer,' she said. 'But I wasn't joking when I said that *you* could be a writer too, Hetty Feather. You have a very vivid imagination and a gift with words. Your invented life history was immensely entertaining.'

'But you didn't believe me.'

'I think if your story was down on paper, you might write with true conviction.'

'Do you think I could really have one of my stories published in a *book*?'

'Not yet a while. I can't quite promise you that, Hetty. We will have to see. You will have to work hard, practising your art. Try writing for at least half an hour each day. I *can* promise I will keep in touch with you and do my best to help you.'

'But I have to go back to the hospital?'

'You do indeed.'

'Matron Bottomly will be so very angry with me,' I said.

'I dare say – but I will do my best to protect you.'

382

Miss Smith gave me a most unladylike wink. 'I am a governor now, Hetty. Your Matron Bottomly has to answer to me.'

Miss Smith gave the money for our sumptuous meal to the waiter, who had been hovering for quite a while. I saw how much money it was.

'My goodness, writers must earn a great deal, Miss Smith!' I said with keen interest.

'Do not get too excited, Hetty. Many writers earn a pittance, or cannot sell their work at all. You might well have to earn your keep as a servant while you hone your craft.'

'I shall start honing for all I am worth,' I said. 'If Ida is still talking to me, I shall beg her for a whole stack of kitchen paper and start writing my story straight away.'

'Ida?'

'She works in the kitchen and has been my dear friend ever since I arrived at the hospital. But I have *not* been a dear friend to her. I don't think she will like me any more now.'

'I am sure she will, Hetty, but just in case, it might be prudent to make a little purchase before we take you back to the hospital,' said Miss Smith.

She took me by the hand and let me up Regent Street and along a little arcade. She stopped outside a stationer's shop. There were wondrous marbled notebooks in the window, patterned with swirling combinations of colour, some sky-blue and purple and pearly pink; some silver and emerald and jade; some scarlet and vivid orange and gold.

'Oh!' I exclaimed, looking at them in awe. I ran my finger over the glass window, following the flow of the design. 'I know the pattern is abstract, but does that swirling shape remind you of anything?'

'It looks like feathers, Hetty,' said Miss Smith. 'How felicitous! You must select one of the notebooks – and perhaps you need a pen?'

'I have an excellent quill pen given to me by my long-lost friend, Polly. Oh, Miss Smith, might I have my very own bottle of ink?' I asked.

We went inside the stationer's and I deliberated deliciously over each and every notebook. Perhaps the purple was the prettiest, the shades of green the most pleasing to the eye – but I chose the notebook with scarlet and orange swirls picked out in gold, because it was as bright as the hair on my head.

The stationer parcelled it up in a special canvas satchel, with a bottle of black ink in its own little leather pouch for safe-keeping. Miss Smith and I had only been acquainted for a matter of hours, but I threw my arms about her and kissed her pale cheek.

She hailed a hansom cab and asked the driver to take us to the Foundling Hospital. I clutched my wondrous present and tried to feel brave – but when we drew up outside the great gates of the hospital, I was trembling.

'Courage, Hetty,' said Miss Smith.

The gatekeeper boggled as we climbed out of the cab. 'Oh my Lord, it's the missing child!' he exclaimed.

'Indeed it is,' said Miss Smith. 'Come along, Hetty dear. Let us seek out Matron Bottomly and tell her your sad tale. Now, Hetty, quick, give me a very brief and *truthful* resumé of the last two days.'

I told her about going to see the wrong circus in Hyde Park, and my omnibus journey to Hampstead Heath, and my encounter with Madame Adeline, and my night under the bush, and my begging in the street, and my ride on the elephant in the Zoological Gardens, and my alarming encounter with the weird gentleman, and my rescue by dear Sissy and subsequent night in her room in the condemned house. I kept it utterly concise, with no picturing whatsoever, but we had to take three turns of the grounds before my tale was fully told.

'My goodness, Hetty, you've certainly had your fair share of adventures. My poor fictional heroines lead very dull lives by comparison!' said Miss Smith.

'Matron Bottomly will be so angry. She will lock me up in the punishment attic for a week,' I said fearfully.

'Wait and see, child,' said Miss Smith. 'Come now, let us confront her.'

We went in through the girls' entrance. The infant foundlings were all filing off to the privies after their darning session. They stopped and stared at me, clutching each other.

'Oh, wonders!' Nurse Winnie cried, dashing up to us. 'It's Hetty Feather back from the dead! Oh, Hetty, God be praised, you're safe!' She seized hold of me and whirled me round, then gave me a kiss on both cheeks.

'There, Hetty! Now tell me, is she one of the cruel nurses who beat you?' said Miss Smith as we proceeded along the corridor towards Matron Bottomly's room.

'Nurse Winnie is a darling,' I admitted. 'But wait till you meet Matron. *She* will not be thankful I am back from the dead. She will very likely *wish* me dead. And buried. And burning to a crisp in H-e-l-l.'

Miss Smith knocked on Matron Bottomly's door and pulled me inside. Matron Bottomly's head jerked up at the sight of me. Her mouth opened comically. She took in my ragged, unkempt state, my missing cap and tippet and apron, my filthy bare feet. She took a deep breath.

'Hetty Feather!' she said. 'I knew *you* would be the child to bring disgrace to the Foundling Hospital!

If you only knew the trouble you've caused! We have never had a child run away before.'

'Oh no, you are very much mistaken!' said Miss Smith quickly. 'Do let me introduce myself, Matron. I am Sarah Smith, newly elected to your board of governors – and very happily I rescued Hetty myself. She did *not* run away, I assure you. She was captured by a band of brigands at the funfair at Hyde Park. They chloroformed the poor child and kept her trussed up in an attic, ready to be shipped overseas.'

Miss Smith leaned forward and hissed dramatically, 'The white slave trade! But I happened to be in the area reporting on slum dwellings and I heard her desperate screams. I rescued her and she begged me to take her back to the hospital. I hope no long-term harm has been done to her – but I fear her confinement will prey on her mind. She must never be confined in a locked room again, her nerves would never stand it.'

It was my turn to marvel at Miss Smith's picturing. I practically applauded when she insisted I must not be locked up! I'm not sure how much Matron Bottomly truly believed – but Miss Smith was a governor and she could not accuse her of lying.

'I feel Hetty Feather is a child of enormous creative potential. I have given her a notebook in which to write. I shall come and visit her regularly and examine her work,' said Miss Smith. 'I am sure I can rely on you, Matron Bottomly, to make sure Hetty is not parted from her notebook. I know you have her welfare at heart.'

Oh, glorious and devious Miss Smith! Matron Bottomly still hates the very sight of me, but she allows me to write write write in this notebook! She has *not* locked me in the punishment attic – though I'm sure she was sorely tempted when Madame Adeline paid a visit to the Foundling Hospital to make sure I'd returned safely!

I have been writing my own story this past year. Miss Smith has been writing too. *A Penny for a Posy* has already been published. I have my own copy, dedicated thus: *To Hetty and Sissy – and in memory of Lil.* Miss Smith tracked them down and paid for a doctor to attend poor little Lil, but sadly he could not help her. However, Miss Smith's rescue organization has found Sissy decent lodgings away from her father, and she is now being trained as a milliner, making neat nosegays for bonnets, so her story ends happily too.

This is *my* story and I promise it is not a work of fiction. I have tried hard not to exaggerate or embroider too much. Miss Smith says very complimentary things about my writing, but says

I have a tendency to be too fanciful. But sometimes the truth is stranger and more wondrous than fiction. I have kept the very best part till last. *I have found my mother!*

I wonder if you have guessed who she is?

I had a very thorough bath the day I returned to the hospital and was given a brand-new uniform and new boots too. I walked into the dining room for supper and a general hubbub broke out, with girls clapping and crying, because everyone had been convinced I'd disappeared for ever. Even Sheila and Monica clasped me close! Little Eliza was beside herself, leaping up at me like a little monkey, her arms about my neck.

However, it was Ida who reacted most dramatically. She took one look at me, turned white as a sheet, and fainted dead away. She had to be carried bodily out of the dining room by two nurses and taken to her room. Her shoe fell off as she was dragged away. I snatched it up and cradled the ugly black brogue as if it was Cinderella's glass slipper.

'I must return Ida's shoe,' I mumbled to a nurse, and fled from the dining room, even though I had not had my supper.

I followed the nurses and poor Ida through the kitchens and down a long corridor to the cramped servants' quarters. Ida's room was as small as the punishment attic and almost as bare. The nurses laid her down on her truckle bed. Ida murmured my name.

'Yes, yes, Hetty Feather's here. She has scared us all but she has turned up like a bad penny,' said one nurse.

'Fancy you taking on so, Ida! You've a kind heart,' said the other nurse. 'There now, you'd better rest. Come along, Hetty, leave Ida to recover.'

'Mayn't I stay for five minutes, just to make sure she doesn't swoon again,' I begged. 'I was so very mean to Ida and I feel so bad about it now. *Please* let me tell her how sorry I am.'

The nurses laughed at me, but let me stay.

'Oh, dear Ida, please be all right,' I whispered.

I smoothed the hair off her forehead and stroked her temple. Her eyes opened. They looked very raw and bloodshot.

'Oh, Ida, your eyes look so sore,' I said, concerned. 'Have you been crying?'

'Of course I've been crying!' Ida said. 'I've been fair demented these last two days. I've been out searching the streets both nights trying to find you. I thought I'd truly lost you and I couldn't bear it. I feared you'd run away because you thought I favoured Sheila, when I was simply making a fuss of her to spite you.'

'And no wonder! I was so horrid to you. Please

forgive me, dearest Ida. You mean the whole world to me,' I declared.

Fresh tears welled in her poor eyes.

'Oh, Ida, don't!' I said, and I hugged her hard, burying my head in her bony shoulder.

Her hands reached up and she wound her fingers in my red hair. 'My little Hetty – my own child,' she murmured.

I raised my head. 'What did you say?' I whispered.

Ida wiped her tears with her fingers, keeping her face covered with her hands. 'Nothing, nothing,' she said.

I took hold of her hands and gently pulled them away so I could see her properly. I looked deep into her eyes and saw the truth. 'You are my *mother*?' I whispered.

'Hush, Hetty, hush! No one must ever know!'

'But . . . but . . .' I saw the strands of our hair side by side on the pillow, Ida's light-brown locks and my fiery red ones.

'Your father has red hair,' Ida whispered.

I clasped her hands. 'Tell me!' I begged.

'His name's Robert – but everyone always called him Bobbie. He was the brightest boy in our village and I loved him with all my heart, though he did not truly care for me. He left to go to sea and voyage round the world.'

'And where is he now, my father?'

'I truly do not know, Hetty. He never came back. He swore he'd write to me but he never did. I waited and waited for him to return – because I realized I was having his baby.'

'Me!'

'Yes, you, Hetty!' Her arms went round me, holding me tightly. 'I did not know what to do. I didn't tell a soul but soon I became so big that people started to notice. My parents could not stand the shame and turned me out.'

'Oh, Ida!'

'I was so lonely, so frightened. I didn't know what to do,' she said, clinging to me. 'I gave birth to you all alone, and you were so terrifyingly tiny, but, oh, so precious. I held you close in my arms all day long and felt I could never ever let you go. But I had no way of supporting us. I did not dare farm you out to some woman while I worked. You were so small and sickly, I knew you would not thrive unless you were cared for most particularly. So I decided it would be best if I took you to the Foundling Hospital.'

'I *wish* you could have kept me, Ida.'

'I wished it too. It was an agony to give you up. I missed you so badly. I nearly lost my mind with wretchedness. I ended up in the workhouse, changing my name so that no one should ever know. It was very hard there, but I did my best to bear it.

Eventually the mistress helped me find a position as a kitchen maid. I worked in that post for a year, but when I knew you were due back from your foster home I applied for work at the hospital. It was my only way of being near you, Hetty. I could never earn enough to buy you back, and the governors would not deem me a fit mother anyway.'

'You are the most fit mother in the world, and the only one I could ever want,' I said fervently.

'It's been such a secret joy these past five years watching you grow, but a torment too, unable to give you a true mother's love. I resolved never to tell you. If anyone found out, I would be sent away in disgrace.'

'Oh, Ida, I will keep our secret, I swear,' I promised. 'But could you tell me just one thing more. Did you give me a name when I was born?'

'I called you a fancy pet name, Sapphire, because your eyes were so blue.'

'Oh my Lord, I pictured that! I *knew* my real mother would have chosen a beautiful name for me! Listen, Ida, I hope to be a writer one day and have my stories published – and then I shall use Sapphire as my pen name. You're not laughing at me, are you?'

'No, my darling, I'm crying because I'm so happy.'

'We will leave the hospital together when I'm

old enough, and my stories will earn lots of money, and I'll find us a fine house, and we will live there together, mother and daughter, just you wait and see.'

'Happily ever after, like the fairy stories,' said Ida, still weeping.

'Happily ever after,' I declared. 'I am absolutely certain!'

Many real children experienced childhoods similar to Hetty's, growing up in the Foundling Hospital. Thomas Coram started this 'Hospital for the Maintenance and Education of Exposed and Deserted Children' in 1739.

This was the first special children's charity in the UK, and over two and a half centuries it rescued more than 27,000 abandoned babies. It continues today simply known as Coram, helping children who are alone or at risk, marginalized at school or without a real home. You can find out more about Coram by visiting **www.coram.org.uk** or see for yourself what life was like for children like Hetty by visiting its Foundling Museum in London and at **www.foundlingmuseum.org.uk**.

For my two best girls

Jacqueline Wilson

SAPPHIRE BATTERSEA

ILLUSTRATED BY
NICK SHARRATT

A new name
A new life for
**HETTY
FEATHER**

CORGI YEARLING

1

My name is Sapphire Battersea. Doesn't that sound beautiful? I write it over and over again on the covers of this private notebook. I stitch a secret S.B. inside the neck of my uniform. I stir a swirly S.B. into the soup when I am helping the cook. I scrub a soapy S.B. when I am cleaning the floor. I whisper my own name in bed at night in the freezing dormitory, and my breath rises and forms the letters in the dark.

I am Sapphire Battersea, but nobody calls me by my real name, not even my dear mother. Mama chose to call me Sapphire because my eyes were so blue when I was born. But even she calls me Hetty now.

'I'm *not* Hetty. It's such a stupid name. It's just a hateful foundling label. I *hate* the way they change all our names, making them up randomly. They don't sound like real names. Hetty Feather! It's ridiculous.'

'You could have had worse,' said Mama. 'Just

think, you could have been *Grizel Grump.*'

Poor Grizel is a girl in little Eliza's year at the Foundling Hospital. Everyone calls her Gristle, and consequently she is always a grump, like her name.

'Sapphire is so elegant, so romantic. It's a perfect name for a writer,' I said, signing it in the air with a flourish.

'Let us hope you become one, then,' said Mama, a little tartly.

'You wait and see. I will publish my memoirs and make our fortune. Miss Smith will help me. My story will be turned into a proper book with gold lettering and a fancy picture on the front, just like all her own Sarah Smith stories published by the Religious Tract.'

'I'm not sure *your* stories would be suitable for a religious press, Hetty,' said Mama, laughing.

'*Sapphire!* Why won't you call me by my true name – the one you chose for me?"

'I suppose Hetty has become a habit, dearie,' said Mama, tweaking my red plait.

'I always call you Mama when we're alone,' I said, a little hurt.

'Yes, but I wish you wouldn't. It's tempting fate. One slip in front of the others and we're done for,' said Mama, and she pulled me close.

'I will never slip, Mama,' I swore fervently. 'No one will ever find out that you are my real mother.'

I hadn't known myself for the first ten long years of my life. Poor Mama had been forced to give me to the Foundling Hospital when I was a little baby because she had no means of supporting me. I was soon fostered out to the country. I lived with a kind family. I loved my foster mother and father and all my foster siblings. I especially adored my foster brother Jem.

I had hero-worshipped him. I treasured the silver sixpence he'd given me when I was taken off to the Foundling Hospital at five. He promised he'd wait for me and marry me one day. I was so little and stupid I actually believed him – until young Eliza arrived at the hospital from the same foster home five years later. She prattled away about *her* dear Jem. I found out that he'd made exactly the same empty promises to her. I couldn't forgive him. I decided to put him out of my mind for ever.

I had found the rigid life of the hospital horribly hard. Some of the nurses were kind, but the two matrons were excessively cruel. I suffered from the attentions of Matron Pigface Peters when I was small, and of Matron Stinking Bottomly when I went into the Seniors. They each went out of their way to punish and humiliate me. I hated them both.

I found it difficult to make friends with the other girls too. I made downright enemies of Sheila and Monica. When Polly came to the hospital, we were like soul mates, but she was adopted by rich folk and we never saw each other again.

My only true friend was Ida, the kitchen maid. I ran away from the hospital on Queen Victoria's Golden Jubilee – and when I came back, Ida was so overwhelmed that she called me her own child when she hugged me. I could scarcely believe it! Ida was my true birth mother. She had skivvied and slaved at the Foundling Hospital for years just so that she could get a glimpse of me every day. She'd slip me an extra potato at dinner, or sprinkle secret sugar on my breakfast porridge. She'd always had a smile or a kind word, and helped me to blossom in that bleak institutional world.

When I became aware of the wondrous truth of our relationship, my whole life changed. I cannot say I became an exemplary foundling. Whether I am Sapphire or Hetty, I still have a temper that lives up to my flaming red hair. But whenever Matron Stinking Bottomly slapped me for impertinence and forced me to scrub the whole length of the hall, I knew Mama was nearby, watching and waiting, burning with sympathy. She'd catch my eye across the crowded dining room at mealtimes, and I'd feel calmed.

Sometimes, when everyone slept in the dormitories, I dared creep right out of the door, along the shadowy landing, down, down, down the great stairs, through kitchens that still smelled of stewed mutton and rice pudding, along the winding corridor to Mama's own tiny bedroom. I'd push open the door and she'd leap up from her bed and hug me hard. We'd sit together and whisper well into the night. Sometimes we'd lie close together on Mama's narrow bed, clasping each other close. I'd trace her dear face in the dark and she'd wind my long plaits around her own neck. We'd feel utterly united, making up for all those many years we'd lived apart.

But then – oh, I can hardly bear to write it. It was all because of Sheila. She was always a light sleeper. She must have woken when I crept through the long dormitory. She didn't call out. She lay there, waiting, and then slid stealthily out of her bed, intent on following me, the sly cat. She was so furtive and silent on her bare feet that I didn't hear her padding behind me. I didn't notice the creak of the stairs as she followed me down to the ground floor.

She stole along behind me all the way to Mama's room. I wonder how long she waited outside, her ear to the door? She suddenly burst in upon us, as Mama and I cuddled close in a fond embrace, clearly visible in the flickering candlelight.

'Whatever are you *doing*, Hetty Feather!' she exclaimed. 'Why are you lying there with *Ida*?'

'Go away! Get out! Get out of Mama's room!' I cried in furious passion.

'*Mama's* room?' said Sheila.

'It is just Hetty's little game,' Mama said quickly, giving me a shake.

But Sheila was no fool. 'You are Hetty's *mother*?' she said.

'No! Like Ida said, it's just my silly game,' I declared, springing off the bed.

Sheila was still staring, open-mouthed. 'Yes, now I see it!' She darted between us, staring rudely. 'You two *are* alike. You're both so small and slight – and you both have blue eyes. Oh my goodness, how extraordinary! Have you known all this time, Hetty? I'd never have thought you could keep such a secret so long,' she said.

It was no use denying it further.

'It's the most private, precious secret! If you dare breathe a word of this to anyone, I'll tear out your tattle-tale tongue and feed it to the pigs,' I said.

'Temper temper!' said Sheila, eyes gleaming. 'So, what will you do for me to keep me sweet and silent?'

'This isn't a schoolgirl game, Sheila,' said Mama, getting out of bed and gripping her by the shoulders. 'I haven't lived this life year after year to have it carelessly destroyed by a spiteful girl. You

404

mustn't tell a soul. If those matrons find out, then we're done for. Swear that you'll keep silent!'

'I won't say a word to anyone, I promise,' said Sheila, but her eyes were still bright. I feared she'd tell Monica the moment she was back in the dormitory.

I'll never know how much she'd have told and whether she'd have deliberately betrayed Mama and me. We were discovered anyway. Mama and I were used to whispering, but Sheila had a high clear voice that travelled far. By terrible chance Matron Pigface Peters had shuffled down to the kitchen, seeking out a midnight snack from the pantry. She heard Sheila repeating, 'Just fancy Ida being your real mother, Hetty!'

Matron Pigface barged her way into Mama's crowded bedroom, a hideous sight in her nightcap and ruffled gown, her greasy hair coiling in true pig's tails about her cheeks. She stared at Mama, at Sheila, at me.

'Repeat what you said just now, Sheila Mayhew!' she commanded.

'I – I don't remember what I said,' Sheila stammered.

'The girls were playing a silly game, Matron. I was about to scold them and send them back to their dormitory,' said Mama.

'Don't lie to me, Ida Battersea!' She was

squinting at her now, then peering at me. 'Can this really be *true*? Are you Hetty Feather's mother?'

'How could I be?' said Ida. 'It's a game, I told you, an idle fancy, because the girls all long for their mothers.'

Matron Pigface Peters dragged me over to the candle, clutching my chin, turning my face this way and that. Then she went to grab hold of Mama.

'Don't you dare touch me! And take your hands off that child too – look, you're hurting her!'

'It's the truth that hurts, Ida Battersea! I see the likeness now! How could you have been so devious? You've been deceiving us for years and years! You were supposed to give up your ill-gotten child for ever – not work here with her glorying in your disgraceful situation. Have you two been secretly communing all this time? It beggars belief! How *dare* you both deceive us like this!'

'It wasn't Hetty's fault, Matron. She didn't know – not for ever so long. I meant no harm. I just wanted a glimpse of her every day – that was enough,' said Mama, starting to sob. 'When she disappeared on the day of the Jubilee, I could hardly contain myself. I worried fit to burst. When she came back at last, I was so relieved I fainted dead away.'

'Oh yes, I remember that!' said Sheila. 'We all

thought you'd died on the spot! So did you tell Hetty then?'

'Hold your tongue, Sheila Mayhew! This is nothing to do with you. Go back to the dormitory this instant. You are to keep utterly silent on this shameful matter,' said Matron Pigface.

'It's not shameful to love your own child!' I said furiously. 'Mama's done nothing wrong.'

'We'll see if the Board of Governors agrees with you! It's my opinion they'll take a very grave view of this deception. I would prepare yourself for instant dismissal, Ida Battersea – with no character reference, so don't expect to get another job in any decent God-fearing establishment. You're morally corrupt and an evil influence on all our girls.'

'How dare you threaten Mama like that!' I cried. 'You wait, Matron Peters! My friend and benefactress Miss Sarah Smith is on the Board of Governors. She will never send my own mama away. *You* will be the one who's sent away, because you're cruel and wicked, and you have no heart at all inside your big fat chest!'

She dragged me away, shouting and screaming. I did not even have time to kiss Mama and say good-bye. I struggled hard, but Matron Pigface slapped me about the head and picked me up bodily. Half the girls from the dormitory were clustered on the stairs, gawping at me.

'Go back to your beds this instant!' Matron Pigface shrieked, and they scuttled away.

She carried on dragging me up another flight of stairs.

'No! No, please don't put me in the punishment room!' I screamed. 'I can't stand it there, you know I can't!'

'You deserve to stay locked up in there for ever!' said Matron Pigface, thrusting me into the terrifying dark cupboard.

'No, please, I beg you! Don't lock me in! Please, I haven't done anything *wrong*!'

'You're the most evil child I've ever come across. You have no shame, show no respect! You act as if you're as good as anyone else. Just remember you're a common foundling, born in sin, without a father. I wouldn't be surprised if you were the spawn of the Devil himself,' she panted, and she locked the door on me.

It was the longest, most agonizing night of my life. I hit the door and walls until my knuckles were bloody – and then I cast myself down on the floor and wept. I called again and again for Mama, but she didn't come. I was frightened they'd locked her up too.

When one of the nurses let me out in the morning, I pushed right past her and ran all the way downstairs to Mama's room ... but she wasn't there! Her cap and apron and print dresses were gone from the pegs on her wall, her brush and comb and her cake of soap and her flannel were gone from her chest. The very pillowcase and sheets had been stripped from her bed, leaving a bare black-and-white striped mattress. There was no trace left of Mama. It was as if she had never existed.

I sobbed myself into a stupor. I could not eat. I could not sleep. I became so fuddled I could barely stagger out of bed. Matron Bottomly and Matron Peters both declared I was faking illness, but I was burning with such a fever that the nurses were frightened and summoned the doctor.

'There is nothing wrong with the child, Dr March,' said Matron Bottomly. 'She simply screamed herself into a passion. I have never known such a wilful child as Hetty Feather. She deserves a good whipping – though of course we would never lay a finger on any of our foundlings,' she added hastily.

Dr March laid the back of his hand on my forehead, then listened to my chest. 'The child is clearly ill, Matron, wilful or not,' he said. 'She's a frail little creature and I fear her chest is weak. She must be kept here in bed, wrapped in wet sheets to lower her fever, and be fed an invalid diet of bread and milk.'

'I think it is criminal to cosset such a wicked girl,' Matron Bottomly murmured to the nurse, but she did not dare disobey the doctor's orders. I was kept isolated in the infirmary. My fever left me after several days but I was still strangely ailing. I could barely sit up in bed. I ate nothing, took just a few sips of water, and lay with my eyes closed, not talking to anyone.

'Come along, Hetty Feather,' said Matron Stinking Bottomly. 'Get up at once.'

'Stir yourself, you lazy girl. We know you're faking,' said Matron Pigface Peters.

They pulled back the sheets but I didn't move, though it was freezing cold.

'Get on your *feet!*' they screamed, and dragged me out of bed.

I stood shivering in my nightgown, while the room whirled violently round and round. The two shouting matrons whirled too, playing a crazy game of ring-a-roses before my eyes. I fainted clean away, cracking my head on the stone floor.

I came round to find blood trickling down my cheek and into the neck of my nightgown. The two matrons were the colour of the infirmary sheets, thinking I had died there and then. Dr March was hastily sent for again. He dabbed at the great gash on my temple, sighing, and told both matrons that it was dangerous to try and rouse me in such a manner.

'But her fever is gone, I am sure. There is nothing wrong with her physically,' said Matron Bottomly.

'Ah, physically, maybe, though she'll be groggy for a couple of days after that bang on the head. No, it's what's going on *inside* her head that concerns me.'

'I'm all too aware of what's going on in that red head of hers. Mischief, lies and total insubordination!' Matron Peters murmured to Matron Bottomly.

Dr March sat beside me, taking my hand in his and patting it gently. I was so overcome by this unexpected kindness I started weeping.

'There now, child. What is troubling you so? What is it you want?'

I swallowed, licked my dry lips and croaked, 'I want *Mama*!'

'Ah, I thought that might be the reason for this bizarre performance,' said Matron Peters. 'Well, want away, Hetty Feather. Your mother has been sent packing and she's never coming back.'

I wept as the word *never* tolled in my head like a mourning bell. I lay in my bed. My head throbbed but I didn't care. I didn't care about anything, only Mama.

Then one morning I had a new visitor. I smelled lemon verbena soap and freshly ironed linen. I

413

opened my eyes and saw the plain neat form of Miss Sarah Smith. She looked at me gravely.

'Oh dear, Hetty,' she said, shaking her head. 'You look like a little ghost!'

'Miss Smith!' I forced my head up off the pillow. The room lurched and tilted but I made a fierce effort to steady myself. 'Oh, Miss Smith, you have to help me!'

'What can I do for you, child?'

'What can you *do*?' I was so desperate I forgot to be polite and deferential. 'You can get Mama back, that's what you can do!'

'I'm afraid I can't do that, my dear,' she said.

'Yes you can! You're on the Board of Governors! You do all that charity work and publish all those books. They will listen to you. Listen to *me*! Mama didn't do anything *wrong*–'

'She had a child out of wedlock, Hetty,' Miss Smith said quietly.

'So did the mother of every foundling in this whole hateful institution!'

'They all gave up their babies to the hospital. They didn't sneak back here under false pretences.'

'Surely that proves just how much Mama loves me. And I love *her*, and I cannot bear it that she's been cast out like a common criminal and denied a character reference.'

Miss Smith tried to interrupt, but I went on

414

talking, sitting bolt upright and shouting now. The infirmary nurse came rushing to restrain me, but Miss Smith stopped her.

'What will poor Mama do? She can't get a new position without a character reference. She's only ever worked here – and three terrible years in the workhouse. What if *they* won't take her back? Then she will be left to fend for herself on the streets. You dare ask me what the matter is! How do you think I feel, knowing my own dear mother is sitting in some mire-filled, squalid gutter, weeping–'

Oh, Hetty, you have such a majestic imagination! Don't get too carried away now! I assure you, your mother is *not* weeping in any mire-filled, squalid gutter. I like that phrase! I might well borrow it for one of my books.'

'Are you *mocking* me?'

'Only a little. I understand your anguish, but it's unfounded. Your mother, Ida, is well provided for. She has a new position already.'

'You're lying!'

The nurse gasped. 'Hetty Feather, how dare you address the lady like that!'

'It's quite all right, Nurse. It's good to see Hetty in a passion. It tells me that she's on the mend already,' said Miss Smith. 'I suggest you go and attend to your other patients, while Hetty and I continue our little chat.'

When the nurse left, with obvious reluctance, Miss Smith put her pale plain face close to mine, looking me straight in the eye. 'Do you really think I'm a liar, Hetty?'

I took a deep breath and then shook my head.

'I will always tell you the truth. Your mother is safe and well, and has a good position. You must trust me.'

'I do trust you, Miss Smith – but I don't trust anyone else. *They* could be lying to you,' I said.

'Hetty, I took it upon myself to raise your mother's case with the Board of Governors. We agreed that we could not possibly create a precedent by keeping Ida in our employ. Many other mothers would start seeking work at the hospital, and that would never do. We've always taken great care that no foundling should be singled out in any way, for treats or praise or special coddling–'

'Hmph! *I* am *constantly* singled out for scoldings and slappings.'

'Yes, and perhaps you deserve them, Miss Hetty Feather! Now listen to me, please. The matrons pressed for instant dismissal, and that was understandable – but it seemed to me singularly unfair to turn Ida away without giving her a good character. She's been an exemplary worker in all her years here, even if it was for a particular reason. She's been hard-working and cheerful, willing to lend a hand with anything. I wrote exactly that in her letter of reference.'

'*You* gave her a character reference! Oh, Miss Smith, thank you, thank you!'

'And I found her a new position too, as a general housekeeper to an elderly lady at Bignor-on-Sea on the south coast. She's an acquaintance of an aunt of mine, an invalid who I'm sure will treat Ida fairly.'

'But the south coast – that's miles and miles away! I shall never see her! Couldn't you have found her a *closer* position, Miss Smith?'

'Sometimes I think you can never be satisfied, Hetty!'

'Can we visit at all?'

'I'm afraid the Board of Governors do not think that a wise idea. But I dare say you will be able to write to each other.'

'Truly? I will get letters from Mama?'

'Yes, I'm sure she will write to you every now and then.'

I'd never had letters before, apart from one from Polly. I'd written my weekly letter home to my foster family. I wasn't sure Mother knew how to write, but Jem certainly did. He had taught me my own lettering when I was barely toddling. I had written for years, but they never once wrote back. Very few of the foundlings received letters, and yet in the junior school we all wrote once a week without fail.

My heart beat harder in my chest. 'Will they give me Mama's letters?' I asked fearfully. 'They don't always give us our letters, I am sure of it.'

I *wasn't* sure – but the expression on Miss Smith's face told me that I'd hit on the truth.

'I do believe there *is* a little censoring. I certainly don't approve, but it's done for well-meaning reasons. Apparently, letters from foster homes are frequently inappropriate or upsetting and would not help the children to settle down at the hospital . . .' Miss Smith's voice wavered.

I seized her hands. 'That's outrageous, Miss Smith, and you know it!'

'Hetty, Hetty, calm down! I do agree with you, it is in most circumstances outrageous, but I do not think there is anything I can do to change matters. It is the custom.'

'Then it's cruel and pointless telling me Mama will write if I can't receive her letters!' I protested.

'Hush now!' She held my hands tightly and put her face close to mine. 'I have given Ida my own address. I will tell her to send all letters to me. I will bring them to you on a regular basis and I will post your replies. That way you will *know* that the letters are being sent – if, of course, you trust me?'

'Oh, Miss Smith, of course I trust you!' I said, and I threw my arms around her.

'Now, now, Hetty, compose yourself. Still, I am pleased to see you are almost back to your old self – in a furious rage one moment and in a fever of excitement the next,' she said, laughing at me. 'If you're truly grateful–'

'I am, I am!'

'Then you must get better quickly and be a good, polite, hard-working girl for your entire future stay at the hospital.'

'I'm not sure I can quite manage that,' I said truthfully.

Miss Smith laughed again. 'Well, do your best, dear,' she said. She called to the nurse. 'I think you'll find that Hetty is on the mend. I have a feeling she'll be able to get up tomorrow. I'm sure she'll definitely be her old self by the end of the week. Isn't that right, Hetty?'

I nodded emphatically. My head ached, and I still felt weak and dizzy when I tried to get up, but I persevered. I ate as much gruel as I could to get stronger, although it didn't taste the same without Mama's loving sprinkles of brown sugar and spoonfuls of cream.

I was still punished when I returned to the schoolroom and my own dormitory, but I didn't care. I listened to the scoldings of Matron Stinking

Bottomly with my head held high. What did I care if she thought me deceitful and dishonest and a disgrace to the whole hospital? I even held my tongue when she said bad things about Mama. I knew she was simply trying to goad me into flying at her, and then she could legitimately fling me in the punishment room. I knew now that Mama was well provided for and would be writing to me, and that special secret knowledge kept me silent and seemingly obedient.

I performed all the extra housework tasks the matron set me. I did not even murmur when she had me scrubbing out the privies.

Sheila came across me performing this unpleasant task. She would normally have laughed delightedly to see me scrubbing with one hand and holding my nose with the other, but this time she hovered anxiously. Then, to my astonishment, she took up another brush and started scrubbing too.

'Whatever are you doing, Sheila?' I asked.

'What does it look like?' said Sheila. 'Ugh! This is disgusting!'

'But why are you helping me? You, of all people?'

'Because I feel badly about you and Ida. I think it was all my fault that Matron Peters came downstairs, poking her nose in. I tripped on the stairs when I was following you. I think she must have woken then.'

'Oh! But even so, you didn't tell on me.'

'I wouldn't tell on my worst enemy,' said Sheila, scrubbing.

'I thought *I* was your worst enemy,' I said.

'Well, there you are, then, I still didn't tell,' said Sheila proudly.

'You're definitely not *my* worst enemy any more. If you carry on helping me perform this disgusting task, I shall have to recategorize you. You will be a dear friend,' I said.

Sheila went a little pink. 'I'm not sure about that, Hetty! But I do feel especially sad that you've lost your mother all over again. And Ida would be a *lovely* mother–'

'She is, she is!'

'You must be so worried about her now.'

'I am. But Mama is strong-willed and very determined. I have a feeling she is safe and in good hands now,' I said.

I did not want to tell her about Miss Smith's reassurances. Sheila might be almost my friend now, but I wasn't sure I trusted her totally.

'I wish I could discover *my* mother,' said Sheila sadly. 'Do you think you will ever see Ida again, Hetty?'

421

'Of course! When I am fourteen I will leave this hateful hospital, and I will search the length and breadth of England until I find her again!' I said fervently.

Miss Smith came to the hospital a few days later, supposedly to check on the state of my health and mark the progress of my memoirs. (She had bought me my beautiful red Italian notebook and encouraged me to start my life story on its smooth creamy paper.) We usually sat in the corner of the schoolroom when Miss Smith visited, under the watchful eye of my teacher, Miss Morley – but this time Miss Smith said I still looked very pale. She fancied a turn in the gardens would do me a power of good.

Miss Morley did not dare protest, because Miss Smith was on the Board of Governors and a well-known, powerful lady to boot.

We went down the stairs and out through the back door, a forbidden joy in itself. We girls went outdoors to 'play' every day, but we had to cluster in the front courtyard, where the big girls strolled and the little ones skipped. All our schoolwork and training happened indoors: reading, writing, counting, sewing, serving, scrubbing – so that we would be competent servants by the age of fourteen.

The boys were going to be soldiers so they were

encouraged outdoors. They did Physical Education every day. They marched up and down, they swung their arms, they ran on the spot. They did not have to perform a single household task. Instead they were marshalled out into the gardens, where they dug and hoed and watered our potatoes and turnips and carrots, our cabbages and kale, our peas and beans, our blackberries and gooseberries.

There were all the senior boys now, digging away in their shirtsleeves. Although they were under the supervision of Old Joe the gardener, they were calling to each other and whistling merry tunes as they worked – while *we* had to work in total silence. If we so much as whispered, we were punished.

'Oh, lucky, lucky boys!' I said to Miss Smith.

'I agree with you, Hetty. Boys seem far more free and fortunate than girls, no matter what their station in life.' She stared over at a tall thin boy standing by himself. Two sturdier fellows were slyly pelting him with potatoes whenever the gardener's back was turned. The boy did not shout or swear or try to retaliate. He simply stood there like some anguished martyred saint, accepting this punishment.

'Poor lad,' said Miss Smith. 'It doesn't seem much fun for him.'

I watched with a heavy heart, biting my lip to stop myself crying out. I knew the boy. He was my dear foster brother, Gideon. I wanted to rush to protect him. I still loved my strange, shy, solitary brother so much, though we scarcely saw each other now that we were at the hospital.

If only I could give the two tormentors a taste of their own medicine. I looked down at the freshly turned earth beside the path. I bent down and grabbed a handful, squeezing it into a muddy lump.

'No, Hetty, no!' said Miss Smith.

'I have to,' I said, and hurled my clod.

It landed most satisfactorily right in the face of the biggest boy. He gave a muffled shriek – unable to cry out loudly with a mouthful of earth. I hoped there were big juicy worms wriggling right down his throat. He bent over, coughing and gagging, while his friend whirled round and round in comical anxiety, wondering from whence the attack had come. All he could see was a stern lady and a small female foundling demurely taking the air in the gardens.

Gideon looked over too, and saw me. I was dressed in our hideous brown uniform, but my cap could not contain all my flaming red hair. I hoped he would wave and smile when he recognized me,

424

but he hung his head and looked more miserable than ever. I had meant to help, but I had only shamed him.

'Oh dear, perhaps I shouldn't have done that,' I murmured.

'Yes, you should be ashamed of yourself, Hetty. Such behaviour!'

'Pointless, stupid behaviour,' I agreed, sighing.

'I am sure Matron Bottomly or Matron Peters would feel you should be severely punished in some particularly painful way. They might think that depriving you of all post is a suitable punishment,' said Miss Smith.

I put my hand in hers. 'But you are not a matron, you are my own dear Miss Smith, and you are going to give me my post, are you not? Oh, do I truly have a letter from Mama?'

Miss Smith patted the pocket of her skirt and smiled at me. We went round the corner to the greenhouses, out of sight of the gardener and all the boys. She reached into her pocket and offered me a small white envelope.

I carefully wiped my muddy hands on the back of my uniform and took it. I was shaking now, my fingers clumsy. I unpeeled the flap, trying not to tear it at all, because it was so very precious – and then pulled out the letter.

18 Saltdean Lane
Bignor-on-Sea
Sussex

My deer little Hetty – no, my brite bloo-eyed Sapphire!

I miss you so my darling child, but if it wernt for the ake in my hart I wuld be happy for I am now working for a lovly old lady Miss Roberts and she is a deer to me, much sweeter than those meen old matrons.

It is a butiful place here. The see is such a site. How I wish you wer with me to take the air and run on the sands. But be of good cheer, you will be out of the hospital befor too long, and then when I have savd enuf muny we will be togever forever deerest child.

With all my love

Your mama Ida

P.S. Please furgiv the look of this letter. I am not used to putting pen to paper and I canot figure out how to spel all the wurds.

I read my letter again and again, though the dear words blurred because my eyes filled with tears.

'Is Ida well?' Miss Smith asked quietly.

'Oh, she sounds very well and likes her position, but she is missing me and, oh my goodness, I am missing her,' I said, holding Mama's letter to my chest.

I did not want to show it to Miss Smith because it was so precious and private, and I could not bear her to see that Mama had a little difficulty with her spelling. Miss Smith seemed to understand. She brought out another envelope from her pocket with a blank piece of paper inside, and a sharpened cedar pencil.

'I thought you might care to reply straight away,' she said.

'Oh, Miss Smith, you are *such* a dear friend!' I said.

We sat down together on the old brick wall. Miss Smith started jotting things down in a small notebook, intent on writing another of her stories, while I scribbled hastily to Mama.

The Foundling Hospital

Oh, Mama, dearest, most special Mama in the entire world,

I am missing you so enormously much. I cannot believe fate has been so unkind to us, tearing us apart again in this way – though if I had

427

been more cautious and Sheila less nosy (though she is sorry now), we would still be together. How lovely of you to write to me. It is such a relief to know you're in a good house with a kind lady – though heavens, Satan himself would seem kind compared with those wicked matrons.

I was taken poorly when you had to leave the hospital, but the doctor was gentle, and Miss Smith was wonderfully reassuring, and I am totally better now, though my heart aches too and I long to have your dear arms around me.

With all my love,

From your own daughter Sapphire (the most beautiful name in the world because you chose it specially for me).

Mama and I have been writing to each other ever since. I have all her precious letters in little bundles tied with silk. Nurse Winnie gave me a yard of narrow green silk ribbon as a secret present when I helped her with her sewing classes for the little ones.

'Remember *your* first darning lesson when you were five, Hetty?' she said, smiling at me. 'You were all fingers and thumbs, you poor little mite, and sewed the toe of your stocking tight to the heel!'

'I was a very stupid little girl, Nurse Winterson,' I said.

'No, no, you were bright as a button. There was always something distinctive about you, Hetty. I knew you would go far.'

'How far is that?' I said, sighing. 'So far that I will scrub people's floors and dust their mantel-pieces for the rest of my working life?'

'I have a feeling you won't be a servant for ever,' said Nurse Winnie. 'And even if you are, you will still lead a very different life from here. Servants have days off, you know. You will be able to do as you please. And pretty servant girls have followers.'

'I dare say – but I'm not the slightest bit pretty,' I said. 'I am the smallest, skinniest girl in my whole year and I have bright red hair.'

'I think your hair is a beautiful colour, dear,' she said – and the next time I helped her she gave me the green ribbon. '*To tie up your bonny red hair,*' she sang, pulling one of my plaits.

Dear Nurse Winnie! She was the only person in the whole hospital I cared for now, apart from Eliza, my little sister. Eliza was brought to my old foster home in the country when she was a babe. I was sent off to the hospital before I turned six – and five years later Eliza followed me.

I had greeted my little foster sister joyfully,

desperate for news of home. It was a hard blow when she spoke of our brother Jem so fondly. I had adored Jem passionately when I was a tiny girl. He had cared for me tenderly and played with me patiently. He had even taught me to read and write . . . He had been like a mother and father to me as well as a foster brother. I'd hoped that one day, far in the future, he'd be my dear husband too. When I played dressing up as a bride, Jem had kissed my finger and promised that he'd put a ring on it one day.

I had believed him utterly. I had thought of him as *my* Jem, but when little Eliza chatted away innocently enough, I realized that he was *her* Jem too. He had played all the same games with her. I could not bear it. I felt he had betrayed me. I stopped writing loving little messages to him in my weekly letters home. There seemed little point in writing anyway, as he never bothered to reply. Though perhaps he *had* written? Miss Smith had actually admitted that many of our letters were confiscated.

Tears sprang to my eyes when I thought of Matron Pigface's trotter-fingers fumbling with my precious letters, tearing them to shreds and tossing them into the fire. I wondered what Jem would have written . . .

No, what did I care? I had been a silly little

child and he had been a kindly lad, that was all.
It was ridiculous to believe that our love had been
real. I would not be wearing my green ribbon for
Jem, or for any other young lad, come to that.
I did not want foolish followers. I only cared for
Mama.

3

I woke very early and sat up in my narrow bed. I
looked down the long dormitory of sleeping girls
in the silvery dawn light. This was the very last
time I would ever see them!

I clasped my hands around my knees, hugging
myself. It was not unduly cold but I shivered in my
nightgown. Today I was leaving the hospital for
ever. Hetty Feather was no more. I would leave her
behind, along with my brown gown and apron and
cuffs and stupid great floppy bonnet.

I peeped down at the basket at the end of my
bed. My new clothes were neatly folded, waiting for
me. I felt a thrill of excitement at the thought of
putting them on, though they were ordinary work
clothes – a plain grey dress and coarse cream apron.
I knew nothing of fashion after all my years of
incarceration in the hospital, but I could always
dream of a real silk dress to match my green ribbon,
long frilled skirts, fine lace, white silk stockings,
and shoes as elegant as Cinderella's glass slippers.

I had no new shoes at all – my hideous brown clumpers still fitted me, so they were deemed suitable for my new position.

I was going as an under-housemaid to a gentleman who lived in the suburbs of London.

'Not just *any* gentleman, Hetty,' Miss Smith had told me excitedly. 'He's a writer! Mr Charles Buchanan.'

'Do you know him, Miss Smith?'

'I know *of* him, dear. He writes children's stories for the Religious Tract, as I do. Very moral tales. He is apparently a very moral *man*. He applied to the hospital because he thought it an act of charity to take a foundling child into his employ – and I did my best to persuade the Board of Governors that you would be an ideal candidate, Hetty. It was a hard task. Matron Bottomly seems to feel that you are quite unsuited to such a worthy gentleman's establishment, but I argued your case, stressing that Mr Buchanan might be a very good influence on you. Why are you staring at me like that? Surely you're pleased?'

'I'm pleased you stood up for me, Miss Smith, of course I am, but if I'm completely truthful I do not really *want* to be this very moral gentleman's servant,' I said.

'Well, whose servant *do* you wish to be?' said Miss Smith, looking aggrieved.

434

'I don't want to be *anyone*'s servant,' I said, folding my arms obstinately.

Miss Smith sighed. 'So how do you propose to earn your living, Hetty?' she asked tartly.

I swallowed hard. Wasn't it obvious? I clung to my own elbows to give me strength to come out with it. 'I – I hoped my memoirs would be published, and I would earn money that way,' I said.

'Oh good Lord, Hetty, how could you possibly think such a thing!'

'Well, you said as much – in a roundabout fashion. You said I had a vivid turn of phrase and excellent powers of description, and a powerful imagination.'

'That's all too true.'

'Well?'

'But that doesn't mean that your memoirs are fit for publication!'

'But why have you praised them so?'

'I wanted to encourage you, my dear. I never dreamed you thought you could publish such a work!'

'I know it's a little childish in parts because I wrote most of it years ago – but I can polish it a lot, maybe rewrite sections. Oh, Miss Smith, *surely* it stands some chance of publication?'

'It's a wonderful piece of work, Hetty, but only as a private journal. It is not *fit* for publication. Be reasonable! Only recollect the things you've written about Matron Peters and Matron Bottomly!'

'But they're true, every last word – I swear it!'

'I dare say, but there would be the most terrible scandal if such a fiercely condemnatory document about such a well-respected charity were published!'

'Well, surely a scandal would be good. It might sell more copies!'

'Hetty, you're incorrigible! You can never publish your memoirs – they're much too bold, too personal, too passionate, too violent, too bitter, too unlady-like, too ungrateful, too every single thing!'

'Then why didn't you tell me this years ago?'

'Because I felt it was very good for you to have a private outlet for your pent-up feelings. I know how hard it's been at the hospital. It's been exception-ally good for you to develop a writing discipline. You have remarkable literary skills, far beyond your age and station, but you must channel them carefully if you ever hope to write for publication. Oh, please don't upset yourself so, dear!'

I had started crying bitterly, utterly cast down. I had so believed my memoirs would be published and make my fortune so that Mama and I could live together without serving a soul.

Miss Smith lent me her lacy handkerchief. When

I continued to cry, she put her arm round me and mopped my face herself. Her kindness softened me, and I tried hard to stop sobbing.

'There now, perhaps you really *will* be a writer some time in the future. But not yet a while, my dear. You can accept this perfect position with Mr Buchanan and be patient. I am sure you will observe good writerly habits if you work in his establishment.'

'I'd sooner work for you, Miss Smith,' I said.

'If you were my servant, I'd expect you to go "Yes, missus," and nod obediently every time I spoke to you,' said Miss Smith.

'Yes, missus,' I said, bobbing her a curtsy – and she burst out laughing.

'I scarcely recognize this new persona, Hetty! Carry on in a similar vein at Mr Buchanan's like a good sensible girl. You really must try to act humbly and do as you're told. I'm starting to feel a little worried about Mr Buchanan. There he is, thinking he's taken on a meek little foundling girl who will be very grateful for her good position. You are a *little* grateful, aren't you, Hetty?'

'Yes, Miss Smith,' I said, because I supposed I was grateful to *her*. I did not see why I should be grateful to anyone else. Even after nine years' hard training at the hospital, I still did not see *why* I had to be content to be a servant.

Every Sunday in the chapel we sang:

> *'The rich man in his castle*
> *The poor man at his gate,*
> *God made them, high or lowly,*
> *And ordered their estate.'*

Why did I have to be stuck being lowly? Why couldn't Mama and I be rich women in our castle?

'You wait, dearest Mama,' I whispered as I sat in bed my last morning. 'I will earn our fortune with my writing one day, no matter what Miss Smith says. Then we *will* have our castle. Well, maybe not a *castle* exactly, but a grand villa with our own pretty bedrooms, where we will live very happily and harmoniously together, just the two of us. We will be rich enough to have a whole troop of servants, but we won't employ a single one. We will not want any poor girls working for us. We will look after ourselves splendidly. I will clean for you, Mama, and you will cook for me, and we will be private and cosy and comfortable.'

I slid out of bed and walked down the long dormitory, past all the sleeping girls. I tiptoed out onto the landing, and then down the long wooden staircase, the grand portraits staring at me sternly.

'Frown all you like. I'm not afraid of you. I shall

never have to stare up at you ever again,' I declared.

I crept right downstairs, across the girls' dining room, the table already set for our meagre breakfast. There was no clattering from the kitchen. The cook must still be sleeping. I moved as silently as a shadow through the great room, which still reeked of yesterday's mutton, and proceeded along the servants' corridor.

I halted outside Mama's room. I could not go in. There was another maid living there now, a large, clumsy girl called Maud. She was harmless enough, but I hated her simply because she had taken Mama's place. I could not stand the thought of her gimcrack possessions littering Mama's chest, her dirty brush and comb on Mama's washstand, her fat, ungainly body sprawled all over Mama's bed.

I stood outside the door, leaning my head against the varnished wood, remembering all the precious times I had spent with Mama within those four walls.

I wrote on the door with my finger: *I love you, Mama*, and then crept away. I returned to my bed undetected. If only I had been so lucky before! We would have had some chance of regular meetings if Mama were still employed at the hospital in London and I were not too far away in the suburbs. A simple bus ride, perhaps.

439

My heart started beating faster at the thought of my journey today. I had Mr Charles Buchanan's address written inside my journal: *8 Lady's Ride, Kingtown*. I had no idea how I would reach this destination. I had only been outside the hospital grounds once, when I was ten – the day of Queen Victoria's Golden Jubilee. We had been escorted all the way to the great children's celebration in Hyde Park. I had seen the circus there, and had run away to try to find my childhood idol, Madame Adeline, the magical spangled woman who had let me sit on one of her rosin-backed horses and had won my heart for ever. I had taken an omnibus ride that day, as bold as brass. I tried hard to remember how I had hailed it and how much money I had paid. What happened when you wanted to get off? Did you ring some kind of bell? How would I know where 8 Lady's Ride was? How would I know anything at all in the outside world?

I remembered how the children in Hyde Park had pointed and jeered at me. Would people still point me out and ridicule me? I clenched my fists. I would make them sorry if they did. I was Sapphire Battersea, and I would show everyone. I was not content to be a common servant. One day my name would be famous, recognized all over London.

I shut my eyes and saw *Sapphire Battersea* in big fancy lettering on advertising posters, *Sapphire*

Battersea in bold print in newspapers. I heard the name *Sapphire Battersea* shouted through loudhailers, *Sapphire Battersea* acclaimed by thousands of mouths.

Then a handbell clanged along the corridor – and I was Hetty Feather again, back in my dismal dormitory. All the girls groaned and yawned and struggled out of their beds, hopping from one bare foot to another on the cold linoleum. They tugged on their brown frocks and fumbled with their aprons and cuffs.

I stood too, pulling on my new grey dress. It smelled so different, fresh and clean. Although the material was brand new, it felt remarkably soft after my thick, itchy uniform. The other girls circled me enviously, stroking the folds, holding out my skirts admiringly, while I brushed and plaited my hair.

'Will you put your hair up now, Hetty?' Emma Baxter asked. She was a kindly, helpful girl who slept in the bed next to mine.

'Of course,' I said, but I had no hairpins, and my flimsy new cap could not easily accommodate all my hair. I tried for two minutes, and then had to give up and keep my schoolgirl plaits hanging down my back.

'Oh dear, you don't look very grown up,' said Emma.

I knew she was speaking the truth. I was no

bigger than the ten-year-olds at the hospital and I didn't look much older either. Emma herself had grown curves, whereas I was as straight up and down as any of the boys.

I drew myself up as tall as I could, my head held high. 'I shall just have to *act* grown up,' I said.

The other girls gathered round to wish me luck. Some sighed enviously, but the timid ones clutched each other, glad that it wasn't their turn just yet.

'Aren't you scared, Hetty? I'd be all of a tremble, going off to the outside and being with all those strangers.'

'I'm not the slightest bit scared,' I lied.

I tried to eat a hearty breakfast in the dining room just to show them. I remembered that Monica had been in such a state she'd had to rush outside to the privies to be sick after a few spoonfuls of porridge. Even fierce Sheila had been very pale, her high forehead wrinkled with anxious frown lines. She had given me a sudden hug after breakfast and murmured, 'Don't ask me why, but I shall miss you, Hetty Feather.'

I did not feel the same way for any of these girls I had grown up with, but I felt a terrible squeezing of my insides when I looked down the long, long table and saw Eliza, craning her neck to peer at me forlornly.

We were not allowed to get up from the breakfast

table till the bell went, but it was dear Nurse Winterson on meal duties, and she was never strict. I clambered off my bench and shot along the room to Eliza. I threw my arms around her and hugged her hard.

'Oh, Hetty!' she wailed, pressing her face against my flat chest. 'I shall not be able to bear it here without you!'

'Of course you will, Eliza. You have many, many friends,' I said, which was true enough. Eliza was a sunny, cheery little creature with curly hair and dimples. Everyone wanted to be her friend. Even the fierce matrons softened when they saw her. No wonder my Jem had found it easy to forget me and lose his heart to Eliza.

Nurse Winnie came over to us. She was shaking her head, but smiling too. 'Now, now, Hetty dear, I know it's your last day, but you know the rules well enough. Go back to your bench, dear.'

Eliza burst into floods of tears.

'Oh, please may I kiss Eliza one more time?' I begged.

'Of course,' said Nurse Winnie. Her own eyes were brimming. 'Do not worry about Eliza, Hetty. I promise I will look out for her.'

I kissed Eliza five or six times on her rosy cheeks, wiping away her tears with the soft cuffs of my new dress. 'There now, darling. Don't take on so. You will be fine,' I promised.

Nurse Winnie put her arm round me as she walked me back to my bench.

'I will miss her so,' I said, struggling not to weep myself. 'But I will not worry about her. It's poor Gideon who breaks my heart. Oh, Nurse Winterson, please, please, please may I go and find him and say goodbye?'

'Oh, come now, Hetty! You know perfectly well that I can't let you go to the boys' quarters!'

'No, but you could perhaps turn your back and not notice if I slip out. I promise I'll be ten minutes at the most. Oh *please*, dear Nurse Winterson. I shall miss *you* so much. You've always been my very favourite nurse.'

'And you've always been the most artful of my girls,' said Nurse Winnie – but she turned her back.

I rushed right out of the room before she could change her mind. I thought I would still have difficulty in getting to the boys' dining room. I passed several nurses, but none of them stopped me. Then I caught sight of myself reflected in a window. I didn't look like Hetty Feather the foundling any more. I looked like a maid in my grey dress, albeit a very miniature version. I stood staring at myself for a full minute, turning this way and that. It was exciting being this new person, but very odd, as if my own head had been stuck on an entirely different body.

The bell rang for the end of breakfast, and I came to my senses and scurried off to the boys' wing. They were swarming out of their dining room, along the hall, up to their classrooms. They were mostly silent, but they still made much more noise than us girls. They stomped harder with their boots and thumped about bizarrely. I looked all about me, jostled as I threaded my way through them. It was so hard to distinguish one particular boy amongst this vast crowd of brown figures. But then I saw him, sloping along by himself, his head bent.

'Gideon! Oh, Gideon!'

He looked over in my direction, his eyes still blank.

'Gideon, it's *me*, Hetty.'

He came rushing towards me and stood over me, a full foot taller than me now, though as little babes we had once fitted together in a basket.

'Oh my goodness, Hetty! You look so different out of uniform. So, are you going today?'

'Yes, I am to be a maid to a gentleman called Mr Buchanan. He writes children's books.'

'You might like it there, then.'

'No I shan't.'

'Well, *I* would like it. I'm leaving at the end of the month, to go to Renshaw Barracks.'

'Oh, Gid, I would give anything to change with

you. It will be such an adventure for you. Just think how fine you will look in a soldier's uniform. You might even get to travel abroad!'

'Yes, what splendid fun – to be shot at and blown to smithereens,' said Gideon bitterly. 'It's all right for you, Hetty. It's so all *wrong* for me. I am a coward.'

'No you're not! You can be ever so strong and brave and stoical. My goodness, you couldn't survive *here* if you weren't.'

'All the other lads mock me. I don't blame them – I'm so very different. It will be worse at the barracks. I've heard such tales.'

I could not bear to see my dear foster brother in such torment. 'Then do not go!' I said. 'You could just walk right out of the hospital! You've got the whole of London to hide in. You're tall and smart. You will be able to bluff your way, find some kind of work and get lodgings. It's so much easier for a boy.'

'I have thought of it often. Perhaps I will find the courage to do that – but I rather think not. I told you, Hetty, I am a coward. We should have swapped places with each other when we were in that baby basket. I should have been the girl and you the boy.'

'Come along there, Smeed! Stop dallying with the servants and get to your lessons, boy,' someone shouted.

Gideon flinched.

446

I held his hand fast. 'Remember, Gideon, I am your dear sister and I love you very much. I will always care for you. Maybe one day when you are on leave, you can come and take me out. I should love to be escorted by a fine soldier in a splendid uniform,' I said earnestly.

'*Gideon Smeed!* Are you listening? Head in the clouds as always! *Move*, or I'll prod you!'

'I have to go, Hetty,' said Gideon desperately.

'Goodbye, dearest Gid. Good luck!' I said, and I reached right up and kissed him on the cheek.

The boys surrounding us jeered and whistled, and Gideon went as red as his waistcoat, but he blew me a very quick kiss in return. Then he went on his way and I wondered if we would ever see each other again.

I felt so cast down that I nearly lost my courage. I almost wished I were staying at the hospital. It was a cold, cheerless place, especially without dear Mama, but it had been my home for nine full years. I tried to have faith in Miss Smith and her writing gentleman, but I wasn't at all sure that this was a good move. Maybe I should take my own advice to Gideon, and make a run for it the moment I stepped outside the hospital gates.

I had survived my two or three days of freedom when I was ten. In many respects I had had splendid adventures – and even earned enough to feed myself too. I was much better equipped now to find myself some desirable employment. Perhaps I should take this one and only chance! I felt badly about Miss Smith, but perhaps she would understand.

I gathered my few possessions in my small brown travelling box, ready to go. But Matron Bottomly called me to her room first. Matron Peters was there too, both of them shaking their heads at me.

'Well, Hetty Feather, you are leaving us at last,' said Matron Stinking Bottomly.

'We will always remember *you*,' said Matron Pigface Peters. 'You are undoubtedly the wildest and most wilful girl we have ever had in our care.'

'You will come down to earth with a bump once you've had a taste of the working world outside,' said Matron Bottomly. 'Beware, Hetty Feather! If you stick to your sulky ways, you will be dismissed for insolence, without a character, and *then* where will you be?'

'Following in the footsteps of your mother, I dare say,' said Matron Peters, and they both sniggered.

'I'll thank you not to bad-mouth my mother,' I said. 'I don't have to listen to either of you ever again. I shall be off now. Goodbye.'

'Goodbye and good riddance!' they said in

unison, like Tweedledum and Tweedledee. Nurse Winnie had read us the two *Alice* books in her sewing class when I was little.

They accompanied me along the landing and down the stairs. Nurse Winnie came running up. She took no notice of either matron and threw her arms around me.

'Good luck, little Hetty! I can't believe it's fourteen whole years since I held you in my arms and tried to comfort you. I've never known a babe scream so much! But I knew even then that you were a very special child, and would go far.'

'Oh, dear Nurse Winnie! Thank you so much for being so very kind to me over the years. I will never forget you,' I said, suddenly close to tears.

'Come *along*, Nurse Winterson. There's no need to single the girl out. She has a high enough opinion of herself already,' Matron Pigface snapped.

'It seems to me you thoroughly spoiled her and ruined her character when she was in the junior school,' said Matron Bottomly. 'It was very hard for me to make a serious impression on such an imp of Satan. You must heed the warnings of the Good Book, Nurse Winterson – spare the rod and spoil the child.'

'That's nonsense!' I cried. 'Nurse Winterson is the only nurse here who shows us real love and care. That's the only way any of us have thrived in this grim prison!'

'Hush your mouth, Hetty Feather! How dare you talk to us like that!'

'I dare say anything I wish, because neither of you have any power over me any more,' I declared.

'Don't be so sure of that! We will be checking up on you vigorously. If you fail to please your new employer, we have the power to call you back to the hospital to retrain you,' Matron Bottomly threatened.

That certainly unnerved me! I didn't want to risk going to Mr Buchanan's now. I'd start afresh, where no one could keep track of me. I wasn't going to be Hetty Feather any more. I was Sapphire Battersea, only child of dear Ida. I would show these pig-faced stinking matrons. I would make my own way in the world, no matter what. I had to make a bolt for it now.

But my spirited plans were instantly thwarted. There was a strange woman lurking in the entrance hall – strange to me, and certainly strange in appearance. She was a very *large* woman. She made even Matron Pigface Peters appear sylph-like. She was dressed in a bizarre dark-red costume that made her resemble an immense slab of bloody meat. She wore a bonnet to match, trimmed with white, like mutton chops with paper frills. I stared at her in astonishment. She seemed equally bewildered by me.

'This scrawny little creature cannot possibly be Hetty Feather!' she said, hands on her hips. 'I thought you said she was fourteen and a good strong girl? This child is barely ten – and her arms and legs look as if they should be in a box of Bryant and May.'

'This is Hetty Feather, ma'am, and her fourteenth birthday was three full months ago – isn't that correct, Hetty?'

I hesitated. I didn't know what to say. I didn't like the look of this great meaty woman at all. I felt a further few weeks in the hospital might even be preferable. What was she doing here? Why had *she* come to fetch me? Where was Mr Buchanan?

'I thought I was going to be Mr Buchanan's servant,' I mumbled.

'Indeed you are, child. *If* you are of age.'

'Speak up, Hetty, and reassure the lady. You've never held your tongue for long previously,' said Matron Bottomly.

'I'm fourteen. I've always been very small.'

'With carrot-coloured hair too! I hope you don't have a temper to match. Lord knows why we've been lumbered with you,' said the meaty one, giving me a prod in the chest. 'Come along then, child. We've got quite a journey ahead of us.'

'Goodbye, Hetty Feather. Try your hardest to be

451

dutiful and diligent. Might I suggest, ma'am, that you treat her severely right from the start. She has wild ways,' said Matron Bottomly.

'Frankly speaking, she could do with a good whipping every now and then,' said Matron Peters.

I glared at them. My lips were pressed tight together. I wouldn't even say goodbye. I clutched my box in both hands. My heart was beating fast. I decided to run for it the moment the great door was opened, but the large woman seized me by the shoulders, her fat fingers digging into my flesh, kneading me like bread. She marched me down the long pathway to the outside gate. I twisted my neck to look one last time at the hospital where I had been locked up for so long. I stared at the barred attic window and saw a ghost of myself looking down.

I shivered in the cold air because I didn't have any kind of mantle or shawl.

'Ah, you're not quite so bold now!' said Mistress Meat. 'You're quivering like a jelly in a mould.'

'I am simply a little cold, ma'am,' I answered, my chin up – but she only laughed at me.

She called to the porter at the gate. 'Is that hansom cab still waiting? Come along, Hetty Feather – he'll be charging us a fortune as it is.'

She hustled me through the gate towards a horse and cab. I couldn't help feeling a little thrill of excitement at the thought of such a journey. She pushed me up inside the cab and followed me close, spreading her dark-red skirts all around me. I had a glimpse of her legs in pink silk stockings, like vast pork sausages. I wriggled away as far as possible in such an enclosed space, while the driver above us clicked to his horse. As it started trotting I heard shouting. I couldn't make out the words clearly, but I was almost sure that someone was calling my name.

I struggled round, half hanging out of the cab window, and saw a young man in brown corduroy running after us, waving his arms and shouting.

'Sit *down*, miss! You don't want to tumble out and break your head,' said the meaty one.

'But that man is calling me! He's waving as if he knows me,' I said, bewildered. 'Please let's stop the cab and see what he wants.'

'Don't be so silly, child. We're not stopping the cab for you to chatter with any Tom, Dick or Harry. We have work to do! I came to fetch you out of kindness, in case you were confused on the journey – but I shall be terribly behind all day long now.'

She commanded the driver to get a move on. We soon rounded the corner of the street, going at such a pace that there was no way the young man could catch us.

Whoever could it have been?

4

I looked long and hard at the meaty woman as we rode along together, squashed up like two pigs in a poke.

'Why are you staring at me? Have I got a smut on my face?' she asked.

'No, ma'am. I was just wondering who you are,' I said truthfully. 'What is your name?'

'I am Mrs Briskett,' she said, announcing her name as proudly as if she were the Queen of England.

Mrs Briskett? Wasn't brisket a type of beef? Oh, what a glorious name for this great bovine woman! I felt the most insistent giggles tickling my inside. I had to clench my teeth and suck my cheeks to stop myself erupting. I set myself to thinking why she was a Mrs Briskett. If she was Mr Buchanan's wife, why did she not bear his name? Was she perhaps a neighbour of his, come to fetch me as a favour?

'Excuse me, ma'am, but do you live at Mr Buchanan's house?'

'Of course I do, you silly girl.'

'And – and *Mr* Briskett?'

'There is no Mr Briskett. It is a courtesy title,' she said.

I thought on. I remembered all the cook's *Police Gazettes* I had secretly read at the hospital.

'Then are you – are you under Mr Buchanan's protection?' I asked.

I thought I'd asked the question delicately, but she coughed and spluttered, her face flushing darker than her bonnet.

'How *dare* you suggest such a thing! I can't believe my own ears!'

'I'm sorry! I didn't mean to cause offence. I didn't understand. I simply thought—'

'I am Mr Buchanan's cook-housekeeper,' said Mrs Briskett. 'I cannot *imagine* how you could possibly have dreamed otherwise. However, you are a poor ignorant orphan, Hetty Feather, so I suppose you simply do not know any better.'

'Oh no, I'm not an orphan, ma'am. I have a very dear mother, Ida Battersea. In fact, I'm not really called Hetty Feather at all – that was just the name the Foundling Hospital inflicted on me. My name is Sapphire Battersea. Please may I be called by that name? It could be my courtesy title.'

'*Sapphire?* What kind of ungodly, fanciful name is that for a little servant girl? Don't be ridiculous, child. Were you christened when you arrived at the Foundling Hospital as a babe?'

'Yes, ma'am.'

'And what name did they christen you?'

I took a deep breath. 'Hetty Feather, but—'

'No buts! That is your name, and you will not be known by any other. Sapphire indeed!'

Yes, Sapphire, Sapphire, Sapphire, I said silently inside my head. *It is a beautiful name and it is my name, and you can 'Hetty Feather' me a thousand times a day, but I know my real name now and you cannot take it away from me.*

'I don't care for that expression on your face, Hetty. I hope you are not a sullen girl. Do you realize how lucky you are to be given this opportunity?'

I felt like the least lucky girl in all the world, but I rearranged my face into an ingratiating smile and nodded vigorously. It was clear that Mrs Briskett had a quick temper and her fingers seemed as sharp as meat hooks. I was sure my shoulders were all covered over with bruises.

The horse slowed down and stopped, and Mrs Briskett nudged me to climb out of the cab. We were in front of a vast, imposing building, practically as big as a palace. It seemed dimly familiar.

'Is this Mr Buchanan's house?' I asked doubtfully.

'Dear goodness, how can you be so stupid, child? This is Waterloo Station! We are continuing our journey by train.' She paused, then said slowly, as if speaking to a simpleton, 'A train is a huge carriage with a massive engine at the front, powered by steam.'

'I know what a train is, Mrs Briskett,' I said with some satisfaction. 'I travelled in one when I left my foster home in the country.'

She snorted. 'You must have been only five or so at the time. I doubt you can remember anything about it.'

'Indeed I can! I remember it all very vividly,' I said. 'Mother took Gideon and me, and we were so sad. My dearest brother Jem came with us to the station, and he told me to be a good brave girl, and he promised he would come and fetch me home one day–' And then I stopped and moaned as if in pain.

'What is it? Did you bite your tongue?'

'Oh, Mrs Briskett, we have to go back!' I said, trying to clamber back into the hansom cab.

'What are you doing? Don't be so tiresome, child. We've finished with the cab. We have to go and catch the train.'

'No! No! I've only just realized – that young man waiting at the gate! It might have been Jem.'

I couldn't be sure. He had been very tall, a good six foot, with the strong shoulders of a man – but of

course my Jem would be nineteen now, no longer a
boy. I had had no contact with him – he hadn't
bothered to answer a single one of my letters –
though Miss Smith had indicated that some at least
of my letters had been confiscated. He had played
fast and loose with me, filling little Eliza's head
with daydreams that he was going to marry her –
but I had been his first love. Perhaps he had
calculated when I was due to leave the hospital, and
had come all the way from the country to meet up
with me? And I had walked straight past him, not
giving him a second glance!

How could I have been so cruelly ignorant? I had
been boasting this very minute to Mrs Briskett
about my powers of recollection, yet I had failed to
recognize my dearest Jem.

'Please, please, *please* let me return,' I cried. 'It
is a matter of life and death. I *have* to see that
young man, the one waiting for me at the hospital
gates.'

'I beg your pardon, missy? You surely cannot
have followers already – you're only a little girl!'

'No, Jem is my *brother* – my foster brother. Oh,
it was him, I am sure of it now. Please, Mrs
Briskett, I will be a good girl for ever – I swear it –
if you'll just let me go back and tell him I haven't
really forgotten him.' I seized hold of her meat-red
sleeve imploringly.

She shook my hand off straight away. 'You're being ridiculous, Hetty Feather. Control yourself, otherwise I shall feel obliged to have a word with the master about your impulsive behaviour. Then you will have the unusual distinction of being dismissed before you have even taken up your position,' she said. She wagged her fat finger in my face. 'This is your last chance!'

I *knew* it was my last chance. I should have dodged away from her and run like the wind all the way back to the hospital – but I hesitated fatally. I did not know my way through the bewilderingly busy streets of London, but that was no excuse. I struggled, but not determinedly enough.

Mrs Briskett marched me into the great noisy station, pushing me so hard in the small of my back that I stumbled in my clumsy boots and nearly fell to the floor. She jerked me up and hauled me up the steps into a carriage. She seemed so powerful I feared she was going to hang me by my feet from the coat-rack like a skinned rabbit – but she thrust me into a corner seat instead, sitting down so close beside me I could not budge.

'There now. Sit quiet and no more nonsense,' she said firmly.

I sat with my eyes closed, thinking back to that moment outside the hospital gates. I tried hard to bring that tall brown figure into focus. Had it *really* been my Jem? I could not be quite so sure now.

I thought back to my early childhood. I remembered Jem lifting me up in his arms, carrying me everywhere. I remembered our times in the treehouse, when he patiently played my childish pretend games. I remembered him teaching me my letters and reading to me night after night. I remembered the way he'd held me tight on that long trip in the wagon, when I was leaving home for ever. I kept my eyes shut, but I could not stop the tears seeping out from beneath my lids and rolling down my cheeks.

'There now, child,' said Mrs Briskett, her voice surprisingly soft. 'Don't you cry now. I can't abide tears. No doubt this is all queer and strange to you. You'll be feeling homesick for the hospital, but that's only natural.'

It would have been exceedingly *un*natural for me to be homesick for the hospital, but it seemed simplest to let her think that. I was amazed by her sudden change of tone. She'd been so tart and testy previously.

She patted my shoulder in a comforting way. 'I remember *my* first position, as a kitchen maid in a huge great house in the country. It was very grand, but it felt so dark and strange and gloomy compared to our cottage at home. I cried myself to sleep for weeks – and I cried in the daytime too because the cook in that kitchen was a truly terrifying creature. That temper! If you chopped the carrots unevenly or curdled the custards, my goodness, she'd start throwing the saucepans at you. The copper ones, mind, so if you didn't duck sharpish you'd be knocked unconscious.'

I blinked at Mrs Briskett in alarm.

'Don't look so fearful, Hetty Feather. That was in the bad old days. Little servant girls are treated with kid gloves now. I won't be throwing any saucepans, so long as you try hard, keep quiet and mind your p's and q's.'

I nodded, though I wasn't at all sure what my p's and q's might be. Problems and queries? I seemed to have a lot of both.

I stared out of the sooty train window as the train chuntered its way out of London. At first I saw ugly great factories spouting thick smoke, then mile after mile of terraced rows of dark little dwellings – but soon these started to thin out. Now I saw green fields and trees all about us.

'Is this the country?' I asked, wondering if I might possibly be near my dear foster home.

'No, no, we're only in Wimbleton – it's a while yet. We've a few stations to go through before we get to Kingtown. That's where Mr Buchanan has his establishment. It's a big fine house too, though not *quite* as large as Waterloo Station.' Mrs Briskett chuckled at my foolishness.

'Is Mr Buchanan a kind man?' I asked timidly, wondering if I might somehow cause offence again by my mild enquiry.

Mrs Briskett remained relaxed, undoing her bonnet strings and giving her grey hair a good scratch. 'Excuse me, dear. My best bonnet's very fine but it certainly sets me itching. Mr Buchanan? Oh, he's kind enough, though he has his little ways, of course. He's a very important writer, you know. You'll often see his articles on education in the newspapers, and there's a whole shelf full of his books in the best bookcase.'

'Might I be able to read one?' I asked.

Mrs Briskett looked at me, her head on one side. 'Can you read then, missy? Proper reading, great long sentences? I've worked with several little girls from the workhouse and they couldn't read to save their lives.'

'I've been reading fluently since I was four years old,' I said proudly. 'My brother Jem taught me.'

I shouldn't have mentioned his name. I felt my lip quivering.

'Well, I'm not sure it's suitable for you to be reading Mr Buchanan's books, though they are all written for children, I believe. It will tickle him to know you've asked – but I don't think there'll be any time for book-reading, Hetty Feather. You'll be helping Sarah and me from six in the morning till ten at night.'

I didn't like the sound of this work regime at all!

'I do so love to read. Could I not read when I go to bed?' I said.

'I'm not having you ruining your eyes and wasting candles,' said Mrs Briskett. 'And if you're doing your job properly, you'll be fast asleep the moment you clamber into your bed.'

'Perhaps I could read during my recess?' I said.

'*Recess?*' said Mrs Briskett, as if she didn't understand the word.

'My playtime,' I said.

The hospital had divided our days rigidly – mostly work and very little play, so it was always particularly important.

'Playtime!' Mrs Briskett chortled. 'Oh, Hetty Feather, you're going to be the death of me! You're not a schoolgirl now. There won't be any playtime for you, my girl. It will be work work work, seven days a week, with Sunday afternoons off *if* you've been a good girl.'

I listened, chastened. It was upsetting to to discover how little I knew about everyday life. The matrons had told me they were preparing me for work, but they had only taught me to darn and scrub floors. These did not seem very useful accomplishments. An hour's darning or scrubbing had seemed interminable. How was I going to keep going all day long? I so wished I could ask Mama's advice. She had tried to prepare me. She had even taken to sending me her best recipes in her weekly letters, just in case they came in useful.

'Do you happen to know if Mr Buchanan likes game pie or beef pudding?' I asked hopefully.

'I dare say,' said Mrs Briskett. 'The master's partial to all kinds of pies and puddings.'

'Then perhaps I could make him one specially?' I suggested. 'I have a very fine recipe.'

But Mrs Briskett was laughing again. 'You – cook? Whatever will you come out with next? *I'm* the cook, missy – you're just the little maid of all work.'

I stared out of the train window again, dispirited. I didn't *want* to be the maid of all work. There were bigger houses built right up close to the railway track now, so I could spy straight into their back gardens. I saw a girl about my own age in a bright blue dress swinging in her garden. Why couldn't I be that girl, kicking up her heels without a care in the world? Why did *I* have to be the maid – and Mama too. Oh, if only we could live in a little house together – *our* home.

I gritted my teeth. I vowed there and then that I would make it come true some day. I knew I could never achieve such a thing on a meagre maid's wage. Even Mrs Briskett could not afford her own establishment. Was Miss Smith really right when she said my memoirs were unpublishable?

'Don't frown, child, it makes you look disagreeable,' said Mrs Briskett, tapping me on the forehead. 'Gather your things up now. We alight at the next station.'

I had hoped that Kingtown would look a little like the country village of my early childhood, but when we emerged from the station I saw we were in a smart town of big emporiums, very much like London itself.

I stared around curiously, startled anew by the noise and bustle, the rattle of the carriages and cabs, the clatter of the folk in the street, the blinding colour of everyone's clothes, when I was so used to the drab brown of our foundling uniform. Even Mrs Briskett's extraordinary dress seemed muted and ordinary amongst the purple and peacock-blue and emerald-green gowns and bonnets.

I whirled round, staring after this lady and that, with their great long skirts swirling about their boots, rows of flounces cascading down their behinds at the back. I had thought my own new dress bright enough, but now it seemed drab in the extreme. I caught a glimpse of myself in a shop window and saw what a scarecrow I looked, my sleeves so long they hid my hands, my skirts skimped and unadorned, my cap bizarre.

'I'm not dressed at all fashionably, am I, Mrs Briskett?' I said forlornly.

'Of course you're not, Hetty Feather. Servants don't follow fashion! You just have to look neat and serviceable,' said Mrs Briskett, but she couldn't help glancing admiringly at her own reflection.

A horse-drawn omnibus went past quickly, the wheels sending a mound of horse dung spraying up in the air, perilously near us on the pavement. Mrs Briskett jumped nimbly aside, mindful of her red skirts.

'That's a *bus*, Hetty Feather,' she announced, as if I were a toddling child.

'I know, Mrs Briskett. I journeyed in one once,' I said. 'Will we be catching a bus now?'

'No, it's only a shortish walk to the master's house. This way!'

I trotted along beside her, looking all around me. I passed several buildings with comical names: the Dog and Fox; the Wheelwright's Arms; the Three Fishes. They all had the same strange, pungent smell. I hung back, peering curiously through the coloured-glass windows.

'Come along, child. You don't want to go peeking into those dens of iniquity,' said Mrs Briskett, giving me a firm tug.

'Dens of iniquity?' I repeated.

'They are public houses. Gin palaces. Wicked places where foolish men waste their money on strong drink and weak women lose their self-respect,' she told me, twitching up her long red skirts, as if she could not bear to share the same pavement with such people.

These horrific dens looked rather cosy places to me, but I knew better than to argue. I was conscious of another even more pungent smell emanating from a huge brick building. I wrinkled my nose. It smelled worse than the hospital privies. Could it possibly be a huge public convenience? I buried my nose in the cuff of my sleeve.

'It's just the tannery, Hetty. Step lively and we'll soon be past,' said Mrs Briskett.

A tannery? When Matron Pigface Peters had been really angry, she'd say, 'I'll tan your hide for you, you cheeky varmint.' Was the tannery a grim place of correction? I shivered.

'You don't know what a tannery is, do you, Hetty Feather?'

'I know it's something dreadful,' I said.

'What? It's where they tan the cow hides to make your boot leather, silly child.'

I peered down at my stout boots. I had had no idea they were made out of dead animals. I felt my

468

toes wiggling in disgust. There was so much I didn't know about the outside world. The hospital had always boasted that they were giving us an excellent education, but now I realized I was as ignorant as a newborn babe where most things were concerned.

I trudged along in my strips of withered cow, breathing more freely as we left the tannery and crossed a large green field. The grass felt soft and springy, so different from the hard pavement. I remembered stamping across fields barefoot when I lived in the country. I felt a pang again, thinking of Jem.

I was distracted by a beautiful grey building with a tall spire and lots of little archways and a grand gothic door. It looked very much like a palace I'd seen pictured in my precious fairy-tale book, a gift from Mama. It had a curious garden, planted with weathered grey slabs of stones instead of flowers and fruit and vegetables.

Mrs Briskett saw me staring, and this time seemed pleased by my interest. 'Yes, Hetty, you will be attending St John's on Sunday afternoon. There's a splendid vicar there. Sarah and I find his sermons very uplifting.'

It wasn't a palace at all. It was a *church*. I had attended chapel every Sunday of my hospital life, but it had looked very different to this.

'Why does the vicar have such a strange stone garden?' I asked

'What?' Mrs Briskett stopped in her tracks. 'Are you being disrespectful, child?'

'No, ma'am.'

'Oh dear Lord, have you never heard of a grave-yard? Those stones mark the graves of all the dead people in this parish.'

'*Dead* people?' I echoed, shocked.

'Don't you know *anything*, Hetty Feather? When you die, you're put in a coffin and buried in a graveyard.'

This was the answer to a long-time puzzle of mine. From time to time children at the hospital had died. My own foster brother Saul had died from influenza. He had simply disappeared overnight. Nurse Winnie told me he'd gone up to Heaven, but I wasn't so sure. Saul had a poorly leg and couldn't walk properly. How could he have journeyed all the way up to Heaven? I'd seen his bony little back enough times when we were bathed together as small children. I knew there were no wings folded away for future use. Besides, I wasn't so sure they'd let Saul into Heaven. He'd certainly never behaved remotely like a little angel.

So *this* is what happened to dead people! They were planted in the garden like potatoes. I stared over the churchyard fearfully. I did not care for this new world at all, with dead animals on my feet and dead people lying all around me. I hoped they stayed safely underground. We had frightened each other at the hospital, telling ghost stories when we went to bed at night. In fact I had done most of the frightening – recycling tales of murder and mayhem from the *Police Gazette*. I'd thoroughly enjoyed myself whispering about poor Minnie who stalked the corridors, a knife stuck in her heart, leaving bloody footprints across the linoleum. What if the dead didn't *stay* dead? They might start growing in the night, heads bursting through the earth, then shoulders, arms, till they were free of earthly clay and could walk the world again.

'Is Mr Buchanan's house near the churchyard?' I asked fearfully.

'We have several streets to go. So come along, child, step out briskly.'

I was happy to do that, even though my arms were aching from holding my box and I was longing to set it down. A boy ran up to us, whistling loudly, carrying an immense laden basket with seeming ease. He was very small, barely my own height, but there was a knowing glint in his brown eyes, and I guessed he was about my age.

'Watcha, Mrs B!' he cried out, walking along with us.

'Mrs Briskett to you, lad,' said Mrs Briskett.

'Who's this, then?' he said, ogling me.

'Don't you be so nosy,' said Mrs Briskett.

'Is she your long-lost daughter, then?' the boy said, chuckling.

'Stop that nonsense! She's Hetty Feather, our new maid. Master thought it time Sarah and I had a little help, seeing as we're getting older and creakier. We were hoping for a big strapping lass – but look at the size of this one!'

'She's little all right,' said the boy. 'I hope you got her half price because she's only half size!'

'Talk about the pot calling the kettle black!' I said, sticking out my chin. 'You're a little runt yourself.'

'Oooh, she speaks – and with a temper to match her flaming hair!' he said, grinning at me.

I pulled a hideous face at him. He stuck out his tongue at me, waggling it vigorously.

'I'll tell Jarvis about your cheek!' Mrs Briskett threatened, but he just laughed and ran off with his huge basket, the muscles in his skinny arms popping.

'Who's that boy, Mrs Briskett?'

'Oh, take no notice, that's just Bertie, the butcher's boy,' she said. 'He delivers all the meat to our neighbourhood. He's not a bad lad, but you have to be firm with him.'

I decided I would be *very* firm. I did not care for

472

silly lads cheeking me. All the same, I could not help marvelling at his strength. I wondered if my own muscles would get stronger now I was out at work. I ached all over and my boots were rubbing my feet sore. I wasn't used to such long walks.

We started trudging up a hill, which made matters worse. I had to lean against a gas lamp to steady my box and get my breath back. But at last, at the summit, Mrs Briskett pointed.

'See the big white house with the stained-glass set in the door? That's your new home, Hetty Feather.'

It was a new, large, three-storeyed house, very grand and imposing.

'It's very fine,' I said.

'Yes, indeed it is,' said Mrs Briskett proudly.

She opened the painted iron gate and we walked up the red-tiled path. I put one foot on the snowy white steps, but Mrs Briskett tugged me back by the hem of my skirt.

'Not the *front* steps, girl! We never, ever go in the front door!'

I stared at her. How were we supposed to get into the house – climb through the windows?

'We go down the area steps at the side!' She grabbed me and steered me towards them. I glimpsed a garden at the back with a great green lawn and an ornate white iron sofa padded with cushions – but I knew enough now to realize I'd never be reclining there.

Mrs Briskett whisked me through the basement door. Suddenly I felt almost at home. The corridor was dark, painted cream and brown. I smelled familiar scents of soda and black lead. I walked into a large kitchen very similar to Mama's old domain at the hospital. I stood there, quivering, because it was so very like, with its scrubbed table and shining pans, and yet not like at all, because Mama wasn't there. There was just Mrs Briskett and a strange pale woman in a print frock, who was sitting at the table eating an enormous hunk of bread and cheese.

'Ah, here you are at last!' she said, springing up. 'Let's have a look at her!'

She seized hold of me, dragging me downwards towards the window so she could get a proper look at me. She pulled a comical face, as if she did not like what she saw. I was tempted to pull a face back, but decided I had better be cautious. She didn't look as cheery as the butcher's boy. If Mrs Briskett reminded me of meat, then this new woman was definitely potatoes. She had a pale, lumpy face with little warts here and there, like eyes in a potato. Her figure resembled a whole sackful of them. Mrs Briskett's whalebone stays kept her figure solid, but if this creature wore corsets, they had long given up attempting to contain her.

'This can't be the new maid!' she said, prodding my face with a finger, turning me left and right.

476

'She's just a child. She can't be old enough, Mrs B.'

'She's fourteen, believe it or not. I know she's a skinny little thing, but we'll just have to fatten her up. Her name's Hetty Feather, though she tries to call herself something outrageous. What was it again, child?'

'My name is Sapphire Battersea,' I announced firmly.

The two women started chuckling as if I'd cracked a joke.

'Oh yes, and I'm the Queen of Sheba,' said Potato Woman, bobbing a mock curtsy. 'Sapphire Battersea indeed!'

'It isn't a comical name at all. I don't know why you're laughing,' I said indignantly.

This made them laugh even more.

'Hoity-toity! Still, what can you expect with that hair? Well, we've been lumbered with a right dud, but I suppose we'll have to make the best of it. Now, listen to me, missy. I'm Sarah, the parlourmaid. Mrs Briskett rules the kitchen, and I rule the rest of the house. You're to do as we say – do you understand? Now, come and have a bite to eat and then I'll take you to meet the master.'

I sat down at the table between the two great women. I stared in astonishment at the food. It was simple enough – cold meat and cheese and bread – but the portions were huge. Mrs Briskett cut me a huge slab of meat that would have fed five foundlings for a week, and buttered me a slice of bread so thickly that my teeth made dents in the yellow when I took a bite. There was strange lumpy brown jam too. I tried a spoonful and spluttered, my eyes streaming.

'What's up, girl?'

'This jam tastes very sharp, ma'am,' I said.

'Jam? It's pickles, you ninny!'

'Don't she know what *pickles* are?' said Sarah.

'This one don't know *anything*. She's so quaint in her ways I'm starting to wonder if she's simple.'

I was too dispirited to argue with her. I had always been the cleverest in my year – well, perhaps first equal when Polly was at the hospital. I was used to thinking myself bright and sharp-witted. Even Matron Pigface Peters and Matron Stinking Bottomly remarked on my intelligence, saying I was as sharp and sly as a cartload of monkeys. But now that I was out in this new topsy-turvy world, I realized I had to start learning all over again. I did not know the simplest things. As a child I had longed to visit the pink and yellow and green foreign lands on the geography map hanging on the classroom wall, but now I realized that my own country was a totally foreign land to me. I did not know the language, the terrain, or any of the customs.

'What's the matter with you now, child?' said Mrs Briskett. 'You're not about to cry again, are you? I told you, I can't abide tears.'

'She's just wanting attention, so take no notice,' said Sarah.

Their talking about me as if I wasn't even there made the tears roll down my face. I could not be Sapphire Battersea here. I wasn't even Hetty Feather. I was simply 'child' or 'girl' or 'missy'. It made me feel very small.

'Come now, no tears,' said Mrs Briskett. 'Have a spoonful of syrup – that'll sweeten you up.'

I still hadn't eaten more than a mouthful of meat and strange pickles, but I took the proffered sticky spoonful and sucked hard. The sweetness soothed me. I licked my lips, remembering the spoonfuls of sugar Mama had once pressed upon me as secret treats.

'Aha, she likes that all right!' said Mrs Briskett. 'That's a good girl. Stop that silly crying now. You don't want to go and see the master all over tearstains – it won't give the right impression at all.'

They fussed over me considerably for this meeting with the master. Sarah took me out through the back door to the privy, and waited for me to relieve myself. The privy was very dark, and as I squatted there, something terrifying ran over my foot.

'Lord save us, stop that squealing! Whatever is it, Hetty Feather?'

'I don't know! Something touched me!'

'Don't be silly, child. It will just have been a spider – or maybe a mouse.'

'Oh! Help!' I screamed louder, and hurtled out of the privy.

The hospital's facilities had been dark and depressing, but they were in their own special building, free of wildlife. I resolved to severely limit my visits to the privy. Maybe I could commandeer a chamber pot and use it privately?

Sarah caught hold of me, dragged me into the scullery, and held a cloth under the tap. She then proceeded to wipe my face fiercely while I wriggled and squirmed.

'Hold still, child – you're covered in soot and smuts from the train!'

'I'm not a baby. I can do my own face!' I protested indignantly.

'You certainly *act* like a baby,' said Sarah. 'And whatever's happened to your hair? You're a right little mophead. Come here!'

She whipped off my cap, combed my hair with her hard fingers, and then pulled it up into a knot, securing it with a couple of pins from her own head. Then she jammed my cap back on, pulling it down to my eyebrows, and twitched at my apron to straighten it.

'There! You still look a funny little creature, but at least you're clean and tidy,' she said. She turned my shoulders to show me off to Mrs Briskett. 'Will she do, Mrs B?'

'She'll have to,' said Mrs Briskett. 'Though I still think she's going to give the master a bit of a surprise.'

Sarah led me out of the kitchen and up the stairs. I was very nervous now, but I took comfort in the fact that I had something in common with this mysterious master. We were both writers. Miss Smith had told him all about me. Maybe he wouldn't treat me like a servant at all. I wouldn't be a maid of all work – of *any* work. Maybe he would let me sit in his study and write beside him. We could have interesting conversations about the joys of composition. Then, at the end of the day, he'd read my stories and give me gentle advice and encouragement.

This idea was so beguiling that I almost believed it. I skipped up the stairs eagerly, scarcely taking in the green embossed wallpaper and the many painted portraits staring down at me, eyebrows raised.

'That's it, look lively,' said Sarah. She led me along a crimson-carpeted landing and gave my face another polish with the hem of her apron. Then she knocked on a door. We stood waiting.

'Yes, yes, yes?' muttered a male voice.

Sarah opened the door and pushed me inside. I thought she would come in with me, but there I was, all alone with this strange new master. For a few seconds I was so dazzled by his room I could scarcely take him in. I felt as if I'd stepped into fairyland. There were books everywhere: books arranged upright on shelves; books piled sideways on the floor; books balanced on desks, tables, even chairs; books lining the floor like a leather carpet. I looked around, mesmerized by beautiful big brown volumes, little crimson pocket books, fancy white vellum, gilt-embossed gift books.

The master sat at the biggest desk behind two huge piles of books. He was a surprisingly small, light man, half the size of Mrs Briskett and Sarah. He wore an odd orange fez with a tassel on his head, and a quilted crimson jacket with gold cord fastenings. I blinked at him, bewildered. He didn't *look* like a gentleman at all. He was dressed like an organ-grinder's monkey. His features were disturbingly simian too, with dark circles under his eyes and wrinkles puckering his face. I had to fight the urge to peer behind his desk to look for a long tail.

I bobbed him a curtsy instead, and arranged my face in a subservient smile. He had rescued me from the hospital, after all. I needed to show true gratitude.

He didn't smile back. He frowned at me, increasing his wrinkles alarmingly. 'Ah! You must be the new maid from the Foundling Hospital. But, oh dear, oh dear, surely you're not old enough for service, child!' he said, in a reedy voice.

I sighed a little. 'I'm fourteen, sir.'

'Good heavens! But you look so poor and puny!'

I felt he was being rather rude, but I realized it wasn't my place to take offence.

'I *am* small, sir, but I am sure I will grow a little,' I said.

'I wanted a good strong girl to help my two servants. They are maturing in years and starting to need assistance.'

'I am very good and very strong,' I said, lying on both counts.

'And you have bright red hair! No wonder Miss Smith was so determined that I take you under my roof. She wouldn't take no for an answer, and I can see why now. No one else would take on a redhead like you – it's asking for trouble. I'm not having any temper tantrums, do you hear me?'

'Certainly not, sir. I never ever give way to temper tantrums,' I declared, telling three lies in less than a minute.

'I should have asked to see you before acceding

to Miss Smith's suggestions. I only agreed because I felt obliged to support a literary colleague.'

'If you please, sir, *I* am a kind of literary colleague too,' I said. 'I have been writing my memoirs. Perhaps Miss Smith spoke of this. I've been showing her my work for years.'

'Ssh, now!' said Mr Buchanan, a finger to his thin lips. 'I am surprised. I thought the hospital would have taught you to speak only when you are spoken to! Yes, Miss Smith did indicate that you have a penchant for romancing. If you work diligently, I might be willing to give you a little guidance in the future. But we will have to see how hard you work, missy, and whether you learn our ways quickly enough. I am taking a grave risk in employing you, but I am a charitable man and keen to do my Christian duty.'

He bobbed his monkey head at me and I nodded back, though I felt my face flaming the colour of my unfortunate hair. I hadn't realized Miss Smith had had to work so hard to get him to employ me. I wasn't specially chosen as a promising candidate for his household. I seemed to be practically un-employable, judging from Mr Buchanan's blunt words. Doubtless he'd prefer any other girl from the hospital – stuttering Mary, slow Freda, even poor mad Jenny.

I did not feel like Sapphire Battersea any more.

I was Hetty Feather, despised by everyone – except my dear mama. I thought of her, longing to pour out my heart to her in a letter. But how was I to send a letter to her now? I had always given my letters to Miss Smith. Would she come and visit me here, in my strange new home? Perhaps not as regularly, if at all.

I thought hard about the vital penny stamps I needed. Mr Buchanan seemed to have run out of things to say to me, and was making dismissive waves at me with his monkey paws.

'Off you go, then, child. Be a good girl and mind Mrs Briskett and Sarah. I'm sure they will instruct you admirably.'

'If you please, sir,' I said. 'I – I will be earning a wage, will I not?'

He peered at me as if I'd said something impertinent. 'Yes, fourteen pounds a year. I negotiated with the Board of Governors at the Foundling Hospital. It's a very generous sum for an untrained child.'

'Yes, sir, certainly, sir – but will I be receiving the generous sum at the end of the week, or the month, or the quarter?' I asked anxiously.

'I cannot see that that is of any consequence to you, Hetty Feather. You do not require any money while you are under my roof. You will receive all your meals free of charge, and I believe Sarah will give you a length of material so you can sew more clothes as you require them.'

'Yes, sir, but I also require several postage stamps,' I said, desperation making me bold.

'Why do you need to correspond with anyone?' he asked.

'I need to write to my mother, sir.' I thought hard. 'I wish to tell her how lucky I am to have been taken on in your household. I want to tell her how kind you have been,' I added artfully.

He looked surprised. 'I wasn't aware that there was any contact between foundling children and their maternal parents,' he said.

'There isn't usually, sir – but my mama is especially concerned,' I said, bobbing a curtsy to seem deferential. 'I would very much like to reassure her that I have an extra special position in a lovely place.'

'I can understand your desire, child. You will be paid quarterly, like Mrs Briskett and Sarah, but I shall take it upon myself to provide you with postage stamps. Here you are, child . . .' He opened his desk drawer and gave me one.

I swallowed again. 'Please, sir – might I have some more?'

I thought this a risk. I did not want to make him angry with me.

To my great relief he chuckled. 'You're a

486

veritable Oliver Twist, Hetty Feather,' he declared.

I wasn't sure who Oliver Twist was, but if he encouraged Mr Buchanan to be generous, then he seemed a fine friend. Mr Buchanan counted me out six stamps, which I seized eagerly, tucking them into my apron pocket.

'Now run along and try not to take any more liberties, child,' he said, though he did not look annoyed.

So I did indeed run. Sarah was waiting for me outside the door.

'I hope you weren't giving the master any cheek, my girl,' she said.

'No indeed. We were getting along like a house on fire,' I said.

Sarah looked at me sideways. 'Don't you get above yourself, missy,' she said. 'Come along. I'll show you all over the house and give you some idea of your duties.'

She took me into the drawing room and dining room, rattling off detailed dusting and polishing and sweeping instructions. I tried to pay attention, but was constantly distracted by the splendour of the house. Every room was crowded with furniture and ornaments and assorted knick-knacks. There were two sofas, four easy chairs, and six uprights in the living room alone. Mr Buchanan only had one behind, and a puny one at that. Why would he need such an immense variety of seats? It would surely take an entire regiment of maids to dust every single item adequately. I'd no idea this was how proper folk lived their lives. I imagined what it would be like to lounge on the purple-velvet chaise longue, to dine at that polished table, to prop my feet on that intricately stitched footstool.

It grew ever more fascinating upstairs, peeping into Mr Buchanan's best bedroom, picturing him in his nightgown and cap tucked up beneath those sheets. I could not help also picturing him getting up in the night and making use of the chamber pot under the bed – though it was disconcerting to be told that it was my job to empty it.

Mr Buchanan's lavatory arrangements were a matter of total astonishment to me, because he also had his very own bathroom with a water closet. Sarah demonstrated how you pulled the chain so that everything was neatly flushed away.

'This is splendid! So why do we use that awful, scary, spidery privy in the garden when we could use this water closet?' I asked.

Sarah looked horrified. 'This is the master's private room! We could not possibly use the same facilities!'

I resolved then and there that when I was set to scrubbing the bathroom, I would quite definitely use the facilities. I pulled the chain again myself, experimenting.

'Stop messing about, Hetty. This isn't a game. Come along now.'

She showed me the best guest bedroom and then the second-best guest bedroom – both seemed incredibly grand to me, especially the beds themselves. I was used to the narrow beds in the hospital. These ones were enormous. I stroked the counterpanes. They felt incredibly soft and silky. Perhaps I could occasionally sneak into one of these guest bedrooms and have a little lie-down?

'Does Mr Buchanan often have guests sleeping in these rooms?' I asked.

'Rarely. The master isn't one for entertaining. He's too engrossed in his work,' said Sarah, leading me up yet another flight of stairs. These had brown linoleum instead of carpet, and there were no paintings looking down at me from the walls.

'These are the attic rooms,' said Sarah. 'You will dust and sweep and polish here too, but you don't need to be quite so particular, because they are only *our* rooms.'

Sarah's room was very small compared to Mr Buchanan's, and the ceiling sloped sharply overhead. Her bed was narrow, her washstand basic, her chest small, with only three drawers. There was no fireplace there so it must be icy cold in winter. She had no ornaments whatsoever – just a brush and comb on her washstand, a Bible by her bed, and one small painting hanging on the wall. It was a portrait of a large lady, not very well executed. She looked like a stiff puppet, not a real woman at all. But Sarah looked up at her and gently touched her cheek, as if she were a real and lovely lady. I knew that gesture, that feeling.

'She is your mother!' I said.

'Yes, dear Mother. My cousin Luke painted her likeness. It's very good, isn't it?'

I thought it very *bad* but for once I knew how to behave. 'Yes, it is. Your mother looks a very fine lady,' I said. 'Does she live far away? Do you get to see her often?'

Sarah's potato face flushed. She shook her head sadly. 'Dear Mother passed away many years ago,' she said, shaking her head. 'I still miss her so much.'

'Oh, Sarah, I'm so sorry,' I whispered.

A sudden new fear clutched at my chest. How would I ever stand it if *my* mama died? I had only known she was my mother for such a cruelly brief time. I could not bear it if she were snatched away from me.

It was the one terrible disadvantage of loving

490

someone. You couldn't bear the idea of being without them. I reckoned up the people I had loved during my fourteen years. I loved Mama most of all, of course. She shone like the sun in my life – but there were stars too. I had loved Nurse Winnie a little, and my dearest friend Polly a great deal. I had cared for young Eliza, and thought wistfully about my whole foster family. I loved them all – though of course Jem was the one I'd truly worshipped and adored.

I thought again about the man waiting outside the hospital. I'd read about the magical method of photography. I wished I had a photograph of that young man so that I could pore over his image and see if he could really be my own dear Jem. I fingered the stamps inside my apron pocket . . .

'Hetty Feather! Don't daydream, girl. Come, I will show you Mrs B's bedroom.'

Mrs Briskett's bedroom was twice the size, with a large bed. A vast pair of bloomers sprawled on the covers, legs akimbo. I felt my mouth twitching, and Sarah herself sniggered, but then straightened her face, looking guilty. Mrs Briskett did not have a portrait of her mama. She had several coloured lithographs of great pink pigs, black-and-white cows, huge woolly sheep and assorted hens and ducks. She seemed to have deliberately surrounded herself with the raw materials of her trade. I wondered if she lay on her big bed looking at these animals by candlelight, plotting massive roasts and stews.

There was only one more room upstairs – a little inconsequential garret with the ceiling sloping severely. I thought it would be *my* room, but it was overly occupied already, stuffed full to bursting with trunks and old chairs and pictures in frames, and box after box of old ornaments and curtains and cushions and whatnots.

'This is the box room, the only room in the house you don't have to bother with,' said Sarah.

'Am I to sleep here?' I asked, in a small voice.

'Of course not, you ninny. I know you're tiny, but I think we'd have difficulty bedding down even a little mouse in here,' said Sarah.

'So where *am* I to sleep?' I said, bewildered, because we'd inspected every single room in the house.

Sarah put her head on one side, looking at me. 'Well . . . perhaps if you curled up very small, you could sleep on the privy floor?'

'*What?*'

Her eyes were twinkling, and as I exclaimed in abject horror, she burst out laughing. 'Oh, Hetty, your face! Dear Lord, you thought I was serious!'

she chortled, clutching her sides and heaving with laughter.

I did not feel inclined to join in. And when she told me where I was in fact to sleep, it didn't seem an especially superior alternative. I was to go to bed in the scullery! This was a little dark room off the kitchen. It had a big lead sink, a wooden draining board, a mangle, hooks for all the assorted dusters, mops, brooms and brushes, and several dark depressing cupboards full of matches and candles and cakes of coal-tar soap, Nixey's Black Lead and Japan lustre shoe-blacking. Sadly, there was no food. Mrs Briskett kept all her edible supplies in the larder, and she locked it up each night with the key she kept round her neck.

There was a small fold-up bed in the last cupboard, and Sarah pulled this out with a flourish. 'There we are, Hetty. Don't look such a sour-puss. See, you have a proper bed, and you can use the sink to wash in.'

I hoped she was joking again, but she was serious this time. I felt my eyes filling with tears.

'Lord help us, what's the matter now?' said Mrs Briskett, coming to inspect my 'bedchamber'.

'I don't want to sleep in the scullery! It's like the punishment room!' I sobbed. 'I haven't done anything wrong yet!'

'Hey, hey, don't be so dramatic. I jolly well hope you *don't* do anything wrong. Little maids have to be as good as gold or else they get dismissed! Sleeping in the scullery isn't a punishment, silly. I slept in the scullery when I had my first job as a kitchen maid,' she said. 'It was practically the self-same bed.'

I looked at her. 'But – but you wouldn't fit it,' I said, between sobs.

Sarah burst out laughing again. I realized I had not been tactful.

'I was a slip of a girl then, missy, not much bigger than you,' said Mrs Briskett, looking offended.

'I am sorry – I didn't mean . . .' I stammered. It was impossible to imagine Mrs Briskett as a slip of a girl. I was sure that she was vast even as a babe in arms. I pictured her in meat-red swaddling clothes, at least half the size of her poor mama . . . I found I was laughing too, but I pretended my snorts were still sobs.

'Now, now, calm down, child, do. I'm going to start baking or we'll have no tea – and Mr Buchanan will start complaining bitterly if he has to do without his cake. You come and sift the flour for me, Hetty, while I change out of my good clothes,' said Mrs Briskett. 'Cheer up, dearie – you know I can't abide tears.'

I did cheer up considerably that afternoon. I had worked with dear Mama in the hospital kitchens, and was quick and capable. I sifted flour, I cut up butter, I cracked open eggs and whisked them to a froth. I measured currants and cherries and walnuts, taking a sly nibble every now and then, while Mrs Briskett was staring at the stove and Sarah's head was bent over her mending.

She set me to darning an old torn nightshirt when I had finished helping with the baking. It seemed strange to hold the nightshirt in my lap, knowing that it had covered Mr Buchanan's bony body, but I darned the worn patch obediently. I had spent nine years darning at the hospital, so it was second nature to me now.

'My, Hetty Feather, that's even neater than I can manage!' said Sarah, peering at the patch. 'Look, Mrs B, you can hardly see the stitches.'

'Well done, dearie,' said Mrs Briskett, patting me on the back with a floury hand.

I felt like bursting into tears again. No one had ever praised me at the hospital.

When Mrs Briskett had made her currant cake and her walnut cake, she laid neat slabs out on a fancy plate, and set a tea tray with a pot of tea, a little jug of milk, a dainty sugar bowl, a pretty cup and saucer. Sarah picked up the tray – and then handed it over to me.

'Why don't you save my legs? You go and serve the master, Hetty,' she said.

She lent me her best cap and fancy white apron with frills, though the cap came down past my eyebrows and the apron hem swept the floor. Sarah and Mrs Briskett laughed heartily at this spectacle, but in a kindly fashion.

I wasn't sure *how* to serve the tea and cake, so Mrs Briskett sat at the kitchen table, frowning and scribbling with her hand, pretending to be the master, while Sarah mimed serving 'him' with his tea and cake, while I watched carefully.

Then Sarah gave me the real tray and sent me on my way. The tray was wooden, covered with a lacy cloth, and heavy. It was a struggle for me to carry it steadily, and as I started up the stairs the teacup rattled on its saucer and the milk slopped out of its jug, but I managed to get all the way up to Mr Buchanan's study without serious incident.

I knew I had to knock on the door before entering, but didn't see how I could do so without growing a third useful hand straight out of my chest. I tried putting my leg right up under the tray to balance it for a second, but it tipped precariously. I was determined to do this properly. I set the tray down on the floor, tapped twice on the door, and when the master eventually murmured something, I opened the door a crack, bent down, hauled the tray upright, edged my bottom through the door, and ended up successfully inside the study.

'I've got your tea and cake, Master,' I said.

'Mm,' he replied absent-mindedly, still writing. He made vague waving gestures with his other hand, indicating that I should set down the tray and serve him. I peered around the room but could not spot a single bare surface for my tray. In the end I had to balance it across two piles of books, but it seemed steady enough.

I served his tea on a tiny corner of his desk and offered him the plate of sliced cake. His hand hovered, first over the walnut, then the currant.

'Which is best, Hetty Feather?' he asked.

'They're both delicious, sir – and I should know because I helped make them,' I said proudly. 'Why don't you take a slice of each?'

He took two slabs – the biggest – and proceeded to eat them, taking alternate bites of each. He made the waving gesture again, this time dismissively.

'Will that be all, sir?' I asked, and he nodded, his mouth full of cake.

I was a little disappointed. I wanted him to say,

'Well done, Hetty. Here's two more postage stamps as a reward – and take this book of fairy stories to read tonight – and here's a blank manuscript book and a fresh quill pen for your memoirs.' But maybe this was overly optimistic. I made do with his grunt, and bobbed out of the room.

When I got down to the kitchen, Sarah patted me on the back and Mrs Briskett cut me my own slice of cake. They were starting to act more like mothers than matrons.

When I trundled my meagre bed out of its cupboard that night, I sat up and wrote a letter to Mama by candlelight. I had helped myself to a good supply of paper and envelopes from the hospital.

> *Do not worry about me, dearest Mama. I will be a good, obedient little servant girl for a while. My new master, Mr Buchanan, is a strange man rather like a monkey, but he has been quite kind to me, I suppose. Mrs Briskett and Sarah have sharp tongues and mock me at times, but they mostly mean well. I am as happy as I can be* **WITHOUT YOU.**

I signed my name with many kisses, and then tucked my letter into an envelope and stuck on my stamp. Then I started a new letter.

Dearest Gideon,

I can't say I LIKE being a servant, but I suppose it's not as bad as I feared. I do so hope that you will find being a soldier is not so bad either. At least you will wear a splendid uniform. Mine is very plain – but then so am I.

Keep well, dearest brother. Remember I am always
Your loving sister,
Hetty

Mrs Briskett had only given me a stub of candle, and it was already flickering – but I reached for another sheet of my precious paper. Because I knew I only had a few minutes before total darkness, I wrote hastily, without time to compose my words.

Dear Jem,

Was it you at the hospital gates???
I am so sorry we did not get time to speak.
But you can write to me at this address. I am a maid here, and it is quite a good house and the people are tolerably kind but I do not think I am cut out to be a servant.
With affection,
Your one-time sister,
Hetty Feather
P.S. Eliza is doing well at the hospital. She is a

good kind child and rarely gets into trouble –
unlike me. She says you are going to marry her
one day. I hope you will be very happy.

I remembered the address accurately enough,
and applied another postage stamp to the envelope.
My candle guttered, and then extinguished itself. I
lay down on my hard little bed. There was a dank
smell of soapsuds and stale cooking, so I had to
cover my nose with my sheets. It was so dark I
could not see my hand before my face, and alarmingly quiet too. I was used to sleeping in a large
room with scores of other girls. I was accustomed to
snores and sighs all night long. I lay tensely, feeling
terribly alone. I tried to picture Mrs Briskett and
Sarah up at the top of the house, and Mr Buchanan
somewhere in the middle, but they seemed very
far away.

I thought of the young man in brown and
wondered if he really was Jem. If so, had he gone all
the way home to the cottage now? I thought
enviously of my foster family, all crammed together
under that thatched roof.

Then, as always, I thought of dear Mama, tucked
up in her faraway home by the sea. I whispered to
her in the night . . . and after a while she seemed
to whisper back to me:

Night-night, Hetty, my love. You've been a good

girl and tried hard, and I'm proud of you. I miss you so much, my darling, but don't worry. We'll be together again some day.

'Some day *soon*,' I murmured, and at last I fell asleep.

6

'Get up, get up, you lazy little girl!'

It was Mrs Briskett, shaking me so hard I had to cling to the sides of my bed, in danger of tumbling to the floor.

'I said you had to be up at six to light the kitchen fire. It's nearly half past now, and I can't start cooking till the stove heats up. We're going to be all behind like a sheep's tail, and I can't bear that! Get up, Hetty Feather!'

I got up and barely sat down again the whole day long. I didn't have time to wash myself properly – just a quick dab. I didn't even brush my hair, I just crammed my cap on top. I scarcely had time to rush to the terrible outside privy.

I was put in a corner to clean Mr Buchanan's boots while Mrs Briskett genuflected in front of the kitchen range. She tried to show me what to do, but it was so complicated and temperamental I couldn't get the hang of it at all. I was sent off in disgrace to sweep and clean the downstairs grates. Then I was given a brush and cloth and polish, to clean the doorstep and brasses. I scrubbed my fingers raw trying to impress, but Sarah was in a bad mood too and sniffed at my efforts. Next I had to haul a huge jug of hot water up the stairs to set on Mr Buchanan's washstand. He was sitting up in his bed, wearing a nightcap instead of a fez, but looking more monkey-like than ever. The sleeves of his nightgown rumpled up, showing excessively hairy thin arms. Maybe that long tail was lurking under the bedcovers after all.

I had to serve him a cup of tea, and then scurry back downstairs to down a cup myself. The kitchen was warm now, and something smelling delicious was sizzling in the pan. I sniffed at it hopefully, suddenly remembering the pigs we kept long ago in my country foster home.

'Don't you go making big eyes at me, Hetty Feather,' Mrs Briskett snapped. 'Lazy girls go without their breakfast.' But she gave me a rasher of wondrous bacon, and a sausage too. I wished I had time to savour them properly, but I had to run to the dining room to serve Mr Buchanan *his* breakfast.

I would have thought a tray would suffice for one gentleman, but oh dear, no. We had to lay a white damask cloth over the table, with the fold exactly in the middle. Sarah fussed over a centrepiece of flowers and ferns, and then set me laying two small knives, two small forks, a dessertspoon, a dish, a plate, and an intricately folded table napkin before Mr Buchanan's chair. I had to refold the wretched napkin three times, and even rearrange the cutlery, because I didn't have the bowls of the spoon on the table and the prongs of the fork upwards. As if it mattered!

Then there was fuss fuss fuss with the salt cellar and pepper box and mustard pot, and the loaf of bread had to be precise upon its platter, and the butter – oh dear goodness, the butter had to be fashioned into a little rose shape with a pair of pats.

We set it all up, with covered hot-water dishes containing enough rashers, sausages, tomatoes and mushrooms to feed an army, plus two boiled eggs in a napkin and a rack of toast. I saw Mr Buchanan left his toast, two rashers, a sausage and several mushrooms when I went to clear the table, and I crammed them all into my mouth quick to keep me going.

I was sent upstairs to clean Mrs Briskett's and Sarah's rooms, and then I did the master's bedroom. He'd used his chamber pot even though he had his splendid water closet a few steps across the landing. I tried out the water closet for myself while I was stuck inside cleaning it. I clung hard to the

505

edge of the seat just in case I was sucked down the hole by a sudden spurt of water – it still seemed eerily mysterious to me.

He'd left his bed for me to strip and make up. Thank goodness the beds in the guest rooms were still pristine, though I had to dust and sweep these rooms too. I was ready to crawl into bed myself, but Mrs Briskett was calling for me, needing me down in the kitchen to peel the potatoes and carrots and chop the cabbage. I chopped my finger too and had to suck it hard to stop it bleeding.

Then I had to see to the fires in the dining room and living room while Sarah flapped around with a duster. While Mr Buchanan was having his lunch, Sarah let me into his study to stoke his own fire, but I wasn't allowed to touch anything else. Sarah dusted here with elaborate care, picking up books and papers reverently and replacing them precisely.

I hoped I might get time to breathe after *my* lunch, and maybe do a bit more fancy darning so that Sarah and Mrs Briskett would marvel at me again – but any chance of that vanished when I spilled a whole pitcher of milk trying to carry it out of the larder with greasy hands. Mrs Briskett smacked me hard about the head and set me to scrubbing the entire floor.

'But my hands are all sore already, Mrs B, and my finger's actually bleeding – look!' I said, thrusting it at her.

'And my heart's bleeding listening to your endless excuses. And don't you go calling me Mrs B: it's Mrs *Briskett*. Let's have a little respect around here. Get going with that scrubbing brush. Milk's the very devil when it spills. I'm not having my kitchen reeking like a dairy. Go to it!'

I started scrubbing, squatting down and wiping the floor cautiously, because my hands were really throbbing.

'Not like that! Get down on your knees and put some elbow grease into it, or you'll go without any supper!' she commanded.

How could I have ever thought she was like a mother! She was even worse than Matron Pigface Peters and Matron Stinking Bottomly. I scrubbed viciously, cursing Mrs Briskett under my breath at every stroke, imagining the flagstones were her big meaty face. I put such effort into it that my behind waggled in the air.

'My, that's a very tempting sight!' said a loud Cockney voice. It was Bertie the butcher's boy, bringing us a basket of meat.

'Less of your cheek, you,' said Mrs Briskett. 'Now, let's have a look at that minced beef. I hope it's not all gristle and bone – I asked for prime mince.'

'It's the finest chopped-up backside of bovine,

Mrs B,' said Bertie. 'Here, have a sniff, it's lovely and fresh.' He offered her a paper of meat as if it were a bunch of roses. She laughed and swatted his hand away, not seeming to mind at all when *he* called her Mrs B.

I muttered miserably to myself that it wasn't fair.

'What's that you're saying, Beautiful?' said the boy.

He squatted down beside me. 'Oh dear, what a face! You must have been a bad girl to be set to scrubbing at this hour! Remember, cleanliness is next to Godliness – so you and the kitchen floor will be wafting around the heavenly clouds one day.'

'One day *soon*, I expect,' I said. 'When I faint from loss of blood, seeing as I have an open wound.' I sucked my poor hacked finger.

'Let's have a look.' Bertie held my grubby hand surprisingly gently and squinted at my finger. 'Call that a cut! Look at mine!'

He spread his left hand out in front of my eyes, fanning his fingers – and I saw that the tops of three of them were entirely missing, not even a vestige of a nail left. He laughed when I gasped.

'Now they really *did* bleed when I chopped the tips off. Old Jarvis minced them up lovely and everyone's cottage pie tasted *real* good that day, with all my prime boy-meat!' He fell about laughing at my face. But three missing fingers were no joke.

'You chopped them right *off*?'

'I'm learning the trade, see. I got a great side of beef, hung onto it tight to stop it rolling around, raised my chopper – down it goes with a great *whack* . . . only my aim was a bit skewed.'

'How awful!'

'No it ain't – not when you're into butchery. My master, old Jarvis, he's got three whole fingers missing – and Samuel and Sidney, his older lads, they've lost one apiece. It's only to be expected. But when you've done it once, it don't half sharpen your aim for the future!'

'I don't think I should care to be a butcher's boy.'

'Yes, well, when I left the workhouse they said to me, Bertie, my boy, do you want to go into Parliament, or do you fancy a career in the city, or maybe you'd like to set yourself up as a gentleman farmer – but do you know something, Beautiful, those jobs didn't appeal to me. Butchery, that's what I thought.'

I felt myself blushing. 'You were in the workhouse?' I exclaimed.

'Yes, and I ain't ashamed of it, either. Weren't my fault my ma ended up there, and I dare say it weren't her fault either, so don't you go looking down on me.'

'Oh, I'm *not*!' I glanced over to see if Mrs

509

Briskett and Sarah were listening, but they were chatting together. Mrs Briskett was busy setting the pieces of meat out on plates and covering them with mesh domes while Sarah started sewing the hem of a tablecloth.

'My mama was in the workhouse too,' I said.

'So you know what it's like,' said Bernie.

'Well, I was brought up in the Foundling Hospital.'

He shook his head. 'A foundling and an orphan. Well, we're a matching pair, ain't we?'

'An orphan? So your mother died?'

'Yup, when I was about ten.'

'You poor thing,' I said.

'Well, I didn't truly know her, did I? We were kept separate, see. We met up on Christmas Day, and that was a rum time, and it meant the world to all of us – but we still had to get through the three hundred and sixty-four other days.'

'So where do you live now, Bertie?'

'I live at the shop – where else? I've got me nice little bed under the counter.' He said it cheerily enough, but I imagined lying all night in the dark with meat dripping bloodily all around me. Perhaps I was more fortunate than I realized, living in the scullery.

'When's your afternoon off, then, Beautiful?' Bertie asked.

'I don't think I get one.'

'Oh, I'll make sure of that. You watch.' He sidled up to Mrs Briskett. He looked smaller than ever beside her huge bulk. 'Like them lovely steaks, Mrs B? They were supposed to be going up to Letchworth Manor, but I swapped them round because you're my favourite customer, and a lady line you appreciates quality.'

'Hark at the lad! He's got the patter, all right, even though he's such a little squirt,' said Mrs Briskett, chuckling.

'You've got an extra kidney too – did you see?'

'What are you after, lad? A slice of my steak-and-kidney pie?'

'Well, *now* you're tempting me! But I was just wondering if I could take your little maid here off your hands on Sunday, seeing as she's a bit down in the dumps.'

'No wonder – she's a careless girl, and needs to be taught a lesson. And on Sunday she'll be coming to church along with us.'

'Of course she will, but what about *after* church? Can't you spare her for an hour or two? I'll bring her back rosy-cheeked in time for supper – how about that?'

'How about you clear off out of my kitchen and stop distracting my little maid,' said Mrs Briskett – but she didn't say no.

Bertie winked at me. 'See you Sunday, then, Beautiful. I'll come calling,' he mouthed.

I shrugged. I wasn't sure I wanted to go off gallivanting with this cheeky Cockney lad, Bertie. He was clearly mocking me, calling me Beautiful. He had obviously forgotten my name.

But when he clattered over, swinging his basket, he called, 'Bye-bye, then, Mrs B. Bye-bye, Sarah Sew-a-fine-seam. And bye-bye, Miss Hetty Feather.'

Mrs Briskett and Sarah tittered.

'My, you're a dark one, Hetty, setting your cap at Jarvis's boy already!' said Mrs Briskett. 'I told you, I don't want you to have no followers. It just causes trouble – and you're not old enough anyway.'

'I don't *want* any followers,' I said, but I found I was a little cheered all the same. I still had miles of stone flags to scrub, and my cut finger was throbbing more sorely than ever, but it didn't seem such a terrible task any more. When I was done at long last, Mrs Briskett fried me a slice of yesterday's currant cake in butter, dusted it with sugar and served it to me on a plate. It tasted truly delicious.

I was set to more work straight afterwards, running up and down stairs tending the fires and fetching hot water. Then Mrs Briskett got it into her head that her saucepans weren't quite clean, and I had to boil them all for half an hour on the range, then attack the enamel pans with a rag and Monkey Brand. It nearly broke my heart when she dirtied them all again cooking Mr Buchanan's dinner.

I was so tired and my hand throbbed so badly I could barely write that night, even though Mrs Briskett gave me another stub of candle. I fancied starting a made-up story, however, if Miss Smith thought my memoirs unpublishable. I picked up my notebook and wrote:

Lady Sapphire was a very kind and liberal mistress. If the cook spilled milk in the kitchen, Lady Sapphire commanded her pet cats to come and lick it up forthwith, a task they enjoyed exceedingly. When the saucepans became just a little bit dirty, Lady Sapphire gave them all away to grateful poor folk and bought an entire fresh set because she didn't want to work her servants unnecessarily hard as they were preparing a special dinner that night. Mr Jarvis the Master Butcher was invited, together with his lady wife, and for a special treat, his loyal but occasionally cheeky apprentice boy, young Bertie. He was very honoured, and bowed and scraped to Lady Sapphire excessively . . .

I fell asleep pondering the number of Cs and Ss

in excessively. I woke up with a crick in my neck and the candle burned out, and then barely slept the rest of the night because I was so worried that I wouldn't be up at six to light the wretched kitchen range.

I was so tired I spent the next day yawning my head off, and when I sat down for my bacon breakfast, I fell fast asleep at the table. But when Sarah went to sort the post I woke up with a start, because there was not one but two letters for *me*!

I knew there would not be a letter back from Gideon. He very probably had not been given *my* letter, and at the Foundling Hospital we were only allowed to reply on Sunday afternoons. But I had a letter back from dear Mama!

My own Hetty,

I am so glad and releeved you have a good posishon, deary, and that theyre being quite kind and sweet to my own gurl. I daresay you will find the work hard, but you're a sensible quik lerner and it makes my hert swell with pride to think of my gurl out in the world, erning her own living. How I wish I culd see you and give you a grate big hug.

All love from your very very afectshonit mother.

P.S. Excuse speling, it's my week point.

514

I held Mama's letter to my chest, I rubbed it against my cheek, I ran my finger along every line, oblivious to Mrs Briskett and Sarah.

'Ah, bless the child,' said Sarah, sniffing. 'How I wish my own dear mama were here to write to me.' She wiped her eyes with the corner of her apron.

'Now don't *you* start, Sarah, you'll set me off – you know I turn to jelly at the sight of tears,' said Mrs Briskett. 'Who's your other letter from, Hetty?'

'I don't know, Mrs Briskett,' I said – although there was something faintly familiar about the firm bold print. I saw the postmark and gave a little gasp. I opened it up, and my eyes skimmed down the page to the signature at the bottom: *Your ever-loving Jem.*

'Oh, my Lord!'

'Well?' said Mrs Briskett.

'It's from – from my foster brother!' I said. 'Do you not remember the young man waiting outside the hospital, Mrs Briskett? I didn't recognize him at first, but it was really him! Oh, if only I had stopped for a few words! I did beg you, remember?'

'You don't consort with family and friends when you're off to start in your first position, Hetty Feather,' said Mrs Briskett. 'Now, put your letters away till later, and go and help Sarah turn out the bedrooms – and no dawdling neither, because

515

there's the potatoes and the carrots to peel, and two pounds of peas to pod, *and* all the Bramleys for my apple pie. He's very fond of my apple pie, is the master.'

I had to tuck Jem's letter away under my apron, where it crackled unread all the long morning. I had to wait until after luncheon. Mrs Briskett found she was running short of sugar and needed cloves for her apple pie, so she sent me off to Dedman's, the grocer's.

'Just find your way back into town and it's the big shop on the corner. You can't miss it,' she said. 'Mind you hurry back though, missy. No daydreaming!'

She wound a shawl round me and watched me from the back door. I ran up the area steps and set off smartly, swinging my arms in a business-like fashion.

'You're going the wrong way, Hetty Feather! Feather*brain*, that's what you are! Go *left* for the town. Dear Lord, what shall I do with you?'

I turned on my heel and walked back the other way, feeling foolish. Mrs Briskett watched me, shaking her head. I hurried to get out of her sight. It felt so very odd to be out alone after all those years of being cooped up in the hospital. It reminded me of the time I ran away, when Queen Victoria had her Golden Jubilee. I supposed I could

run away now. Run away where though? Run away
. . . home?

I took the unread letter from under my apron,
leaned against the park railings, and read it
through.

Dear Hetty,

*Yes, it WAS me at the hospital gates. I could
not believe it when you walked straight past me.
I had pictured our meeting for so long and I had
always seen us running into each other's arms. I
was so dumbfounded I couldn't move. I just
stood there dithering until it was too late. I
wondered if you felt too grand to speak to me
now, walking along with the lady in her red town
gown. I feared you had forgotten me altogether,
though you swore you'd remember me for ever!*

*When Mother received notification from the
hospital, saying you were leaving to go into
service on 14th May, I decided I would come all
the way to London to wish you well. I so hoped we
might be able to spend a little time together. I've
longed to know how you are faring. You looked
quite the grown-up young lady, but still my little
Hetty too.*

*Do you not remember those rare times we had
together when you were little? Do you remember
our secret squirrel tree? We had so many dear*

funny little games. They were such happy times.

Please write and tell me how you are doing, and reassure me that you still keep a place in your heart for

Your affectionate foster brother,

Jem

I seemed to have been holding my breath the whole time I was reading the letter. I breathed out, my head throbbing, having to cling to the railings to stay upright.

Your *affectionate* brother Jem. My own dear Jem, the sweet boy who had once meant all the world to me. But he still hadn't mentioned Eliza, though I had specifically quizzed him in my letter. Had he not made *her* his own special darling after I'd left home? He'd filled her little head with nonsense too – *our* nonsense, all my own imaginary games.

It had felt like such a betrayal that I'd resolved never to think of Jem again. I thought he must long ago have forgotten me – and yet he had journeyed all the way from the country to see me. He must have got up before dawn, travelling on the milk train, and then somehow found his way through the busy streets of London to the hospital. He had waited there. I had walked straight past.

Oh Lordy, how could I have been so stupid? I was

the one standing dithering now, wondering what to do. I could beg on the streets until I had enough for the train fare, and then rush back home to my dear Jem . . . But what then? I still had to earn my living. My foster sisters Rosie and Big Eliza had had to go into service. If I walked out of my position with Mr Buchanan, I would never get a character reference. And what would Mama say to that?

I sighed and leaned against the park railings – and then shrieked when a very wet tongue licked the back of my hand through the bars. I whirled round, shrieking, and waved my arms in fear and horror at the huge slavering beast attempting to swallow my hand for breakfast. Was it a small bear? A black panther? A wolf?

'Help! Help!' I shrieked.

'Hey, hey, don't take fright! Tommy wouldn't hurt a flea, little miss,' an old man cried.

'Are you sure?' I said, still backing away rapidly and wiping my assaulted hand. 'What kind of an animal is it?'

The old man looked at me as if I were completely mad. ''Tis only a Labrador, miss.'

When I failed to look reassured he shook his head sorrowfully. 'A *dog*, miss,' he said, in the clear loud tone you'd use for a lunatic.

Oh dear, a dog! I could not believe I had reacted so ridiculously. I had seen pictures of dogs in books.

I remembered Rover in one of the elementary readers in the Infants at the hospital, but Rover had been a scrappy little creature, not a great fiend with enormous jaws. Had there not been dogs on the farm, then? I thought hard and remembered something running like the wind, barking at all the sheep. I had run too, rolling around in the grass, oblivious to his snapping jaws. What was the matter with me? How had I been fearless at four when I was so cowed now, barely able to say boo to a goose?

I reached through the park railings and very gingerly patted Tommy's big black head. He panted happily, drooling in delight. 'Good boy,' I murmured faintly.

Then I tucked Jem's letter away beside Mama's, bade the old man goodbye, and set off into town. It still felt as if I were trekking through steamy jungles, trudging over arid deserts, wading through crocodile-infested rivers as I made my way down the quiet suburban streets. I wondered if I'd ever get used to life outside the hospital. I didn't seem to have any sense of direction whatsoever, and had to ask twice before I found my way to the main shops – and then ask a third time before I got to Dedman's, the luxury grocer's.

This was such a delightful emporium that I forgot all my fear and trepidation and tiptoed around the dark interior, gazing in awe at the shining jars of jam and fruit and pickles, the sugar loaves, the great wheels of cheese, the glazed sides of bacon, the huge sacks of rice and sultanas and prunes. A little boy had run away from his nurse-maid and was kneeling in front of these sacks, delightedly scooping up great handfuls of dried fruit. I had to clench my fists to stop myself joining him. I remembered stealing just two or three sultanas when I was helping in the hospital kitchen – and the stinging punishment inflicted by Matron Stinking Bottomly when she caught me red-handed and sticky-fingered.

'How can I help you, young missy?' said a tall man with a drooping moustache and a white apron right down to his boots.

I murmured a request for cloves and sugar, and he weighed them out and handed them to me in a brown paper parcel. 'That'll be sixpence halfpenny, please.'

I stared at him. Of course, I had to pay for them – but I didn't have any money! I felt myself blushing crimson. The tall man stroked his moustache expectantly while I shifted from one foot to the other. Was I going to have to trail home and ask for the money from Mrs Briskett and then come all the way back again?

'Which account shall I charge, missy?' the man

asked.

'Oh! Well, I work for a Mr Buchanan—'

'Then it'll be Mrs Briskett's account,' he said, nodding his head as if I were a very lucky girl. 'Mrs Briskett will train you up nicely. She's an excellent woman. As indeed is Miss Sarah. She's a very fine parlourmaid. You tell her I'm looking forward to seeing her at our Sunday evening soiree.'

Yes, sir,' I said, and backed out of the shop, after one more longing glance at the dried fruit sacks.

Good Lord, was Sarah *courting*? And if so, why was it right for her to see the moustache man on a Sunday, and wrong for me to see Bertie the butcher's boy? Not that I *wanted* to go for a stroll with Bertie. I was not interested in boys.

I felt the bib of my apron so that my letters crackled inside. What about Jem? Was I 'interested' in him? I thought back yet again to those moments at the hospital gates. I wished I could step back in time and have another go at leaving the hospital.

Yes, I'm coming out the gates with Mrs Briskett in her meaty red attire, and there is this tall, good-looking young man in rustic corduroy. Our eyes meet.

'Oh my goodness, it's Jem! My dear long-lost brother Jem!' I say, so that Mrs Briskett cannot possibly object.

'My dear little Hetty, I knew you wouldn't forget

me,' Jem breathes.

'Bless you, dearies,' says Mrs Briskett. 'Here, let us repair to a tea room – we can all have a bite to eat, and you two can catch up with each other, and then . . . and then . . .'

And then indeed! As if Mrs Briskett would permit such a meeting in any case. I resolved to write a longer, more regretful letter to Jem that night – and one to Mama too, of course.

I actually managed to find my way home without having to ask for directions even once. Tommy was still careering around the park, the old man throwing sticks for him. The dog bounded over in my direction, and I couldn't help prickling with alarm all over again, but I managed to wave at him nonchalantly enough.

I reached Mr Buchanan's house feeling reasonably proud of myself, but Mrs Briskett was frowning.

'Dear goodness, girl, did you travel to Timbuktu for the cloves and sugar? I've had my pastry ready for hours!'

'Don't be cross with me, Mrs Briskett,' I said. 'Oh, isn't Dedman's a wondrous shop!'

'What's that you've got all over your dress, young lady?' Sarah asked, brushing at me. I was covered with rust from leaning against the park railings. 'Dear goodness, can't you keep clean for two minutes? You've got to wear that dress till you make yourself another one, so think on and try to keep it spotless.'

'Mr Dedman sent you a special message, Sarah,' I said softly, not sure she'd want Mrs Briskett to overhear.

Mrs Briskett snorted all the same. 'Mr *Dedman* sent her a message?' she said. 'I very much doubt it, seeing as, true to his name, he's been a dead man these past ten years.'

'Well, *someone* sent you a message. A tall man with a funny moustache. He said he thought you an excellent woman and was looking forward to seeing you at your Sunday soiree.'

Mrs Briskett snorted so loudly this time that stuff came out of her nose and she had to grab her pocket handkerchief and mop it up hastily.

'Really, Mrs B,' said Sarah, looking offended. 'I hope you're not laughing at me.'

'Perhaps you'll hear a message from a *real* dead man!' said Mrs Briskett, tapping Sarah over the knuckles with her wooden spoon.

'Do not mock things you don't understand,' said Sarah huffily, and swept from the room.

'Hoity-toity!' Mrs Briskett called after her, but she looked a little worried now. 'Dear Lord, that girl needs her head examined. I don't hold with that sort of caper. It's not right, and no one can convince me otherwise.'

'What sort of caper? What did the message mean? What's going on?' I asked, all agog.

'Ask me no questions and I'll tell you no lies,' said Mrs Briskett, and wouldn't say another word.

When I tried asking Sarah later, she shook her head at me too. 'It's private, Hetty. You wouldn't understand,' she said. 'Now button your lip and get on with your work.'

I certainly *didn't* understand. I didn't understand so many things about this strange outside world. It felt as if I'd stepped out of the hospital onto another planet.

7

I saw very little of Mr Buchanan each day, though I became all too intimate with his personal linen and his chamber pot. Mrs Briskett and Sarah still sent me up to his cluttered study to serve afternoon tea, but after our first conversation and my bold request for stamps, we did not talk further. I knocked at his door at four o'clock, and then edged my way into his room, bearing my tray of freshly brewed tea and *wondrous* cakes: Victoria sponge, orange and lemon cake, chocolate gateau, cherry and sultana slices, fruit tartlets, iced butterfly cakes – oh, the joys of Mrs Briskett's baking!

Mr Buchanan rarely looked up from his blotchy manuscript as I entered the study. When I returned half an hour later to collect his tray, most of his cakes were nibbled, but he frequently left a slab here, a slice here.

'Don't you want to finish up all your cake, sir?' I asked.

'Mm?' Mr Buchanan squinted at me through his

527

spectacles as if he wasn't quite sure who I was. He smacked his thin lips ruminatively, considering. 'No, not just at the moment. I am far too busy writing.'

Now, I considered myself an overly eager writer, but it never interfered with *my* appetite. How could the wretched man leave a large slice of sponge utterly untouched? This was a particularly beguiling sponge too, positively oozing raspberry jam and thick buttercream! Mrs Briskett commented on his increased appetite, however, because *somehow* his plate of cake diminished radically as I carried his tray back to the kitchen. I nodded happily, licking away the crumbs from my mouth.

I wished Mr Buchanan could somehow be winkled out of his study. He shuffled in even before breakfast, and was frequently muttering away there late at night. Sarah sighed and shook her head because she could rarely give it a little dust, let alone subject it to a proper weekly turn-out. I sighed too, because I was all too aware of the stamps in his desk drawer.

I wrote weekly to dearest Mama, and I also seemed to have embarked on a regular correspondence with Jem. (More about this later!) I badly needed stamps, and Mr Buchanan had many. I couldn't help thinking that perhaps he wouldn't miss just a couple.

I knew that stealing was wrong – a very, very bad

thing to do – but I didn't see that I had any alternative. Well, during the daytime, I thought that, and had the actual theft all worked out in my mind: I would wait until Mr Buchanan vacated his room at last – on a visit to his publishers? A meal at the chop house with an old friend? A stroll around the garden to clear his head? Even a fleeting trip to his splendid water closet? There *had* to be some opportunity when I could whisk into his room, duster in hand. Even if Sarah accompanied me, it should not be too difficult for me to slide that little desk drawer open beneath my duster, and grab a handful of precious stamps. I even practised the action, two fingers raised beneath the imaginary duster, two fingers intent on pulling the little knob of the door and lifting out the stamps.

By day I could rehearse this eagerly – but every night I dreamed I'd actually performed the deed. I did not get caught by Sarah or Mr Buchanan himself, but I felt *observed* all the same. I had attended chapel at the hospital every week for nine whole years. It had been drummed into me that God was omnipresent. I imagined a Supreme Being striding through the city on colossal legs, bending down and applying his huge holy orb to the window of Mr Buchanan's study. He'd shake his great and glorious head in horror. He'd not threaten me with Hell. No, far worse: he'd grow great angel's wings, fly straight to Mama and tell her that her only child was a common thief. Mama would shake with tears of shame – and I'd wake up with tears running down my own cheeks.

I could not do it. But I *so* needed those stamps. As soon as I had my first quarter's wages I could purchase my own and replenish them, I reasoned to myself. But that was months away. Perhaps I could simply *ask* Mr Buchanan for more stamps? But he'd been reluctant to give me more than one; he had clearly thought himself excessively generous to give me a handful. Would he not think me ungratefully greedy if I begged for more?

I could explain truthfully enough that I was devoted to Mama. I could even say that she was not very well. In one of her letters she had mentioned that she had a slight cough and had entreated me to wrap up as warmly as possible and rub goosegrease on my chest to prevent myself from catching a similar chill. I could exaggerate her illness and say I was unduly worried about her. But this might tempt the Superior Being to smite her in order to punish me. And I now had *two* correspondents. Even if Mr Buchanan was excessively understanding about my need to write regularly to Mama because she was my dear relation, he would never slot Jem into the same category, even though he was my foster brother.

I resolved all the same to *try* asking Mr Buchanan for more stamps. He could always say no. It wasn't a *crime* to ask, unlike stealing.

My hands were trembling the next day as I lugged the tea tray upstairs (containing a pot of Earl Grey with lemon slices, several portions of buttered malt bread, and a scone fresh out of the oven, with a little pot of strawberry jam and another of whipped cream – I hoped Mr Buchanan's appetite was birdlike today).

I put down the tray, took a deep breath, and knocked smartly on the door. I was a little *too* smart. I clearly made Mr Buchanan start, because he cried out. When I went into his room, I discovered he'd blotched his page with ink.

'What's the matter with you, Hetty? You banged on the door like a veritable thunderbolt. Now look at this page! I shall have to copy it all over again.' He blotted and sighed, while I endeavoured to find a resting place for his tea and cakes.

I saw over his shoulder that he was in the habit of making blots even without sharp knocks at his door. Although he had a whole sheaf of blotting paper, he did not use it effectively, because several pages were badly smudged. Even where they were totally unsullied, it would be a terrible task to figure out more than a few words because his handwriting was such a spidery scrawl.

'Goodness, sir, how do your publishers read your stories?' I asked.

'With great difficulty! They complain bitterly, and suggest I find myself a secretary to copy out my manuscript in a fair hand. I am sure it will incur too much expense, however, and I would find working with some young lady too much of a distraction,' said Mr Buchanan, wiping his spectacles, smearing them more thoroughly in the process.

My heart started thumping. 'Would you find *me* a distraction, sir?' I asked, bowing my head and hunching my shoulders, trying to make myself seem even smaller, so that he might see me as part of the study – an inkstand, say, or a volume of poetry.

Mr Buchanan blinked at me.

'*I* could transcribe your work, sir, a little at a time. I have a very clear hand, and I never ever blot. We used to get our knuckles rapped at the hospital if we blotted, and it made us extra careful.'

'But what of your duties around the house?'

'Oh, I am sure I could fit in an hour or so in the afternoons, when I would otherwise be mending. I could get up early and go to bed later to fit in any sewing. Sarah says I am very neat at darning,' I added, wanting to put myself in the best possible light.

Mr Buchanan sipped his tea and nibbled a

corner of his malt bread, contemplating. 'Give me an example of this fine hand, Hetty Feather,' he said, holding out his pen and a clean sheet of paper.

'Certainly, sir,' I said.

I had nowhere to sit, and hardly any room to rest the paper, but I dipped the pen confidently in the ink, tapping it on the edge of the bottle, making sure it was not so full that it would drip and not so empty that it might scratch. I commenced writing in a clear, careful copperplate:

Dear Mr Buchanan,

Please let Hetty Feather copy out your stories for you. She has an excellent hand, as you can see for yourself. You will not regret it, I promise you.

Yours respectfully,

Hetty Feather, maid of all work and potential excellent secretary

Mr Buchanan read it out loud, giving the sparse hair under his fez a little scratch, so that he seemed more monkey-like than ever – especially when he gave a little screech and bared all his teeth: this was laughter!

'Very well, I am convinced. If Mrs Briskett and Sarah can spare you for an hour every afternoon, then you may come and copy my work. It may help you with your own compositions, child. You will have a chance to study my grammar and learn complex vocabulary.'

'Yes, sir – and that will *almost* be reward enough in itself.'

'*Almost?*' He peered at me, chin on clasped hands.

'Well, sir, you did say that employing a secretary would incur considerable extra expense—'

He frowned at me. 'You surely aren't suggesting that I pay you an extra wage, Hetty Feather?' he enquired.

'Oh no, sir, that would be ridiculously impertinent,' I said quickly. 'But perhaps you might see fit to proffer me with a very tiny reward every now and then?'

'A *reward*?'

'Perhaps a stamp?'

'A stamp?' (There he was, boasting about his vocabulary and grammar, but all he seemed capable of was repeating *my* nouns).

'Or two? Or three or four or five?' I said, risking all. 'I write to Mama a great deal, sir, and I have already used up the stamps you so generously gave me.'

He took another morsel of malt bread. 'Mm. Well, I will give you a weekly stamp allowance, Hetty Feather, so long as you work quietly and neatly and do not neglect your household

534

duties. Now, off you go. Take the tray with you.'

'But you've scarcely touched your tea, sir.'

'I have had sufficient, thank you.'

So I took his tray and dawdled on my way back to the kitchen, celebrating my stamp-earning success by eating his scone smothered with a jarful of jam and a jug full of cream.

Mrs Briskett and Sarah were astonished when I told them of my new duties.

'How can a little orphan like you write posh enough to please the master?' Mrs Briskett said indignantly.

'I'm *not* an orphan. I have a lovely dear mama,' I said.

'Show us this writing, then, Hetty,' said Sarah, fetching the kitchen pencil and some brown wrapping paper.

'Well, I really need ink and proper paper,' I said.

'Ah!' said Sarah, convinced I couldn't follow through.

'But I will do my best to demonstrate even so,' I said.

I wrote, in an excessively swirly and elaborate hand:

I am Hetty Feather and I am a maid of all work, and Mrs Briskett and Sarah are very kind to me and teach me my duties.

Mrs Briskett and Sarah read my message aloud, slowly, almost as if it were a struggle. Sarah said each word a beat behind Mrs Briskett.

'Can't you read properly, Sarah?' I asked, astonished.

'Of course I can read,' she said, pouting. 'It's just you write in such a fancy way. It's hard to make out the lettering.'

'But she does write it lovely,' said Mrs Briskett. 'You're a funny little slyboots, Hetty Feather. You've only been here five minutes and you're ingratiating yourself with the master something chronic.'

'Yes, what's your little game, Hetty? Why would you take on all this extra fancy writing work. Is it just to show off to the rest of us?' said Sarah.

'No, of course not,' I said fiercely, though perhaps this accounted for ten per cent of my motivation. 'I seized the opportunity so that I could ask a favour from Mr Buchanan.'

'Aha!' said Sarah. 'So we're right, Mrs B! What sort of favour, eh?'

'Stamps,' I said.

They peered at me.

'So I can write regularly to Mama.'

'Oh, my dear – oh, *now* I understand!' said Sarah. 'Would that I could write to my own mother! Isn't that touching, Mrs B?'

536

'Yes, I suppose it is,' said Mrs Briskett, beaming at me. 'What a dear good daughter you are, Hetty Feather. Here, sit yourself down, and try one of my scones. They're fresh out of the oven and extra light today. See, even Mr Buchanan has eaten his up, every crumb.'

So I sat and ate my second scone, glowing. I hadn't told a lie at all. I just hadn't told them that I was also writing to Jem.

My initial reply had been brief:

Dear Jem,

    Of course I remember everything about my little-girlhood. I remember our special squirrel tree. I remember every single one of our special games. They meant a great deal to me. Every night at the hospital I would think of the happy times we spent.

    I know little Eliza thinks of almost identical happy times. She is convinced you will be waiting for HER when she is fourteen.

    Kind regards,

    Your sister Hetty

There! I thought that would show him. I did not really expect to hear back from him. But within a *day* I received another reply. Luckily it was one of my tasks to collect the letters when they fluttered through the letterbox onto the hall mat. I saw several dull-looking bills and circulars to be served up to Mr Buchanan on a little silver tray like sweet-meats – but also a letter addressed to me in Jem's distinctive hand.

Dear Hetty,

I think from the tone of your letter that you are angry with me. Surely it is not because I tried so hard to be a good brother to little Eliza? I was so achingly lonely after you'd gone to the hospital. I don't think you have any idea how much I missed you. Eliza was a restless baby who cried a great deal. I had always had a knack of soothing you, so I did my best to calm her too – and as she got older I did sometimes play 'our' games with her, to amuse her and console myself. She is a sweet child and I was very fond of her – but she never meant anywhere near as much to me as you. You must know that.

Please tell me more about your new position and whether it truly suits you.

With deepest affection I am still
Your Jem

I read this letter many times. It was like a salve to a deep wound. So Jem truly preferred me to Eliza! I felt a thrill of happiness – and then a prickle of guilt. Poor little Eliza, still fantasizing about Jem marrying her one day. Jem should never have let her think that. He had not behaved admirably – but he said he had been so lonely. *Achingly* lonely. For me!

I found myself whirling round and round the rooms as I dusted, running up the stairs two at a time, singing cheerily as I scrubbed and peeled and polished.

Jem still cared about me. He was still my secret sweetheart. And maybe one day . . .

8

I went with Mrs Briskett and Sarah to the servants' church service early on Sunday afternoon. It was a chance for me to peer around and see many new people. I stared in dismay at all the other girls. I felt so plain and shabby in my grey print frock and borrowed shawl. Mrs Briskett was wearing her meat-red costume, and Sarah sported an alarmingly purple velvet dress and mantle, fringed and tassled.

I did not care for either of their outfits, but I hung my head miserably all the same. I did not even have a bonnet, and had to cover my hair with my borrowed shawl.

'Dear, dear, we'll have to fashion you a proper Sunday outfit, Hetty,' said Mrs Briskett, twitching at my dress. 'If I gave you my old Sunday best, Sarah, do you think you could cut it down so it fitted young Hetty?'

'I'll see what I can do,' said Sarah. 'There, Hetty! Say thank you to Mrs B. What a kind offer!'

'Thank you very much, both of you,' I said. I very much hoped Mrs Briskett's former Sunday best wasn't red.

They sat me between them, spreading their skirts as if they wanted to hide me. I felt like an ugly little weed between two great overblown roses. When the service started, they pulled me up for the hymns and pushed me down for the reading of the lesson, though I had been attending church services weekly for nine years and knew exactly what to do. Mrs Briskett and Sarah nodded approvingly to each other when I sang each hymn without looking at the words and muttered the correct responses to the prayers.

'Well, you might look a drab mite in your work clothes, but you *act* like a good little Christian,' Mrs Briskett whispered.

She meant it as a compliment, but I felt more self-conscious than ever. There were two girls in the pew in front who kept looking round and nudging each other and giggling, clearly amused by me. When Mrs Briskett and Sarah closed their eyes at the start of a prayer, I pulled a hideous face at the girls. They both squealed, and an older lady leaned over and tapped them hard on their fancy bonnets, much to my satisfaction.

When it came to his sermon, the vicar in St John's droned on for an unconscionable time. I yawned and fidgeted and picked the hangnails of my sore fingers. He told us how lucky we were to serve our masters and mistresses, because that way we were serving God. We might be lowly servants here on earth, but if we were humble and hard-working, we'd step up through Heaven's gate and as angels lead a grand life free of toil. I did not find this argument particularly convincing. Why was it *our* place to serve here on earth? Why couldn't we all take it in turns?

I imagined sitting in Mr Buchanan's padded wing chair in his study, reading and writing at my leisure, while he dusted and scrubbed. It was a delightful idea, and I smiled.

'Look at little Hetty taking it all in, bless her,' Mrs Briskett whispered to Sarah.

She gave me a penny from her purse to put in the collection plate. I rather badly wanted to keep the penny for myself, and wondered if I could keep it tucked in the palm of my hand. I remembered the lucky sixpence Jem had given me the day I left for the hospital. I'd kept it in my mouth, I was so determined not to relinquish it. I had eventually hidden it in the knob of my bed-stead – but someone had stolen it long ago. I wondered if Jem had given Eliza a sixpence too.

I held my hand over the plate, clenching my palm muscles to keep hold of the penny, but Mrs

Briskett gave me a little nudge, waiting to hear a clink. I let go of the coin with a sigh.

We walked home from church – and there, sitting on the area steps, was Bertie the butcher's boy.

I felt my face going the colour of Mrs Briskett's costume. I hadn't thought he would really come calling for me. I rather wished he hadn't. I had Jem now, so I didn't want any other boy in my life, thank you very much.

'What are you doing sitting here, making my steps look untidy, boy?' said Mrs Briskett.

'Ain't it obvious, Mrs B? I've been waiting to see you three lovely ladies come home from church,' said Bertie. He blinked his eyes in an exaggerated fashion. 'My, you're a dazzling sight – enough to unsettle a simple lad like me.'

'You're simple, all right,' said Sarah, swatting at him with her hymn book.

'Why weren't you in church too, you bad boy?' said Mrs Briskett.

'Is the church a place for miserable sinners, Mrs B?'

'Of course it is!'

'Ah, but you see, I'm *not* a miserable sinner. I'm a very cheerful little saint, so I don't need no churching, do I?'

'You need a good hiding, that's what you need,'

said Sarah, untying her bonnet strings. 'Don't you let our Hetty go walking with that boy, Mrs B – or he'll lead her astray.'

'I don't have any evil intentions!' said Bertie indignantly. 'I just want to show her around a little, her being brought up in that queer hospital. She needs to see a bit more of the world than your kitchen and scullery, Mrs B, excellent and immaculate though they are.'

'Listen to him!' said Mrs Briskett. 'He's got such a way with words he sets your head spinning. Well, take young Hetty off for a nice little walk, then. Just for an hour or two, mind. We have early supper now, seeing as *one* of us chooses to go out gallivant-ing of a Sunday evening, meddling with all sorts.'

'I'll thank you to hold your tongue and mind your own business, Mrs B,' said Sarah haughtily, and flounced indoors.

'That gullible girl,' said Mrs Briskett, sighing and sucking her teeth. 'Now, you behave yourself, young Hetty, and be back here by half past five – well, six at the latest. And you behave yourself too, boy, or I'll be after you and I'll box your ears good and proper.' She bustled through the back door, still issuing dire warnings.

Bertie rolled his eyes at me. 'Them two old birds, fuss fuss fuss! How do you stand it, Hetty?'

'They're all right. They mean well,' I said

awkwardly. I didn't like them fussing either, but I found I didn't care to hear Bertie criticizing them. In a short space of time they'd become almost like family.

'Come on, then,' said he, stepping out jauntily.

He was wearing *his* Sunday best – a brown suit, a little tight, and shiny in the seat, with such a stiff starched collar he had to hold his head up high the whole time. His unruly hair was slicked down flat, perhaps with perfume, because he smelled power-fully sweet.

Two smirking young girls from church walked past arm in arm, tossing their heads in their dainty bonnets and swishing their fine velvet skirts. They obviously knew Bertie, because they nudged each other and grinned and giggled – and then turned their noses up at me. I pulled a ferocious face again, but I didn't smooth it out quickly enough. Bertie saw and stared at me.

'Well, that's a happy face! What are you looking like that for?'

'I'm not pulling a face at you. I'm pulling a face at them,' I said, nodding over my shoulder at the girls.

'Why's that, then?' said Bertie, swaggering. 'Did you see them making those sheep's eyes at me? Don't take it to heart, Hetty. I can't help if they're a little bit sweet on me. They work in the draper's over the road from us, so we're on nodding terms, but there's nothing serious between us, I swear.'

'Don't be so full of yourself, it's very annoying. I didn't give a hoot about the way they were looking at *you*. I minded the way they looked at *me*.'

'What way was that, Hetty?' He sounded puzzled, as if he truly didn't have any idea.

'They looked down their pretty little noses because I'm small and plain and haven't got any bright fancy Sunday clothes. I just have to go out in my drab daily work dress.'

'What?' said Bertie. 'Look, I *like* you being so small. It makes me feel almost big, see. And you've got a dear little face, with the biggest blue eyes.'

'Yes, they are my best feature. Sapphire blue.'

'There you are, then. And you don't need any bright fancy clothes, not with your flaming hair. It's all the colour you need.'

'Do you really think so?' I said.

'Course I do. Now come on, step lively, we've a long way to go, and if I don't get you back by six o'clock, old Mother Briskett will chop the rest of my fingers off and serve them up in a fricassé on toast.'

I walked beside him, almost running to keep up with his brisk step.

'So do you think my blue eyes make up for my being plain?' I asked, after a minute.

Bertie burst out laughing. 'My, for a little orphan girl you act like a princess at times, wanting all the compliments,' he said.

'I'm *not* an orphan.'

'All right, all right – you're not an orphan. And you're not plain neither. You're pretty as a picture. Happy now?'

I found I *was* happy as I stepped out beside him. I peered around at all the people on the pavement: girls walking with linked arms, boys in small clusters, couples walking along sedately, with little children running ahead bowling hoops. It still seemed so extraordinary that people were free to wander where they wanted, while all the foundlings were locked up in the hospital month after month, year after year.

'What's up *now*?' said Bertie, seeing my expression change.

'Nothing. I was just thinking back—'

'No, you don't want to do that. The trick is to think *forward*, see. Come on, Hetty, step out.'

'Where are we going, then?'

'You'll see when we get there – but you'll like it, I promise.'

'Is it . . . the country?'

'What? No, don't be silly, I'm a city lad. I don't want to take you where it's all messy and muddy, and the folk are a bit backward and suck straws, and all the men lumber about in them frocks.'

'*Smocks.*'

'Well, they look ridiculous on a gent, whatever you call them. Great lummocks, they look.'

'No they don't!' I said fiercely. I remembered my foster father's smock – the warm earthy smell of it, the tickle of the stitching against my cheek when I cuddled up close. It had seemed the most manly of garments then. I wondered if Jem wore a smock nowadays.

'You know nothing about the country and country ways,' I said to Bertie. 'It's beautiful in the country.' I thought of the cottage where I'd lived for five happy years. It shimmered in my mind – the cosy thatch, the roses and hollyhocks, the open fire, the inglenook, the little bedrooms under the eaves. I had to sniff to stop myself bursting into tears.

'Hey now, don't upset yourself! I didn't mean to cause any offence. Heaven save us if we're arguing already!'

'I lived in the country when I was a little girl,' I said.

'Well, that's fine and dandy, then. You can be my little Hetty Hayseed. Just blink those sapphire-blue eyes and look happy again, eh?'

'My mother was going to call me Sapphire,' I said proudly. 'That was her secret name for me.'

'Really? Gawd knows what *my* mother's name for me was. Trouble, most likely – or Mr-Bawl-his-head-off,' said Bertie.

We walked past the park where I'd met Tommy, the huge hound. I looked for him hopefully, wanting to show off that I knew such a fierce animal, but he wasn't bounding around today. There was a cricket match taking place, so we peered through the railings to watch for a minute or two.

'Seems like it's the slowest game on the planet,' said Bertie. 'Still, the chaps look good in their fancy whites. Are you a sporty girl, Hetty? You look like a whippy little thing. Good at running, are you?'

'I don't know,' I said. 'The girls at the hospital didn't do sports, only the boys. I think perhaps I'd *like* to run.'

'Well, when we get out of town you'll get a chance to run, I promise.'

We went along the main shopping street.

'There's Dedman's the grocer. I've shopped there,' I said proudly.

'I'll show you my shop, shall I – though it don't look right all shut up on a Sunday, without all the meat hanging outside.' Bertie pointed out Jarvis the master butcher's, and showed me all the other shops too, telling me tales of all the folk who worked there. I yawned ostentatiously when he spoke about the draper's shop, and silly simpering Kitty and Ivy who worked there.

'You seem to know everyone, Bertie,' I said.

'That's right, I do. But they don't know *me*. They just think I'm Jarvis's boy, the cheeky lad who gives them lip. They don't even know my name, most of them.'

'You told me your name straight off.'

'Yes, because I knew you were different. I sensed it as soon as I saw you. We're children of circumstance, you and me, Hetty. We're going to have to make our own way in the world.'

'That's right,' I said, smiling at him.

'Come on, then – not too far to go now.'

The shops petered out. We went down shabby alleyways, past warehouses and a reeking fishery.

'Is *this* your favourite place?' I asked, wrinkling my nose.

'Patience, Miss Sarcastic. You'll like it, you really will,' said Bertie.

He led me onwards, down further alleyways, and then under the bridge by the railway. It was very dark.

'Bertie?' I said nervously.

'It's fine,' he said, taking my hand. 'It echoes – listen: *Hello, Hetty Feather!*'

Ten Bertie voices shouted hello from every angle. I laughed, and ten Hettys laughed too.

'*I'm not Hetty, I'm Sapphire Battersea!*' I shouted at the top of my lungs – and the darkness sang out my special name in a magnificent chorus.

Then we were out on the other side of the bridge, and it was as if we'd stepped into another world entirely. We were down by the river. I'd seen the Thames before, but only in the middle of London, slick with grease and stinking to high heaven. The river here was fresh and sparkling, and little rowing boats and canoes bobbed up and down on the waves.

We were in a long green park by the riverside, crowded with Sunday-afternoon revellers enjoying the sunshine.

'Take a little run, Hetty!' said Bertie.

I hitched up my skirt and charged ahead. I thought I was running fast, but Bertie easily overtook me. We stopped to catch our breath, both of us laughing. There was a little stand in the middle of the grass with a brass band playing, the men in stripped blazers and straw hats. Couples sat on little white chairs, and children ran about, whirling round and round to the music.

Bertie and I sat and listened too. He sang along with the music – saucy words to jolly tunes.

'Don't you know this one too, Hetty?'

'I've only ever heard hymns or harvest songs,' I said.

'I'll take you to the music hall one day,' Bertie promised. 'Fancy a boat ride now?'

'Can we really?'

'You bet we can!'

He paid for the hire of a rowing boat for half an hour. It was great fun getting into the boat, because it tipped like crazy and we wobbled about. Bertie very nearly tumbled in headfirst, clearly not quite as experienced a boatman as he was making out.

I seized the oars excitedly.

'That's my job!' said Bertie.

'Oh, let me try, please!' I begged.

It wasn't as simple as I'd thought. It proved really hard work just pulling the oars together through the water. My arms couldn't pull with equal strength, and the boat started spinning in a circle.

'You're making me dizzy,' Bertie laughed. 'Come on, let me show you.'

He took the oars and rowed us swiftly along beside the river bank. 'You just sit back and enjoy yourself,' he said.

I was a little irritated, but I sat back obediently, trailing my hand in the water. There were so many boats bobbing about us that I kept calling out, worried we'd crash, but Bertie steered us in and out and round about, and soon we were gliding along in deeper waters.

'Can't I have another go now, please, Bertie?' I begged.

He let me try again, and I started to get the hang of it at last, though every now and then my oar missed the water altogether or I 'caught a crab'.

'You're doing very well, Hetty, but it looks bad, a puny little girl rowing a strong lad like me. Let me take charge to save my blushes,' said Bertie, removing his jacket and rolling up his sleeves.

'You just want to show off those muscles,' I said, but I let him have his way.

He rowed us swiftly to a little island in the middle of the river, where he moored the boat. 'There, let's have a bit of rest here. You could have a little paddle if you wanted, Hetty.'

'I think I'll do just that! Turn your back while I take off my stockings, then.'

I kicked off my ugly boots, rolled down my itchy woollen stockings and stepped into the water. It came up to my knees, so I had to hold my dress up to stop the hem getting soaked.

'You'd better keep your back turned, Bertie,' I said, capering about.

He peeked at me, of course, but I didn't get cross. I didn't really care. It just felt so delicious to have my hot sore feet in the cold water. I remembered paddling in the stream with Jem years back, and felt a fierce pang for him now. I wished I was with *him* – and yet Bertie was fun too, far better company than I'd thought he'd be.

He smiled at me from the grassy bank, waving his arms about to ease them. He was barely an inch taller than me, but he really did have great strong muscles – which of course he flexed ostentatiously when he saw me watching.

'You're like a little water baby,' he said as I splashed about. 'Why don't you go right in swimming?'

'For two pins I would,' I said, wishing I was young enough to tumble in nearly naked like some little children further up the bank.

'You're a girl and a half, you are, Hetty. So, you like my special place, yes?'

'I like it very much,' I said, coming to sit beside him.

'And do you like *me*?' he asked, looking me straight in the eye.

'I reckon I do like you, Bertie,' I said, but when he tried to take my hand, I swatted his away. 'None of that now! No romancing!'

'Go on, Hetty, just let me put my arm round you – to keep you from falling in.'

'You're the one in danger of falling in if you don't

watch out,' I said, giving him a little poke. The sweet smell of his perfume was overpowering in the heat.

'What's up? Why are you wrinkling that little nose of yours?' he asked.

'I thought it was ladies who were meant to wear the perfume,' I said.

He wriggled, looking uncomfortable. 'Sorry. I do stink a bit, I know. I just poured Jarvis's pomade all over me because I didn't want to smell of meat, see.'

'Oh, Bertie.' I took his hand voluntarily now. 'You smell fine. Thank you for bringing me here. It's truly lovely.'

'I'd like a little house here, right on the island. Wouldn't it be grand to wake up to the sound of water lapping all around? I've often toyed with the idea of throwing in my job with old Jarvis and running off to sea,' he said dreamily.

'My father was a sailor,' I said. 'Well, so I've been told. I've never met him. He ran off before I was born.'

'My pa did likewise. I don't even know who he was. Could have been Old Nick for all I know or care. Well, lovely as it is, I'd better get you back. We'll have to hurry to get you home by six or Mrs B will have my guts for garters.'

'Do you care what she says, then?'

'Course I don't – but I want her to let you out *next* Sunday – and the Sunday after that, and all the Sundays following. I've taken a fancy to you, Hetty Feather. You're my girl now.'

I wasn't sure I should go along with this. Wasn't I *Jem*'s girl?

'You know I'm only just fourteen,' I said.

'And I'm fifteen, and so we're just the right ages for each other,' said Bertie. 'Don't worry, Hetty, I promise I won't lead you astray.'

'I'd like to see you try!' I said, jumping back into the boat.

It rocked violently, so that I had to sit down abruptly and cling to the sides.

'Whoops! You nearly went for a swim after all!' said Bertie.

He rowed us back to the boathouse and then brought us both a hokey-pokey to eat on our way home. I bit into my iced cream, and shuddered as the cold ran up my teeth and all round my gums.

'Don't bite it, girl – lick it!' said Bertie, showing me how.

I licked and licked and licked.

'What do you think of it?' he asked.

'It's heavenly!' I said, grinning all over my face.

An old couple passing by laughed at me. 'She

looks as if she's never tasted iced cream before!' said the old woman, chuckling.

'Well, she hasn't. She's a poor little orphan girl only just out of the Foundling Hospital,' said Bertie.

'Oh, bless her,' said the old man, fumbling in his waistcoat pocket. 'Here's a threepenny, dearie. Treat yourself to another.'

I was shocked speechless, staring at the silver threepenny bit in the palm of my hand.

'Well, there's a turn-up!' said Bertie.

'I'm *not* an orphan! How many times do I have to tell you?' I said.

'Go and give him his threepence back, then,' said Bertie.

'No fear! It's mine,' I said, popping it into my pocket.

'Oh well, you can buy the lollipops next week,' said Bertie.

When we got back to Mr Buchanan's home, he squeezed my hand. 'There will be a next week, won't there, Hetty?' he said.

'Yes . . . please!'

'I'll deliver you back, then,' said Bertie.

Sarah was in her purple bonnet, all ready for her mysterious assignation.

'You can take off that bonnet and have a spot of supper before you go, or you'll be coming over poorly,' said Mrs Briskett, consulting her pocket watch. 'And what time do you call this, then?' she said, frowning at us.

'I call it one minute to six, Mrs B,' said Bertie.

'I thought I told you half past five?'

'Or six at the latest, and here we are now – six just about to chime. Punctual to the finest degree!'

'Hmph!' said Mrs Briskett, but she invited Bertie to stay for our oyster patty supper.

Sarah only nibbled the edge of hers, and then got up from the table determinedly. 'I'm sorry, Mrs B, but I'm that het up I can't eat.'

Mrs Briskett tutted at her, but let her go. 'Take care now! Don't get too over-excited, you know it's not good for you,' she said.

Bertie and I exchanged glances, while Sarah blushed.

'Where are you going, Sarah?' Bertie asked. 'Are you seeing that fine policeman fellow I've seen eyeing you up and down appreciatively?'

Sarah snorted at him. 'The very idea!' she said, but she seemed too preoccupied to get properly indignant. She waved goodbye to us, tying up the drawstrings of her bag.

'Don't waste all your hard-earned money now,' said Mrs Briskett.

'Surely the gentleman is paying for you, Sarah –

or by definition he ain't a gentleman,' said Bertie.

'You mind your own business, you cocky little urchin,' said Sarah. 'I'm off now.' She looked at Mrs Briskett. 'Wish me luck, Mrs B!'

'I'll do no such thing. You're a very foolish girl, and I don't approve,' said Mrs Briskett – but as Sarah went out of the back door, she called, 'Good luck, even so!'

'Come on, Mrs B, out with it! What's Sarah's secret? We're all agog!' said Bertie.

'It's nothing to do with you, lad. My lips are sealed. Now, finish your patty and be off with you.'

'Such excellent patties too, Mrs B. Hetty's lucky to be able to learn from you,' said Bertie.

'I know you're just trying to sweet-talk me, Mr Honey-tongue. Go on – scoot!'

Bertie crammed the last of his patty in his mouth. He stood up, gave Mrs Briskett a little bow – and blew a kiss to me as he went out of the door.

'I saw that!' said Mrs Briskett. 'I'm not sure I should let you near that boy, Hetty. I've no idea what he'll get up to. No, correction: I've got plenty of ideas, and none of them good. Come along, help me clear the table. Then you can copy out a few receipts for me, seeing as you've got this famously excellent handwriting.'

I meekly did as I was told. Mrs Briskett was all of a fidget, fussing around the kitchen, starting to turn out her larder but losing heart halfway through. She kept sighing. I wondered if she were wishing she had a Sunday outing too.

'Did Mr Briskett pass away a long time ago, Mrs Briskett?' I asked.

'What? There was never any such person! I told you, it's a courtesy title.'

'Did you ever have a sweetheart, Mrs B?'

'Mrs *Briskett*! No, I've never had no time for men,' she said. 'You can't trust them. You're a case in point. It's clear some bad lad led your poor mother astray.'

'Mrs Briskett, *is* that man in the grocer's shop Sarah's sweetheart?'

Mrs Briskett rolled her eyes. 'Of course not, Hetty. That gentleman happens to be respectably married.'

'Then why is she seeing him? Where do they go?'

Mrs Briskett tapped my nose with her finger. 'Ask no questions and you'll be told no lies,' she said.

'The matrons always used to say that to me at the hospital,' I said.

'I'm not surprised. You're a terrible girl for questions, Hetty Feather.'

'How else am I to find out about things?' I said.

'There aren't many answers worth knowing,' said Mrs Briskett, sorting jars of sour pickles. Her

mouth was puckered, as if she were actually sucking them. I wondered what it would be like to be
Mrs Briskett, with no family at all, cooking tempting and tasty dishes for one pernickety old
gentleman who rarely cleared his plate.

'Do you *like* working here, Mrs Briskett?'

'Questions, questions! You can't seem to help it!
Yes, of course I do. You can't go much higher than
this – cook-housekeeper in a lovely villa. I started
off as a kitchen maid when I first went into service,
but the cook was a regular harridan and scared the
life out of me. Then I worked for a young couple,
but the missus was too flighty and didn't give me no
direction. Then I worked in another home where
the missus was the exact opposite, telling me what
to do all day long. I used to hear her voice nag-
nag-nagging even in my dreams. And *then* I came to
work for the master here, and what a joy it is
to have no missus whatsoever.'

'But, Mrs Briskett, wouldn't you like to *be* a
missus one day?'

Mrs Briskett stared at me as if I'd suggested she
become an Indian Princess or an opera singer. 'Of
course not, Hetty. I hope you're not going to turn
out to be one of those girls with ideas above their
station.'

I went to bed that night, determined to keep all
my ideas above my station. I wrote a long letter to

Mama, telling her that I'd been to church and had a jolly boat trip with a new chum. I did not specify exactly who this new chum was. I wrote to Jem too, and I described the boat trip – but I thought it best not to mention any chum at all.

I got into the habit of copying Mr Buchanan's writing every day. At first it was hard work deciphering all his curlicues and squiggles, but after a few days I grew used to his style and could copy quickly and easily. I could not say his work *read* quickly and easily. He used such long convoluted sentences that you lost all sense of what he was saying. He spent page after page laboriously describing every little detail. His characters rarely talked to each other, and when they did, it was with the stiff erudition of elderly clergymen, even though they were children. They were quite the most tedious children too, forever quoting the Bible to each other and pointing out morals.

I had read Miss Smith's stories with huge enjoyment, but Mr Buchanan's tales were so turgid that I yawned as I copied them.

'Did you not get enough sleep, Hetty? That was a fearsome yawn!' said Mr Buchanan sharply.

'I'm sorry, sir. I – I'm just a little tired today,' I said, pressing my lips together.

'You're making good progress with your copying. You will have the manuscript ready for the publisher by the end of the month. Now, I have to cast my mind about and find a subject for a new story . . .' He paused. I realized he was expecting me to show some interest in this project.

'You're very industrious, sir,' I said dutifully.

'I have to work hard because, alas, my stories do not sell particularly well,' he said.

'Oh goodness, sir, I wonder why,' I said – though I knew very well!

'I think they are written in too fine a literary style,' said Mr Buchanan. 'And my characters are well-brought-up young ladies and gentlemen. Perhaps I should copy your friend Miss Smith and write about street waifs. *Her* stories are immensely popular.'

'Miss Smith goes out into the London streets, sir, and interviews the children there,' I said.

'I dare say. And very admirable too. But you are surely not suggesting I do likewise?'

I tried to picture Mr Buchanan picking his way fastidiously across muddy pavements, summoning street children imperiously. They'd simply jeer at him. They might even throw stones.

'Perhaps not, sir,' I said.

'I believe that was how Miss Smith met *you*, Hetty,' said Mr Buchanan.

'Yes, sir,' I said.

'Well, child, perhaps you can tell me a few tales from the past? He was looking at me hopefully, his nose twitching.

'What, right this minute, sir?'

'Can you not remember clearly enough?'

'Oh, I can remember every single detail, sir. Besides, I wrote it all down in my memoirs.'

'Ah yes. Your memoirs. Do you still have them, Hetty?'

'Yes I do. I was hoping Miss Smith might help me to get them published – but when she read them, she said it wasn't possible because they sounded too harsh and ungrateful. It would upset the Board of Governors.'

'I see, I see. Yes, you should show immense respect and gratitude, child. If the hospital had not taken you back, you might well be in the gutter now, living a life of wretched depravity. Instead of which you are safe and warm and well fed in a good Christian home, with not a care in the world.'

I had many, many, many cares – up at dawn, scrubbing my fingers raw, emptying his horrid chamber pot, working like a dog all day long, copying his stilted stories just to earn stamps to keep in touch with my dear mama . . . My eyes filled with angry tears.

'Ah yes! I can see you are ashamed of your ingratitude, Hetty. But never mind, I dare say your childish literary efforts at least helped you to learn the lessons of application and discipline – and after so much practice you now write in a quick clear hand. Well, continue with your good work.'

I carried on copying his dire tale, my eyes crossing with boredom as little Miss Mimsie Marie and young Master Twaddle Tommy gave a penny to a starving, shivering beggar child and then went home to toast their toes in front of a roaring fire and stuff their smug little faces with buttered muffins.

When Mr Buchanan's clock chimed five, I put down my pen and picked up his tea tray, ready to return to the kitchen.

'That's a good girl, Hetty. Run along now,' said Mr Buchanan – but then, as I was going out of the door, he called me back.

'I feel you should be encouraged, child. Show me these memoirs of yours. I will see if I can help you with your literary style. Perhaps you can rewrite a few passages. It will be an invaluable lesson for you, Hetty.'

'So – so you think there might be a chance of getting my memoirs published after all?' I said, my heart beating fast.

'Now you're being ridiculous, child.' He saw my

face fall, and checked himself. 'But perhaps, if we reworked some part together, it might be possible to publish a small extract. I could perhaps write an article about foundlings for a newspaper or journal, with a paragraph from you – the first-hand account, as it were.'

I pondered. This wasn't at all what I wanted. It certainly wouldn't make my fortune so that I could free Mama from service and buy a fine home where we might live happily ever after, just the two of us. But a small extract in a newspaper was better than no publication at all . . . and perhaps some forward-thinking, truth-discerning radical publishing person might be so taken aback by the extract that they sought me out and offered me a publishing contract for the entire work.

'Well, child, stop gawping, and go and get these little memoirs. I will see if I can find time to glance at it tonight,' said Mr Buchanan.

I scuttled off downstairs with his tea tray, so excited I didn't even finish his half-eaten cherry cake and shortbread. I slammed the tray down on the kitchen table and rushed to the scullery.

'What's up with you, girl? You're not just leaving the tray there, are you, right where I want to roll out my pastry for tonight's steak-and-kidney pie? And deal with the dirty crockery! It's not going to wash itself now, is it?'

'In a minute, Mrs Briskett. I'm just running an errand for the master,' I said, taking my memoirs out of my shabby box. The red cover was faded now, and the spine broken. I had got into a fight with Sheila in the dormitory, and she had seized my precious manuscript book and thrown it the length of the room, the spiteful girl.

'What's that scrappy book, then?' asked Sarah, following me.

'My memoirs,' I said, holding it tight against my chest as if it were my own dear child.

'Your mem-what?' said Sarah. 'You're such a tiresome girl for saying fancy stuff no ordinary folk can understand.'

'It's like a journal. It contains the story of my life,' I said grandly, my chin in the air.

I hoped Sarah would be suitably impressed, but she burst out laughing – and when she told Mrs Briskett, *she* started chuckling too.

'The story of your life, young Hetty!' she said. 'You're a caution! You haven't even *had* a life yet – you're still knee-high to a grasshopper, and you've been stuck in that hospital all the time.'

'I have experienced many momentous things,' I said indignantly.

This made them splutter more.

'Oh yes? What exactly have you experienced, eh?' said Sarah. 'Met the Queen, have you? Sailed all round the world? Flown up in the sky to say how d'ye do to the Man in the Moon?'

'I *have* met the Queen, as a matter of fact – or very nearly – on the day of her Golden Jubilee,' I said haughtily. 'That was certainly a momentous day for me, in more ways than one. So you can both stop tee-hee-heeing. I am going to see the master.'

I swept out of the scullery in what I hoped was a dignified manner, but I tripped over the bucket in the corner, which somewhat spoiled the effect. Mrs Briskett and Sarah laughed so hard they had to hold each other to stay standing.

I went up the stairs clutching my memoirs, starting to have qualms. I badly wanted to see my work published. Imagine hundreds, maybe thousands, of people reading it! That thought made me thrill with pride – but I felt very shy and shivery at the thought of one person in particular perusing every line. I suddenly did not want Mr Buchanan reading my memoirs. It would be like taking off all my clothes before him while he blinked at me beadily through his spectacles.

I paused halfway up the stairs, clutching my book to my chest. I couldn't do it. I'd tell Mr Buchanan that I'd lost it somehow. I had to protect it. But then he suddenly poked his head out of the study door and peered down at me.

571

'There you are, Hetty! I was wondering where you'd got to. Bring me these memoirs, child.'

'I – I couldn't find them, sir,' I said.

'What? Nonsense – there they are, you're holding the book right there! Bring it to me immediately.'

'But – but it's a poor thing, sir – written years ago when I was a small girl. You will find it very tedious.'

'I dare say, but I want to help you, child. Hand it over.'

I wanted to fling it far down the stairs, out of harm's way, but instead I handed it over like an automaton. Mr Buchanan bobbed back inside his study, pocketing my memoirs.

I felt very queer and strange all evening, thinking of him turning the pages, reading every little detail about my life. I asked Sarah what mood the master seemed to be in when she served him supper.

'A funny mood – very vague, almost vacant. He read as he ate, picking up his cutlery without concentrating, so that he tried to cut into his pie with his fork.'

'Yes, but vague in a good way or bad? Was he frowning?'

'How can I tell, when the master has such a wrinkled forehead?'

'You're worrying that he doesn't like these

precious memoirs of yours, aren't you, Hetty?' said Mrs Briskett. 'What sort of things did you write in them, eh?'

'All sorts of things,' I said miserably.

'Well, I hope you haven't confessed to anything too dreadful, or the master will be obliged to dismiss you forthwith, and I'd have to start all over again with a new girl just as you're starting to train up nicely,' said Mrs Briskett.

I couldn't concentrate on my letter-writing when I went to bed that night. I blew out my stub of candle and lay twitching in the dark, imagining Mr Buchanan two floors up, his nose in my notebook, glasses glinting as he read his way through my life.

I tossed and turned all night, and got up long before Mrs Briskett and Sarah. When they came down, I had the fire lit, the tea piping hot in the pot, and fried eggs and bacon sizzling in the pan.

They patted me on the head and told me I was a good girl.

'A good girl who's had very momentous experiences,' Sarah couldn't resist adding.

When she came back from serving Mr Buchanan his breakfast, I fell upon her.

'What was the master doing, Sarah?'

'What? Eating his breakfast, silly.'

'Is he reading?'

'Mm? Yes, and a very bad habit it is. He gets so

absorbed he'll likely drop egg and bacon all down his front, and I shall be the poor soul who has to try to get the stains out.'

'*What* was he reading, Sarah?'

'*I* don't know. I'm not in the habit of snatching his book up so as I can see the title.'

'It was a book, then? It wasn't . . . ?'

'Your illustrious memoirs? Yes, I believe it was – and of course . . . it's coming back to me now . . . he held it up solemnly and said to me, "Sarah, this is a veritable masterpiece. I'm going to have it bound in finest leather with gold-embossed lettering."'

I was sure she was teasing me, but I couldn't help hoping that she *might* just be telling the truth.

'He really seemed to like it?' I asked tremulously.

Sarah and Mrs Briskett laughed their silly fat heads off. I tossed my own head and stomped off to clean the bedrooms. Mr Buchanan was in his study with the door closed. I longed to peep in and see for myself if my memoirs intrigued or irritated him. Perhaps he had already cast them aside on one of his cluttered tables. They would be entirely forgotten and I would lose even this extremely slim chance of publication . . .

I was in such a fever about my wretched memoirs I couldn't settle to anything. I think Sarah was a little sorry she had mocked me so, because she let me work on my Sunday dress after lunch instead of helping her sides-to-middle a pile of worn sheets. Mrs Briskett had donated her Sunday outfit of several years ago. It was emerald-green velvet, startlingly bright, but Mrs Briskett and Sarah said it set off my red hair a treat. The velvet had gone shiny at the back, worn smooth by Mrs Briskett's formidable bottom, but there was so much material that Sarah helped me cut the pieces for a frock from the unsullied front.

She fashioned me a pattern too, but she based it on my work dresses and they seemed very plain to me. I had looked very carefully at the girls in the street on Sunday. I wanted a fitted bodice and a waist.

'Then you will need stays, Hetty!' said Sarah.

I saw that she had a point, but I couldn't possibly make do with Mrs Briskett's second-best whalebone stays – indeed, you could comfortably fit a whale itself inside them. I would just have to hold my breath, suck in my stomach and stick out my meagre chest in my new dress.

I had observed a faded pair of curtains in the mending pile in Sarah's cupboard. They had dark gold tassels and trimmings. I decided on a few secret snips so that my dress could have the perfect finishing touches.

I wondered what Bertie would think of me in my new frock. I smiled as I stitched, because it was very pleasant to be liked, and it diverted me a little from fretting about Mr Buchanan – but then Mrs Briskett started preparing his afternoon tea: little cucumber sandwiches and honey cake. It was time for me to go and confront him!

I trembled so much that the cup and saucer and plate played a tune on the tray as I stumbled up the stairs. When I knocked on the study door, my hand was slippery with sweat.

'Come in,' Mr Buchanan called.

I'm not sure what I expected. My thoughts ran wildly between two options: he would either seize me, strike me, tell me I was a wicked, ungrateful girl to tell such tales of the hospital and turn me out of his house forthwith – *or* he might clasp me to his bosom and tell me I had written a compelling work of genius, not a word of which needed changing, and he would see that it was published immediately.

He did not react in either of these ways. He barely raised his head. He was scribbling in his spidery writing in a new manuscript book. He did not stop when I balanced the tray precariously on an edge of his cluttered desk. I poured his tea and handed it to him. His hand went out for it automatically, but he was still intent on his writing and he spilled half of it. He jumped as scalding tea shot up his smoking-jacket sleeve.

'Oh, take care, sir, you'll burn yourself,' I said.

'Yes, yes. I'm fine, it's fine,' he said, flapping his wet sleeve.

'Shall I fetch you a dry jacket, sir?'

'No, no, don't fuss.' He carried on writing, reaching out blindly again and stuffing a sandwich into his mouth. He could just as easily have stuffed the plate in instead, and crunched up the china with equal absent-mindedness.

'You seem very busy, sir,' I said.

'I am indeed, Hetty Feather. I have started writing my new book.'

I glanced at the page in front of him. His handwriting was even more blotched and sloped at a bizarre angle.

'Take care not to get too carried away, sir – or even I won't be able to read it,' I said. 'I'll make a start on it as soon as I've finished copying your other work.'

Mr Buchanan suddenly snapped to attention. 'That won't be necessary, Hetty. I think it's better if I make a fair copy myself – then I can alter sentences as I go, rearrange paragraphs, et cetera. It will take longer but will be far more satisfactory in the long run.'

I stared at him, appalled.

'Don't look so stricken! You can still continue with the old manuscript. You must not take this personally. You've worked hard, I grant you, and you write a very legible hand, if a little childish in appearance.'

'But what about my stamps?'

'What? Oh, your postage stamps! Yes, you can have the agreed ration until you finish the manuscript.' He reached into his desk drawer, and took out the stamp box. 'In fact, I will continue to provide you with stamps whenever you ask, so long as you don't take it into your head to communicate with every child in the Foundling Hospital.' He handed me another four stamps.

'Thank you, sir. That's very generous of you. And don't worry, it's just so I can write to Mama.' I silently mouthed 'and Jem' when he started writing again, for honesty's sake.

Mr Buchanan gave me the old manuscript and a spare pen, and I started writing too, but I couldn't settle properly to my task. I kept peering around the room, looking for my memoirs. It was so difficult to detect in this mad chamber, crammed to the ceiling with books and papers and manuscripts. I craned to look in the wastepaper basket, wondering if he'd tossed my poor work in there.

'Do you have a crick in your neck, Hetty?' Mr Buchanan asked.

'Oh no, sir, I was just looking . . . I couldn't help wondering . . .' I couldn't wait any longer. 'What did you think of my memoirs, sir?'

Mr Buchanan removed his fez to scratch his head vigorously. Then he set the quaint hat back on his head at a comical angle, wrinkling his nose to hitch up his spectacles.

Tell me, you ridiculous little monkey man! I screeched inside my head, but I clamped my lips together to keep the words inside.

'Oh yes, your "memoirs",' said Mr Buchanan. He said the word as if it were ridiculous, and I felt the blood flooding my face. 'Mm, well, it was certainly a substantial effort, Hetty. I hadn't realized it would be so long, when you have led such a short life.'

'But what did you think of the content, sir?'

'It was quite . . . startling. I'm surprised at you, child. You showed shameful ingratitude to your benefactors. Some of the passages about your good matrons were quite scandalous. Miss Smith was absolutely correct. Though vividly written, the manuscript is unpublishable.'

'But it's the truth, sir.'

'Nonsense! It's the truth as you perceive it – a childish tirade by an angry, undeserving creature, utterly self-absorbed and far too passionate. I am ashamed of you, Hetty. I cannot understand how you could write this.'

'Then give me my memoirs back, sir,' I said defiantly.

'When I am less distracted by my own work, I

will glance at it again. Perhaps there might be a few simple passages we can work on. Your childhood in the country might make a pleasing pastoral piece. People like to read about simple country bumpkins.'

'They're not simple country bumpkins,' I said hotly. 'They're my family.'

'Of course, of course,' he said soothingly. 'And perhaps, when I'm not quite as busy, I'll help you to construct a written portrait that will do them justice. Now, I think you'd better run back to the kitchen, Hetty. I don't want you to copy any more today. I need a little space to continue my new story. You're distracting me.'

I peered all around.

'What is it now?'

'I'm looking for my memoirs. Can I have my book back, please?'

'I shall keep it safely here in my room, and if I have a spare moment in the next few weeks, I shall give it another glance.'

'Oh no, sir!'

'Are you arguing with me, Hetty Feather?'

'No, sir. Well, yes, sir, I suppose I am, because I want my memoirs back. They're mine, and I feel uncomfortable without them.'

'You're being ridiculous, girl. The book is safe in my room.'

'But *where*, sir? I can't see it anywhere. It's not on your desk, or on your shelves, or any of the piles of books.'

'I have it safe, I assure you.'

'Then *please* may I have it back?'

'Of course you may, in the fullness of time, when I have finished looking at it.'

'But that's not fair!' I wailed, stamping my foot in my passion. 'It's my book and I want it back *now*!'

'Hetty Feather!' Sarah came bursting in through the door, skirts flying. 'Whatever are you up to, shouting at the master! Forgive her, sir – she's just a wilful, ignorant orphan who does not yet know her place.'

'I am not an *orphan*!' I screamed as Sarah picked me up in her huge arms, heaved me over her shoulder like a coal sack, and bore me away.

10

Sarah carried me all the way back down two flights of stairs to the kitchen and then dumped me on the rag rug in front of the range. Mrs Briskett stared at us both in astonishment, up to her elbows in uncooked pastry.

'Oh my Lord, whatever's the matter, Sarah?' she gasped, wringing her doughy hands.

'Hetty Feather's taken leave of her senses! I was seeing to the fires on the first floor when I heard this rumpus upstairs. She was shrieking at the master!'

'Oh, Hetty, how could you! *Shrieking*, you say, Sarah?'

'Like a banshee! Is that not right, Hetty? Whatever possessed you?'

'He's got my memoirs and he won't give them back!'

'What? You're working yourself into a passion over a scribbling notebook? Have some sense, girl! The master will give you notice now.'

'Just as I was getting fond of you, child! How could you lose your temper like that?'

'It's the red hair – they're all the same. Stop that noise at *once*, Hetty Feather, or I'll give you such a slapping,' said Sarah, shaking me.

'But he's stolen it from me!'

'Why on earth would the master do that, you silly girl? He's got countless notebooks of his own.'

'He said he wanted to keep it a while, so he could improve certain passages,' I sobbed.

'Well, surely that's what you wanted, is it not?' said Mrs Briskett, perplexed.

'Yes, but *I* want to look after it, not him. It's *mine*.'

'I've never heard such nonsense in my life!'

I couldn't make either of them understand. My memoirs meant so much to me. I'd had so little that was truly my own at the hospital. I'd worked so hard at them. It was as if little pieces of myself were stuck to the pages of that notebook, my very blood mixed in with the ink. But though I put this into words as passionately as I could, they still seemed shocked at me – and I couldn't implore the master again because they would not let me near him.

At first they were both sure he would ring for me and dismiss me on the spot, but when he'd done nothing by the next day, they decided he *might* have forgiven me because I was young and inexperienced.

'And you can't *help* having that awful red hair, can you, dear?' said Mrs Briskett. She pulled my cap down so that it brushed my eyebrows, to hide as much hair as she could.

I was allowed to do all my usual chores, though forbidden to serve the master his afternoon tea. If Sarah thought she heard the master's step nearby while we were making his bed or scrubbing his bathtub, she would whisk me hastily out of the way.

I wrote a long tale of woe to Mama, telling her all about it. She was very tender and comforting when she replied, but in many ways seemed to take the same attitude as Mrs Briskett and Sarah.

Try to stay out of his way, Hetty dear, and when you do evenchooly bump into him stair at the flor and look as meak as posibol. In all other respecs this seems a good posishun so you must KEEP it. This leter is sent with all the love in the world from yore own dear Mama

But she added a P.S.: *You can allways surch for yore memoirs when dusting his studdy and shov it down yore apron quik.*

I *did* search, but I couldn't find my memoirs in any of the piles of books. Greatly daring, I tried the little drawer in his desk where he kept the stamps – but it was stuck fast. He had locked it! I wondered if he had crammed the book in there. It would just about fit. But there was no key in the lock, and I couldn't find one anywhere in his trinket tray.

I was fretting miserably about it the next morning, when Bertie called with his meat basket.

'Hey, Mrs Briskett, wait till you see the side of beef I've got for your Sunday lunch! If you make one of your Yorkshire puddings, it'll be a meal fit for the old Queen herself. It'll put you in such a good mood I dare say you'll let Hetty here stay out an extra hour – isn't that right?'

'Young Hetty isn't allowed out on Sunday at all, boy, let alone an extra hour. She's disgraced herself good and proper, she has,' said Mrs Briskett.

Bertie raised his eyebrows. 'Cor, Hetty, what've you *done*!'

'She's severely cheeked the master, when he's been so kind as to take an interest in her, that's what she's *done*,' said Sarah.

'Oooh, what did you say, Hetty?' asked Bertie, grinning.

'I simply asked for my property back,' I said haughtily.

'No, no, missy! There was no *asking*! When I heard, you was shrieking your head off and stamping your foot,' said Sarah.

'What a girl!' said Bertie admiringly. 'But you haven't lost your position, have you, Hetty?'

'She's very lucky not to,' said Mrs Briskett.

'It's only because the master's preoccupied with his work. He's always like this when he starts a new story. I once splashed red-hot soup into his lap when I was serving his supper and he barely flinched, he was so busy scribbling in his notebook,' said Sarah.

'He's no right to purloin *my* notebook,' I said.

'Here, perhaps he's pinching all your ideas, Hetty,' said Bertie.

Mrs Briskett and Sarah laughed heartily, as if he'd made the funniest joke in the world. I did not find this amusing, but at least it softened them up. Mrs Briskett relented over my Sunday-night curfew, though she issued so many conditions and commands she set my head spinning.

I had added incentive to finish sewing my Sunday dress. I sat up half Saturday night adding the finishing touches by flickering candlelight and was consequently so tired I nearly fell asleep during the sermon, my head nid-nodding while Mrs Briskett and Sarah took it in turns to give me a sharp poke.

It was wonderful, though, to parade into and out of church in my new green frock with its gold trimmings. I saw some of the younger maids giving it the eye, and I was sure they were looking envious. I could have done with a decent pair of white stockings instead of my old holey grey ones, and my stout boots were much too hobbledehoy. I looked at a girl wearing pale-grey kid boots with little heels and pearl buttons, and longed to possess a similar pair. I looked down at Mrs Briskett's feet and then at Sarah's, but *their* boots were almost as ugly and serviceable as my own, so there was no point hoping for their cast-offs; besides, their feet were twice the size of mine so I'd be shuffling around like a clown.

I remembered the clowns that I'd seen at Tanglefield's Travelling Circus. My stomach gave a little twist as I thought of Madame Adeline and her troupe of rosin-backed horses. I'd been a very little girl when I'd first seen her perform. I thought she looked like a fairy in her pink sparkly outfit, her long locks flowing, the most beautiful woman in the world. When I ran away from the hospital and found her again, I realized that she was a sad old lady beneath her wig and thick make-up. I wondered if she was still performing.

Bertie was waiting on the area steps, wearing his best brown suit, but not quite so perfumed this time. He rolled his eyes when he saw my new dress.

'My, Hetty, that's a fine outfit you're wearing!' he said.

'She made it herself, every stitch,' said Sarah.

'One of *my* old Sunday outfits, bless her. I always loved that bright green – but it looks even better on

588

young Hetty, with her red hair,' said Mrs Briskett.

They both beamed at me proudly while I fidgeted before them. I couldn't work out how to react to them at all. I was used to people who loved me (like Mama and my old foster family) or people who loathed me (like Matron Pigface Peters and Matron Stinking Bottomly). Mrs Briskett and Sarah ticked me off almost as much as the matrons – but they seemed genuinely fond of me already.

I wondered whether I should give them a hug goodbye. Perhaps they would think it outrageous. I was sure *Bertie* would welcome a hug, but I wasn't sure it would be wise.

'You look a total sweetheart in that lovely green dress, Hetty,' he said, spinning me round.

Was he saying I was *his* sweetheart? My heart started thumping inside my tight velvet bodice. I knew Jem assumed I was *his* sweetheart. His last letter to me had made it plain:

My dear Hetty,

What a pair of sillies we are. I thought you had forgotten all about your dear Jem – and you thought I had forgotten YOU, transferring my affections to little Eliza. I will always love her dearly as my young sister – but I hope that you and I will find the deeper love of true sweethearts in the fullness of time.

Of course you're very young, still a child, and we are forced to live many cruel miles apart. But I am nothing if not patient, Hetty. I will work hard and save hard, biding my time. In two or three years' time I should be ready to branch out on my own, and then . . . well, we shall see!

Take care, my own sweet girl, and write often to your

Very loving Jem

I did not need to carry the letter on my person. I had read it so many times by flickering candlelight that I knew every word by heart. Yet even though I knew it so well, I didn't know what to make of it. I was thrilled, of course. It was exciting to think that I inspired such deep feelings in such a fine man. But this was the trouble. I'd known Jem the *boy*. When I thought of him, I still saw him as an earnest, fresh-faced ten-year-old, his hair tousled, his clothes torn, his boots muddy.

I could not match that Jem with the tall man in corduroy waiting outside the hospital. I remembered so many sweet things the boy Jem had said to me – but this heartfelt love letter unnerved me. Since I forced myself to stop thinking about Jem the year I was ten, he had grown shadowy, almost unreal, like a character in a storybook. Now it seemed almost as if Robin Hood or Dick Whittington were writing to me.

What would he think if he saw me walking hand in hand down the street with Bertie? I blushed and tried to wriggle my fingers free.

'Hey, keep hold, Hetty!' he said, curling his own fingers to keep mine safe.

'I – I'm not sure I should be holding your hand,' I murmured.

'And why's that? Do you suddenly think you're too grand for me in your fancy dress?'

'No, of course not! It's just . . . well, to be utterly truthful, Bertie, I think I have another sweetheart already.'

Bertie dropped my hand and stared at me. 'Well, that was quick work! You've only been out of that hospital place five minutes!'

'No, this is a long-ago sweetheart, when I lived in the country when I was little.'

'How little?'

'When I was five and Jem was ten.'

Bertie burst out laughing. 'Oh, come on, Hetty!'

'I know, it sounds so silly, but he was my dear brother and so kind to me.'

'You can't be sweethearts with your *brother*.'

'He's not a real brother by blood, he's my foster brother. His name's Jem and – and we always used to play we would get married one day.'

'Look, when I was five I wanted to marry the pretty little girl with plaits I glimpsed at church on Sundays, *and* the maid with the rosy cheeks who served us porridge at breakfast, *and* the kind old dame who sat me on her lap when she taught me my letters.'

'Yes, but he does still care for me, Bertie. He's started writing to me.'

'But can he come and see you and take you out of a Sunday?'

'No.'

'So what would you rather do – sit at home in your scullery week after week, or come out with me and have fun?'

'Oh, Bertie! I want to come out with you and have fun, of course I do – but I feel bad about Jem. He says he'll wait patiently for me, even if it's years.'

'Come off it! How old is this Jem? He must be . . . nineteen now. You're telling me a grown man of nineteen is happy to moon about, daydreaming about a little girl he's not seen for goodness knows how many years. Is he soft in the head, this Jem?'

'No!'

'Is he very plain? Very thin or very stout? Is he missing a limb or two?'

'*No!* He's strong and tall and good-looking.'

'Then don't you think he might have half the

village after him, if he's such a catch? I bet he's got a sweetheart at home.'

'Jem would always be true to me,' I said, but my voice wavered.

I remembered all Jem's sweet-talk with little Eliza, spinning her the same stories.

'Aha!' said Bertie, seeing my face. 'You're not so sure now, are you? Come on, Hetty, stop your nonsense. Don't spoil things. I'm taking you somewhere special today.'

'To the river?'

'No, that was *last* week. *This* week we're going on a little expedition. I've got an even better surprise.'

We walked down into town and then hopped on a bus for a ten-minute ride. We sat squashed up together on the top, the wind in our hair, looking over a high wall into green parklands. Then, far in the distance, I saw shimmering reds and yellows and bright blues. I heard music. I sniffed savoury smells.

'What is it? What *is* this place? Oh, it's not a circus, is it?' I asked, quivering.

'No, it's a fair. There are swings and merry-go-rounds with carved horses and—'

'I know what a fair is. I've been to one,' I said, remembering the children's fair in Hyde Park on the day of the Golden Jubilee.

'There! I thought it would be such a surprise,' said Bertie, looking very disappointed.

'Oh it is, it is – a *lovely* surprise,' I reassured him, standing up eagerly to see better. The bus lurched and I nearly toppled over.

'Careful!' said Bertie, grabbing me. He stroked the gold fringing on my bodice. 'This is very pretty. Did you really make it all yourself?'

'Yes, every stitch,' I said proudly.

I remembered my first darning lesson at the hospital when I was five: how I'd pricked myself with the needle a dozen times, and bunched the toes up together. Perhaps the hospital had taught me something useful, then?

I stared at the other girls all about me as I got off the bus. I was pleased to see that my dress looked almost as stylish as theirs – though some of their dresses hung a little differently, sticking out at the back. At first I thought that all the girls, though otherwise slender, simply had big fat bottoms – but surely they couldn't all have such protruding rears?

'Bertie, why do those girls' dresses stick out in that way?' I asked.

Bertie seemed to be the fount of all knowledge, but this time he shrugged his shoulders. 'Search me, Hetty. Ask one. *I* can't, I'll get my face slapped.'

I wasn't sure I dared – but when we were waiting in the queue to climb up inside the great red and yellow helter-skelter, we got talking to the couple in front. Bertie knew the boy, who worked in the draper's in the next town. His girl worked there too, and clearly made use of the shop's wares, because her dress was sewn all over with ruffles and ribbons, with little jet beads around her cuffs. I admired these, and she admired my gold fringing. She clapped her hands when I told her I'd whipped it off an old curtain.

I peered at the very prominent bump at the back of her dress. 'I love the way your dress hangs at the back,' I said, describing a curve with my hands.

'What? Oh, you mean my bustle!' she giggled.

'Ah! So, this bustle – is it stitched into the dress?'

She brought her head close to mine. 'It's a special pad. We sell them at our shop for five shillings,' she whispered.

Five shillings! But I didn't need to *buy* one. I could surely fashion a pad out of anything. I thought of all the cushions cluttering every chair and sofa at Mr Buchanan's. No one would notice if just one went missing . . .

Then we were inside the helter-skelter, climbing up and up the stairs in the dark. The draper's couple kept pausing above us, so that I blundered right into the girl's wretched bustle.

'What are they playing at?' I said to Bertie.

'Oh, I know exactly what they're playing at,' said Bertie. 'We could play that game too.'

'You'd better not try!' I said, and when he did indeed try to put his arms round me, I gave him a sharp poke with my elbow.

When we got to the top of the helter-skelter, I felt dizzy up so high, right above the gaudy canopies of the fair, able to see for miles across the wooded parklands. I clutched hold of Bertie in spite of myself.

'There now, Hetty, I've got you tight,' he said.

He sat down on a mat and pulled me onto his lap. Then someone gave us a shove in the back. We were suddenly whizzing round and round and round, at such a rate and with so many bumps I thought we might fly straight off the slide – but Bertie was true to his word, holding onto me tightly, his hands gripping my waist. We hurtled right down to the end of the slide and shot off onto the grass, tumbling in an undignified heap, screaming and laughing.

'That was good, eh, Hetty?' said Bertie, pulling me upright.

'Yes, it was wonderful,' I said, jumping up and down and clapping my hands.

'You're a marvellous girl, up for any kind of lark,' said Bertie. 'Right, I'm going to win you a coconut as a reward.'

We went to the coconut shy and he tried his hardest, aiming three balls at the hairy coconuts balanced on sticks. He hit one with his last throw, but he couldn't topple it.

'It's a cheat. They must be stuck on!' he said, red in the face with effort.

'Can I have a go?' I begged.

'It's a waste of time. You can't shift the beggars,' said Bertie.

'Please!'

'You're so obstinate!' he said, but he paid a penny for me to have a go too.

I tried my best. I missed completely with my first shot. I hit a coconut with my second ball – and it wobbled a little but stayed balanced on its stick.

'There, what did I say?' said Bertie.

I took aim with my last ball. I pictured Matron Pigface Peters' head on the stick and *hurled* the ball with all my strength. It struck the coconut with such force that it shot straight up – and then toppled to the ground.

'There! I did it! We've got a coconut, Bertie!' I shouted triumphantly.

Bertie didn't look too thrilled, though everyone else around laughed and clapped me.

'So what do we *do* with this nut? How do we eat it?' I asked.

'Crack it open,' said Bertie.

597

'How do we do that?'

'You're such a strong girl I should think you could do it with your teeth,' he snapped.

'What? Oh, Bertie, don't be cross with me. I thought you *wanted* to win a coconut. Are you cross with me for spending all your pennies?'

'I've got heaps more, silly. I'm just cross because *I* wanted to win it for you. Bit of manly pride and all that. Come over to the darts stall. I dare say you can win us a china ornament or a goldfish in a bowl.'

'Will you be even crosser if I do?' I said.

'Probably!' said Bertie, but he was smiling now.

'Seriously though, I feel so bad that I haven't any money for rides. I won't get paid for a couple of months yet.'

'I've got heaps for both of us,' said Bertie, patting his jingling pocket. 'I saved all my tips this week, *and* mowed Mr Jarvis's big garden for an extra shilling, so we're rich. So is it darts now, Hetty?'

'I think I'd sooner go on that wonderful merry-go-round,' I said.

'Excellent!'

We stood watching for a whole turn so that I could work out which horse I liked best. They were all painted different colours – black and brown and grey like real horses, with great manes and flowing tails of proper horsehair. There was one splendid white beast with a black patch on his eye, just like Madame Adeline's Pirate from that long-ago circus. I knew he was the one.

I pointed him out to Bertie, and as soon as the music slowed, he leaped onto the boards, dodging round other eager boys, and claimed the white horse as ours. He helped me up so that I could cling to the mane, while he sat at the back, holding the twisting golden pole.

The lad came for his pennies, the music started, and we were off, whirling round and round. It was almost as good as cantering about the ring on that real horse with Madame Adeline. I dug my heels into Pirate's painted flanks and threw my head back. My clumsily arranged hair lost half its pins and came tumbling down past my shoulders.

When we stumbled off the merry-go-round at last, deliciously dizzy, I tried to pin my hair back into place.

'Leave it, Hetty, it looks lovely loose like that,' said Bertie.

'It makes me look younger than ever,' I said, sticking pins in willy-nilly.

'What's the matter with looking young? You don't want to look like a wrinkled old lady, do you? You look all right to me. Better than all right.' He touched a stray lock of hair, stroking it gently. I was very glad I'd taken the trouble to lather it thoroughly with Pears soap last night, even though it meant going to bed with sopping wet hair.

'You've got lovely hair, Hetty,' said Bertie.

'It's red, though. Everyone hates red hair,' I said.

'I think it suits you. It's grand – so bright it dazzles your eyes.'

'I think my eyes are my best feature. They're sapphire-blue, do you see? My mama called me Sapphire before she had to give me away . . .' I hesitated. 'You can call me Sapphire, if you like.'

'Sapphire. Mmm. Sapphire, Sapphire, Sapphire. Do you know what? I think Hetty suits you better.' Bertie jingled the change in his pocket. 'What next, eh? We can have another go on the merry-go-round – or try the swing boats – or I could buy us a poke of fried potatoes?'

I thought hard. 'How about the darts stall? You win us something this time,' I suggested.

So we tried our luck. With his second dart Bertie scored a bull's-eye and we could choose any prize on the stand. I circled round and round, in an agony of indecision.

'Have a goldfish. It matches your hair exactly, dearie,' said the man running the stall.

'Don't you cast aspersions on my sweetheart's hair,' said Bertie.

This time I didn't contradict him.

'Why don't you pick an ornament, Hetty?' Bertie suggested.

'Good idea,' I said – but I still had to deliberate long and hard.

Eventually I chose a little black-and-white dog with floppy ears and an earnest expression. 'He's lovely, Bertie. Thank you so much,' I said. 'Well, if I've got a present, you must have my coconut.'

'No, you take it home and share it with Mrs B and Sarah. That'll please them – and that way Mrs B will let you out next Sunday without any argle-bargle, so long as you behave! What were you *doing*, shouting at your master? If I tried that trick with Jarvis he'd box my ears. Here, Hetty, this notebook of yours – do you record everything in it?'

'Things that take my fancy,' I said.

'Will you write about me in it?' Bertie asked eagerly.

'Perhaps,' I told him.

11

We were a little late getting home, and I got severely ticked off by Mrs Briskett. Sarah had already gone out for her mysterious Sunday evening engagement. I felt a little sorry for Mrs Briskett all the same, stuck indoors all afternoon and evening, so I produced my coconut.

'Here's a little present, Mrs B,' I said.

'Mrs Briskett to you! You're just trying to get round me, you bad girl,' she said, but she took it all the same.

She made a hole in it and poured out strange watery 'milk'. I didn't care for it at all, but Mrs Briskett drank it up eagerly.

'It works wonders for the complexion, coconut milk,' she said.

I stared at Mrs Briskett's big red face, wondering if she was about to sprout bristly brown whiskers like the coconut, but nothing untoward happened.

She took her rolling pin, put the coconut on the

floor, and attacked it vigorously. It smashed into small pieces, exposing the white inside. I gingerly tried the white meat.

'Ah! I like this part!' I said, crunching happily.

Mrs Briskett tucked in too.

'We'll leave some for Sarah when she comes back, won't we?'

'Of course we will,' said Mrs Briskett, setting a fair portion aside on a saucer. 'But I don't think she'll be back till late.'

'Mrs Briskett, do tell me – *are* Sarah and that strange man with the moustache . . . sweethearts?'

Mrs Briskett snorted. 'Oh, Hetty Feather, whatever will you come out with next? The very idea! And I don't know what Mrs Arthur Brown would say if she thought her hubby was stepping out with our Sarah.'

'Then why does she see him every Sunday?'

'She doesn't just see Mr Brown, she's with a lot of other like-minded folk. But they don't go to see each other. They're there to meet up with something very queer. Oh, it gives me the shivers just to think of it.'

'What is it? Tell me, Mrs Briskett! Who do they meet?'

'I couldn't possibly say,' said Mrs Briskett. 'But I don't approve. I don't approve *at all*.' She gave a genteel shudder.

I was more bewildered than ever. Was she seriously suggesting that Sarah and Mr Brown, two rigidly respectable people, were somehow behaving in a reprehensible manner? I thought back to the vicar's sermon in church. He had spoken out against the music hall, suggesting that it was not a suitable place for serious God-fearing folk – not quite a den of iniquity like a public house, but disturbing all the same. I wasn't sure what happened in this mysterious music hall. I pictured Sarah gaudily made-up and provocatively dressed, singing a saucy song as she strutted across the stage, pursued by Mr Brown, waggling his eyebrows and twirling his moustache. This fancy was so comical I couldn't help snorting with laughter.

'It's not funny, Hetty. I'm seriously worried about Sarah. It's taken hold of her and she won't listen to reason,' said Mrs Briskett.

Then perhaps Sarah went to a public house after all? Again, I had only a very hazy idea of what they were like inside. I pictured Sarah slumped on a bench, downing a tankard of gin, while Mr Brown drank straight from the bottle, dribbling all down his droopy moustache. I snorted again – and then hurried off to the scullery to avoid another scolding. I made up my tiny bed and sat with half a candle, writing letters.

I wrote several pages to Mama, telling her about

my new dress in some detail, and my plans for the pad at the back to turn myself into a fashion plate. I also told her about my trip to the fairground with Bertie – *but don't worry, Mama, he is just a friend. I know I am much too young for sweethearts, but he is fun to be with and he seems to like me.*

I reassured her that I was in perfect health. She was always asking if I was eating properly, wondering if I had even the slightest cough. The doctor at the hospital had once said I had a weak chest, so Mama still worried terribly.

I wrote to Jem too, but this letter was considerably shorter. I knew he probably wouldn't be interested in my new dress, and whether it should have a pad at the back or not. I did tell him briefly about my trip to the fair, but I did not mention Bertie as such. I said I went to the fair with a friend, and carefully did not specify the sex.

This only took a paragraph. I did not know what else to write. I kept trying to conjure up Jem's adult face – but although I could picture that tall figure in brown corduroy, his features were a blur. It seemed safer to think of the long-ago Jem, so I filled my page asking if he ever strolled past the special tree where we'd played endless games of house together? Did he still fish in the stream where I'd paddled? Did he plough with Saxon and Sam, the two Shire horses I'd once taken such delight in feeding chunks of carrot?

I was wide awake and still had some candle left. I wished I could write a letter to Gideon, but I didn't know where he was. He would have left the hospital by now and would be shut up in some far-away barracks, learning how to be a soldier. I ached for him, wishing I had some way of protecting him.

The letter to Jem had reminded me too much of the past. I thought of that little dark country cottage with all of us children tumbling around inside. Gideon had always come off worst in any free-for-all. He came last in our running races, though he had long legs like a colt. Our brother Saul could beat him, even though he was on crutches. I fingered my ribs automatically when I thought of Saul. He had had a terrible trick of poking me with the sharp end of his stick, leaving me all over bruises. Mother always insisted we be kind to Saul, but she forgot to tell *him* to be kind to *us*.

I knew it was a sin, but I had thoroughly disliked my brother Saul. Still, I had been very sad when he died of the influenza at the hospital.

I shivered. I did not want to think of the hospital any more. I might not be living the life of my dreams, publishing my memoirs and providing for dear Mama – but my new life as a servant with

Mrs Briskett and Sarah in Mr Monkey Buchanan's house was so, so, so much better than being shut up in the cold, forbidding hospital. And my Sunday afternoons with Bertie were positively delightful.

I wondered whether to start a new memoir book now that Mr Buchanan had purloined my old one. His wastepaper basket was often stuffed with crumpled discarded pages. I could straighten them out, maybe even smooth them with Sarah's flatiron. Then I could stitch them together, strike through every sentence of his spidery scribble, and start my own memoirs on the blank backs.

No, perhaps I would always be too sharply truthful for autobiography. I could attempt a work of fiction instead – a novel about a young girl with eyes as blue as sapphires – but she would be tall and shapely and have tumbling blonde curls. Perhaps she had been brought up in a strict and severe (unnamed) institution and cruelly treated by terrible matrons. She'd be sent off at the tender age of fourteen to earn her living as a maid, in spite of her intelligence and obvious potential, and feel cast down by the dreary routine of being a general servant. But then she meets her true sweetheart, a former workhouse inmate, now cheerily earning his living as . . . a baker's boy . . . ? I blushed in the darkness of the scullery, ashamed to have let myself get so carried away. I blew out my guttering candle and tried to settle.

I heard Mrs Brisket's footsteps as she paced backwards and forwards across the scrubbed flags of the kitchen floor. Every now and then she muttered to herself and sighed. It was clear that Sarah was still not home.

Then I heard the clop of hooves outside in the road, anxious voices, and sudden footsteps. There was a knock on the back door, then Mrs Brisket's sudden exclamation:

'Oh my Lord, Sarah, whatever's happened!'

I jumped out of bed and ran into the kitchen. There was Sarah, swaying in her purple Sunday best, her eyes rolling, her mouth open, propped up by Mr Brown and a cabbie. Good heavens, was she really *drunk*?

'Sarah, Sarah, Sarah, look at the state of you!' said Mrs Brisket, seizing hold of her and pushing her onto a kitchen chair.

'She was certainly in no state to get herself home,' said Mr Brown. 'I had to take it upon myself to call a cab for her.'

'I'm so sorry, Mr Brown. Oh, Sarah, you silly girl! I knew this would happen!'

'She paid for a special materialization – and it worked, it worked tremendously. Sarah was ecstatic. There's no other word to describe it;

609

ecstatic! But then it all became too much for her, and she went into a swoon, quite overcome. She rendered herself incapable of getting out of the house, let alone coming all the way home. I had to practically carry her out of the cab – and she's not a light woman,' Mr Brown said ruefully.

'Oh dear, I do hope you haven't done yourself an injury, Mr Brown. Thank you so much for looking after our Sarah. Please allow me to pay for the cab,' said Mrs Briskett.

'No, no, I won't hear of it. What's a cab fare between friends? But I'm just giving you fair warning – on Sunday evenings Sarah really needs to be accompanied by a lady friend who can look after her, perhaps loosen her clothing if she's overcome once more. I've tried my best, but there are limits to the attention I can decently pay her. Do I make myself clear?'

'Clear as day, Mr Brown,' said Mrs Briskett. 'Thank you very much, gentlemen. I'll take over now.'

She bustled about Sarah, undoing her bonnet and the collar of her dress. Mr Brown and the cabbie wiped the sweat off their brows and made a hasty retreat.

Mrs Briskett frowned at me. 'Don't just stand there gawping, Hetty. Run for the smelling salts – in the cupboard over there.'

610

I rummaged in the cupboard, while Mrs Briskett plunged her hand right inside Sarah's bodice. There was a sudden snap, and Sarah breathed out and almost overflowed her Sunday dress.

'There, I've got her stays undone – that should help,' said Mrs Briskett. 'Where are those salts, Hetty?'

I thrust a packet of Saxa salt at her and she sighed irritably.

'*Smelling* salts, you stupid girl. The dark blue bottle in the corner!'

She grabbed the bottle from me, uncorked it, and waved it under Sarah's nose. Sarah's head jerked, her eyes blinked, and she let out a gasp.

'There now, Sarah, take a deep breath. Oh my Lord, you've given us such a fright!'

'Is she very drunk, Mrs Briskett?' I asked.

'Drunk?' Mrs Briskett stared at me. 'Hetty Feather, what a thing to say!'

'*Drunk!*' Sarah echoed. This accusation shocked her back to total consciousness. 'The very idea! I haven't had a drop of alcohol since Christmas, apart from a dribble of sherry in your trifle, Mrs B, and no one can count that against me.'

'Now, now, take no notice of the stupid girl. Of course we know you're not drunk. Don't go up-setting yourself further. I'll make a nice cup of tea to settle you. Come on now.'

611

Mrs Briskett nodded at me to put the kettle on the range, while she knelt down and unbuttoned Sarah's boots. 'There now, wiggle your tootsies.'

'You're ever so good to me, Mrs B.'

'Well, you're a dear girl, even if you get carried away by strange fancies. It's not good for you, though, getting yourself in such a state. Look at you, swooning all the way home! These sessions are getting too much for you. You'll do yourself a mischief. Plus you're spending all your wretched savings! Promise me you won't go any more.'

'Oh, I *have* to go, Mrs B! Tonight was so wonderful, a true miracle! I saw her! I felt her hands upon me! My own dear mother!' Sarah breathed, and then her eyes rolled as she swooned again.

'Her mother?' I said as Mrs Briskett wafted the smelling salts under her nose once more. The sharp stench made my own eyes water. 'But I thought her mother was dead!'

'Exactly. Dead and buried. And that's where she should stay,' said Mrs Briskett.

'You mean . . . she's a ghost?' I whispered.

'Something similar. I don't think it's right or Christian. We shouldn't meddle with ghouls and ghosts. If we get them to pop out at us, how do we know we can ever be shot of them?' Mrs Briskett looked all about her, as if an eerie spectral being were lurking in a corner of the kitchen.

'She's not a ghoul or a ghost!' Sarah murmured, mopping her forehead. 'She's a beautiful spirit. She speaks to me through Madame Berenice.'

'Is she a circus lady?' I asked, thinking of dear Madame Adeline.

Sarah looked affronted, but Mrs Briskett nodded grimly.

'She's exactly *like* a circus lady, performing her tricks while Sarah and all her silly cronies sit around in a circle, marvelling. And paying through the nose for the experience,' she said.

Sarah rose unsteadily to her feet. 'I'll thank you to keep your opinions to yourself, Mrs B. You've been very kind, but I'll not stop to hear you talk of Madame Berenice in such a manner. She's a saint of a woman. She simply wants to comfort poor grieving souls by bringing us messages from the spirit world. It beats me why you won't come too, and hear a few words from your own mother,' she said.

'I heard enough words from her when she was in this world – and few of them were kind ones,' said Mrs Briskett. 'Now sit down again, Sarah, or you'll *fall* down.'

'I'm going to my room,' Sarah said, and staggered across the kitchen.

'Oh, the obstinacy of the silly girl,' said Mrs Briskett. 'Come, Hetty, we'll have to take hold of her or she'll get halfway up those stairs and then tumble all the way down.'

So the two of us battled with the bulging bulk of poor Sarah, heaving her right up to her room at the top of the house. We were all three breathing very heavily by this time.

'There now!' Mrs Briskett panted, propelling Sarah towards her bed. 'Light her candle, Hetty, so we can see what we're doing.'

I did as I was told. In the wavering light we all saw the image of Sarah's mother on the wall.

'Oh! Oh, Mother dear!' said Sarah, sitting down heavily on her bed, weeping.

'Now, now, don't upset yourself,' said Mrs Briskett, busily unbuttoning her.

'These are tears of joy, Mrs B, tears of joy,' Sarah murmured. 'Joy that we're reunited at last.'

I found Sarah's white nightgown and put it over her head for decency while Mrs Briskett struggled with all her buttons and hooks and manoeuvred her lumpy body out of her bodice and stays. When her quivering flesh was entirely freed at last, Mrs Briskett pushed her gently back on her bed and pulled the covers up over her.

'There now. Go to sleep, Sarah, there's a good girl,' she said, tucking her up as tenderly as if she were her mother herself.

Sarah obediently closed her eyes, and we backed out of the door.

Mrs Briskett breathed a great sigh of relief. 'My Lord, it affected her badly this time!'

'*What* did? *How* did she see her mother?' I thought of the gravestones by the church. 'She didn't . . . she didn't *dig her up*?'

Mrs Briskett shook her head at me. 'Don't be ridiculous, Hetty. All right, I'll tell you – not that I know much, mind. I'll come down with you and have another cup of tea. It's fearfully late but it'll take me hours to get to sleep after this to-do.'

So we sat down together in the dark kitchen and sipped tea while Mrs Briskett explained properly.

'Sarah goes to see Madame Berenice every Sunday. This Madame calls herself a spiritualist-medium. She says she's in touch with the spirit world.'

'*Is* she?'

'Well, who's to say? Sarah clearly believes so – and Mr Brown and all the other folk who go there and give Madame Berenice half their hard-earned wages. They're all that desperate to see their long-departed loved ones. Mr Brown lost his only son to influenza years ago and wants to get in touch with him. *Mrs* Brown holds no truck with this kind of caper and neither do I. It's not decent, nor Christian, trying to meddle with the Lord's will. If you're dead you're dead, and you should jolly well stay dead, not come back and start haunting people. It doesn't do any good. Look at the state of Sarah tonight. Oh, she'll be that mortified in the morning!'

'But what does this Madame Berenice *do*, Mrs B? How does she get in touch with the spirit world?'

'Don't ask me, Hetty. All Sarah will say is that they sit around in a ring in a darkened room, and then this Madame Berenice goes into a trance and starts talking in strange voices.' Mrs Briskett shivered. 'You wouldn't get me in that circle for a million pounds!'

I lay awake thinking about it long after I'd gone back to bed. It seemed a very strange idea to me – but then *everything* seemed strange to me in this crazy outside world.

I was woken by the sound of crockery in the kitchen. When I ran in, I saw Sarah bustling about, laying breakfast, neat in her dark work dress and white cap and apron.

'How do, Hetty,' she said cheerily. 'I thought I'd give Mrs B a little lie-in this morning, seeing as she was up till all hours on account of yours truly!'

She didn't sound the slightest bit embarrassed. She danced about the kitchen, treating the stone flags like a polished ballroom floor. She looked comical, of course – a great lumpy parlourmaid waltzing around with the breadboard and the teapot – but I couldn't laugh at her, not when she looked so wondrously happy. She buttered the good crust on the end of the loaf, spread it with Mrs Briskett's deluxe strawberry jam specially kept for the master's scones, and handed it to me.

'Get that down you, you skinny little ha'p'orth,' she said.

'My mama always gave me special little treats when I was at the hospital,' I said.

'Mothers are the very best, aren't they, Hetty!' said Sarah.

Mrs Briskett was in a good mood too, having had an hour's lie-in, so she decided to let me have a turn at baking, showing me how to make an apple pie. It was fresh out the oven when Bertie came with our meat delivery of mince and chops and a rib of beef.

He sniffed appreciatively at the sight of the big pie, its golden pastry oozing apples, cloves and cinnamon. 'My, that looks a sight for sore eyes, Mrs B,' he said enthusiastically. 'You're a wonderful cook, ma'am, especially in the pie department.'

'It's not *my* pie, Bertie. Young Hetty made it. She's got a very light hand with her pastry. I doubt I could do better myself.'

'*Hetty* baked it!' said Bertie, looking astonished.

'Don't act so surprised!' I said. 'Can he have a tiny taste, Mrs Briskett?'

'I don't see why not,' she said. 'In fact we'll all try a slice.'

She cut us a liberal piece each and ladled on a spoonful of cream too. 'Here, Sarah, you need some good food inside you after all that swooning last night.'

'You were swooning, Sarah?' said Bertie. 'Why's that? Do you have a pash on some fine fellow? Ooh, was it the thought of meeting up with me today? Well, I'm very flattered, Sarah, but I'm afraid I'm already taken. You'd definitely be in with a chance, but I'm that feared of Hetty here I daren't cross her.'

'Stop your cheek and try her pie, lad. It's very good,' said Sarah, munching.

He took a large bite of pie, and then pretended to choke. He clutched his throat, eyes popping, staggering around the kitchen as if poisoned.

'I'll *throw* the pie at you if you don't behave,' I sniffed.

Bertie stopped playing the fool and took another big bite. 'It's actually absolutely delicious, Hetty! Total knockout! My, you'll make someone a lovely little wife one day!'

'No I won't! I'm not going to be anyone's wife, little or otherwise,' I said, tasting my own portion of pie. It truly *was* delicious. 'I shall make my own way in life,' I declared indistinctly through a big mouthful.

'Won't you be lonely, Hetty?' said Bertie.

'Not at all. I shall set up home with my mama,' I said.

'Oh, bless the child,' said Sarah. 'Would that I could do the same.'

'Now careful, Hetty, you'll set her off again,' said Mrs Briskett. 'We don't want her swooning all over the place.'

'I am perfectly well, thank you, Mrs B,' said Sarah with dignity.

'Oh yes, it looked like it last night!'

'I was overcome because I was so happy to be reunited with my beloved mother, to feel her own hands upon me, her lips kissing my brow! I am so very glad I met Madame Berenice!'

'Oh, that spiritualist lady?' said Bertie. 'I deliver to her: fillet steak, crown of lamb, capons – even a goose, though it ain't Christmas! Seeing all them ghosties must work up a grand appetite.'

'Don't you mock what you don't understand,' said Sarah, swatting him with a tea towel. 'Madame Berenice is a true saint, working so hard to reunite us with our loved ones. Is your mother living, Bertie?'

'No, she passed on when I was just a little lad,' said Bertie.

'You're still a little lad now,' said Sarah, tucking into the rest of her pie. 'This is exceptionally good,

Hetty. I think your cooking days are numbered, Mrs B.'

'Hmph!' said Mrs Briskett. 'You watch your tongue, Sarah. Young Hetty's got a long way to go yet.'

'I'm just teasing, Mrs B,' said Sarah. She turned back to Bertie. 'So, Bertie, would you not like to hear your dear mother's voice?'

'I don't think I'd recognize it, Sarah, so it would be a waste of time. But I'm pleased you get to hear *your* mother.'

'She touched me last night! I asked for a special materialization, and she manifested herself right there in the room, before my very eyes.'

'You thought you really saw her?'

'I know I did! She touched me. She kissed me on the forehead!' said Sarah.

'Well, that's grand, Sarah, simply grand,' said Bertie. His eyes swivelled to me and his eyebrows shot up.

'Do hush now, Sarah,' Mrs Briskett begged. 'You shouldn't talk so much about such things.'

'I want to tell the world, Mrs B! I am not the slightest bit embarrassed. It's like a miracle. I'm a changed woman. Why won't you be pleased for me?'

'We're all thrilled for you, Sarah,' said Bertie. 'Do you reckon you're a changed woman too, Mrs B? If so, why don't you let Hetty and me stay out walking a little later next Sunday evening? After all, you let Sarah stay out late with her dear departed mother, as it were. It's only fair, don't you see?'

'*I'm* not a changed woman – and I'm not a stupid one either,' said Mrs Briskett. 'No one's taking any liberties, especially not you! You're to bring Hetty back at six sharp, do you hear me?'

'But it won't be long enough! I've got great plans. I want to take Hetty somewhere really special this time. She deserves to see a bit of London, Mrs B, seeing as she's been a poor little foundling girl locked up in that hospital all those years. I'm intent on showing her the sights, all them historic buildings up London way – *educating* her.'

'I know young lads' intentions – and if you don't stop this cheek, you won't take her out at all,' said Mrs Briskett, with such a note of finality that even Bertie saw there was no point in arguing.

12

I wondered happily on and off all week where Bertie would take me on Sunday. He was there waiting for me when we got home from church, but he didn't have his ready smile. His shoulders were hunched. Even his hair lay limp upon his head without benefit of pomade.

'Bertie? What's the matter?' I said as we walked away from Mrs Briskett and Sarah. 'Where are we going today?'

'I'm not sure we're going anywhere, Hetty,' he said flatly.

I looked at him. Oh goodness, didn't he like me any more? Had he found another sweetheart? I was horrified. I wanted to be Bertie's special one-and-only girl – although didn't I have another sweetheart myself? I'd only known him a few weeks, but I realized he'd become important to me. I'd thought he was keen on me. He liked me: he liked me being small, he liked me being spirited, he liked my apple pie, he even liked my red hair.

'What do you mean, we're not going anywhere?' I said, my voice cracking because my throat was so tight.

Bertie looked down at his boots. 'I haven't got any money, Hetty,' he mumbled, pulling out his empty pockets to show me. 'I had such plans. I was aiming to take you up to London today.'

'Yes, to show me the historic buildings.'

'No – to show you the Western Gardens up at Earl's Court. Folk say it's wonderful there, even better than the fair. There's a band, and it's all decked out in fairy lights, ever so pretty. I knew I'd need quite a lot of cash for two train fares and all the amusements, so I volunteered for more gardening jobs. I started a nice little sideline with my meat customers. If I saw their garden looked a tad untidy, I'd ask if they needed anyone to mow their lawn. It all seemed to be working out excellently . . .' His voice tailed away.

'But then?' I said.

'The parlourmaid from Whiteacres, a big house over in Berryland – she said her mistress was fretting. Her gardener's hurt his back and the weeds were getting on her nerves – so I says, like an idiot, "Well, I'll do your weeding, ma'am."'

'You're many things, Bertie, but you're not an idiot.'

'Wait till you hear me out, Hetty. So after work yesterday I go round to Whiteacres, and I reckoned I had a good hour before the light started to fade, so I kneel down and set to weeding. I worked real hard, pulling and pulling – and then gathers them all up neatly and puts them in a sack, leaving everything spick and span, thinking the mistress might give me an extra tip for tidiness. Then the parlourmaid comes out, looks at my nice tidy bare bed and starts shrieking her head off. It turns out I'd uprooted all her prize shrubs along with the wretched weeds. I thought everything green had to be a weed. I didn't realize they were waiting to flower later. Only now they're not. They're all dead, in the sack. And to stop her missus telling tales to Jarvis the butcher and then him giving *me* the sack, I've had to hand over all my savings towards new plants – *and* I have to pay her a shilling a week till she reckons I've paid for the lot. You're not *laughing*, are you, Hetty?'

'I'm sorry!' I said, spluttering. 'Oh, poor Bertie. You were trying so hard too. But you have to admit, it's just a little bit funny.'

'It's not funny in the slightest, because I can't take you out now, on account of the fact I ain't got no spare cash – and I won't have for weeks and weeks according to that mean old maid.'

'We can still walk out together, silly.'

'But that's all we *can* do, walk. I haven't got the cash for a rowing boat, or even a hokey-pokey – don't you understand?'

'Of course I do. But we can still walk – and talk. And *next* week I'll bake us a pie and we'll have a little picnic – how about that?'

'Oh, Hetty! I thought you'd be cross with me and want to go out walking with some other lad with a pocketful of cash who'd treat you properly,' said Bertie. 'You're a diamond girl, did you know that?'

'I'm a *sapphire* girl,' I said. 'Come on, let's go for a walk in the park. We can always pretend it's those gardens. I was always picturing when I was young.'

'When you were at the hospital?'

'No, before that. I doubt anyone could picture at the hospital – it was too dreadful. I meant when I was little, in the country. I used to have this special tree. We called it our squirrel house . . .' My voice trailed away when I saw Bertie's expression.

'You and that Jem?' he said.

'All of us children,' I said, though of course I'd meant just Jem and me. I didn't want to think of Jem. I'd had another letter from him yesterday. He had told me all about Mother and Father and the farm, and how Rosie was engaged to be married, and Nat was doing very well in the army, and he hoped he'd maybe meet up with Gideon one day. It was a letter just like Jem himself, strong and straightforward, tender and concerned. It ended: *I am thinking of the future, Hetty. Our future, together. With love from Jem.*

626

I had tried hard to picture Jem himself, but somehow I could only see him as a child, with a boy's voice, not as the man I knew he was. And it was impossible to picture him now, when I was walking along with Bertie, doing my best to console him.

'You're thinking of that Jem, aren't you?' said Bertie suspiciously.

'No I'm not,' I lied. 'I'm thinking of the pleasure gardens – *these* pleasure gardens,' I continued as we walked through the gates into the plain green park. 'Oh, see the fairy lights on the trees, Bertie, and little coloured lanterns – look!' I waved my hand at the ordinary plane trees, then pointed to a scrubby patch of grass. 'See, there's a rose bower for sweethearts – and little boys are walking around with trays of gingerbread and we can simply help ourselves—'

'This sounds better than the Western Gardens!'

'*Much* better. And over there' – I pointed vaguely into thin air – 'is a pleasure dome, like in "Kubla Khan".'

'What's Kubla Watsit when it's at home?'

'It's a strange poem. I'm not sure I understand it, but I love the way it's written. Nurse Winnie lent me this book of poetry once. I wish I still had it.'

'Hasn't that weird old stick Buchanan any poetry books? I don't suppose he could lend you one?' said Bertie.

'He's barely speaking to me since I got cross with him for taking my memoirs. He still has them, Bertie, but he doesn't mention them. Sarah says she'll give me what for if I bring it up again. She says it's not my place to make demands on the master. Oh, Bertie, don't you just *hate* having to know your place?'

'Well, I can picture too, Hetty. I can picture right into the future, when I'll be . . .'

'A master butcher like Mr Jarvis?'

'Definitely *not* a butcher. I live, breathe and eat meat, and it's started to turn my stomach. No, I'll live on your apple pies, Hetty – and I won't be no butcher.'

'Well, I don't think you'd better be a gardener,' I said, giggling.

He gave me a look, but then he laughed too.

'So what do you see yourself as, Bertie?'

He suddenly looked shy. 'You'll laugh at me!'

'No I won't. Well, I'll try not to. Go on, tell. It doesn't matter if it can't come true, it's only picturing. I have all manner of madcap fantasies. I see myself as a famous author, Sapphire Battersea, writing a few pages every day, living in a house even bigger than Mr Buchanan's, keeping my mama in luxury. Or – or I could be Sapphire the circus lady in pink, with spangly tights, riding my troupe of rosin-backed horses, while hundreds gasp and clap. Or perhaps I might even be Sapphire the sailor, crossing the seven seas with the wind in my hair, gulls screaming overhead, dolphins swimming along beside the ship. There! Now you can laugh at me!'

'Well, *I* picture myself on stage in a fancy toff suit, with a little straw hat to tilt at a jaunty angle.'

'An actor?'

'Not a Shakespearean actor, spouting all sorts of stuff you can't understand. No, comedy's more my line. Or maybe a music-hall turn – comical, with a saucy song, maybe even a little dance.' He did a little tap dance on the grass, his feet flashing. He landed elegantly with a 'Ta-*da*!' his arms held high.

'Bravo!' I said, and clapped him. 'You're good at it, Bertie, really good.'

'I thought I might act like a bit of a charmer with the ladies. I could call my act Flirty Bertie – and as I'm so small, it would work really well if I shared the routine with a very *tall* girl, to make it more comic like, but still touching. A pity *you're* not tall, Hetty – it would be grand to do a double act with you. Have you ever fancied treading the boards yourself?'

'I'm not sure! The vicar said that music halls were very bad places – but I think they sound like fun,' I said.

'They're *great* fun. I think you'd love them. I'll take you there some day – when I've got some cash!

Maybe it will inspire you, seeing as you're a bit of a writer. You could write a play yourself and then star in it,' said Bertie. 'I could have a part too, couldn't I?'

'You could play the leading man, definitely,' I said. 'And my brother could act in it too.'

'That Jem?' said Bertie, frowning.

'No! *Not* Jem. I'm sure he'd hate the very idea. Jem wouldn't ever be anything but a farmer, I'm sure of it. No, my brother Gideon. He was at the hospital with me, though we scarcely ever saw each other. Poor Gideon, he's not at all like other boys. He's always so timid and fearful. But one Christmas he was chosen to be the angel in our nativity tableau in chapel. There he was, right up high, arms in the air, and this look of utter radiance.' I thought of Gideon now, and shivered.

'What is it?' said Bertie.

'He's gone to be a soldier, and I fear he will very much dislike a soldier's life. He was terribly teased at the hospital. It's such a worry, having brothers. Do you have any, Bertie?'

'Not that I know of. Nor sisters either. It's easier that way. I can just look after myself.'

'Did the other boys ever pick on you when you were at the workhouse?' I asked, my voice lowered.

'Of course they did,' said Bertie cheerfully enough.

'Because you were small?'

'We was *all* small, seeing as we didn't get enough to eat and worked a twelve-hour day from when we were ten. But the older ones picked on the younger ones. I learned to dodge and duck, and then I built myself up a bit. I did a drill every morning, pumping myself up like a little strongman, hanging off the tops of doors to increase my arm muscles. In time I could take on even the biggest boys and get the better of them all. Hanging like this, Hetty!'

Bertie leaped right up and caught hold of the branch of a tree at the edge of the park. He hung on, swinging his legs vigorously, then pulled himself up until his chin was on the branch. He stayed wobbling there, his face purple with effort, obviously expecting applause.

'Ah, *now* you're picturing you're Bertie the monkey. Shall I offer you a banana?' I said.

He laughed and tumbled down, then capered about me, making silly chattering monkey noises.

'I shall take you to the Zoological Gardens where you belong,' I said. 'Look, they're just over here. Shall I put you in your cage?'

'I'll have a ride on Jumbo the elephant first,' said Bertie.

'I've *had* a ride on that elephant, truly!' I said proudly.

We sat down under the trees and I told him how

I'd run away on the day of the Queen's Golden Jubilee.

'But you never saw the old lady herself?' said Bertie. 'Well, we must rectify that. I spy the palace shining in the sunshine just over there. Let's join Her Majesty for afternoon tea.'

'*What* a good idea! Well, I'll very quickly fashion myself a new dress – *not* one of Mrs Briskett's cast-offs. I'll select a subtle sky-blue, with lace at the neck, and lace mittens to match, and I'll have pale-grey kid boots with little pearl buttons.'

'I'll have them kid boots and all,' said Bertie, examining the loose sole of his old brown boot. 'And a toff's suit, please, with one of them starched shirts with the high collars.'

'Yes, it will be so starched you'll feel as if you're wearing a suit of armour. This *might* get you into trouble when we're ushered into Her Majesty's drawing room. You will be expected to bow down low, but of course your starched shirt will keep you resolutely upright. There is a grave danger Her Majesty will take offence and summon her guards, and they will march you off to her dungeons.'

'Buckingham Palace doesn't *have* dungeons!'

'These are *secret* dungeons down in the sewers, and they will shut you in a rat-infested cage and you will cast yourself down in the mire and moan piteously.'

'This is a really cheery story!'

'Ssh, I'm coming to the best part. Meanwhile I am imploring the Queen to forgive you, confessing that I've over-starched your shirt, and she will laugh heartily and instruct her guards to release you immediately.'

'All cowering and covered in rat muck – even my starched shirt!'

'So the Queen commands that you be taken to her private bathroom and you luxuriate in her very own bathtub. The taps have little gold crowns and the royal crest is printed on the porcelain. Here, did you know Mr Buchanan has his own water closet and we're not ever allowed to use it – but I do secretly sometimes.'

Bertie roared with laughter. 'I bet you do, Hetty. And I use the Queen's very own personal facility while I'm washing off all the sewer slime.'

'And then a maid gives you a whole new outfit – toff gentleman's clothes with a fancy waistcoat and everything, but they all belonged to Prince Albert so they're miles too big for you. The maid has to pad you out with big cushions.'

'Oh yes, turn me into a figure of fun now.'

'Yes, but it's to a purpose! You come waddling back, clean again, but positively spherical. Her Majesty starts chortling away, because you look so comical, so you take advantage of this, see, and do a funny dance, waddling even more, and bowing low and then bouncing back again. She laughs and laughs and says you should be on the stage – and guess what, Bertie, there's a special Royal Command Performance at the theatre, and *you* are top of the bill: Great Big Bertie, the talk of all London – how about that?'

'That's just fine and dandy, Hetty. You're a grand girl for telling stories!' he said.

When we set off for home at five to six, Bertie squeezed my hand as we walked along the road. 'I thought this afternoon was going to be a disaster, but it's been the best ever, and it's all down to you, Hetty. You're a girl in a million.'

I felt myself glowing. It was so lovely to be appreciated, the centre of attention. I had always felt so *crushed* at the hospital. It had often scared me when I looked at all the hundreds of other girls in their identical brown uniforms and white caps and tippets. It was hard to hang onto the fact that I was *me*, Hetty, different from all the others.

'You're a *boy* in a million, Bertie,' I said. As no one seemed to be passing, I threw my arms around his neck and gave him a quick hug.

'Hetty!' he said, going crimson – but he looked tremendously pleased.

He delivered me back to number eight Lady's Ride on the very dot of six – but I discovered Sarah and Mrs Briskett in the midst of such a to-do I don't think they even noticed. Sarah was in her Sunday purple, bonnet on, trying to get out of the door, but Mrs Briskett was hanging onto her arm, imploring her not to go.

'You must stay home safe, Sarah. I'm *ordering* you!'

'You can't give me orders, Mrs B, and you know it. I'm free to do what I want – and I know what that is!'

'Very well then, girl, I'm not ordering, I'm imploring. Heaven help us, I'm *begging* you to stay at home,' said Mrs Briskett.

'Don't be so ridiculous, Mrs B. How could I possibly keep away! I'm going to pay for another materialization. I can't wait to see Mother again.'

'Yes, and you'll swoon again too, and Mr Brown made it plain he didn't feel it was fitting for him to look after you in such a state.'

'Then come with me, Mrs B!' said Sarah. 'If you'll only come too, you'll see why it's so important to me. It could be important to you too. You could be reunited with all *your* loved ones who have passed over.'

'As if I'd go along with such an idea! I think the dead should stay shut up in their graves, where they belong. It's not decent, stirring them up like this. It's downright blasphemous!'

'How dare you! I've never blasphemed in my life! And it's the sweetest, most holy experience, communicating with my own mother. I lost her when I was only fourteen, and she was all the world to me. I missed her so when I was sent away into service. I never dreamed I'd not see her sweet face again.'

I shivered, thinking about my own mama. 'I'll go with you, Sarah,' I said, taking hold of her hand.

They both looked at me, astonished, as if the table had started talking.

'Don't be so foolish, Hetty!' said Mrs Briskett.

'Why is that foolish, Mrs B? It's the most beautiful experience, going to one of Madame Berenice's seances.'

'You can't take a *child*!'

'Hetty's old enough to be sensible,' said Sarah.

'*You're* a lot older, and yet I can't make you see sense,' said Mrs Briskett. 'Oh, very well, go then, and take Hetty too, even though she'll likely scream herself senseless.'

'I won't scream, I promise,' I said. I was starting to feel very excited. I had no real idea of what happened at a seance, but it certainly sounded interesting. I was a little frightened at the thought of Sarah's mother emanating out of thin air, but I was sure she'd be paying more attention to Sarah than to me.

It would be a wonderful story to tell Bertie next time I saw him – and an extra outing seemed much more attractive than staying home in the scullery,

636

writing dutiful letters to Mama and Jem. I *wanted* to write to Mama, but I still didn't know whether to tell her all about Bertie or not, so my letters were shorter and more stilted than usual. I knew absolutely that I shouldn't tell Jem about Bertie, so my letters to him were shorter still – though his were getting longer.

'I will go with Sarah and behave very sensibly, and if she swoons again I will take care of her and find us a cab home,' I said.

Mrs Briskett shook her head and sighed, but Sarah put her arms around me.

'There, you're a dear little girl. Come along then. My, you cut a fine figure in that dress.'

'I still don't hold with such shenanigans,' said Mrs Briskett, but she went to the money jar she kept in the larder, right at the back on the top shelf, took out half a crown, tied it up in a handkerchief, and gave it to me.

'That will cover the cab fare, just in case,' she said, tucking it up my velvet cuff.

I smiled at her gratefully and gave Sarah a little nod. 'We'll be fine,' I said grandly.

'Well, don't say I didn't warn you,' said Mrs Briskett, folding her arms. 'It's not right and fitting, meddling with the supernatural. It's just a form of witchcraft, that's what *I* say.'

'Well, we don't care what *she* says, do we, Hetty?' Sarah murmured to me and we set off.

13

We walked away from the town, along a stream, down many winding lanes. I tried to take note of the way we were going in case I had to steer Sarah back, but I soon became muddled. I was surprised when we stopped in front of a relatively modest cottage with an ordinary suburban garden. It had a little privet hedge, a patch of emerald-green lawn, and a bright flowerbed of marigolds and geraniums edged with scallop shells.

Sarah led me up the red and black tiled garden path and pulled the bell by the front door. A tall pale woman in black answered the door.

'Is she Madame Berenice, or her servant?' I whispered to Sarah.

'No, no. She is Emily. I believe she is Madame Berenice's sister. She will serve us refreshments afterwards.'

'Afterwards!' I repeated excitedly.

Emily took our shawls silently. Sarah pressed a little envelope of money into her hand and murmured something about materialization. Emily nodded, and still without speaking led us into a very dark room, the curtains shrouded with thick black velvet. I expected her to light a lamp but she went away again.

It was so very dark after the bright evening sunshine that for a moment or two I could see nothing, but I sensed we weren't alone. No one spoke, but I could hear someone breathing, someone rustling. I could smell liniment and floral scent. I gradually began to make out a small group of people sitting on chairs set around a table in a circle. There was tall thin Mr Brown from Dedman's grocery, sitting very erect; two elderly ladies, both in black – and a woman with compelling dark eyes wearing a strange feathered turban and extravagant robes. I did not need Sarah to introduce me. She was clearly Madame Berenice.

'Sit down, Sarah,' she said, in a deep voice. 'And who is the little person with you?'

'This is Hetty Feather, Madame Berenice. She is our new little maid, come to help me home if necessary,' Sarah whispered deferentially. 'I've asked for another materialization, madame. I do hope that's convenient?'

'I will do my best, but as you know, there are no guarantees. Our spirit friends are very sensitive, especially when there is a stranger in their midst.'

She was staring at me intently in the darkness, and I couldn't help squirming.

'Would you like Hetty to wait outside, madame?' Sarah asked.

'Oh no, please may I stay!' I said, determined not to miss out on anything.

'Are you a believer, Hetty Feather?' asked Madame Berenice.

I wasn't quite sure what she meant. 'I go to church every Sunday,' I said.

'Do you believe in the psychic sciences, child?'

'I – I'm not sure what they *are*,' I said.

'She's very ignorant, madame. She's a foundling, brought up at the hospital. She knows very little, but she's a good helpful girl, eager to learn,' said Sarah.

'There is no greater wonder in all nature than the communication between the spirit world and our own,' said Madame Berenice. She uttered her words with great expression, as if she were on stage. 'Have you lost a loved one, Hetty Feather?'

'I've lost my dear mama,' I said huskily.

'No, no, Hetty, your mother is still living,' said Sarah. 'Madame Berenice is asking you if any of your dear friends and family have passed away.'

'I don't think so,' I said, a little flustered.

'Can't we get on with the seance, Madame Berenice?' Mr Brown said.

'Calm yourself, sir. There must be no impatience, no restlessness, or the spirits won't come,' Madame Berenice rebuked him. 'Sit within the circle, Hetty Feather.'

I tried to find an empty chair in the darkness, and tripped over a footstool in my blunderings.

'Hetty! Sit *down*! You're keeping Madame Berenice waiting,' Sarah hissed.

'I can't help it. I can't *see*,' I whispered. 'Why can't we draw the curtains a little?'

'We need total darkness, child,' said Madame Berenice. 'Those dwelling in the spiritual sphere are shy and wary of our world. It is a harsh, crude environment, and we have to be considerate. If we are lucky enough to achieve a total materialization again—'

'Oh please, *please*!' Sarah begged.

'Then it would be like exposing a newborn baby to blinding light,' Madame Berenice continued. 'We have to be in harmony with the creation of all animal structures, as they are created in the darkness of the womb. Now, are we all ready?'

I found a spare chair at last and sat down abruptly.

'Let us join hands and see if the spirits will come to us today.'

I had to hold hands on one side with Sarah, which felt odd, and on the other side with Mr

Brown, which felt even odder. They both gripped tightly, almost crushing my fingers. I had a sudden intense tickle on my nose, but I couldn't wriggle either hand free to give it a good scratch. I was trapped in this silent circle in this musty dark room.

'Is there anybody there?' Madame Berenice asked, her voice even deeper.

I held my breath, but nobody answered.

'Is . . . there . . . anybody . . . there?' she cried, again and again, for a full five minutes.

Nothing happened. There was silence, though Madame Berenice was breathing heavily now, as if running to catch a train.

'Speak now, dear spirits,' she gasped – and then suddenly gave a little scream.

I jumped, and had to bite my lips to stop myself giggling hysterically.

'Hello, dear Father!' Madame Berenice lisped, in a strangely high-pitched baby voice.

'It is my Cedric!' Mr Brown choked, crushing my fingers.

'Yes, Father! I have come to tell you how happy I am,' the weird little voice squeaked.

'Will you ask my little lad if he's in any pain now?' Mr Brown asked.

'There is no pain in the spirit world, dear Father.'

'Oh, thank God! So could you ask if he is keeping up with his schooling? He was always such a bright little lad.'

'I know all the secrets of the spirit spheres, Father. I have no need of earthly schooling,' said Cedric.

'So what do you do all day, Cedric?' I asked eagerly.

I wanted to know if he flew around the world, manifesting himself in and out of houses at whim, or whether he hovered in the same spot in space, waiting to be summoned. But Sarah shook my arm fiercely, practically detaching it from my shoulder.

'You mustn't speak directly to the spirits, Hetty!' she hissed. 'Besides, he's not *your* loved one's spirit. Be quiet at once, and let poor Mr Brown commune properly.'

'Could you tell him how much his mother and I miss him?' Mr Brown asked, his voice hoarse with emotion.

'But I am always with you, Father. Please give my love to Mother,' Cedric squeaked, his voice so high-pitched it made Madame Berenice gasp.

'Oh, the Lord be praised,' Mr Brown said, and the rest of the circle murmured this too. His hand was hot and damp and I could feel him shaking.

I did not know what to make of all this. Mr Brown clearly thought a miracle had taken place and that his dead little boy had actually spoken to him. The voice hadn't really *sounded* like a little boy. It had sounded like a middle-aged lady *pretending* to be a child. Perhaps it was inevitable that Cedric would sound like Madame Berenice if he were using her as an earthly vehicle.

She was gasping again, almost as if she were having a seizure.

'Could you ask my Cedric if he could visit us in our own home?' Mr Brown asked desperately.

'I am . . . sorry – Cedric is . . . fading,' Madame Berenice panted. 'The spirits are jostling with each other for attention tonight. Oh, it's very wonderful, but a terrible strain. Who is this now? Pray speak clearly.'

'Is it Mother? Oh please, let it be my mother,' Sarah begged.

But it wasn't Sarah's mother this time, it was a dear friend of one of the old ladies. She spoke in a quavery voice, and told us that she had fully recovered her health now, and did not even cough. Then the other old lady spoke to *her* dear departed friend, who said that she was feeling fit and well too, and that she was reunited with her little cat now, and very happy.

It was almost like listening to real old ladies conversing in a shop queue, and it all went on for so long that I began to feel restless. Both my hands were numb now, as Sarah and Mr Brown were still clutching them fiercely, and the room was oppressively hot and dark.

Madame Berenice began her throaty gasping again.

'Is it Mother *this* time?' Sarah begged.

'I think . . . yes, I think it is,' Madame Berenice panted.

'Can you ask her if she'll come here to me again? Oh please – it meant the world to me.'

'I – am – coming – Sarah,' said another strange whispery voice from Madame Berenice's lips.

'Oh, Mother!' Sarah said, half standing in her eagerness.

'Sit still, my child. Sit very still, all of you,' Madame Berenice interrupted. Then she gave a final gasp and fell face down on the tablecloth.

'Oh my Lord!' I whispered, fearing she had died too, and gone to join all her spirit friends in person. I wondered why everyone was still sitting there, not trying to revive her. Then I saw a wisp of strange white smoke, and glimpsed a figure all in white gliding slowly across the room. I could barely breathe for shock. The white figure was moving slowly but surely in my direction. I could see her more clearly now, though her face was obscured by a white veil. Sarah shivered, making little moaning noises. The apparition glided onwards. I ducked my head as she came nearer, terrified she might speak to me, or maybe slide straight through me – but she was only concerned with Sarah.

'My little girl,' she said, in an eerie whispery voice.

'Mother!' Sarah sobbed.

She wasn't a little girl at all, she was a great lump of a woman, and yet somehow she seemed to be shrinking back to childhood again. I could picture her in a pinafore, her hair down her back, tears running down her round moon face.

'Oh, my mother!'

I found there were tears blurring my own eyes as the white figure hovered beside her. She gently touched Sarah's head with her fingertips, then bent and kissed her.

'Oh, Madame Berenice, please may she stay just a little longer?' Sarah begged.

'No, my dear, her visits must be brief. I think her psychic essence is already fading – yes, fading . . .'

'Goodbye – but not for long,' the white figure whispered.

'Let us close our eyes and give thanks to our spirit friends,' said Madame Berenice.

We all closed our eyes and murmured thank you, while Sarah sobbed convulsively. When we opened our eyes, the spirit was gone.

'Oh thank you, thank you!' said Sarah, weeping and sniffing.

She clearly needed the handkerchief that was tucked up my sleeve, so I tried wriggling my hand free.

'Do not break the circle! There is still a spirit there, clamouring to be heard,' Madame Berenice snapped.

I gripped hands again, peering around the circle in surprise. It was difficult to see properly in the dark, but it seemed as if everyone had had their visit. Sarah's mother materializing had been the star spirit turn. Was there to be some sort of encore?

'Who is there?' Madame Berenice asked. 'Oh, oh, it is a young boy!' she answered herself. 'A little stranger determined to make himself known. Who do you wish to communicate with, child?'

He whispered something indistinctly, his voice high and reedy. We all had to strain to hear him.

'Try again, try again,' Madame Berenice commanded.

The whispering was a little louder this time.

'Hetty! Hetty Feather!' the ghostly voice hissed.

'Oh, Hetty, dear!' Sarah said. 'It's a spirit come to talk to you!'

'No! No, I don't want him to,' I said.

'There is no need to be frightened, child,'

Madame Berenice tried to reassure me. 'Just relax and clear your mind. You said you did not have anyone dwelling in the spirit realm, but you were clearly wrong. I will try to connect more intensely.' She breathed heavily in and out, while my mind whirled. Who could it be?

'It's not – not a brother, is it?' I said, panicking. Oh dear Lord, was it Gideon? Had some terrible accident happened at the barracks? Had Gideon found it so unbearable he had taken his own life?'

'It *can't* be Gideon,' I whispered.

'Have you forgotten me, Hetty Feather?' said the voice, sounding reproachful.

Then there was a sudden rap beneath the table – a tap-tap-tapping, like a stick . . . or a crutch!

'Saul!' I screamed.

I had never loved Saul the way a sister should. We had always fought. I had been made to feel deeply ashamed because he had a withered leg and it was very bad to torment a crippled boy – though Saul tormented *me* for all he was worth. He had lived with Gideon in the boy's wing, but he had died of influenza.

I had been so anxious that Gideon might die, because he was so unhappy and weak and delicate. I hadn't even thought about Saul dying. Now here I was, years later, making the same mistake all over again. I had almost forgotten Saul – but he had not forgotten me! He was here now, coming to get me!

'No! No, no, no!' I screamed.

I wrenched my hands away from Sarah and Mr Brown, and ran from the room. I was down the hallway, out of the door, through the garden gate and halfway down the road before Sarah caught up with me.

'Oh, Hetty, come *here*!' she cried, and she threw her arms around me.

'No! I won't go back!'

'It's all right, I won't make you. Don't worry, dear, I know it can be overwhelming at first. But the spirits are our friends, Hetty, our dear loved ones returning to us. Oh, did you see my dear mother, as distinct as anything?'

'Yes, I am happy for you – but I don't want to see my brother Saul!'

I kept thinking I could hear the tap of his crutch, even out here in the gentle twilight. I was in such a state that we had to take a hansom cab home for my benefit.

Mrs Briskett was waiting for us in the kitchen. When she saw me shaking, she shook her head furiously. 'That's the giddy limit, Sarah! If you want to waste all your hard-earned savings and make a spectacle of yourself in that spooky place, then that's your affair, but I won't have you reducing the child to such a state. Just look at her, poor little lamb.'

Mrs Briskett sat me down and made me a cup of tea and a slice of bread and butter in an effort to calm my nerves. I was still shivering so much that my teeth clanked against the cup and I could barely swallow my bread.

The two women put me to bed with an extra coverlet and a hot-water pig. They sat on either side of me, patting my hands, until at last the shivering subsided. I drifted off to sleep – but Saul pursued me in all my dreams that night, his crutch tap-tap-tapping as he searched for me.

14

'I am sorry if I got you into trouble with Mrs B, Sarah,' I said the next day as we made Mr Buchanan's bed together.

'Oh well, it wasn't really your fault, Hetty. You were just that worked up and over-excited. It happens frequently at Madame Berenice's sessions. You're a girl who's for ever working herself into a passion, anyways – but I know you can't help that. Your temperament's fiery, just like your red hair.'

'Perhaps I can work on it, Sarah. I feel it is time I learned to stay composed.'

'That'll be the day, Hetty!' said Sarah. 'Smooth out the creases your side of that sheet now. Hurry up – we should just about have time to do the master's study while he's still having his breakfast.'

We went into Mr Buchanan's study together. He had clearly already been working on a story that morning. Papers were scattered across his desk, and several were screwed into little balls in his wastepaper basket.

'Dear, dear, he's always like this at the beginning of a story. He makes so many false starts,' said Sarah, dabbing at a fresh inkstain on his desk.

I squatted down beside the wastepaper basket, picking up the crumpled pieces of paper and smoothing them out, thinking that I could use the unwritten sides for my own stories. I had in my hands a discarded version of his first page. I started reading – and my hands shook.

My name is Emerald Greenwich. Is that not the most beautiful name in the world? My dearest mama called me Emerald because my eyes are deep emerald-green. Oh, how I miss my mama now. I know she committed a grievous moral sin when she bore me out of wedlock, but she repented abjectly, and suffered greatly when she handed me in to the fine Christian guardians at the Foundling Hospital.

I spent a few years with some simple country folk, but my true education began when I returned to that splendid institution and learned the hard but necessary lessons of obedience and humility. I am afraid I still find it a struggle to hold my tongue and remember my place, but I am

learning from the kindly example of my
benefactor and employer—'

'*Kindly!* He has stolen my story – all of it, bla-
tantly! How dare he! How *dare* he!' I shrieked.

Sarah looked at me, astonished. 'Hetty? For
heaven's sake, child, lower your voice! The master
will hear!'

'I don't care if he does. He is a wicked hypocritical thief! I tell you, Sarah, he has stolen my
story.' I was shaking so badly I could barely stand
upright. I seized the wastepaper basket and shook
the entire contents over his desk.

'Hetty! Have you gone mad? Dear heaven, stop it
this instant. Get back to the kitchen.' Sarah tried to
grab hold of me, struggling with me so that we both
toppled over with a thump.

'What on *earth* is going on?' Mr Buchanan came
stamping into his study, his napkin tucked into his
shirt, a fork still in one hand.

'Oh, I'm sorry, sir, beg pardon, sir, the poor child
is having some kind of fit. Let me carry her away
until she recovers,' said Sarah, struggling to her
knees.

I had had all the breath knocked out of me, but
I still could not keep quiet.

'You wicked, evil, terrible thief!' I screamed

hoarsely at Mr Buchanan. 'You said my story was coarse and unacceptable and no one would ever publish it. And now I know why! *You've* taken it, *you're* writing it! You're just changing the names and putting in long words and mealy-mouthed moral comments, but it's still *my* story.'

'Cease this ridiculous insubordinate babbling at once, or I shall turn you out of my house immediately,' said Mr Buchanan.

Sarah tried to clamp her hand right over my mouth. 'Oh no, sir, take pity on her. She doesn't know what she's saying. It's as if the Devil himself has got hold of her tongue,' she said.

I prised her fingers away, refusing to be restrained. 'I do *so* know what I'm saying! You've stolen *my* memoirs, *my* life! You're a wicked thief. You think you're so saintly, but I think you're going straight to Hell with all the other devils!'

'That's it! Go and pack your bags. I will not have you in my house another minute. I am dismissing you forthwith,' said Mr Buchanan.

'No, no, please!' Sarah begged.

'Without a character reference!' added Mr Buchanan.

'But, sir, how will she get another position without one?' said Sarah.

'That's not my concern,' he said.

'No, you are just concerned with stealing a poor girl's work!' I shouted.

'Remove this terrible fishwife child from my presence,' said Mr Buchanan to Sarah.

'Not until you give me back my memoirs! I'll not have you copying any more of them. Give them back to me!' I cried. 'Give them back this instant or I'll . . . I'll fetch a policeman!'

'Hetty, Hetty, *hush*!' said Sarah, struggling with me.

'Lord save us, what's happening?' said Mrs Briskett, running into the study, her great bulk knocking over columns of books to the left and the right. 'Oh, Hetty Feather, was that you shrieking at the master?'

'I am not her master. She is no longer in my employment. Be so good as to turn her out of this house immediately. I will not be shouted at and abused by a wretched foundling child, especially when I've shown her every kindness!' He was shouting too, his fez slipping sideways as he jerked his head in emphasis.

'I won't go! Not without my memoirs! They're my property. You shall not steal them. Give them *back*!'

'I don't know what you're talking about, you evil-tongued little harpy.'

'Yes you do. You took them from me. Give them back – please, *please*! That book means the whole world to me. It's my life, mine and Mama's.' I was crying now, tears of pure rage.

Mr Buchanan was breathing heavily, sweat standing out on his wrinkled brow. 'You've clearly taken leave of your senses. I know nothing of these so-called memoirs. Now get out of my study this instant.'

'You *liar*!' I shouted.

Mrs Briskett gasped and crossed herself piously. She tried to seize hold of me, but I clung to a corner of Mr Buchanan's desk, screaming.

'If you please, sir, she means that little red note-book, scribbled all over. Are you sure you don't still have it?' said Sarah bravely.

'I am *quite* sure – and if you don't hold your tongue, you will find yourself dismissed as well,' said Mr Buchanan, puffing himself up like a little bullfrog. A button on his waistcoat burst and his watch popped out of his pocket. It dangled there on his watch chain, along with an onyx seal and a little silver key. The key to his *desk drawer*?

It was no use asking politely. This was my only chance. I darted forward and snatched at the chain, tugging so hard that it broke. I had the key in my hand before he could stop me. I slotted it straight

658

into the desk drawer – and there, inside, were two notebooks. One contained my own precious memoirs – and the other was an entirely new manuscript. I whipped open the first page.

Emerald Greenwich – the Story of a Foundling Child . . . by Chas. G. Buchanan

'There!' I said, clutching my own memoirs. 'I *knew* it! You *did* steal my memoirs! You're using them for your own story!'

'Oh, sir!' said Sarah, looking shocked.

'Now now, Sarah – be warned!' said Mrs Briskett anxiously.

'Of course I haven't stolen your ridiculous memoirs, Hetty Feather! I had no idea you called your pathetic little journal by such a grand title. "Memoirs" indeed!'

'You've copied some of it out, and put it under your name!'

'Yes, I *have* started copying out a new version. I have taken the time and trouble to try to improve your work, to show you the correct way to go about composition. I was then intending to go over it with you, carefully instructing you. Yet *this* is the way you repay me, screaming ludicrous accusations at me and attacking my person, actually breaking my watch chain. Just wait till I report these events to the hospital!'

'No, *you* just wait till I report to Miss Smith on the Board of Governors that you've stolen my memoirs. Look, you've written your name by the title – that's absolute proof!'

I tried to snatch that manuscript too, but Mr Buchanan was too quick for me this time. He picked it up and beat me hard about the head with it, sending me reeling.

'Now, leave these premises immediately, Hetty Feather,' he said. 'Take her out of my sight this instant or I shall fetch a policeman myself. I shall report your behaviour and show him the broken links of my watch chain, and you will go straight to prison. It's the best place for you, you wicked, ungrateful girl.'

'Quick, Mrs B! Let's get her out!' said Sarah.

They took hold of me, each with a hand in my armpit, and hauled me out bodily, my feet scarcely brushing the floor – though I still had my memoirs clasped to my chest. They dragged me down all the stairs to the kitchen and then let me go.

'Oh, Hetty, what have you *done*! He'll never take you back now, no matter how we beg,' said Sarah, starting to cry.

'I wouldn't stay here now even if *he* begged *me*,'

I said fiercely, my head held high.

'But what will you do, you silly child? You'll never get another position as a servant without a character reference,' said Mrs Briskett, wringing her hands.

'I will – I will try my hand at something *other* than service,' I said grandly, though my heart was beating fast. 'I will make my own way in the world. Somehow.'

'But where will you sleep tonight?' Sarah asked.

'She will have to go back to the hospital,' said Mrs Briskett.

'I am not going back there, not ever. I'd sooner walk the streets,' I declared.

'Oh, Hetty, if only you weren't so headstrong!' said Sarah. 'You have no idea what life can be like for young girls cast out without a character. So many girls come to a bad end, through no real fault of their own.'

'I won't come to a bad end, I promise,' I said.

'But what will you *do*?'

I thought desperately. I remembered when I'd run away before. I'd sold flowers on the street with Sissy, and then Miss Smith had found me. Miss Smith had told us about one of her charities, set up to help destitute young girls. I supposed *I* was destitute now. The very word made me shudder.

'I shall go to London and see my friend Miss Smith. She will help me,' I said firmly. 'Don't worry, Sarah, I will be fine.'

'Of course I'll worry! You're like a little sister to me now,' said Sarah, and she gave me a hug.

'A very *bad* little sister,' said Mrs Briskett, but she came and hugged me too.

I felt like a very small slice of ham in the midst of a very large sandwich, but I was so touched by their concern and kindness that I had to fight not to cry.

I went to the scullery to pack my box – my retrieved memoirs, my books, my little fairground china dog, my letters from Mama and Jem, my writing paper and envelopes, my brushes, my spare maid's dress, my nightgown. They all fitted neatly inside. But what about my green Sunday outfit? I tried folding it this way and that, but it was heavy velvet and I could not make it small enough.

'Wait, Hetty!' said Sarah. She ran all the way upstairs and came panting back with her own leather suitcase with a strap. 'You may have this. Mother gave it to me when I first went into service.'

'But I can't take it, Sarah – not if it was a present from your mother.'

'I have no need of it now. I've nowhere to go. Mother would want you to have it, I am sure, especially now, when . . . when the two of you have met,' said Sarah shyly.

I gave her another hug, feeling dreadful that I had never quite appreciated her properly. I was surprised by Mrs Briskett too, because when I went back into the kitchen with the packed suitcase, I found she'd made me up a veritable picnic in a big paper bag.

'It's so kind of you, Mrs Briskett! It will keep me going all day long.'

'You'll also need this.' She went to the larder and took down her jar of housekeeping money. I thought she'd count me out a few shillings – but she gave me the whole jarful.

'I can't take it!'

'Of course you can. You'll likely need every penny. You'll be able to stay somewhere small but decent for a few days until this Miss Smith can find you work.'

'Oh, Mrs B!'

'Mrs Briskett to you, missy! Now, mind you write and let us know how you're getting on. We'll worry ourselves sick about you till we hear, won't we, Sarah?'

'Oh, we will, we will,' said Sarah, giving me another hug.

'You're sure you know the way to the station? You must ask for a ticket to Waterloo – that's the

London station. When you arrive there, use some of your money on a hansom cab, do you hear, Hetty? And if you get lost up in town, then look for a policeman and ask him the way. Take care now!'

'Oh don't! She looks so little. We can't let her go!' said Sarah. She stared around wildly. 'Can't we hide her somewhere, here in the house? Just for a day or two, while we sort things out for her?'

Mrs Briskett frowned, clearly wavering. But then the bell from Mr Buchanan's study started jingling fiercely.

'Oh! Oh, maybe master's changed his mind! You be ready to say you're very very sorry, Hetty,' said Sarah, straightening her cap and gown and rushing out of the kitchen to the stairs.

'I'm *not* sorry. It's the master who did something wrong, not me!' I said – but I was wavering too. Now that my temper was ebbing away I was start- ing to feel very, very scared. Perhaps I *would* apologize. I didn't need to mean the words. Inside my head I could scream that Mr Buchanan was a dishonest, hypocritical thief, just so long as I didn't say it out loud. Then I could stay in my position with Mrs Briskett and Sarah, where I felt so safe and cared for.

But it was no use. Sarah came back, chalk-faced and tearful. 'Oh, he won't relent!' she said. 'He

664

asked if Hetty had gone, and when I said she was still doing her packing, he said he would have her physically thrown out on the street if she wasn't gone in the next five minutes!'

'I'd like to see him try! He's just a withered little monkey man! He couldn't lift me, for I'd scream and kick and hit him,' I declared.

'Hush, Hetty. Stop that silly talk! The master will fetch someone to do it. You might get hurt. You'd best go straight away,' said Mrs Briskett.

'He says he'll be watching from his window to make sure he's seen the back of you,' said Sarah.

'Then I'll show him my blooming back,' I said. I had one last hug with Sarah and gave Mrs Briskett a shy kiss. 'Thank you so much for looking after me,' I said.

Mrs Briskett's face started wobbling. Great tears rolled down her cheeks. 'Oh my, *now* look! You've set me off – and I can't abide crying!' she sobbed.

'Then don't cry, Mrs Briskett, please. I shall be fine. Goodbye, my dear friends.'

I took Sarah's mother's suitcase and my bag of goodies, and walked swiftly out of the kitchen, through the scullery and down the back passage. I opened the door to the area steps and climbed up onto the pavement. There was Mr Buchanan peering down at me, still looking outraged. He actually shook his monkey fist at me.

Well, I'd show him. I pulled the most ferocious face up at him, and made a strange gesture with my fingers – I'd seen the boys do this at the hospital. I hoped it was rude. Certainly, judging by the expression on his face, it had considerable effect. Then I sauntered down the road, my head in the air, as if I was simply out for a Sunday stroll.

Oh, my Lord – what was I going to do about Bertie? As soon as I was out of sight of the house, I slowed down and started shivering. It seemed as if I would never see Bertie again. I thought of our happy Sunday jaunts, and I had to squeeze my eyes shut to stop myself crying on the street.

Then something large and warm and boisterous bounced straight into me. It knocked the suitcase and paper bag out of my arms, and licked my face with a very big wet tongue.

'Tommy! Down, boy! *Down*, I say. I know you like the little missy, but you'll frighten her!'

It was Tommy the black Labrador, with his kindly old gentleman owner.

'Are you all right, little missy? Tommy doesn't mean any harm. He's just pleased to see you and desperate to get to his lovely park.'

'I'm fine,' I said, stroking Tommy's soft head.

'But, oh dear, he's made you drop all your belongings. Here, let me help.' The old man bent down and picked up my bag of goodies, luckily so tightly folded over by Mrs Briskett that none had spilled. He handed me the suitcase. 'Going off on a journey, are you, little missy?' he said. 'Going home to visit your mother, is that it?'

I started at him. Of course! I was sure I had more than enough money for a train trip to the coast and one night's board and lodging. I would go to see Mama!

'Yes, you're right,' I said. 'You're absolutely right. I'm going to visit Mama.'

'She'll be so pleased to see you,' he said sweetly.

I wasn't quite so sure. She'd be pretty horrified if she knew I'd broken Mr Buchanan's watch chain and stuck my tongue out at him. I wouldn't necessarily tell her the whole story. But before I set off on my journey I had to find someone else.

I said goodbye to the old man, gave Tommy another stroke, and set off for the town, stopping to wipe my face thoroughly with my handkerchief once I was out of sight.

I went past the draper's shop, pausing momentarily to glare at Ivy and Kitty behind the counter. Then I walked up to the butcher's shop. I knew it was very foolish of me, but I was a little scared to go inside. The front of the shop was hung with poultry, their yellow claws dangling purposefully, as if ready to scratch the customers' heads. The sides of the shop were draped with a furry frond of hares and rabbits, their eyes staring mournfully, their little mouths dripping blood.

I wasn't used to such an alarmingly close encounter with so many dead animals. In fact, the more I stared, the more certain I was that I could never enjoy a rabbit pie or a chicken stew ever again. I ran past the poor dead creatures into the shop, to face further scenes of carnage. Great sides of beef and lamb hung from steel hooks, and a huge pig's head leered at me from the table, an apple in its mouth. Parts of its body were arranged in a grisly pattern all around it: belly and chops and kidneys, and a very long string of sausages.

The smell of meat was unpleasantly overpowering. I breathed shallowly, feeling so sorry for Bertie. I could see no sign of him, and hoped he wasn't out delivering.

I tried to avert my eyes, and joined the queue of folk waiting to give their orders. My arms ached holding my food package and the suitcase, but I didn't want to set them down on the floor. I couldn't sully Sarah's mother's suitcase with bloodstained sawdust.

I waited as seemingly half of Kingtown deliberated over their mince and mutton, while Jarvis the butcher and his two bigger lads listened and gave advice. They barely had a full set of fingers between them, but they still chopped chunks of meat with alarming speed and gusto. I found I was clenching my own fists anxiously on their behalf.

At last I was at the front of the queue, facing Mr Jarvis himself, a man as large and fat and red as his own sides of beef.

'How can I help you, little missy? Who's the cook in your household?'

'Well, it's Mrs Briskett, but I'm not—'

'Oh, Mrs Briskett! Lovely lady, but particular, and that suits me fine because I am too. So how can I help you? The meat the boy delivered yesterday was up to scratch, was it not? Is there company coming? Does she need a capon or a crown of lamb?'

'No, no, sir, it's – it's your boy I want. Bertie. Is he here? May I have a quick word with him?' I whispered.

Mr Jarvis stood stock-still. He cupped his hand to his ear in a pantomime gesture. 'Say that again!' he said. He nudged the other two lads. They stopped chopping. 'Listen to this!'

I took a deep breath. 'Please may I talk to Bertie?' I repeated.

The lads nudged each other and sniggered.

'What do you think this is, girl? A parlour where young lovers can do their courting?' Mr Jarvis bellowed, for the benefit of the entire queue behind me.

'I'm sorry, sir, of course not, sir, but it is a matter of urgency,' I said.

'A matter of *urgency*?' Mr Jarvis boomed. The whole street must be hearing him now – even Ivy and Kitty in their draper's shop. 'This *must* be young love. You want to see our Bertie *urgently*, do you?'

The lads burst out laughing. I started crying, in rage and humiliation.

'I only wanted to say goodbye,' I sobbed. 'I can't see that's so outrageous. Please tell him I came calling. My name is Hetty Feather.' I turned on my heel and tried to push past all the customers.

'Hey! Wait, missy. Don't cry now,' said Mr Jarvis, relenting. 'He's in the back, doing the offal. Go and say your goodbyes then, but be quick about it.'

He gestured for me to bob under the counter. I squeezed through and scurried out through a door at the back of the shop. I found myself standing in a bloody battlefield. Dead animals in varying states were strewn over a counter, some with their heads and hides still in place. Bertie was standing there in an apron and trousers, no shirt at all, busy disembowelling these creatures, pulling all kinds of disgusting gleaming things out of their bodies.

'Hetty!' he said, shocked. He went scarlet. 'Oh, Hetty, don't look! I don't want you to see me doing this! Why did the old man let you through?'

'I begged him. I've come to say goodbye.'

'What?' He saw the suitcase and realized I was serious. 'Why? What's happened?'

'Mr Buchanan's dismissed me.'

'He never! But what did you *do*?'

'I shouted at him because I found out he's been copying my memoirs. I broke his watch chain getting the key to his desk, and I said he was a cruel, wicked, hypocritical thief who would end up going to Hell.'

'Well, that's telling him! So he won't have given you a character.'

'No.'

'Oh, Hetty. What will you do, then?'

'I'm going to see Mama. She lives by the seaside. She might know of a position near her. Then we could see more of each other, which would be wonderful.'

'No! All right, go and see your mother, but then come back! We have to have our Sundays together. You're still my sweetheart! I'll keep my eyes and ears open on my rounds – I go all over the town, right? I'll see if anyone's wanting a likely girl. I'll recommend you. You leave it to me, Hetty.'

'Well, it's very good of you, Bertie, but—'

'No buts! See here, you're not planning to go back to the country, are you? Are you going to see that foster brother you write to?'

'I don't see how I can go back. There's no work for a girl in the village. All my foster sisters went into service.'

'Good! You're not a country girl. You belong in the city, with me.'

'Come back here now, missy, you've had long enough. And you, lad – I hope you're not slacking!' Mr Jarvis called.

'I'd better go,' I said quickly. 'I don't want to get you into trouble.'

'Do take care, Hetty. Write as soon as you can to let me know where you are. Oh Lord, I want to take you in my arms, but how can I like this?' He gestured with his slimy hands, looking at them in disgust. 'What must you think of me!'

'I think you're my sweetheart,' I said. I leaned across the loathsome carcass on the table, and swiftly kissed his flushed cheek.

Then I rushed out of the room, bobbed a grateful curtsy to Mr Jarvis, and whisked out of the shop, while everyone stared, and a few clapped and cheered.

I hurried though the town, trying to tell myself

that everything was fine. I was simply going to have a little holiday and see Mama at long last. But I couldn't help feeling very queer and shaky, even so.

15

I changed out of my grubby work dress and cap and apron while locked inside the ladies' waiting room at the station. I felt better and braver in my emerald best dress, and my skimpy work clothes were much lighter to carry.

The third-class rail ticket cost a great deal of money, much more than I'd reckoned. The housekeeping jar was a lot lighter when I put it back in my case. It was very unnerving reaching Waterloo and having to negotiate my way up and down the platforms to find the correct locomotive for Bignor, but I managed it successfully.

I hadn't realized that it would be such a *long* train journey to the coast. I fidgeted a great deal as I gazed out of the window. England was much larger than I'd realized. I stared until my eyes blurred, but I still hadn't glimpsed any great expanse of water.

I opened Mrs Briskett's parcel for some lunch, and then carried on nibbling on and off throughout the journey. A grim-faced lady sitting next to me sniffed in disgust and twitched her skirts away from me, acting as if I were spilling crumbs all over her. It was certainly a temptation.

A much sweeter family joined the train at Arundel: a jolly father in a straw hat and blazer, a pale mother with a babe in arms, and two girls in sailor suits, one my age, one about eight or nine. They all smiled at me, and the two sailor girls started chatting as if we were old friends, telling me they were having an early seaside holiday and it was going to be great fun.

I offered the girls a slice of Mrs Briskett's short-bread and talked to them a little. They were astonished when I said I'd never been to the seaside before.

'We go to Bignor every single year. We think it's the most splendid tip-top place ever,' said the older girl. 'We go bathing every day, and listen to the band and watch the pierrots. Oh, you will *love* it! Where will you stay? We always go to the same lodgings near the promenade. Maisie and I can see the sea from our bedroom window.'

'Where are *your* mama and papa?' asked Maisie. 'Are you travelling all on your *own*? How queer!'

'Maisie!' the mother rebuked her gently. She smiled at me. 'Are you going on a visit, perhaps?'

'Yes, to see my mama.'

'Oh, that's lovely, dear.'

'Why don't you live with your mama, then?' asked the older girl.

'Charlotte!' the mother said, shaking her head. 'You girls! Stop plaguing your new friend with your questions.'

'My mama works in Bignor,' I said.

'Your mama *works*! Why's that?'

'That's enough, girls!' said their mother, looking a little uncomfortable.

They weren't a very *grand* family. They were only travelling third class like me, and their clothes were a little shabby. I could see the telltale black line around the skirts of both girls where their hems had been let down, and although their boots were highly polished, they were cracked and down-at-heel. Even so, there was a *huge* divide between us. That little baby sleeping in the mother's arms would grow up safe within a family. She would be able to stay a child well into her teens. She would never be told it was her place to be a servant.

The baby was starting to get fretful, and wouldn't be soothed, though the mother rocked her tenderly. 'Hush now,' she said, over and over, but the baby wouldn't hush at all.

The father tried tickling her and then talking to her sternly, which made the baby cry harder. The girls chatted to each other, clearly not expecting to take their turn as nursemaid.

'Let me take her,' I offered.

'I'm afraid she's very querulous, poor lamb,' said the mother. 'I'm not sure you'll be able to quieten her. Sometimes she cries for hours. I think it's the colic.'

I was used to little babies. In my last year at the hospital I had spent many hours in the nursery, helping care for the newborn foundlings before they were despatched to foster homes in the country.

'Come to Hetty, baby,' I said, picking her up from her mother's arms.

She had a cross red face, her forehead wrinkled as if she had every care in the world. The silly little thing did not know how lucky she was. I held her upright and pressed her against me, patting her back.

'There now. Do you have a sore stomach? This will make it feel better,' I said.

I walked up and down the carriage, rocking her against me. She stopped screaming, snuffled several times, and then quietened altogether.

'Oh my! You've worked wonders!' said the papa.

'You're very good with babies, dear,' said the mother. 'There, Charlotte, there, Maisie! See how nicely she's soothed your little sister!'

I took a deep breath, aware of a sudden glorious solution to my situation. 'I would be very happy to be your nursemaid,' I said.

I meant it in all seriousness, but the family all

678

laughed merrily, as if I were joking.

'I – I would not cost very much,' I ventured further, but this made them laugh even harder.

I felt I could not pursue the point any further. I continued to walk the baby. She stayed fast asleep, even when the train drew into the station at Bignor-on-Sea at last. I carried the baby very carefully down the steps to the platform, my suitcase hanging off one arm. The father went dashing off to supervise the removal of the family's luggage from the guard's van. I waited with the rest of the family. Maisie was jumping up and down excitedly, declaring, 'I can smell the sea already!' She was so convincing that I imagined the water lapping against the brick walls of the station.

'I hope there's time for a bathe before tea!' said Charlotte. 'Will you have a bathe too? Wait till you see what it's like, Hetty! Do you have your own bathing dress? If not, you can hire one on the beach.'

'I expect I will do that,' I said.

'And you'll need a bucket and spade! Maisie and I always make sandcastles. It's absolutely ripping fun. We made such a splendid castle last year, with a proper moat, and then the sea came in and filled it up, and we made stained-glass windows out of fruit drops. Maisie had to lick them first, which was a little disgusting, but she didn't mind at all—'

'Charlotte, calm down!' said her mother, smiling at her. She reached for the baby. 'Thank you so much for looking after little Flora. I've never known her so contented.'

'It was a pleasure,' I said solemnly. My arms felt very empty when I gave her back.

'Well . . .' The mama was looking around at the crowds on the platform. 'Can you see your mama anywhere? She *will* be meeting you, won't she?'

'Oh, she doesn't know I'm coming. It's a surprise,' I said.

'Do know where to find her? Perhaps you might care to walk part of the way with us?'

'Oh, yes please!' I said.

We walked out of the station in a little procession, the papa alongside the porter, who had a huge trolley full of their luggage, then the mama and the baby, and then Charlotte and Maisie on either side of me, talking nineteen to the dozen, telling me all about the seaside.

'Where *is* it?' I asked, because we were in a perfectly ordinary street, though the light was brighter than usual and the air felt fresh and clear.

'Just down there! Oh, mama, may we run ahead just a little and show Hetty the sea?' asked Charlotte.

'Of course,' said their mama.

The girls both surged forward, skirts flying. I

ran along beside them, my case bumping awkwardly against my legs.

'Take care, girls!' she called.

I felt truly part of their family – not a nursemaid, more like a sister. I started picturing our life together. We'd have our annual jolly seaside holiday in Bignor, and then we would go back to our home in Arundel. I would go to school with Charlotte and Maisie, and help their mama with the baby when I was at home. We'd all do the cooking and the dusting and the scrubbing and the mending. I'd have my own comfortable little bed in the girls' room. I would never be stuck all alone in the scullery.

Charlotte and Maisie raced round a corner. I heard them whooping triumphantly. I followed them, and then stopped short, my heart thudding. I'd seen pictures of the sea in books, each wave carefully cross-hatched to give a life-like impression. I'd seen the Thames, which had seemed vast enough after the country stream of my childhood. But nothing had prepared me for the immensity of this sea glittering before me in the sunlight.

I had fancied it would be a dense blue like the wash of colour in my picture-book illustration, but this was a bright silvery grey, an entire sparkling world of water. I turned my head to the left and to the right, and it was still there, as far as I could see.

I dropped my suitcase and stretched my arms wide, trying to take it all in.

'Isn't it glorious?' said Charlotte.

'Yes, it is truly wonderful,' I breathed.

The sea blurred to a rainbow shimmer because I was crying now, overcome by the beauty of this vast stretch of water. I scrubbed at my eyes with my handkerchief.

'Don't be sad,' said Maisie, putting her hand in mine.

'I'm not sad, I'm happy,' I said, laughing shakily.

'You do like it here, don't you?' she asked.

'I think it's the most beautiful place in the whole world,' I said. My heart rejoiced that Mama lived here now and could see the sea every single day.

I suddenly wanted to see her so urgently that I trembled all over. I feared she would be angry and distressed when I told her that I'd lost my position, but I didn't care about her scolding me now. I just wanted to be with her.

'I must go now,' I said.

I said goodbye to Charlotte and Maisie, and they kissed me as if we were firm friends. I waved to the papa and the mama and the baby, then I picked up my suitcase and started running right along the sea front. I didn't know where Mama's road was, and the first two people I asked did not know either, but then I came across a painted notice board with a map of Bignor clearly laid out. There was even a helpful little arrow labelled YOU ARE HERE! I pictured a half-inch Hetty standing on her allotted spot, and walked her up and down the roads until, right at the edge of town, I came across Saltdean Lane. I'd written it on so many envelopes under the dear name of Ida Battersea.

I stared at the map until my eyes watered again, memorizing the way, and then I set off along the promenade. This was a fairyland town with a pier jutting out into the sea, kiosks of strange seafood, and bathing machines all along the beach. Even the streetlamps were painted a pretty pale green, and the paving stones beneath my feet were rose-pink.

I had to turn off the promenade down Victoria Avenue, and the streets immediately reverted to plain grey, but I didn't care – I was running now, so eager to see Mama that I didn't pause for breath until I reached Saltdean Lane at last. The houses weren't as large and grand as Mr Buchanan's in Lady's Ride. I liked them better – pretty villas painted cream and apricot and lilac, with bright flowers in their gardens.

I counted each house until I found number eighteen. It was cream, with white window frames and a blue door, very fresh and pretty, with pink hydrangeas in tubs on either side of the doorstep.

I was utterly delighted to see that Mama's house

was the prettiest in the whole lane. I went up the neat tiled path, shaking with excitement. I knew better now than to knock at the front door. There were no area steps, so I slipped down the side of the house and rapped lightly on the back door. I waited, my heart thumping.

Then the door opened. There was Mama! I knew she was my own dear Mama – of course I did – but she looked so different. She had always been little and slight, like me, but now she seemed some-how to have shrunk. Her dress hung loose on her, and her tiny wrists and hands stuck out of the cuffs, looking like little claws. Her dear face was so thin now that her cheekbones showed in sharp lines.

'Oh, Mama!' I said, throwing down my case and clasping her close.

'Hetty! Oh, Hetty, is it really you? You look a picture in that dress! Darling, what are you doing here?' she gasped, and then she started coughing.

She thrust me away from her quickly, putting a handkerchief to her mouth. She coughed and coughed, her faced reddening, the veins standing out on her forehead, her whole body racked.

'Oh, Mama,' I whispered.

I steered her very gently inside and sat her down on a kitchen chair, then fetched my case from the doorstep. I ran the tap at the sink, pouring Mama a glass of water, and gave it to her. She tried to drink, the glass clinking against her teeth, and gradually the terrible coughing stopped. Her eyes were watering, and little beads of sweat stood out on her forehead. I took a teacloth, held it under the cold tap, and then pressed it against her burning temples.

'You're ill, Mama, very ill. You definitely have a fever – and that cough! Why aren't you in bed? Come, let me help you. Where do you sleep?'

'No, no, I can't possibly go to bed,' Mama said weakly. 'I'm fine now. It was just a coughing fit. The surprise of seeing you!'

'But you've got so thin! Why didn't you *tell* me you were ill when you wrote?'

'I didn't want to worry you. I'm *not* ill, not really. I just have a troublesome cough, but I'm in the best place possible, breathing in this good sea air. Some days I feel really well, truly.'

'Will you stop trying to be so brave! It's *me*, Mama! You can be honest with me.'

I knew next to nothing about sickness and disease, but even so I knew that Mama was gravely ill. 'Is it – is it influenza?' I whispered.

I had suffered a bout of influenza once myself and had been very ill for days, along with many other children at the hospital. My crippled foster brother Saul had died from the disease. So had Cedric, Mr Brown's little boy.

'Oh, Mama, don't die! You can't die!' I said, bursting into tears.

'Don't, Hetty! I'm perfectly all right, I swear I am. I haven't got influenza, I promise you.'

'Have you seen a doctor?'

'Well . . .' Mama hesitated. 'There's nothing a doctor can really do for me, dear. But I go to the pharmacy and he makes me up a cough linctus. That helps considerably. But never mind *me*. What are you doing here? How did you get Mr Buchanan to give you permission to visit me?'

'Well . . .' It was my turn to be evasive now. I didn't really want to tell Mama the whole story, especially now she was so fragile. 'Mr Buchanan is – is an unusual sort of employer. He knows how much you mean to me and how badly I've been missing you. He said I could have a little holiday with you. Isn't that lovely?'

But I could never fool Mama, ill or not.

'A little holiday, my eye! Oh, Hetty, child, what's happened? You haven't lost your position already, have you? He has given you a character reference, hasn't he?' Mama started coughing again in her agitation.

'Let me make us both a pot of tea and then I'll tell you all about it,' I said.

'Oh Lord, I must take Miss Roberts *her* tea. She'll be waking from her afternoon nap any moment, and she gets agitated if I don't have it ready for her.'

'But doesn't she realize you're ill?'

'No! Well, she must hear me coughing sometimes, but she doesn't comment. I take a spoonful of linctus every time I have to talk to her, and that helps a little.'

'But doesn't she see how pale and thin you've got?'

'She's an old lady, Hetty. She has cataracts and can barely see her own hand in front of her face.'

Mama looked like an old lady herself as she shuffled around the kitchen preparing a tea tray. She let me make the pot of tea, but she cut wafer-thin slices of bread and butter and arranged them in tiny triangles on the plate, with a pot of blackberry jam.

'I gathered the blackberries myself and then made the jam,' Mama said proudly. 'You shall have a big slice in a moment, darling. Though I don't think you deserve it. You've clearly been a very bad girl. I thought you were happy working for this Mr Buchanan. You liked it that he was a writer.'

'I've never liked him. He thinks he's a great writer, but his stories are dull dull dull. And then he took my memoirs, Mama – *my* story, *our* story – and was using it to write his own story. So I confronted him.'

'Hmm! You don't "confront" your employer, Hetty.'

'*Sapphire!* Won't you call me by my true name, Mama?'

'Sapphire, Hetty, whichever name. You're still my dear, headstrong, wilful daughter, and goodness knows what I'm going to do with you!' said Mama.

A bell on the wall suddenly jangled, making us both jump. Mama started coughing again, holding her handkerchief over her face. 'She's . . . awake! Wants . . . tea!' she gasped.

'Oh, Mama, you poor thing, don't try to talk. Look, sit down. Can't I take the old girl her wretched tea? If she's half blind, maybe she won't notice it's me and not you.'

'Don't talk . . . so daft,' said Mama. She gave one last cough, clutching the handkerchief, then crumpled it up quickly and tucked it in her apron.

'Mama?'

She ignored me, took the tray, and carried it out of the kitchen, her poor stick arms taut and straining. I couldn't bear it and tried to take the tray off her, but she glared at me ferociously and I had to give way. I watched her walk slowly up the stairs, her breath rasping, shoulders hunched. Oh dear Lord, this was my lovely young mother, my Ida, who had raced up and down the steep stairs at the hospital and lugged great vats of porridge around.

When she came back, scarcely able to draw breath, I sat her down and poured her a cup of tea. I urged her to eat her own bread and jam, but she said she wasn't hungry.

'You *must* eat, Mama. Look how thin you are,' I said, taking her poor little hands in mine. They were cold, though when I felt her forehead, it was still burning.

'Mama, please. I can't bear to see you looking so frail and exhausted. You're very ill, no matter what you say. You *must* go to bed – and *I* must call a doctor.'

'I can't go to bed, Hetty dear. I have to make the supper. And we certainly can't call the doctor. He charges a fortune! There's nothing he can do for me anyway. I shall take another dose of my linctus. The only other medicine I need is you, my darling girl. Oh, Hetty, I still can't believe you're actually here!'

I stopped trying to press Mama and helped her cook supper. I made an apple pie to show off my pastry skills, and basked in Mama's praise.

'Perhaps we might get you a job as a little cook after all!' she said. 'Miss Smith might be able to set you up again.'

I kept quiet. I wasn't going back to Miss Smith. I wasn't going to be a cook. I wasn't going anywhere now. I was going to stay right here and look after Mama.

16

Mama let me stay in her room that night. I crept quietly up the stairs, my shoes in my hand, while Mama gave Miss Roberts her night-time cup of cocoa and settled her in her bed.

Mama's room was up in the attic. It made me want to weep, seeing all her modest possessions again: her little violet vase, her brush and comb, her special soap, her bundle of letters from me. She had a narrow iron bed, but I was sure there was just about room for two, especially if we wound our arms around each other. But Mama wouldn't hear of it.

She fetched fresh linen from the press, a cushion from the sofa in the drawing room, and a thick cashmere shawl belonging to Miss Roberts.

'Here, Hetty, I'll make you up a separate little bed fit for a queen,' she said.

'It's lovely, Mama, but I'd sooner sleep with you.'

'No, darling.'

'But why? I used to creep into your bed sometimes back at the hospital.'

'I don't want you too near me, in case . . . in case you catch my cough,' said Mama, and she wouldn't be swayed.

So I bedded down in my cosy nest on the floor, and Mama lay on her bed. I edged nearer in the night and put my arm up, so that I could just about reach her hand.

'You'll give yourself dreadful pins and needles,' she whispered.

'I don't care if I get pins and needles all over. I need to hold onto you. Oh, Mama, I've missed you so.'

'And I have missed you, my Hetty,' said Mama.

We clung tightly to each other's hand. I think Mama might have been crying. I know I was.

I woke very early. Mama was coughing, her hands clamped over her mouth to muffle the sounds. I got up and propped her up on my cushion as well as her pillows. It eased her chest slightly and made her cough less.

'Better now, Mama?'

'Much better, sweetheart,' she whispered. 'Now, I have been trying to work out the best way to get you a new position. I'm wondering whether I should write to Miss Smith to explain the situation, though I know my spelling leaves a lot to be desired. I don't want to let you down, Hetty.'

'You could never let me down, Mama! But I don't see that there's much point telling Miss Smith. I am sure she will take Mr Buchanan's side, I just know it. He'll tell her lies about keeping my memoirs to help improve my grammar and writing style.'

'But she must be fond of you. She's taken such an interest in you these last few years, and she's been so kind forwarding all our letters. I'm sure she might give you a character to help you find another position.'

'The only position I want is right here, Mama. I want to be with you.'

'And I want that too, darling, with all my heart, but I'm not sure how we can keep you hidden away day after day. Miss Roberts is infirm, but she still totters from room to room using her walking stick. If she were to come upon you unawares, she'd be very shocked – and then *I* would lose my position.'

'But you've said she's a kind old lady. If you told her you've been reunited with your long-lost daughter, surely she'd be happy for you and *want* us to be together? I could work for her too. I would fetch and carry and do her sewing. I could even write her letters for her.'

'Hetty, Hetty, you still don't understand the ways of the world. I am her *servant*. I'm not expected to have a daughter, especially one born out of wedlock. She would think it terribly lax and immoral to condone such a situation.'

'I think it's terribly lax and immoral of *her* to let

you wait on her hand and foot. Even if she's totally blind, she can surely *hear* how ill you are every time you cough,' I said hotly.

'Ssh! She'll hear you,' said Mama. She swung her legs out of bed and tried to get up, but the movement made her cough again. Her hand searched all round the bed as she shook and gasped, looking for her handkerchief. She found it at last and held it to her mouth, while I stood beside her helplessly, patting her poor heaving back. She was so thin that her shoulder blades were as sharp as knives.

'Please, Mama, get back into bed,' I begged, but she wouldn't listen. She stood up, still coughing, staggering over to her washstand in her old night-gown. She stood with one hand clutching the tiled top, her knuckles white. She gave one last heave. I saw the handkerchief at her lips suddenly darken with bright blood.

'Mama!' I stared in terror. She tried to hide the handkerchief, but it was too late.

'You're coughing blood!'

'Only a little, because it's such a hacking cough. Oh, Hetty, don't stare like that. See, the cough has stopped. I'm better now.'

I had a pain in my own chest, my heart beating fast. This wasn't just a troublesome cough. This was far more sinister. I knew what I had to do now. I wouldn't tell Mama because she'd argue with me

694

and get agitated.

We both washed and dressed, and then I crept downstairs with Mama and helped her light the range and prepare breakfast.

'You're such a grand, capable girl now, Hetty. I'm so proud of you,' said Mama.

Miss Roberts stayed in bed to have her breakfast, and then fell asleep again as she read the morning newspaper. I peeped round her bedroom door to catch a glimpse of her. She was a stout little old lady who looked as if she'd been stuffed with pillows. I couldn't tell how many chins she had when she was awake, but she had at least four when lying down dozing. Her mouth was open, showing just two teeth at the top and two at the bottom, like a baby. She was wearing a large flounced nightcap, but from the curled grey wig on its stand on her dressing table I guessed she was as bald as a baby too. She was certainly as helpless as an infant. Mama had to help her wash and dress and visit the WC. It seemed so desperately unfair when Mama was the one who was so ill.

I was determined Mama was going to have the best medical treatment, no matter how costly. I tipped out the entire contents of the housekeeping jar and tied all the coins in a handkerchief in my pocket. I was careful not to chink the coins, not wanting Mama to hear.

When Miss Roberts woke for her mid-morning cup of Camp coffee, I knew Mama was going to be busy getting her up and dressed and ready for luncheon.

'May I go out for a little walk, Mama?' I asked.

'Of course you can, Hetty. It will do you good to have some air. Take care to watch where you're going, though. I don't want you to get lost,' said Mama.

As if I would ever lose my dear Mama now! I set off on my search, walking down to the sea front. I was momentarily distracted by the beach. There were children already playing on the pale sands. I had an urge to rip off my shoes and stockings and run around too. There were bathing machines lined up right along the sands, and quite a few folk bobbing up and down in the waves in maroon and navy bathing dresses, their faces red with sunburn. I'd never swum, but it looked splendid fun.

I watched for a minute, and then looked around. I saw an old gentleman laboriously pushing an elderly lady in a bathchair. They looked as if they must visit a doctor regularly.

'Excuse me, sir, madam,' I said, bobbing them a polite little curtsy. 'Might you know where there is a good doctor here in Bignor?'

'Are you poorly, little lass? You look as fit as a fiddle to me,' said the old man.

'It's my mama. She's got a very bad cough. She urgently needs a doctor,' I said.

'Then our Dr Jenkins is the man for her. I had a terrible throat this winter and he made a new man of me. He stopped me coughing in no time,' said the old man. 'Dr Jenkins, twenty-two Magnolia Square.'

'What's that you're telling her?' said the old lady, rearing up in her bath chair and squinting at me. 'She's a little maid, Henry. She'd never be able to afford Dr Jenkins.'

'Oh yes I can, ma'am,' I said, and I marched off, jingling the coins in my pocket.

I went back down the promenade to the painted map and found Magnolia Square easily enough. The houses were tall and grand, with beautiful pink flowering trees in their front gardens. I found number twenty-two – and there was a gentleman walking briskly down the steps, carrying a black bag.

I'd seen a black bag like that before, when the doctor was called to the hospital. I'd been very ill, but he had made me better.

'Oh please, sir, are you Dr Jenkins?' I asked, rushing up to him.

'I am indeed, my dear. I'm off on my rounds now.'

'Oh please, could you call at number eighteen Saltdean Lane? It's very urgent!'

'Is your mistress ill?'

'No, it's Mama – but don't worry, I have lots of money and can pay you royally.'

His mouth quivered. 'What ails your mama, child?'

'She has a very frightening cough, so much that she spits blood. She's grown very thin and tired, and has a burning fever,' I gabbled.

Dr Jenkins looked grave now. 'I will fit her in at the end of my rounds.'

'Oh thank you! Number eighteen – you won't forget? And do you think you will be able to make her better?'

'I will do what I can to help her,' he said.

'Shall I give you the money now?' I said, fumbling for my handkerchief of coins.

'No, no, wait until I've seen your mama. Number eighteen Saltdean Lane – you see, I haven't forgotten.'

I ran all the way back to Mama's house, in spite of the hidden coins jingling in my pocket. I glanced up at the windows of number eighteen and there was Miss Roberts, dressed now, peering down at me. I had to look away quickly and walk on down the road purposefully, then steal back ten minutes later. There was no sign of her now. I nipped round to the back door and tapped softly for Mama.

'There you are, dearie! My, your walk has done you good. You've got lovely pink cheeks! But we'll have to find you a sunhat. Redheads burn easily –

they've got such fine white skin.'

'Have I really got fine skin, Mama? I thought my blue eyes were my only good feature.'

'You're fine all over, Hetty – the best girl in the whole world – though you're not good, you're very, very bad, cheeking your master so terribly. But I've been thinking carefully about your predicament.'

'Mama, I told you, I'm not contacting Miss Smith. I'm not leaving you now.'

'Listen to me, Hetty! I've been thinking hard while I've been fussing round Miss Roberts. She's got several old lady friends she takes tea with from time to time. I hear them all a-moaning and a-grumbling about their own maids. They've all got to the stage where they need nurses as well as maids, but they don't want to pay a double wage. I've heard them say that Miss Roberts is a very lucky lady having me—'

'And she *is*!'

'So I was wondering—' Mama broke off to cough, her face flushing painfully. 'Perhaps we could find you a position with one of these old girls – and then we could write to Miss Smith and ask if *she* could give you a character, like she did me.'

'Oh, Mama! What would she put? *Hetty Feather has a temper to match her red hair. She shrieks like a banshee if thwarted. She attacks her employer if he confiscates her property.* These old ladies might be a bit dotty, but surely they'd not be impressed by that.'

'I agree with you! I know we can't expect Miss Smith to tell an outright lie, but she could temper her words a little. She could write something like: *Hetty Feather is a warm-hearted, willing girl who works well and will be very true and loyal if treated kindly.*'

'*You* give me a character, Mama!'

'I wish I could! There's no better daughter in the whole world,' said Mama. Then she started coughing again – so badly that she had to sit down at the kitchen table. I ran to get her linctus and poured her two great spoonfuls, but it didn't seem to have any effect. By the time the paroxysm stopped we were both in tears.

I took Mama in my arms and held her tightly. I could feel all her little sparrow bones. She was trembling, but she relaxed against me for a moment, and then feebly tried to push me away.

'Don't get too near, Hetty,' she whispered. 'I'd tear my own heart out if I infected you.'

'It's all right, Mama. Don't worry. We're going to get you well again,' I said fiercely. 'Just you wait.'

I was on tenterhooks for the rest of the morning, waiting for Dr Jenkins to come calling. But he didn't come and didn't come and didn't come.

Mama cooked Miss Roberts a mutton chop for her lunch, with a little mashed potato. We had a big plate of mash sprinkled with grated cheese – though Mama barely touched hers.

'You must eat, Mama. You've got so thin,' I said. I tried holding the fork to her lips, coaxing her like a baby.

When we'd done the washing-up together, Mama set about writing a letter to Miss Smith. I saw how long it took her to spell out the simplest words and my heart ached for her.

'You must tell me when I make mistakes, Hetty. I know I'm very ignorant,' she said, blushing.

'No you're not! You write a lovely letter,' I lied firmly.

Then at last I heard a knocking at the front door.

'I'll go!' I said, jumping up.

'No! No, Hetty, let me—' said Mama, struggling to her feet, but it made her cough again, and she had to cling to the table to stay upright.

I ran through the kitchen and out into the hallway to the front door. I flung it open, and there was Dr Jenkins, carrying his black bag.

'You came after all!' I said.

'I am a man of my word,' he said. 'Now, where is the patient?'

He looked towards the stairs, expecting to be taken up to a bedroom, but I led him down the hallway and through to the kitchen.

'Hetty!' Mama gasped. 'What are you *doing*, showing the gentleman into the kitchen! I'm so sorry, sir. I'll take you to the drawing room directly. Have you come to see Miss Roberts?'

'No, I rather think I've come to see you,' said Dr Jenkins. 'You don't look at all well, my dear.' He put a hand on Mama's forehead. 'You have a fever – and I heard you coughing when I was in the hall.'

'No, sir, not me. I am fine,' Mama insisted, looked terribly flustered.

'It's all right, Mama. Tell the gentleman all your symptoms. I've fetched him for you. He's a doctor so he'll make you better.'

'Oh, Hetty, what have you *done*?' said Mama, starting to cry.

'Mama, don't. You *need* a doctor. And don't worry about money – I'm going to pay. Look, I have lots of money hidden in my handkerchief.'

'Hush, child,' said Dr Jenkins. 'Perhaps you can make us a cup of tea while I examine your mother.'

I did as I was told. Mama continued weeping while he listened to her chest and asked her many questions. She answered in a monotone, barely polite, but the doctor treated her gently, with respect.

'I think you know my diagnosis, don't you?' he said eventually, sitting down beside Mama and sipping his tea.

Mama nodded.

'You have an advanced case of phthisis,' Dr Jenkins said quietly.

'What's that? Please, is it serious, Doctor?' I asked fearfully, hating the hissing sound of the sinister little word.

'I'm afraid it is, Hetty. Your mother is consumptive, and has been for some while. It's a wonder she has been able to keep her position,' he said.

'But I'm going to lose it now, aren't I?' Mama said, and started coughing again.

He waited until the paroxysms stopped. 'My dear, how *can* you carry on in this state? And you know and I know that I have to tell your mistress.'

'And *you* know and *I* know that she will cast me out, and I will have nowhere to go. I doubt even the workhouse will take me in this state,' said Mama.

'I am going to see if I can admit you to the local infirmary,' said Dr Jenkins. 'There is a special ward for consumptive patients.'

'And will they make Mama better there?' I asked.

'They will give her every care,' he said.

'Yes, but can they *cure* her?' I said desperately.

'I think you are going to have to be a good brave girl, Hetty, and learn one of life's saddest lessons. We often lose the people we love the most.'

17

I wouldn't believe it. I tried not to let Mama believe it either.

'You're not going to die, Mama. I won't let you! I will care for you and feed you and nurse you, and do every single thing for you so that you never have to move, and then you won't cough, and then you will get better, just you wait and see,' I declared.

But Mama just shook her head very sadly, without even enough spirit to argue with me. She was proved horribly right about Miss Roberts. Mama had cared for her so devotedly – but as soon as the doctor broke the news to her that Mama had consumption, she panicked.

'She must leave this house immediately!' she screamed, so loudly that Mama and I could hear her downstairs. 'I can't have any sickness here! She might infect me! I will have to have the whole house thoroughly cleansed and disinfected. I will have to go to the trouble of training a new maid in my ways, and I'm a sick old woman myself. Oh, *why* did she have to do this to me? How will I ever get a maid to replace Ida?'

'What a selfish, wicked woman!' I exclaimed. 'She doesn't give a thought for *you*, Mama.'

'She's simply frightened,' said Mama. 'Go to her, Hetty. Here's your chance. Tell her that *you* will care for her.'

'I'm not working for her!' I cried.

'Hetty, please, will you try? One of us has to work – and it looks as if I am finished.'

'*Don't!* All right, Mama, I will go and talk to her.'

I'd sooner have worked for Matron Stinking Bottomly than for this self-centred, wretched woman who didn't have a word of compassion for my dear sick mama – but I could not deny her anything now.

'Try to be very polite!' said Mama.

I went up the stairs and knocked on her door.

'Who's that? If it's you, Ida, you can't come in! I daren't risk the infection – and I mustn't upset myself. I am a sick woman, aren't I, Doctor?'

I swallowed hard while he murmured to her. I wanted to burst in and boot her right out of bed, but I entered her room quietly, and bobbed her a deferential curtsy.

'Ah, the little daughter,' said Dr Jenkins.

'Whose daughter? *Ida's?*'

'Yes, ma'am – and I can take over Mama's duties while she's in the infirmary,' I said meekly. 'I have been trained as a servant and can cook and clean. Please let me assist you, ma'am. I am quick to learn.'

'There now, Miss Roberts!' said Dr Jenkins. 'Here is the answer to your prayers.'

'No, no, absolutely not! Don't let that girl come near me! She might have the infection too. And I can't have a child born out of wedlock in my house. I'm sorry, but I have my Christian principles.'

'And I have *my* principles, ma'am,' I shouted, unable to help myself now. 'I am *glad* you will not take me on. You pretend to be a good woman, but you haven't got an ounce of compassion in your withered heart. You are so taken up with your own trivial concerns that you didn't even *notice* that Mama was coughing herself to death. She's cared so dutifully for you, and yet you just want to turn her out onto the streets. You talk of Christian principles! I think you're going to get a horrible surprise when you go knocking on St Peter's gate in Heaven. He'll shake his head at you and turn you away, just you wait and see!'

I stamped out of the room, down the stairs, back to Mama in the kitchen.

'I couldn't quite hear – but that didn't *sound* very polite,' Mama said weakly.

'Oh, Mama, I did try, truly, but she didn't want me,' I said.

'Then we're done for,' Mama said weakly. 'We're both homeless.'

'No, we're *not*. That Dr Jenkins seems a kind gentleman. I'm sure he'll do his best to get you into the infirmary,' I said.

'I *try* to be kind – and I'm going to take your mama directly to the infirmary in my carriage,' Dr Jenkins said, following me into the kitchen. 'Why don't you get your mother's things packed up, my dear?'

It took only a few minutes to pack Mama's possessions into a box. She had just two changes of clothes, her nightgown, her washing things, her brush and comb, her little violet vase, and a satin pouch embroidered with one word: HETTY. I found all the letters I'd ever written to her inside, tied up in neat bundles with ribbon, plus all the childish presents I'd made for her, right back to a little ill-sewn heart. I wept then to see that she'd treasured them so carefully.

I carried Mama's box and my own suitcase, and we left Miss Roberts's house with the doctor. Mama tried to go to Miss Roberts to say goodbye, but she would not let her over her bedroom threshold and screamed at her to go away. Even so, Mama insisted on going to the neighbouring cottage, asking for the mistress there and begging her to send her maid to assist Miss Roberts.

The doctor took us to the infirmary in his carriage.

'I really can't go to this infirmary,' Mama protested weakly. 'I must try to find some kind of shelter for Hetty and me. I can still work if I put my mind to it.' But she started coughing again, that harsh hacking cough she couldn't control. Then she choked, and the terrifying bright blood stained her handkerchief.

'You cannot possibly work, my dear,' said Dr Jenkins. 'All you can do is rest now.'

The carriage drew up outside a large grey building that reminded me uncomfortably of my own hospital.

'Wait here, both of you,' said the doctor, and he hurried inside.

'I'm so, so sorry, Mama,' I said tearfully. 'I thought the doctor might be able to make you better. I didn't dream that dreadful woman would throw you out. I didn't realize.'

'I know, Hetty, I know,' Mama said, resting her poor burning head on my shoulder. 'Oh, darling, what use am I to you as a mother? Perhaps I should have given you up for good when you were a baby and never tried to be near you. I've just brought you heartache and grief.'

'You've given me great love. You're the best mother in the whole world. You mustn't worry about a thing now. You're going to get better, I promise you are. I'm going to visit you every day, and buy you little treats and care for you – just the way you did for me when I was little. But I'm big now, Mama, and can look out for myself, so you mustn't worry.'

'You, *big*? You'll always be my light-as-a-feather

Hetty,' said Mama.

'Sapphire,' I said.

'Sapphire,' said Mama, very gently touching my eyelids with her fingertips. 'When you were born, I wrapped you in a shawl and held you in my arms. You didn't cry or sleep like most babies. You just lay there, a tiny little thing, and looked up solemnly with your big blue eyes. You didn't seem like a stranger at all – it was as if I'd known you for ever.'

We clung to each other. Then Dr Jenkins came back, accompanied by a nurse in a high white hat and a starched apron. Her uniform reminded me of the matrons at the hospital and I was scared, but she helped Mama out of the carriage gently enough.

'Come along, you poor dear. Let us get you comfortable in bed,' she said.

'There now, young woman,' said Dr Jenkins to me. 'They will take care of your mother. They have put aside a bed for her, and she can stay there until – until she needs it no longer.'

'Thank you, sir.' I fumbled for my handkerchief. 'Exactly how much do I owe you, Dr Jenkins?'

He looked down at me, hesitating.

'It's all right, I have a great deal of money here. I can pay you the full amount, I'm sure,' I said.

'You keep your money, my dear,' said Dr Jenkins. 'I think you're going to need every penny.'

'That's – that's exceptionally kind of you, sir. I

am deeply indebted to you,' I said. I was trying to sound very grown up and business-like, but he shook his head sorrowfully, and patted me on the head as if I were a little child.

I scurried after Mama and the nurse. When I caught them up at the infirmary entrance, the nurse looked shocked to see me.

'No, no, dear. You're not allowed in here,' she said.

'But I have to go with Mama!'

'I'm taking her to the fever ward. Our patients are kept in complete isolation,' said the nurse.

'But *you* can go with her!'

'Yes, but *I* am a nurse!' she said.

'Then let me be a nurse too!' I said.

'Don't be ridiculous, child!'

'Please, please, please, can I just see where Mama's bed will be, and help her into it?' I said. I dropped to my knees. 'Look, I am *begging* you. *Please.*'

'Oh, very well, you can come in for five minutes, but then you must go. If Sister catches you there, I shall get into serious trouble,' she said.

So I walked with the nurse and Mama down long corridors smelling strongly of iodoform. Then, at last, at the very end of the building, we went through a door into a long room with beds lined up on either side.

'It's just like the dormitory at the hospital,

Mama!' I said.

I peered fearfully at the folk in the beds. They were mostly lying neat and still beneath their grey blankets, as if their limbs had been as firmly tucked in as their sheets. The few sitting propped up on pillows were all wearing bright red bed jackets. Perhaps they were provided to make the patients look bright and cheerful, but the colour only emphasized their sallow faces.

'You will have this bed here. It's in the best place of all, by the window. There, you have a sea view!' said the nurse, as if this were a special seaside hotel.

The window was opened a few inches, rattling a little in the strong breeze blowing from the sea.

'Won't Mama be in a draught?' I asked anxiously.

'She will get lots of sea air, and that will be very good for her lungs,' said the nurse. 'Now, go behind that curtain and take off your clothes. I'll provide you with infirmary linen. You won't need your own nightgown. In fact you won't need any of your things here. Your daughter can take them away.'

'I'll keep my letters,' Mama said firmly.

When I'd helped her into the plain white nightgown and garish bed jacket, she clutched the satin pouch to her chest.

I helped her gently into bed, smoothing her hair and pulling the bed jacket up around her thin neck.

The nurse provided her with a little china spittoon and a large handkerchief.

Mama and I stared at each other. Tears spilled down our cheeks.

'Oh, Hetty,' Mama whispered.

'There now, time to rest,' said the nurse, trying to straighten Mama's clenched fists. 'Say goodbye now.'

'This isn't goodbye for ever, Mama,' I said fiercely. 'You're going to get better, do you hear me? And I'm going to find a place for us to live and we'll be together at last, you and me. That's the way it's going to be, I promise.'

'But . . . now . . . I think you will have to . . . go to Miss Smith,' Mama gasped, starting to cough.

'No, I'm going to stay here. Don't worry, Mama, I have a plan. I will find a position here, and every day I will come to the infirmary before it gets dark. If I can't creep in somehow, I will stand in the grounds and I will wave to you at your window to show you that I'm fine. And you will wave back to me. Will you do that, Mama?'

'I will, darling,' Mama said between coughs.

I wiped her brow for her, kissed her hot forehead, and then ran out of the ward. I ran down the grim corridors, out of the infirmary, down the road, right onto the sands. I laid my head on my suitcase, clutched Mama's box, and cried my heart out.

'**H**etty? Hetty, is that you?'
I sat up, dazed, squinting in the sunlight. I didn't have any idea how long I'd been lying there on the sands. I'd cried for so long, but then I must have fallen asleep. Perhaps I was still dreaming now, because a strangely familiar child was squatting beside me, calling my name and looking at me with concern – and yet I felt sure I didn't have a friend in the world.

'Hetty, don't you remember me? I'm Maisie. We met on the train,' she said, tucking her hair behind her ears.

I stared at her. I'd only met her a day ago, and yet it seemed like months and months. I'd been travelling with such joy and optimism, so happy at the thought of seeing Mama. Yet now she was incarcerated in the infirmary, and though I hoped otherwise, I wasn't sure she would ever walk out. I had been trying so hard to do the best thing by calling the doctor, but maybe it would have been better to do nothing. Then Mama would at least have had her position and we could have been together. Miss Roberts might never have noticed I was there.

I started crying so bitterly that Maisie looked frightened.

'Don't cry so, Hetty, please! What's the matter? Are you lost? I am lost, but I don't mind a bit. I went for a paddle in the sea and I wandered in the water a little because it was so delightful, but when I went back up the beach, I couldn't find Mama and the others. I've been walking along the sands looking and looking for them, but *I'm* not crying one bit, see. I'm trying to be a big brave girl.'

'You *are* a big brave girl,' I said, wiping my eyes. I took several deep breaths, trying hard to calm myself. 'There now, I'm not crying either, not any more. Let me gather up my things and we'll walk along the sands together and I'm sure we'll find your family soon.'

I stood up, grasped my suitcase and Mama's box, and we started trudging along the beach together. Maisie set off to the right, but I felt sure she was going the wrong way.

'No, Maisie, I think your family will be *this* way, near the pier. I think you've been walking away from them all this time.'

'I'm not always very good at knowing which way

to go,' Maisie admitted. 'Will you stay with me until we find them again, Hetty?'

'Of course I will.'

'Shall I carry that box for you, as you have your suitcase?'

'No, I can manage it perfectly myself,' I said. My arms were aching, but I could not bear to relinquish Mama's box.

We travelled further along the beach. I had sand in my boots now, chafing my feet uncomfortably. Maisie had the advantage, running along in bare feet, her sailor dress tucked up comfortably in her drawers.

'This is such an adventure, isn't it, Hetty?' she said, giving a little skip.

I tried to smile at her. I wished with all my heart I could be a blessed child like Maisie, when the worst thing that could happen to her was getting lost on a beach. And she wasn't even lost any more, because I suddenly spotted a familiar little family. The mama was calling anxiously, clutching the baby, the papa was striding up and down, his head turning this way and that, and the big sister was running to the sea and back, gazing wildly about her.

'See, Maisie? There's your family,' I said.

'Oh! Yes, so it is! And see how they are searching for me!' said Maisie. She started running. 'Mama!

Papa! Charlotte! Here I am! Don't worry, I'm not a bit lost now.'

I watched her run over to them, and saw how her papa picked her up and whirled her round and round, her mama gave her a big kiss, and her sister Charlotte hugged her hard.

I felt tears pricking my eyes all over again. I turned my head and started walking quickly away – but I heard the family calling my name, and then thudding footsteps across the sand. It was Charlotte. She gave me a hug too, as if I were part of the family.

'Dear Hetty! Maisie says you found her. We're so grateful. We were all going frantic. Won't you come and let Mama and Papa thank you properly?'

She took my hand in hers and led me back to the little group.

'Well done, Hetty! We were looking everywhere for our silly little girl,' said the papa. 'How can we reward you?'

'Yes, we are considerably in your debt,' said the mama. 'I was nearly going out of my mind with worry. But what about *your* mother, Hetty? Have you not found her yet, dear?'

'Oh yes, I have, but – but she is very ill, and now she is in the infirmary and – and I don't know what to do,' I said, sobbing.

'My poor child!' She gave the baby to Charlotte and put her arms round me. I laid my head on her soft muslin blouse and wept, while she patted me gently on the back.

'There, now,' she said softly.

'I'm so sorry! It's just – I don't know what to do!'

'I know what you're going to do. You're going to come back to our lodgings and have supper with us,' said Papa.

'Yes, yes, yes!' said Charlotte and Maisie.

So I walked back with them to their lodgings, a big pink-washed house in a street leading off the promenade. I was still crying, and cowered away when their landlady came to the door. I knew I must look a terrible sight in my grubby dress, my face covered in tears and my nose running.

I thought they would send me to the kitchen to beg a morsel there – but not a bit of it.

'This little girl is a friend of ours, Mrs Brooke,' the mama said firmly. 'She will be having supper with us.'

'Certainly, Mrs Greenwood,' said the landlady, though she took in my cheap maid's dress and raised an eyebrow.

'Come, girls, let us tidy ourselves before supper,' said the mama.

She led the way upstairs to their rooms. She and

her husband shared a big blue bedroom, while Flora the baby had a cot beside their bed. The girls' room was next door, a pretty pink, with two single beds with patchwork quilts, and a proper dressing table and a washstand with pink-and-white patterned china.

Mrs Brooke brought jugs of hot water for each room and we washed in turn. The girls put on fresh clean sailor dresses, while I wore my Sunday green velvet. I felt it was too hot and formal for the seaside but the girls admired it enormously, stroking the velvet and fingering the yellow fringing.

'I would give anything to wear such a grown-up dress,' said Charlotte enviously. 'And you're allowed to put your hair up too, Hetty!'

'It doesn't stay pinned up for long though,' I said, and I brushed it out loose so that it fell a long way past my shoulders.

'You look like the lovely advertisement for Edwards' "Harlene" Hair Restorer!' said Charlotte.

'Oh, let me have a turn brushing it!' Maisie begged. Her own hair was limp and straggly, and she marvelled at mine.

'I wish I had lovely long hair like yours, Hetty! It's just like a mermaid's.' She pulled my green skirts tight around my legs. 'There, now you have a mermaid's tail too!'

I could hear the baby wailing fretfully, so I decided to make myself useful and went and knocked next door.

'Excuse me, Mrs Greenwood – would you like me to take care of the baby while you get ready in peace?' I offered.

'Why, Hetty, you're such a kind girl!' she said. 'All right, dear, see if you can work your magic with little Flora all over again. I have changed her napkin so I don't know why she's crying so. Perhaps you might ask Mrs Brooke to prepare her another bottle of boiled milk?'

'Certainly,' I carried the cross little baby carefully down the stairs and found my way to the kitchen.

Mrs Brooke was cutting thin slices of bread and butter, while fat yellow slabs of smoked haddock poached pungently on the stove.

'Please may I have a bottle for the baby?' I asked.

'Certainly . . . miss,' she said. The word came out grudgingly, but she said it all the same.

I took the bottle of baby milk and fed Flora in the window seat of the sitting room. She was clearly thirsty because she attacked the bottle with great vigour, making comically loud sucking sounds. I held her close, wondering at her intent little face, her long lashes and tiny delicate ears. I especially liked her perfect little toes peeping out beneath her rucked-up petticoats.

I thought of poor dear Mama and how she'd been forced to give me away when I was even younger than little Flora, denied the chance of holding me close like this.

We had had so short a time together. She had missed my first five years altogether, she had kept a wary distance when I came back to the hospital – and then she'd been cruelly banished. I'd planned for us to be together when I was grown up. I'd thought we'd have many, many precious years ahead, enough to make up for the sad time apart, but now . . .

I started crying again. Flora stopped sucking and stared up at me, her forehead puckering. She waved her tiny starfish hands, almost as if she were trying to comfort me.

'I'm sorry, little Flora,' I whispered, sniffing. 'I'll try to concentrate on you again.'

She drained her bottle completely, her eyes closing as she took the last few mouthfuls. She gave several contented sighs, snuggled her head right into my chest, and fell fast asleep. I held her close, and wouldn't put her down even when Mrs Brooke banged a gong and the family assembled in the dining room for supper.

I ate a few morsels of fish carefully with one hand while still holding the baby. There was fruit pie for pudding. The pastry was a little pale and uninteresting compared to my own. I was in such a turmoil I could eat very little.

'There now, children! Are you quite full now?' said Mr Greenwood, consulting his pocket watch. 'Good heavens, is that the time? Off to bed with you this minute!'

'Oh, Papa, *please* mayn't we stay up a little longer! It's still sunny outside. Are you *sure* it's bedtime?' Maisie wailed, as if the world were suddenly coming to an end.

Mr Greenwood's mouth twitched under his moustache, and Charlotte burst out laughing.

'Oh, Maisie, can't you tell when Papa is joking?'

'Don't you remember, Maisie?' Mrs Greenwood said, fondly pinching her daughter's cheek. 'We always go for a little walk along the sea front after supper.'

'Oh, so we do! Oh hurray, hurray!' said Maisie.

So we all went for a walk. I insisted on carrying little Flora, who was muffled in another shawl against the sea breeze. My heart beat hard against the baby, thinking that at any moment they would say goodbye to me and send me on my way to nowhere – but they seemed to take my company for granted. I left my suitcase and Mama's box back at the boarding house so at least I had an excuse for returning with them.

We set off down the road to the sea front.

'Now, which way shall we go, my dears?' said Mr Greenwood, standing before the painted map.

'Oh, please,' I whispered, my mouth so dry I could barely make myself heard. 'Could we – oh, could we—?'

'Let's see the pierrots!' Charlotte shouted.

'No, no, let's listen to the band,' Maisie clamoured.

'We can do both – *and* take a little stroll along the pier,' said Mr Greenwood.

Mrs Greenwood was looking at me. 'Where did *you* want to go, Hetty?' she asked.

'I – I wondered if I might possibly just run along to the infirmary. Perhaps Mama will be looking out of her window. I should so like to reassure her that I am all right.'

'You're a good thoughtful girl, Hetty. We will come with you, and then perhaps your mother will see you're among friends,' she said.

'Among very *dear* friends,' I said. 'Oh please, may we?'

It was a good fifteen minutes' walk away. I knew

724

everyone must be longing to see all their favourite seaside entertainments but they walked cheerfully beside me. Maisie skipped in circles, while Charlotte talked nineteen to the dozen about her school, and her best friends, and her favourite teachers, and the very worst cruel teacher ever, who made even great girls of Charlotte's age stand in a corner with a dunce's cap upon their heads. I did not think this very cruel at all compared to Matron Stinking Bottomly and Matron Pigface Peters, but I simply nodded or shook my head or tutted at appropriate times.

'Where do *you* go to school, Hetty?' Charlotte asked.

'I have left school now,' I said, truthfully enough.

'Oh, you lucky thing! How I wish I could leave school too, but Papa says it's important for a girl to have a good education, worst luck!'

I still nodded from time to time, but I was no longer listening to her sweet silly prattle. Inside my head I was chanting, *Mama, Mama, Mama*.

We approached the grim grey infirmary, and I stared hopefully up at the windows, but they all seemed so dark. I could not see in it at all, or tell whether anyone was looking out.

'I have to go *closer*,' I said, and I ran into the garden, through the shrubbery, looking around frantically, wondering if I could still work out which was the right window. Then I reached it at last and looked through the glass. I could see the ward. I could see the row of beds. Oh glory – *there* was Mama, propped up on her pillows in the garish red bed jacket, her face chalk-white, her eyes shadowed with dark circles. She was staring anxiously at the window, and when she saw me, her whole face lit up.

I smiled and blew kisses and held little Flora up, making her wave her tiny fist, hoping that Mama would think I had miraculously found a new position as a nursemaid. Mama seemed astonished at the sight, and tried to swing her legs out of bed to run to the window, but this made her cough. A nurse approached her bed and pushed her back against her pillows, but she did it gently, and she wiped Mama's brow when the coughing fit subsided at last.

I sent Mama a final kiss and she weakly blew a kiss back to me. '*I love you!*' I said – and her own lips mouthed the three words with me.

Then I ran back to the Greenwoods, hugging little Flora hard. 'I saw her! She was looking out for me,' I said, tears running down my cheeks.

'I'm so glad you saw her, Hetty,' said Mrs Greenwood. 'Now, dear, Mr Greenwood and I have had a little discussion. We will be happy to look after you for the next fortnight while we are in Bignor. You can share a room with the girls. I am sure Mrs Brooke will have a spare settle bed.'

'So – so can I be your nursemaid after all?' I said, dazed.

'No, we don't want you to be a nursemaid, though it will indeed be lovely if you continue to care for Flora so splendidly. We want you to stay with us as our guest, our little friend.'

19

The Greenwoods were so kind to me. I couldn't quite believe they were real. It was almost as if I'd made them up. I felt as if I'd made *myself* up too. I wasn't Hetty Feather any more. I wasn't even Sapphire Battersea. I wasn't a foundling child. I wasn't a maid. I was a little Greenwood girl now.

I helped look after baby Flora, which was no hardship at all. I'd grown to love this funny little baby, and although lugging her around everywhere made my arms tired, it somehow helped the ache in my heart. But caring for Flora was seen as a favour, certainly not a duty. I had no duties at all – this was the strangest part.

I didn't have to get up early and fight with the range and prepare breakfast. We didn't have to slip out of our soft beds until seven thirty. I woke around six even so, because it had become such a habit.

I lay still, thinking of Mama, lying just a few streets away. I sent her many loving thoughts and liked to fancy she was sending hers back to me. I felt as if we were somehow having our own private conversation through the ether.

Then Mrs Greenwood would put her head in, her hair still tumbling around her shoulders. She wore a tartan shawl over her long nightgown, and looked more like Charlotte and Maisie's big sister than their mother.

'Time to get up, girls,' she said, softly and sleepily, and she'd stoop over each tousled head and kiss their cheeks. She gave me a little pat on the shoulder at first, but after a few days I got a kiss too. We'd take turns getting washed and queuing for the water closet. It wasn't quite as grand as Mr Buchanan's, but serviceable enough, and no sign of any spiders!

Then we'd dress to go down to breakfast. I didn't have a frock suitable for the seaside. My green velvet was too warm and elaborate, and I didn't want to spoil it on the sands, yet my plain grey maid's dresses showed the whole world that I was really a servant.

'I think you had better borrow one of Charlotte's dresses,' said Mrs Greenwood. 'You don't mind, do you, Charlotte?'

'Of course I don't! It will be fun to see Hetty in one of my frocks. Come, Hetty, have a look. See which one you like the best.'

I couldn't believe she could cheerfully offer me the pick of her wardrobe. At the Foundling Hospital we had never willingly shared anything, not even a tangerine at Christmas, a sweet from a visitor, an undarned pair of stockings. We guarded such treasures fiercely for ourselves. And it wasn't as if Charlotte or Maisie had any number of fine frocks. The Greenwoods weren't rich at all. I learned that Mr Greenwood was an ordinary clerk in an Arundel insurance office, though the Greenwood female folk were as proud of him as if he were King of Arundel Castle.

I am not sure if they were a religious family or not. We did not attend church on Sunday, but perhaps this was because it wasn't part of seaside routine. I know one thing: the Greenwoods were the most truly kind and Christian-like people I had ever known.

I picked a pale primrose muslin from Charlotte's wardrobe. It was a little long and loose on me, but I thought it quite beautiful. Charlotte and Maisie clapped their hands when I shyly paraded in front of them in my new gown.

'It looks lovely on you, Hetty – much better than on me,' said Charlotte generously.

'Yes, I totally agree, and it won't matter if it's a bit long, because you can tuck your skirts up in your drawers on the beach,' said Maisie.

Charlotte tried to lend me a pair of her shoes as well, but they were several sizes too big, while Maisie's were too small.

They sold very cheap white sand-shoes at a stall on the promenade. I wondered about buying myself a pair, but I didn't feel I could waste any of my precious hoard of coins. I knew I'd be fending for myself again after this fortnight. I wore my hideous old boots the length of the street from the lodgings to the sea, then I whipped them off and ran around barefoot.

Mrs Greenwood saw me gazing at the sand-shoe stall every day and asked me quietly if I'd like a pair, but I shook my head resolutely. The Greenwoods were already spending a lot of money on me, though they insisted it was a mere trifle. I'm not sure if they came to an arrangement with Mrs Brooke about my bed and board. I fervently hoped it wasn't too exorbitant.

Mr Greenwood paid for me to have a daily donkey ride with Charlotte and Maisie. Oh, those dear, funny, patient donkeys! They were led about by a strange man who barked out fierce instructions to all us children: 'Sit very still! Don't feed the donkeys! Don't ever kick them. Don't tweak their ears!' But when he spoke to his five donkeys, his voice was soft and crooning, and he patted their noses gently.

They had special names: Rosie, Maudie, Sally, Jessie and Polly. I always chose to ride on Polly, because I had had a dear friend Polly at the hospital. Polly-Donkey was the smallest and sweetest, ash-grey with a dark cross on her back. She seemed to like me too, and gave me a little whinnying greeting when I patted her. Perhaps it was because I lived up to my name and was light as a feather! Charlotte and Maisie were quite slight too, but some of the children on the beach were great stout creatures and it must have been hard for the little donkeys to bear them on their backs.

Mr Greenwood paid for the use of a bathing machine too, and the hire of a ridiculous swimming costume for me with long drawers and a frilled hat. Charlotte and Maisie were a little timid when it came to climbing down the steps and immersing themselves in the sea, but I couldn't wait. The cold was a shock – and the salty taste another – but I managed to keep my head above the waves most of the time. I did not know how to swim. I splashed wildly with my arms and legs but I did not progress anywhere. However, I found that if I lay on my back and stuck out my stomach, I could float!

'Look at Hetty! She's a real mermaid now!' Maisie shouted.

Mrs Greenwood didn't take to the water at all. She sat decorously on the sands with baby Flora, but Mr Greenwood bathed with us. He looked very comical in his striped costume, but he swam with strength and dignity. He also played the fool, pretending to be a whale and spouting a great plume of water into the air, while Maisie clapped her hands and squealed.

'Aren't papas *silly*!' Charlotte said to me.

I could only smile, because I did not have one. I did not think Mr Greenwood silly at all, I thought him excessively kind and generous. On hot sunny days he bought hokey-pokey ice creams for all of us. Mine was delicious, but it reminded me terribly of Bertie. I had not written properly to him, because I could not bear to tell him that Mama was so ill. I simply sent him a postcard of the sea front with a brief message: *Dear Bertie, Wish you were here. Love Hetty.* I wrote exactly the same message on another postcard to Jem. I did not put a return address on either because I did not have one. I stuck my last two stamps on the cards and posted them.

Whenever the tide was out, Charlotte, Maisie and I made sandcastles, sharing big wooden spades. Maisie got bored of digging very quickly, but she was good at finding shells to pattern our castles. She loved to run into the sea for pail after pail of water to fill the moat around the base of each building.

While we worked, I made up a story that we were three fairy princesses, each with her own castle. We took turns telling how our castles were decorated inside. Charlotte wanted marble throughout, with a four-poster bed with velvet curtains. Maisie wanted her walls studded with pearls, and she had a pearl dressing-table set to brush her long wavy princess hair. I chose coral for my palace, shiny and strange, in myriad patterns. I had a soft seaweed-green sofa stuffed with duck's down, where I reclined in a coral-pink embroidered tea gown, writing my memoirs.

'Aren't any of you princesses going to run off with handsome princes?' said Mr Greenwood, eavesdropping on our chatter.

Charlotte and Maisie giggled coyly.

'I might just run off with Michael Fairhill,' Maisie said, grinning.

'Oh no, Maisie, that's not fair! Michael's *my* sweetheart,' said Charlotte.

'Girls, girls, don't talk that way,' said Mrs Greenwood. 'Michael is our next-door neighbours' son, Hetty. He's a dear kind boy and he's played patiently with my girls since they were babies, but he's nineteen now, so of course he's not really their sweetheart.'

'He is so, Mama,' said Maisie. 'In fact I am perfectly sure he is going to marry me when I am a little older.'

'No he is not. He's going to marry *me*, because I'm the eldest,' said Charlotte.

'Stop squabbling, girls! You sound ridiculously like the Ugly Sisters!' said Mr Greenwood. He looked at me. 'What about you, Cinderella? Do you have a sweetheart?'

I hesitated, blushing.

'She does, she does – look at her cheeks! She's gone scarlet! What is his name, Hetty?' said Maisie.

'Well, I have *two* sweethearts,' I said.

This made them both squeal.

'Who, who? Tell us their names!' said Charlotte.

'Well, there's Bertie . . . and there's Jem,' I said.

'And which one do you like the best?' Maisie asked.

'I'm not sure,' I said truthfully. 'I do like them both.'

'So which one will you run off with?' Maisie demanded.

'I don't think I'm going to run off with anyone. I shall stay in my coral palace, and Mama shall come and live with me, and I shall nurse her until she's completely better,' I said.

I knelt there on the sand, my head bent so they should not see the tears in my eyes. Charlotte put her arm round me even so, and Maisie nestled close and took my hand.

'Perhaps she really will be a little better today,' Charlotte said.

Every evening after supper the whole family walked with me to the infirmary. I was bolder now, but I still couldn't get into her ward. Every time I tried to sneak in through the entrance and down the long corridor, a nurse caught me and marched me back out again. However, when the nurse in charge of the ward was having her supper in a side room, I could call softly through the open window. Mama would slip out of bed and come right up to the window, her hand clamped over her mouth to stop herself coughing. She'd reach through the gap at the bottom and we'd clasp hands tight. I'd pass her the long loving letters I wrote each night. I'd bring her tiny presents too: an embroidered handkerchief, a pretty shell I'd found on the beach, a plaited lock of my hair.

Mama was so weak she'd often start crying. I was worried about her getting chilled if she stayed at the window too long, but her eyes shone whenever she saw me. She whispered feverishly that my visits meant the whole world to her. She couldn't talk to me properly for fear of coughing and alerting the nurse, so I talked to her instead, telling her again and again that I loved her. I promised she was going to get better, and then we would live together. Meanwhile she mustn't worry about me at all. I said I was very happy with my dear Greenwood family.

I didn't tell Mama they were only here for a holiday because I knew she'd fret over what would happen next. I tried to put it out of my mind myself, though I often woke with a start in the middle of the night, terrified.

During the day I somehow managed to put most of my troubles out of my mind. The evenings were especially sweet. After seeing Mama I'd feel reassured, ready for the rest of our walk. Sometimes we promenaded on the pier, though Maisie was afraid of the gaps in the planks of wood and started whimpering. She worried that they would give way, and she would fall right through into the surging sea. Mr Greenwood had to give her a piggyback to get her to venture right to the end of the pier.

I loved to go there myself. I'd clutch the railings and stare out to sea and imagine myself sailing away beyond the horizon. There was an advertising poster on a kiosk on the pier for Argosy cigarettes, with a bold woman in a white cap and navy nautical dress sailing her yacht with a triumphant look in her eyes. She wasn't a woman who knew her place. She didn't *have* a place – she was as free as the wind in her hair and the waves beneath her.

There was a machine that told fortunes on the pier. Mr Greenwood paid a penny each for us all to have a go. Charlotte and Maisie got exactly the same fortunes, printed on little pink cards:

You are fair of face
A form full of grace
Wedding bells chime
True love divine!

This made them both squeal and claim Michael Fairhill as their future husband.

'Now it's your turn, Hetty!'

My fortune card was bright sapphire-blue and it said:

You have far to go
A life of woe
But your wishes come true
Happily for you!

'Oh, Hetty, perhaps Bertie or Jem will marry you!' said Maisie. 'Then everything will end happily. Which will you choose?'

'Neither! I know what I wish for,' I said, clutching my little blue card until the edges cut into my hand.

One evening we went to see the pierrots – a little troupe of performers in white clown outfits. The next day on the sands, Charlotte and Maisie and I gave our own 'Pierrot' concert to Mr and Mrs Greenwood. I even fashioned a tiny pierrot costume for little Flora. I held her in my arms and made her bob up and down, performing her own baby song and dance.

Another evening Mr Greenwood paid for us all to sit before the big octagonal bandstand and listen to the music. I did not know any of the songs, but all the Greenwoods sang along while the band played. They were a military band in smart uniform with gleaming gold epaulettes. I hoped that Gideon might be able to join a similar band.

We also went to see Mr Clarendon's Seaside Curiosities. I had noticed a distinctive red-and-white striped tent pitched at the end of the promenade and had very much hoped it might be a circus.

'No, no, Hetty, it's not a circus, it's a freak show,' said Charlotte. 'Oh, Papa, please may we go and see the curiosities?'

'I'm not sure it's suitable for young girls,' Mrs Greenwood said quickly. 'And please don't use that word, Charlotte, it sounds unpleasant.'

'What should we call the freaks, then, Mama?' Maisie asked.

'You shouldn't call them anything. They're poor unfortunate people who cannot help the way they look,' said Mrs Greenwood.

'Now don't get upset, my dear,' said Mr Greenwood. 'I think Mr Clarendon's folk rely on trickery and make-up. I'm sure there's not a genuine freak amongst them.'

'Please, what *is* a freak?' I asked.

'Perhaps we will have to show you,' said Mr Greenwood.

'It's truly not a suitable show for children. I regret that we took Charlotte and Maisie last year. It is sad and tawdry and vulgar,' said Mrs Greenwood.

'Yes, and we *loved* it!' said Charlotte. '*Please* let us take Hetty, Mama!'

Mrs Greenwood weakened, but she wouldn't come in with us. She sat on a nearby bench with little Flora, while the girls and I eagerly approached the entrance to the tent. Mr Clarendon himself stood there, bizarrely dressed in a bright scarlet suit with a bowler hat of the same hue tipped sideways on his head. He spoke into a loudhailer, instructing passersby to roll up and see the astonishing sights inside.

'Prepare to be truly amazed,' he said as Mr Greenwood paid for all of us.

He tipped his bowler to Mr Greenwood and smiled at us girls. He gave me a particular wink which disconcerted me. I did not know if I would like Mr Clarendon's freaks or not, but I decided I did not care for him.

The tent was divided into little rooms, one leading to another. The first was a little disappointing. It consisted of a display of not-very-remarkable seaside objects: a very large preserved fish with doleful eyes; some fancy seashells; a crab with enormous claws; a display of stuffed seagulls suspended precariously on wires; and a moth-eaten stuffed seal with a woebegone expression.

Charlotte and Maisie circled these exhibits a little impatiently. 'Wait till you see the *next* room, Hetty – and the one after that!' they said, taking my hands and hurrying me along.

We moved through the flap to the next room. There was a real man sitting on a chair, wearing only his trousers, hoisted up with a pair of black braces. His entire body was covered in detailed blue pictures, as if he were a human comical paper. There were even pictures engraved up his bald head.

There was a sign above him: HENRY, THE MAN WITH ONE HUNDRED TATTOOS. I stared at him, fascinated. I squinted very carefully at each picture. I tried counting, but there were too many, and perhaps there were more lurking beneath his trousers. I would never know if there truly were one hundred. Were they *real*?

'Perhaps they are just painted on?' I whispered to Charlotte.

'Lick your finger and try to rub one off, missy!' said Henry.

I jumped, and declined his invitation – but I circled him several times, still marvelling. His arms bloomed with bouquets, his chest sported strange ladies and slithery snakes, and an eagle perched permanently right on the top of his head. Exotic wild creatures stampeded across his shoulder-blades: lions, tigers, even a great buffalo with a Red Indian warrior upon his back.

'Come this way, Hetty – there's lots more to see!' said Charlotte.

We encountered Pirate Pete, Scourge of the Seven Seas, in the next room. I studied him with great interest. He looked just like a storybook pirate, with gold earrings and a kerchief tied around his long coarse hair. He had a patch over one eye, a wooden peg leg, and a real parrot on his shoulder. Maisie tried to stroke the parrot but it pecked at her irritably.

In the next room we gazed upwards in awe at Fantastic Freda, the Female Giant. Her placard said she was seven foot high, but she was standing on a large upturned bucket, which added many inches to her height. Her girth was impressive too.

She was wearing a vast blue-and-white striped bathing dress, straining at the seams. She struck several poses, miming swimming, while a little gang of boys clapped admiringly. Some shouted rude comments, and Fantastic Freda smiled and rattled her collecting cup in a saucy fashion – but her eyes looked very sad.

'My, I'd forgotten all about Fantastic Freda,' said Mr Greenwood, blinking up at her. 'Amazing woman!' He pulled Maisie's hair. 'See what happens when you eat too many hokey-pokeys!'

Charlotte had already rounded the corner to observe Harold, the Two-Headed Marvel. I took a deep breath when I saw him. He wore a full cape with two identical heads poking out at the top. He stared at me with four eyes – but as I tiptoed nearer, I saw that only one pair of his eyes swivelled in my direction. The second pair shone like glass and did not move. The second nose was as large and smooth as its twin, but the nostrils didn't quiver. The second pair of lips were slightly open, but they didn't smile. The second head was a perfect wax model stuck through a hole in a cape and set fair and square on the shoulders. The real head was carried at an angle, leering at us in a disconcerting fashion.

Maisie laughed a little hysterically, convinced that both heads were real. She declared she loved the double-headed phenomenon best of all the curiosities, but in the middle of the night she woke up screaming.

'The man with two heads is looking at me!' she shrieked, loud enough to wake the dead.

Charlotte and I tried to comfort her, but she didn't calm down until Mrs Greenwood came running in from the next room. Maisie slept in her parents' bed that night, but woke up cheerfully enough in the morning – and that evening begged to view Mr Clarendon's Curiosities all over again!

20

Time seemed suspended during that first strange seaside week with the Greenwoods. The second week hurtled by in a flash. Suddenly it was Friday, their last day. We went to the beach as usual, but we came back early in the afternoon so that they could start packing their trunks. I helped Charlotte and Maisie collect together their under-things and stockings and fold all their dresses. I took off the pale primrose dress and put on my own grey print with a sinking heart.

I heard Flora fussing in the next room, so I went to see if I could hold her and keep her quiet while Mr and Mrs Greenwood did their packing.

'You're such a good helpful girl, Hetty,' said Mrs Greenwood. 'I don't know how we're going to manage without you.'

'You've almost become a part of our family this holiday,' said Mr Greenwood.

I bent my head over little Flora and clutched her tightly to stop myself crying. I took her back to the girls' room and walked her up and down. She relaxed against me, making contented little sucking noises. I rubbed my cheek against her downy head and patted her back.

'Dear little Flora,' I whispered.

I heard Mr and Mrs Greenwood talking to each other earnestly next door, but their voices were lowered so I could not hear what they were saying. After a few minutes they came in the room together, looking solemn.

'Hetty, dear, we've been conferring together, Mr Greenwood and I,' said Mrs Greenwood.

'We were wondering . . . how would you feel about coming home with us to Arundel?' said Mr Greenwood.

'Oh, Papa, what a wonderful idea!' said Maisie.

'Oh *yes*, Papa, it would be lovely to have Hetty for a sister,' said Charlotte.

I burst into tears now, still clutching Flora, but shaking uncontrollably.

'There now, Hetty, I'll take baby,' said Mrs Greenwood gently.

'Don't cry so, Hetty. Don't you *want* to be our sister?' said Charlotte.

'I – I want it more than anything,' I sobbed.

'There, then! It's settled,' said Mr Greenwood, clapping his hands. 'You will be like another daughter to us.'

'I would like that tremendously, but – but I am *already* a daughter to dear Mama. I have to stay here and see her every day at the infirmary,' I said.

'I understand, Hetty – but I think it would ease your poor mama's suffering to know that you are safe, with a good family to care for you,' said Mrs Greenwood.

'I know that's exactly what Mama would want, but even so, I *have* to stay and see her, because . . . because she might not be here much longer.' I said the words in a whisper, hardly able to bear to say them aloud.

'You poor dear child,' said Mrs Greenwood. 'But where will you stay if you won't come with us?'

'I have a little money to see me through a few days, and then I shall look for work here,' I said resolutely.

'Then we will give you a character reference. I will write it this very minute. I shall say you are the most excellent little nursemaid,' said Mr Greenwood.

'And we will give you our address,' said Mrs Greenwood. 'If you need a home when – when the time comes, then promise you will come to us.'

I promised and thanked them fervently. I was so overcome that I could scarcely eat my supper. I could not believe that they could be so good and kind and generous. There was a part of me that wanted to seize this extraordinary opportunity right away. I was aware that it was a spur-of-the-moment offer. If they reflected on matters back in their own home, they might well change their minds, albeit reluctantly.

They weren't a wealthy family and I knew they lived in a modest house. Charlotte and Maisie had described it to me in detail. I would have to share a room with the girls and it would be a terrible squash for them. What would they do with me? Would they send me to school with Charlotte or send me out to work? I wasn't a real daughter, and yet I was too close to them now to be a proper servant. I was always being told I didn't know my place. I could see that I didn't really *have* a place in the Greenwood family, though we might all wish I did.

In any case I couldn't go with them now and leave Mama. I packed my suitcase too, because I couldn't stay on at their lodgings. The Greenwoods begged Mrs Brooke to let me have a room there for a few nights, but she said she had a new family with six children and a nursemaid coming on Saturday afternoon and there wouldn't be room for even a mouse to bed down.

So on Saturday I walked with the Greenwoods to the railway station, the summoned porter pushing all their luggage. I hugged them all in turn and we said our goodbyes. Mr Greenwood was the only one of us who didn't cry – and even he seemed more moist-eyed than usual.

I waved to them until the train had chuffed its way out of the station. When the white smoke cleared, I looked around the platform hurriedly, seeking out arriving holidaymakers with small children.

There were several families travelling first class, but they all had their own nannies and nursemaids with them. I hastened to the guard's van, where they were unloading all the trunks and cases, and sought out less stylish families without travelling servants. There was one family with three little fair children who looked promising. The youngest was wailing dismally while its mother patted it in-effectually. I darted forward.

'Excuse me, ma'am. I don't want to seem for-ward, but I'm very good at handling babies. May I quieten the little one for you?' I asked eagerly.

The mama looked horrified and backed away from me, acting as if I were about to snatch her ewe lamb away for ever.

'I don't mean any harm, ma'am. Please let me offer my services as a nurserymaid while you are on holiday. I have an excellent character reference.'

'Will you go away at once and stop pestering my wife or I'll be forced to call a policeman,' said the father, looking fierce.

I sloped off, humiliated, and approached another family with twin boys, but they seemed equally suspicious. When I started talking to a third family, a station porter came up and seized hold of me by my collar, practically choking me.

'I don't know what you're playing at, miss, but there's no hawking or begging allowed on this station, so I must ask you to move on,' he said firmly, and dragged me outside.

I still didn't give up. I watched for families making their way to lodging houses near the promenade and offered my services to each one, but they all regarded me with suspicion. I tried again when the next London trainload arrived, with equal lack of success.

I tried another tactic, walking up and down the streets of Bignor, knocking on every likely door, begging for work.

'I will turn my hand to anything. I am an excellent nursemaid, but I am an experienced parlourmaid too, and a competent cook – I'm particularly good at pastry. Please may I work for you? I have a good character and I'll be content with the smallest of salaries. Oh please, will you take me in?'

I gabbled some version of this spiel again and again. Folk frequently shut the door in my face. One kindly cook let me sit in her kitchen and made me a cup of tea, but then even she sent me on my way. By mid afternoon I was exhausted, but I wouldn't give up. I tried the shops instead, seeing if any might be willing to take me on, but people shook their heads again and again.

When it was nearly time to see Mama, I paid a penny to use a public convenience and washed my face and brushed my hair, trying to spruce myself up a little lest I alarm her. I struggled along the road to the infirmary with my suitcase.

I went right up to the window and Mama crept out of bed. We stood together, only the pane of glass between us. I kissed her lips and laid my hand against hers. We stood motionless for a minute or two, gazing deep into each other's eyes. Then a nurse came and pulled Mama back to bed. She tapped on the window for me to be gone.

I did not go straight away. I walked round the walls of the infirmary to the main entrance and approached another nurse there.

'No children are allowed in here, dear,' she said briskly.

'I'm not a child,' I said, standing on tiptoe. 'I'm a working girl. In fact I would like to work *here*. Perhaps I could train as a nurse?'

'Nonsense! You're far too young.'

'I'm sixteen, nearly seventeen,' I lied.

'Run along now and stop wasting my time.'

'I'll do any kind of work. I could do the cleaning.

I'm very used to scrubbing floors. Or I could help in the kitchen. I practically cooked single-handed in my last household,' I gabbled. 'Or perhaps there is a children's ward. I'm very experienced with babies. I have a good character reference. Please let me show it to you.'

'Go *away*, you silly girl. Why won't you take no for an answer?'

'Because I'm desperate!' I snapped.

'Well, this is no place for young girls, working or otherwise. Come along, out you go.'

She sent me firmly on my way. I trudged along the promenade, lugging my suitcase, wondering what on earth I was going to do now. I had spent all day looking for work and had got nowhere. I was so tired I sat on my suitcase for a while, gazing about me despairingly. When I ran away from the hospital I had done a little begging. I hadn't even needed to ask for money, I had just looked mournful – but no one seemed to understand the concept of begging in Bignor. People barely gave me a second glance.

I had also sold flowers with Sissy, but there was no sign of any flower sellers along the promenade.

How else could I earn money? There seemed no way at all. At least I had enough left for a couple of nights' lodging. I decided I'd better look for a cheap room now.

I wandered back along the sea front, utterly weary,

scarcely able to put one foot in front of the other. I remembered all the happy times running along beside Charlotte and Maisie, strolling on the pier, listening to the band, marvelling at Mr Clarendon's Seaside Curiosities . . . and then it suddenly came to me.

I marched along with sudden determination until I reached the red-and-white pavilion tent. Mr Clarendon stood outside in his bizarre scarlet suit and bowler hat, talking through his megaphone.

'Roll up, roll up! Come and encounter the greatest collection of living breathing curiosities you'll ever see in a month of Sundays! Marvel at Henry, with his hundred tattoos, gasp at Fantastic Freda, the Female Giant—'

'Excuse me, sir,' I said.

'Would you like a sixpenny ticket, little miss?'

'No, I have already been in and seen all the people inside. I was wondering, sir – would you like a brand-new attraction?'

He stared at me. 'What might you have in mind, missy?'

'I could be . . . Emerald, the Amazing Pocket-Sized Mermaid, half girl, half fish,' I said.

'And how are you going to be a mermaid, missy? I don't see no tail, I see two little feet in shabby boots.'

'If I come back tomorrow as Emerald the Mermaid, will you take me on?'

He looked me up and down, his eyes narrowed. I reached up and unpinned my hair, so that it fell past my shoulders in a long red wave. His lips twitched.

'I'll have to see your costume first. I'm not making no promises. But I reckon you *could* be a draw.'

'How much would you pay me?'

'That depends on the takings, girl. We'd have to negotiate.'

'Very well. I'll be back tomorrow,' I said.

I did not like him very much. I especially did not like the way he looked me up and down. But if this was my only way of earning money so I could stay on in Bignor, then I'd have to put up with it.

Now I needed a roof over my head. I did not try any of the lodging houses near Mrs Brooke's. I deliberately walked away from the sea and picked a street of tumbledown houses on the far side of town with ROOMS TO LET signs.

I took the first one available. It was an attic room with a narrow bed and the sheets looked distressingly dirty, but I was too tired to seek anything better. The landlady was as grimy as the bedding, her hair lank, her fingernails black, her dress shiny with grease stains. But she was kind enough, and brought me up a supper tray: cold sausage, and a slice of bread and dripping, with a

756

mug of tea. I did not like to think of her filthy fingers touching the food, but I was so hungry I ate it all the same. Though the sheets were grey, I got into bed willingly enough, and fell asleep as soon as my head touched the grubby pillow.

I was up early the next day, my money counted out and wrapped in my handkerchief. As soon as the shops were open I went to the nearest draper's. I bought a sharp pair of scissors, a tape measure, a paper of pins and needles, and a reel of green cotton. I thought some more, and selected a packet of pearl beads, another of green sequins, and some fancy green braid. I thought again, and had a couple of yards of cheap pale-pink muslin measured out, with matching pink cotton thread.

'Is that it now, missy?' said the draper's assistant, rolling her eyes.

'Yes, thank you. Please wrap them all in a paper parcel for me,' I said briskly.

I went down the street until I found a fish-monger's. I asked him for two scallop shells, then I purchased a tube of strong adhesive glue from the stationer's shop. There! I had everything I needed now.

I went back to my grimy attic room, sat cross-legged on the floor, and set about constructing my mermaid costume. I measured myself with the tape measure first, and then sketched out shapes on the pages of an old newspaper. When I was sure I had the pattern right, I laid my green velvet gown out on the grubby carpet and seized the scissors. It took me several minutes before I had the courage to make the first cut. It was my only decent dress, the costume I'd fashioned with such care. I wasn't even sure that my idea was going to work. I didn't have enough material to cut out a proper tail in one piece. I took off the redundant trimmings, pinned the newspaper pattern in place, and started snipping out the shapes to make a mermaid's tail. I had to fiddle around, cutting a patch here, a length there, and somehow try to fit all the pieces of the puzzle together to make the tail. It was a tiresome, complicated procedure. Several times I held the ruined velvet to my cheek and wept bitterly, but then I carried on with my task.

I stitched and stitched until my hands were sore and pricked, but slowly, slowly, the mermaid's tail grew. When the basic shape was stitched together at last, I stuck my legs cautiously into it. Thank goodness it fitted as snugly and smoothly as a glove. I sewed green brocade in stiffened strips to the fork at the end of the tail, and then started the tedious chore of stitching handfuls of little pearls and sequins into place to give the tail the shimmering effect of scales.

My eyes were twitching now and my hands

cramped, but I still had to make my top. The mermaids I had seen in picture books were naked, though their long hair more or less preserved their decency. I wasn't sure my hair was quite long and thick enough, and I wanted to make *certain* I preserved my decency, so I sewed myself a pink gauze bodice and carefully stuck a scallop shell at either side to cover my chest (not that I yet had anything much to cover!). I sewed more pearls around the edges, and then assembled the entire costume, brushed out my hair, and peered at myself in the spotted mirror on the wall. I wasn't sure I looked *utterly* convincing, but then again, neither had Harold the Two-Headed Marvel. I looked decorative – and I guessed that might be Mr Clarendon's primary requirement.

I packed my costume very carefully into Sarah's mother's invaluable suitcase, and set off. I walked over to the infirmary first, and peered through the window. Mama was lying back on her pillows, coughing and coughing. My heart turned over at the sight of her. She saw me and tried to get up, but I shook my head fiercely, gesturing to her to stay in bed. I mouthed *I love you* over and over again, and blew her kisses. Mama managed to stop coughing long enough to smile valiantly and blow kisses back.

I set off for Mr Clarendon's Seaside Curiosities

with renewed determination. Every step I took I whispered, *I love you, Mama, I love you, Mama, I love you, Mama*, trying to give myself courage. I still felt shy and frightened when I approached the red-and-white pavilion. Mr Clarendon was outside in his ridiculous red suit, inviting all the passersby to roll up.

I stood beside him, waiting for him to reach the end of his spiel. He eyed me up and down again.

'You still don't look like a mermaid to me,' he said, waggling his eyebrows in a way that was meant to be amusing.

'I need to change into my costume, Mr Clarendon,' I said. 'You can't expect a mermaid with a tail to walk down the street.'

'Ooh, hoity-toity!' he said, chuckling. 'Well, come this way, missy. I'll escort you to your dressing room.'

I followed him through the tent, past the fish and seagulls and sad seal, past the tattoed man, Pirate Pete and his parrot, Freda the Female Giant and Harold the Two-Headed Marvel. They did not have much of an audience as yet and were lounging around, scratching and yawning. Freda saw me and nodded down at me in a friendly fashion, waving her great hand. I waved mine back, trying hard to stay composed.

The 'dressing room' was a curtained-off cramped corner at the back of the tent.

'Come on, then, little mermaid, give us a swish of your tail,' said Mr Clarendon. He stood there rubbing his hands together.

'I cannot change in front of you, sir,' I said. 'Surely you realize it wouldn't be decent. Please go away and return in five minutes.'

'You're a fiery little snippet!' he said. 'You don't order me around. I'm the one who gives the orders. I'm the boss of this establishment.'

'Yes, sir, and I very much hope you will be *my* boss – but I would still appreciate a little privacy.'

I stood firm, and he shrugged his shoulders, sighed, and walked off, though I sensed he had not gone very far away. I hoped he wasn't peeping.

I unsnapped the suitcase, pulled off my dress, and inserted myself into the elaborate tail and pink bodice. I could not walk in my costume. I could not even stand. I lay down gingerly on the dirty tarpaulin. I let my hair down and combed it vigorously, trying to look as fetching as possible.

Then I called out: 'Roll up, roll up, come and see the new attraction at Mr Clarendon's Seaside Curiosities! Marvel at Emerald, the Amazing Pocket-Sized Mermaid.'

Mr Clarendon came bustling in, laughing – and then stopped short when he saw me. My heart started beating fast but I forced myself to lie still, lounging on the squalid flooring as if it were the sandy shore. I combed my hair, arching my back, and moved my legs so that my tail twitched.

'You little beauty!' he said, walking around me, peering at me from every angle. 'Where did you get your costume from, tiddler? Are you on the stage?'

I took this as an immense compliment, and murmured something ambiguous. If he thought I was professional, maybe he'd pay me more.

'So you'll exhibit me, then, Mr Clarendon?'

'I'll say! I think we can build you up into quite a little novelty. We can make you a suitable setting – have you lying on a pile of sand, spread a bit of sea-weed around, a few shells, to get the right atmosphere. I think you'll pull the lads in even more than Freda.'

'So how much will you pay me?'

'Half a crown a week – if the takings are good. A florin if they're not.'

'What? I could get more than that as a maid!'

'Well, go and get it then, little girlie.'

'But – but I'm not sure I can live on that.'

'You'll get tips. Wink at the fellows and they'll start raining coins, you'll see. And you can have free lodging with the rest of us. You can share with Freda.'

I did not like the idea of winking at the fellows. I did not see that there would be much room for me in lodgings if I had to share with a giant. Even so, joining this strange group of sad souls seemed my only viable option now.

'I'll join your troupe, then,' I said.

'That's the ticket! You'll have every morning off. Folk don't seem to have the stomach for freaks straight after breakfast. We open at two, but you'll be here at one forty-five to change into your costume. Then we go straight through till midnight.'

'Ten hours!'

'You'll have five-minute breaks at four and nine, and a half-hour for supper at six thirty.'

'Can I go out during my supper break?'

'Well, you're not going to get far in that costume, are you?' he said, 'No, you'll take your supper here, like all the others.'

I sat up straight. 'I'm not like all the others. I'll go without supper if necessary – but I must go and see someone at that time every day. I'll make sure I'm back at seven sharp, in costume. Is that a deal, Mr Clarendon?'

'I told you, I'm the one who makes the deals, not you,' he said, but he held out his hand and we shook on it.

21

So I started my bizarre new career as Emerald, the Amazing Pocket-Sized Mermaid. I moved into the lodging house with Mr Clarendon and the rest of his Curiosities. Mr Clarendon had an entire suite of rooms all to himself on the first floor. The rest of us had to make do in small cramped bedrooms – but at least they were clean, with washed linen.

I barely said a word to the tattooed man or the pirate or two-headed Harold. They would drink together late into the night and only surface at noon, shuffling up and down the stairs in under-vests and trousers, bleary-eyed and smelling of stale beer. The tattooed man and the pirate seemed more interested in each other, but Harold leered at me with his real head, and I learned to whisk myself away from him quickly to avoid his pats and pinches.

I hated him, and disliked the other men, including Mr Clarendon – but I grew to love Freda! I had been a little frightened of her at first, because she was so very large, even when not standing on a bucket. She had been given a double bed to accommodate her vast size. I was told I had to share it with her. I was very anxious about this, scared that she might suddenly turn in the bed and squash me flat. I resolved to sleep on the floor with a blanket.

When we went upstairs together after my first very long and gruelling afternoon and evening as Emerald, Freda was kindness itself.

'You poor little baby, you must be exhausted,' she said. 'But what a little star you are! All the boys were beside themselves!'

'They crowded round you too,' I said.

'Ah, but they only want to mock me,' said Freda sadly.

'No, I heard someone say that you're a fine figure of a woman,' I said.

'Fine figure of a freak, more like,' said Freda. 'But you're a real little beauty, Emerald.'

I did not tell her my real name. I did not want anyone ever knowing that Hetty Feather – or Sapphire Battersea, indeed – was now a performing curiosity in a freak show. I pretended to Mama that I had found a respectable position as a nursery-maid. I did not write to Bertie or Jem any more. I knew what they would think of me, though I was not doing anything so very wrong, and my costume was perfectly respectable, if exotic.

'I am not the slightest bit beautiful, Freda,' I said 'I have red hair, and I am much too little and scrawny.'

'I am so tall and stout no one even notices my hair,' said Freda. She took off her flounced bathing hat and let her hair down. It was fine fair hair, but a little sparse – it barely covered her huge shoulders. She crouched down to try and look in the mirror to brush it. She knelt instead of sitting on the chair – she was probably fearful of breaking it. She was scarcely able to move, trapped in this tiny room, and I felt so sorry for her.

'Here, may I brush you hair for you?' I offered timidly. 'It is such a fine shade of yellow. It's very becoming, Freda.'

Her hairbrush was the smallest size. All her possessions were tiny and dainty: her little pot of rose face cream, her papier-mâché trinket box, her cherub candlestick. I realized that vast Freda had a tiny feminine creature imprisoned inside her. I turned round so that she could undress modestly, though I have to confess I took a tiny peek. Her body was even more extraordinary when liberated from her bathing costume. She quickly hid her huge pink bulk with her nightgown. It barely reached her knees, though it would have trailed on the ground like a bride's train on me.

I put on my own nightgown, and Freda

exclaimed at the simple lazy daisies I had embroidered on the bodice.

'They're so pretty, Emerald!'

'I will embroider some on your nightgown,
Freda,' I offered.

She got into bed, trying very hard to keep to her
side, but she couldn't help spreading over the
mattress, taking up nearly all the room. Her poor
huge feet stuck out at the end. They were sadly
callused because she was forced to walk barefoot:
no shoes were big enough for her.

It now seemed like an insult to lie on the floor
with a blanket, so I crept into bed beside her. She
was holding herself rigid, scarcely drawing breath.

'I fear you have nowhere near enough room,
Emerald,' she said sadly.

'No, no, I am perfectly fine, Freda,' I said,
though I was clinging to the edge.

She blew out her candle – and in the darkness we
became two ordinary girls. Freda asked me what
had brought me to Bignor, and I told her about
Mama. I cried a little, and Freda cautiously patted
my shoulder with a huge hand.

I asked Freda if she had a mama, privately
wondering if she might be even more enormous
than her daughter.

'I lost my dear mama when I was ten, and
already a foot taller than her,' she said. 'None of my

family are similarly afflicted. My father and brothers are normal height and my mother was tiny like you – but she loved me dearly and never reproached me for growing to such a size.'

'Oh, Freda! Of course she didn't! How could you help growing?'

'My father was ashamed of me. He kept me in a dark cupboard for months after Mama died, hoping it might restrict my growth.'

'How terrible!'

'And then, when I was fourteen, he sold me to a travelling fair, to be displayed as a freak of nature.' Freda sighed and the whole bed trembled. 'It was very hard at first, but now I am used to it. Mr Clarendon is kinder than most and treats me fairly enough. It is a little lonely at times, living with so many strange men – but now I have you for company, Emerald! You must not be frightened of me, even though I am so very big and queer-looking.'

'I am not the slightest bit frightened of you, Freda dear – and I am charmed to share a room with such a kind, gentle lady,' I said, and I meant every word.

As the weeks went by we grew as close as sisters. We breakfasted together while the men were still fast asleep. Freda did not care to stroll along the promenade because people would stare so and shout after her, but she liked to sit in the garden at the back of the lodgings and get a little fresh air that way. I'd sit with her and we'd chat while I sewed.

I embroidered little pink roses around the neck and cuffs and hem of Freda's large nightgown, which utterly delighted her. I was making a lot of money from tips, so I decided to make Freda a proper present. I went back to the draper's shop and bought several yards of blue silk and set about fashioning her a proper lady's costume. She had only her bathing dress and her nightgown and a shabby man's coat to keep her warm in winter. She cried with joy when she held the lengths of silk and felt their softness.

'But they are far too fine for me, Emerald. I will tear them to shreds.'

'Not if I make you a costume that fits you properly. I will sew it very carefully, with tiny strong stitches. Just be patient, Freda. You are going to have such a beautiful dress, I promise.'

I did my very best to keep my word. I had to stand on a borrowed ladder to measure Freda from her shoulders to her ankles, and we both blushed painfully when I had to stretch the tape to measure her chest and waist and hips, but once these indignities were out of the way and I could start sewing, we had an extremely companionable time together.

Freda offered to read aloud to me from the little

fairy-tale books Mama had given me. I had never let anyone else even touch them before, but I found it curiously soothing for Freda to read in her soft husky voice, holding the tiny tales reverently in her huge hands. I became agitated when she started reading the tale of Jack the Giant Killer – but Freda was fascinated, astonished to discover a story about distant relatives. She didn't mind that the giants were all treated as villains by the anonymous author. She seemed to like it that they were very fierce and tried to catch little people and feed them to their ogre children.

When she'd read her way through all the tales, I did my best to make up a few fairy stories myself featuring Fearless Freda and tiny Emerald Mermaid. She loved these stories so much that I wrote them down for her when I'd finished her costume at last.

Oh, how she loved her blue silk costume! She trembled all over when I made the final fitting, stroking her own arms, marvelling at the softness of the silk. I detached the mirror from the wall and held it up for her so that she could see herself in sections, and she gave little squeals of joy.

I could not fashion her real kid or leather boots to set off her dress because I did not have the right skills – nor indeed, tools – but I managed to make her matching blue silk gaiters that came up to her calves. I reinforced the soles with thickest cardboard, stuck on with my glue.

'I'm afraid you won't be able to walk very far in them, Freda,' I said regretfully, but she still seemed delighted.

She wore her new costume very proudly while on display at the curiosity tent. Mr Clarendon made her a new painted background of the promenade, with tiny figures all pointing and exclaiming at the very fine figure of Fantastic Freda, the Fashionable Female Giant.

He had made me a backdrop too – of blue sea and yellow sand – and he displayed me on a pile of real sand stolen from the beach. Folk marvelled at Freda, but I knew I was now the main attraction. I think it was only the very little children who believed I was a real mermaid – but all the lads and gentlemen clustered around me eagerly, and even their ladies clapped their hands and declared I was as pretty as a picture.

I simpered and smiled for all I was worth, even when some of the louder lads made extremely uncouth remarks about me, because I wanted them to stuff my housekeeping jar with tips. I kept it by my side, painted with sea anemones and decorative fish, and by the end of each evening it was crammed to the brim. Every time someone dropped another coin into the jar with a satisfying clink I thought of

Mama and how it meant I could stay close to her.

I bought her little delicacies every day, and bribed a kind ward orderly at the infirmary to take them in to her: little jars of custard cream, small bottles of fortified wine, a perfect bunch of hothouse grapes. Mama always smiled and nodded and mouthed her thanks to me when I looked at her through the window – but she seemed to be getting thinner and thinner, and even when she lay as still as a statue in bed, the coughing tore her apart.

Then, one terrible evening, she started haemorrhaging as she coughed, blood seeping through her fingers as she clutched her mouth. I heaved the heavy glass window upwards with sudden desperate strength, climbed right through, and ran to her bed. As she coughed and bled, I held her tight and stroked her, and told her that I loved her over and over again, until she was still at last. I held her poor lifeless body and would not let her go. The nurses let me stay there on the bed with Mama, knowing they could not prise me away.

I went on whispering to her, even though I knew she could no longer hear me. I told her that she was the best mother in the whole world. I went through all the tender kindnesses she'd shown me through the years at the hospital, until the ward grew dark.

Then a nurse came and whispered softly, 'We must tidy your dear mother, child.'

I helped wash her and comb her tousled hair. The nurse snipped me off a lock to keep for ever. We gave Mama a clean nightgown and folded her poor thin arms neatly over her sunken chest. I tucked the satin pouch containing my letters under her fingers so that she might read them in Heaven and remember just how much I loved her.

'We will have to make the funeral arrangements,' said the nurse. 'I expect it will have to be a pauper's funeral . . .'

'No! No, I will pay for Mama to have a proper decent funeral,' I said firmly.

I went to the undertaker's with my jar of tip money – to find it still wasn't nearly enough. Dear Freda insisted on giving me the rest. It wasn't a grand funeral. At the undertaker's they outlined various options: beautiful ornate oak caskets with golden handles, black carriages drawn by a matching pair of black horses with plumes, professional mourners in top hats and tails . . . I selected the simplest funeral possible: a plain coffin, a horse and cart to carry it to the graveyard, and no paid mourners at all – only me.

I didn't have any money left for a length of black material to make a decent funeral dress. I had to content myself with a black velvet ribbon tied round my sleeve. But I promise you no professional mourner grieved more profoundly. I murmured the responses with heartfelt concentration, I threw a posy of wild flowers down on Mama's coffin, and when the ceremony was over, I knelt by the raw earth and wept for hours.

Eventually the vicar came over to me, bent down, and rested his hand on my shoulder. 'Try not to grieve so, child. Your mother is at peace now,' he said gently.

I could not imagine Mama at peace. I saw her twitching restlessly, racked with that terrible cough. 'Mama suffered so dreadfully,' I sobbed.

'She is free of earthly pain now,' said the vicar. 'Go home now, child.'

Where *was* my home? I was only here because of Mama. I did not belong anywhere without her.

I stayed for another few weeks, working for Mr Clarendon at his curiosity tent. I went through all the motions required of me – combing my hair, making eye contact with the customers, arching my back to look my best, twitching my velvet tail, smiling all the while. Tips were plentiful, and I smiled again as I carried my full jar back to the lodgings – but I cried every night cradled in Freda's great gentle arms. I smiled until I had enough to pay Freda back for her loan, and then I told her I must leave.

'I shall miss you so, Freda. You are my dearest friend in all the world. But I cannot stay here now.

It is too miserable without Mama,' I told her.

'I understand, Emerald, but oh, I shall miss you so. I have never had a friend before,' Freda said.

'I shall be your friend even if we are apart. I shall come back to Bignor every summer, I promise – and each time I'll make you a new silk dress.'

'But where will you go, Emerald?'

I had thought about it long and hard while lying on my mound of sand performing my mermaid mime. I had various options. I could go to Miss Smith in London and beg her to help me. I knew this was the most sensible idea, but I was not sure I could bear to do this. I did not want to apologize for my behaviour at Mr Buchanan's. I did not want to grovel until she took pity on me and found me a similar position. I was especially frightened that she would make me return to the hospital while she was seeking this position for me.

I could seek out the Greenwood family in Arundel and see if their offer still held – but somehow I shrank from this too. Our fortnight together already had a strange dream-like quality, as if it hadn't really happened. Even if they welcomed me into their home, I wasn't sure it was what I wanted now. Too much had happened to me this summer. I was not sure I could be a child again with Charlotte and Maisie. I felt too old and too sad to play games any more.

I could go back to see Bertie – dear valiant Bertie, who said I was his sweetheart. But we weren't *real* sweethearts. We certainly weren't old enough to set up home together. We could picture for all we were worth on our Sunday afternoons together, but he was still stuck in that reeking butcher's shop every day, up to his elbows in gore. It would be years and years before we had saved up enough money for a little house of our own – and did I really *want* that with Bertie? I'd wanted to share a house with *Mama*. I did not want to live in any house without her.

I'd had a real home once, long ago – that dear cottage in the country. I had a mother there too. She had been fierce with me sometimes, and paddled me royally, but I knew she loved me in her own way. I felt a real longing for her warm strong arms. I had been part of that family once. Jem had written to me again and again. He had made it plain that he wanted me back. I had doubted him, but he had stayed constant in his love. He longed for me – even though he did not really *know* me any more. He only knew that fierce, funny little five-year-old who had played at his side.

I was not sure I wanted to go back now. I wanted to go *forward*.

'Oh, Mama, what shall I *do* ?' I asked the empty air. 'If only I could ask you.'

And then I knew where I had to go.

22

The train journey on Sunday seemed endless. I had bought myself a cheese roll and an apple at the station, but they were poor substitutes for Mrs Briskett's picnic. I was exhausted and very hungry and thirsty by the time I got to Waterloo Station. I stared longingly at all the food stalls, but I did not want to spend so much as another penny now. I was not sure how much my evening might cost. It might take all my money.

I negotiated my way around the station and found a train bound for Kingtown. I remembered making the journey with Mrs Briskett when I left the hospital. It seemed many years ago, and yet it was only a matter of months. I'd been so young and innocent then, so full of hope. Everything had seemed so bizarre and new and puzzling, but I'd had the thought of Mama sustaining me. She had seemed so far away then – but it was so much worse now, when she'd gone away for ever.

I shut my eyes and pressed my lips together. I

779

would not let myself think that. I had to believe that Mama was still here – soon I might even be talking to her . . .

It seemed so strange stepping out of Kingtown station early that evening. I thought of Bertie and longed to see him. Did he still care for me – or had he forgotten about me already? Was he out walking with some other girl today? I thought of Kitty and Ivy in the draper's shop. Had Bertie taken Kitty out in the rowing boat, along the river to our secret island? Was he strolling in the park with Ivy, picturing for all he was worth?

No, surely Kitty would squeal and fidget and capsize the boat – and dim Ivy could not conjure up any fancies worth a farthing. I tossed my head. Bertie might well find it difficult to find a girl to replace me.

But I was not here to try to find Bertie. I walked along the familiar roads until I reached Lady's Ride. I passed Mr Buchanan's splendid big house, peering up at his study window. I was ready to thumb my nose at him, but there was no sign of little Monkey Man. I looked at the area steps and wondered whether to slip in to see dear old Mrs Briskett – but it was getting late and I didn't think there was time. I was sure I would see Sarah shortly.

I walked on, trying hard to remember the way,

once anxiously tracing my steps when I took a wrong turning. At last I found myself in the little street of cottages with bright flowers in the gardens. I counted along to the right one and walked up the garden path. I saw that the blinds at the windows were closely drawn.

I took a deep breath and knocked on the door. After a few moments the same tall dark woman, Emily, opened it and gazed at me enquiringly.

'Good evening. Is Madame Berenice holding a seance tonight?'

'Yes, she is. Please come in.' Emily looked at me closely in the dimly lit hall. 'I think you have visited us before . . .'

'Yes, with Sarah.'

'Ah! You are the little girl who ran away! I believe your brother made contact from the spirit world and it frightened you a little.'

'It frightened me a great deal! I never cared for that brother.'

'But you wish to communicate with him again?'

'No! No, I'm here because – my dear mama has died and I'm desperate to make contact with her again.'

'Oh, you poor child. Well, I'm sure Madame Berenice will do her very best. Would you care to leave your remuneration on the silver plate on the hallstand? It will be five shillings to hear her voice, and ten for an actual materialization. I'm afraid there are no guarantees, though. The spirits are contrary creatures and won't always come when they are bidden.'

'I understand,' I said, counting my coins. 'There!' I let a handful of threepennies, sixpennies and shillings clatter down on the plate.

Emily's dark eyes flickered over the coins, clearly counting. 'Yes, that will be sufficient,' she said. 'Follow me.'

She led me into the darkened room. Just like last time, I could barely distinguish anything. I sensed, rather than saw, my fellow clients.

'Come and join us, child,' said the deep, thrilling voice of Madame Berenice.

I felt my way to the chairs around the table.

'Hetty! Is that you?' Sarah whispered. She reached out and took my hand. 'Oh, Hetty, how we've worried over you! How are you, dear? Did you come here specially to find me?'

'I – I came here to find . . . someone else,' I said. 'Oh, Sarah, my mama . . .' I couldn't continue, but she understood, and gripped my hand harder.

'Oh, you poor child! I am so sorry. But you have come to the right place. You will be wondrously comforted,' she said.

Emily was whispering to Madame Berenice.

'I believe you have requested a materialization,

Hetty?' said Madame Berenice. 'I'm afraid Sarah has requested one too, but there can only be one each night. There is no greater wonder in all nature, but it takes immense effort to summon up psycho-plastic matter. I cannot possibly manage two such projections in quick succession.'

'Let it be Hetty's materialization, Madame Berenice,' said Sarah. 'I have experienced this wonder many times.'

'That is very generous of you, Sarah,' said Madame Berenice.

'Thank you! Thank you so much!' I said, giving Sarah a hug.

'Now now, settle down, child. Let us all concentrate. The spirits are restless tonight, eager to communicate. We will join hands anew and see who visits us first.'

I sat between Sarah and an old lady who clung to me with her dry little mittened hand. I could dimly see the old lady on her other side, and the drooping figure of Mr Brown. There were three other women. It was going to be a very long evening. My heart pounded in my chest. Would Mama come? Would she speak to me? Would I see her dear face again?

'Is there anybody there?' Madame Berenice asked throatily. 'Yes! Yes, there is a child here, an eager young chap.' Her own voice became little and piping. 'Hello, Father dear!'

'It's my Cedric!' said Mr Brown, choking with emotion.

We sat in our circle while little Cedric chatted inconsequentially and Mr Brown shed happy tears. Then long-lost sweethearts and cherished companions took it in turns to commune. They talked of heavenly peace and shining light and cosmic harmony, but they didn't say anything specific about their spirit world. They were all very loving, but their messages seemed unbearably tedious as time ticked slowly by in the dark, stifling room. They enquired genteelly about someone's cough or bad back. One of the old ladies in the spirit world explained to her friend in the room exactly how to make a beneficial peppermint tisane.

I fidgeted desperately, willing her to *hurry up*. My mama might be waiting to get a word in while we were being solemnly instructed to add a teaspoon of sugar to each pint of peppermint.

I managed to curb my impatience when it was Sarah's turn at last, and her mama spoke to her softly and warmly, as if big lumpy Sarah were a small girl again. I could scarcely breathe now. It was *my* turn! Would *my* mama cross over from her new home in the spirit world to talk to me?

'Is there anybody there – a new spirit, anxious to reassure her little daughter?' Madame Berenice asked.

There was no answer.

'Is there anybody there?' Madame Berenice repeated.

We waited, again in vain.

I gave a little sob, and Sarah's hand tightened over mine.

'Won't you come, Mama?' I whispered in the dark.

'Hush, child. The spirits can only communicate through me,' said Madame Berenice. 'We must all stay holding hands, shut our eyes, and pray for a materialization. I sense a presence – but the spirits are shy, especially when asked to materialize.'

We held hands, we shut our eyes, we waited. Then I was aware of a slight rustle of material. I opened my eyes. An indistinct figure, all in misty white, was standing near us, very slowly moving towards me. Her face was obscured by a long white veil.

'Is it *you*, Mama?' I asked. 'Oh, Madame Berenice, is it really my mama?'

'It is your own dear mother, Hetty,' a strange, eerie voice whispered.

'You sound so – so different, Mama. Are you all right? Are you still coughing?'

'There are no ailments in the spirit world, my dear. I am in perfect health now. I am very happy. You must not grieve for me, Hetty.'

She glided nearer. She walked with slow strange grace, her skirts rustling.

Mama had always walked with quick darting steps.

She bent down before me. She was tall and stately.

Mama was scarcely taller than me.

She bent nearer and I smelled her rose cologne.

Mama never used cologne in her life – she simply smelled of her own sweet warm flesh.

She kissed me on the forehead with smooth cool lips.

Mama's lips were chapped and rough because she licked them anxiously – and she never kissed my brow. She kissed my cheeks and lips, and sometimes the tip of my nose when she was being playful.

'Mama?' I said.

'My dear little child.'

I wasn't her dear little child at all. She wasn't my mama. I started trembling. I knew who she was – Emily, the tall woman who had let me in and taken my money. Madame Berenice's sister – and accomplice. I wanted to rip her white floating veil from her head, switch on the light, and expose her to all the people sitting there so stupidly, paying their money week after week for a fraudulent trick. But somehow I held myself rigid. I bit my lips in an effort not to fly into a temper.

All these people sitting with me in the dark believed utterly. My dear friend Sarah lived for these moments with her 'mother'. She had given up her chance of a materialization tonight for my sake. I could not take away the most precious consolation of her hard life.

So I held my tongue while the ghastly false Mama kissed me again and circled the table, and the others cried out and marvelled. She told me to be a good brave girl, and she promised to watch over me and visit me often on Sunday evenings. Then Madame Berenice told us to close our eyes again and give thanks for this marvellous materialization from the spirit world.

I kept my eyes open and watched the white woman steal silently out of the door. I waited while Madame Berenice murmured some spirit mumbo-jumbo, taking short rapid breaths as if she'd been running. Then she called out for light. Emily returned, bearing a lamp. She was dressed all in black now. She had obviously thrust her ghostly white garments into some cupboard. It seemed quite clear to me that she was the apparition pretending to be Mama. She had the same stance, the same walk, even the same smell – but all the others were totally oblivious to this. They marvelled at the success of the evening and crowded around me joyfully.

Sarah gave me a warm hug. 'I'm so very happy for you, Hetty,' she said.

The others patted me fondly and congratulated me.

'Say thank you nicely to Madame, Hetty,' said Sarah. 'She has worked so hard on your behalf.'

I stared at Madame Berenice. She was worse than Mr Clarendon. At least he only charged a few pennies per person, and he didn't just prey on the bereaved. I bent forward and whispered into her turbaned ear, so that only she could hear me: 'You're a wicked old fraud. I want my ten shillings back!'

She looked at me with narrowed eyes, her rouged lips set in a strained smile. She did not acknowledge me in any way – but at the door on the way out, Emily took me a little roughly by the shoulder and thrust a ten-shilling note at me.

'Take it and never come back,' she hissed.

Then Sarah caught me up, still so innocently happy for me. I had to keep up the pretence, though inside my heart was breaking. I so wished I'd been convinced by the clumsy materialization, but I was too close to dear Mama to be fooled by a charlatan.

Sarah burbled on and on about *her* dear mother. I listened sadly, trying my best to make encouraging responses.

'But you must tell me all about you now, Hetty

dear. How have you been keeping? Have you got a
new position? Come back and have a cup of tea with
Mrs B and me and tell us everything!'

Sarah was so persuasive, linking her arm in
mine, smiling at me fondly as if I were her long-lost
sister, that I took her up on her offer. I had nowhere
else to go, after all.

It seemed very strange approaching Mr
Buchanan's house and going down the area steps.
Sarah looked anxiously up at the dimly lit study
window, but Mr Buchanan was safely at his desk
out of sight. Sarah put her finger to her lips even so,
and I tiptoed down the steps as if I were her silent
shadow.

The kitchen smelled warmly and wonderfully of
savoury pie. The table was all set for supper. Mrs
Briskett was busy cutting the pie into slices. She
paused dramatically when she caught sight of me,
and then rushed towards me, mercifully dropping
the knife before embracing me, hugging me hard
against her upholstered chest.

But there was another person in the kitchen – a
pretty little fair girl with big blue eyes, almost as
blue as my own.

'Who are you?' I asked, taken aback.

She smiled sweetly at me. 'I am Rose-May. I
know exactly who *you* are. You're naughty Hetty
Feather! I've heard such tales about you!'

'Rose-May's our new little maid,' said Mrs Briskett, and she gave her a fond pat on her curly head. 'She's shaping up nicely now.'

'Mrs Briskett and I have been making rabbit pie,' said Rose-May. 'Won't you try a slice, Hetty?'

I looked at the steaming pie, the pastry crust crisply golden, risen high, a fancy edging pricked all the way around. 'Did you do the pastry?' I asked Rose-May.

She nodded proudly, flexing her fingers. 'Mrs Briskett says I have a really light touch,' she declared.

'Well, isn't that just fine and dandy,' I said. I looked at Sarah, who was taking off her bonnet, still flushed with excitement after her encounter with her mama. 'Why did you not accompany Sarah to Madame Berenice's?' I asked prissy little Rose-May. 'Did she not ask you? *I* used to go with her to make sure she didn't have a swooning fit.'

'I care about Sarah, of course, but I couldn't possibly go with her to that meeting. I am a Baptist, and we don't hold with spirit meetings and such-like,' said Rose-May.

'Rose-May's very devout,' said Sarah, sounding a little in awe of her.

'Mr Buchanan sent me to the Baptist Society to find a new maid of all work. He wanted to find a good meek girl who wouldn't cause any trouble,' said Mrs Briskett. 'He didn't want to risk another foundling! But tell me, Hetty, what are you doing here? Did you meet up with our Sarah by chance?'

'Hush now, Mrs B, poor Hetty's been through a great deal. Her mother passed over this summer.'

'Oh, dear child, I'm so sorry,' said Mrs Briskett.

'But Hetty has been reunited with her dear mother this evening. Isn't that wonderful?' said Sarah, still flushed and glowing with the excitement of it all.

'I'm not so sure *wonderful* is the word I'd use,' said Mrs Briskett. 'Look at the state of the poor girl. White as a sheet, and skinnier than ever.' She steered me gently to the table and sat me down on the bench. 'Eat some pie, child,' she commanded.

'Poor Hetty!' said Rose-May. She bent her head, clasped her hands, and said piously, 'For what we are about to receive, may we be truly grateful. Amen.'

I *was* truly grateful to be offered a slice of pie, and I suppose it tasted delicious, but I found it hard to eat. I chewed long and hard on the rabbit meat, but I couldn't seem to make it go down.

'Don't you like rabbit pie, Hetty?' said Mrs Briskett. 'Young Bertie brought us such a nice fat rabbit, ready skinned.'

'He said he'd make me a little fur tippet out of all his rabbit skins,' Rose-May said, giggling. 'Like Baby Bunting.'

I stared at her sweet simpering little face. I wanted to push it straight into the wretched pie. My stomach heaved.

'Excuse me,' I gasped, my hand over my mouth.

I ran out of the kitchen, making for the horrible privy out in the back yard. I heard Sarah asking if I was all right, and Rose-May wondering if she should run after me, and Mrs Briskett saying, 'Poor little thing, she really *is* an orphan now.'

I got to the privy just in time, for I was violently sick. Then I stood outside in the dark, staring up at the crescent moon, tears running down my face. I could not bear to go back into the kitchen. I didn't belong there any more. I did not belong with anyone. I wasn't special to anyone at all, only Mama – and now I had lost her for ever. I was an orphan.

You are NOT an orphan!

It was Mama's voice, clear and distinct, as if she were standing right beside me in the moonlight.

'Oh, Mama, is it really *you*?'

Of course it's me, you silly girl. Don't you know your own Mama?

'But – but *how* is it you? Did Madame Berenice conjure you up after all?'

That dreadful turbaned charlatan! As if I'd ever lower myself to speak through HER! Now listen to me, girl. You are NOT an orphan. You still have one parent alive.

'You mean . . . ?'

Why don't you try to find your father?

'But – but you said he doesn't even know I exist.'

Then perhaps it's time to tell him!

'But, Mama—'

No buts.

'I'm not sure I *want* a father. I want *you*. I want to feel your arms around me! Can't you materialize somehow?'

We don't need materializations, darling. YOUR arms are around ME – because I am in your heart.

I crossed my hands over my chest. I felt my heart beating wildly, blood throbbing through my body, so that I tingled all over. I stood there, still crying, though I was happy now. I wasn't alone any more.

'Thank you, Mama,' I whispered into the dark.

I'll always be with you, Hetty.

'I'm not Hetty any more, Mama, I am Sapphire Battersea – and I'm going to find my father.'

Read on for a sneak preview of the third story
featuring Hetty Feather,

EMERALD STAR

1

'What are you doing here, child? This is no place for a little lass like you. Come on, tell me your name.'

I drew myself up as tall as I could, standing on tiptoe in my clumpy boots.

'I'm not a child,' I said haughtily, though I knew I was so small and slight I did not look anywhere near fourteen. 'My name is . . .' But then I hesitated foolishly.

My name is Hetty Feather, but I had never felt it was my *real* name. It was a comical name chosen at random when Mama handed me to the matron at the Foundling Hospital when I was only a few days old. I had been christened Hetty Feather in the hospital chapel and people had been calling me that name in irritation and anger ever since. I was not a placid child and found it hard to stick to the rigid rules and regulations of the hospital. My hot temper and wild spirit made me stand out from all the other foundlings as clearly as my bright red hair.

I was plain, the smallest and slightest in my year, and cursed with my carrot hair – but I did have bright blue eyes, my one good feature. I fancied my mama might have called me Sapphire if she'd been able to keep me. When at last I found her, I discovered she really had wondered about naming me her little Sapphire.

I tried to call myself Sapphire Battersea when I left the hospital to go into service, proudly adopting Mama's distinctive surname. But they laughed at me in my new position and said Sapphire wasn't a servant's name. I did not *want* to be a servant. When I was dismissed in disgrace, I ran away to Mama, only to discover the dreadful truth – that she was dying of consumption. I had to earn my living all that sad summer by the sea, when I visited her daily. I could not find any respectable work at all so I chose a disreputable job instead. I fashioned my beautiful green velvet Sunday best dress into a mermaid costume and joined Mr Clarendon's Seaside Curiosities as a star attraction. I was Emerald the Amazing Pocket-Sized Mermaid. My new dear friend, Freda the Female Giant, called me Emerald every day.

'*Are you deaf or simple? What is your name?*' the innkeeper repeated.

I did not want to call myself Hetty Feather. I did not care for the name – and the governors at the

2

Foundling Hospital might well be trying to track me down. I longed to say that my name was Sapphire Battersea, but I had to be wary in this new strange village. This was where my dear mother had been brought up. Folk might recognize the name and run to tell my father. I wanted to seek him out myself and break my news gently.

The innkeeper tossed his head and turned to walk away.

'I am Emerald,' I blurted out.

The old men leaning on the sticky bar sniggered into their foaming pints.

'Emerald?' the innkeeper repeated. 'What sort of a name is that?'

'A fine distinctive name,' I said.

'What about a surname then?'

'I am Emerald . . . Star,' I announced, giving birth to my new self right that moment.

'Emerald Star!' said the innkeeper.

This time the old men laughed openly.

'She's cracked in the head!' he said to them, and they guffawed and drank and spat contemptuously in the sawdust at their feet.

'I'll thank you not to mock,' I said. 'Emerald Star is my stage name. I am very well known in the south. In fact people pay to come and see me.'

'What do you do then, Emerald Star?' the innkeeper asked, an unpleasant tone to his voice.

3

'I perform upon the stage,' I said.

I wasn't exactly lying. When I exhibited myself as Emerald the Amazing Pocket-Sized Mermaid, it was upon a sturdy plinth, so that people did not have to bend down to see me reclining there, twitching my green velvet tail on a little pile of sand.

The word 'stage' made the men's heads rock. They set down their pints and stared at me as if I were about to perform then and there. Some looked smugly disapproving.

'So she's one of they actresses,' said one, and tutted with his two teeth.

'Are you a turn at the music hall then, lass?' asked another with interest. 'I go regular on a Saturday night over at Brackenly. I've seen them all – Simon Spangles, little Dolly Daydream, Georgie and His Talking Doll, the Romulus Brothers, Lily Lark . . . Great acts, all of them. But I've never seen you.'

'I'm not a travelling player. I perform on the *London* stage,' I insisted, telling a terrible lie.

'You don't look like one of them theatricals, all painted faces and high-pitched voices,' said the innkeeper.

'More's the pity,' said one of the old men. 'What sort of a costume's *that*?' He pointed to my drab grey dress. 'You're nothing but a little maid, spinning us all fairy stories. I don't believe a word of it.'

'Believe what you want. I don't care at all. My

4

business is not with you.' I turned to the innkeeper. 'My business is with *you*, sir.'

'She wants her pint of porter!' said the old man, chuckling.

'I simply want a bite to eat and a room for the night,' I said. 'I have adequate funds.' I patted my full pocket. 'And you advertise both on the sign outside.'

It was the only sign I'd seen. I'd tramped the length and breadth of this bleak little Yorkshire village searching for rooms. It was a seaside of sorts, but it did not seem to have hotels and hostelries. Beautiful Bignor on the south coast had these aplenty, and every second house had lodgings. It had bathing machines along the beach, and pierrots and hokey-pokey men and all manner of amusements. This bleak village of Monksby had a small harbour and a stinking fish market and a few streets of mean dwellings. Now it was past ten o'clock, the only place with any light and life was this Fisherman's Inn.

I was desperately tired. I had been travelling all day, cooped up in the third-class railway carriage, my heart beating wildly at the thought of finding my father. I was not sure quite how I would manage this. I did not even know his last name. Mama had simply called him Bobbie. I had not liked to ask her all the hundreds of questions humming in my head

5

because she found it so painful talking about her past.

'Give the child a room, Tobias, and stop persecuting the poor little thing,' said the woman behind the bar. She was big and tough, with a great crooked nose like a picture of a witch in a storybook. She looked very frightening – but she was nodding at me kindly. 'Look at her – she's swaying on her feet with tiredness, and all you men can do is turn her into a little guy. You come with me, dear.'

'Thank you, ma'am,' I said meekly.

'Who are you to issue invitations, Lizzie? Do you own this inn?' said Tobias.

'No, but I own a human heart, and this girl needs food and drink and a bed for the night,' she said, and beckoned me behind the bar.

I ducked under the wooden top and Lizzie led me through a door into a gloomy kitchen at the back.

'You're shivering, child. I'd light a fire but old Tobias won't admit summer's over now. Here, put this on.' She took her own grey woollen shawl and wrapped it tight around my shoulders. I had proudly held my own when Tobias and the old men were baiting me, but Lizzie's simple little act of kindness made the tears start trickling down my face.

'There now,' she said, giving me a pat. She sat me at the table and bustled around the kitchen. She took a saucepan from the sink and tried to scrape it out. 'He had a fish stew for his supper but he's cleared the pot. I'll have to scratch around for something cold for you.'

She found a loaf in a crock and cut me two thick slices of bread and a generous chunk of cheese. They were both a little stale but I ate them gratefully enough. Instead of a cup of tea she fetched me a pint of ale from the bar.

'There now, this will warm you up,' she said.

I did not care for the taste at all, but I drank a few sips obediently. When Lizzie saw I was leaving most of it, she downed it herself, and wiped the froth off her lips appreciatively.

'Now, I'll show you the privy. I'm afraid it's not very nice – you know what men are like, and you sound like a London lass, used to fancy ways,' she said, lighting a candle and leading me by the hand.

The privy was unspeakably disgusting. Perhaps it was as well I couldn't see it properly in the dark. Still, I had no choice but to use it and then wash my hands thoroughly at the outside pump. Lizzie led me back inside and up the stairs. I was shivering now, and so tired I could barely carry my small suitcase.

'Let me give you a hand with that,' said Lizzie, taking it from me. 'Is this all your worldly belongings? You haven't run away, have you?'

'Not exactly. I – I am running *to* someone,' I said.

'Not a sweetheart, I hope?' said Lizzie. 'Never trust a man – a shilling's your best friend.'

'No, he's family, not a sweetheart,' I whispered.

'That's better. Though how come you're looking for family round here? You don't come from these parts, do you?'

'I think my mother did,' I said. I looked hard at Lizzie, trying to gauge her age. The lines on her face were set hard and deep and she looked many years older than my dear little mama – though in the last few desperate months of her life *she* had aged visibly too.

'She was called Ida,' I said, clutching hold of Lizzie, suddenly desperate, and deciding I could trust her. 'Ida Battersea.'

I willed Lizzie's face to soften, to say, *Oh my goodness, Ida Battersea! She was my dear friend.*

But she shook her head. 'Can't say I've ever heard of her, dear. Anyway, let's find you a room. Tobias has three or four guest rooms up here, though they're seldom in use. We'll find you the best one, eh?'

The rooms all looked the same to me – bare and basic, with a stripped narrow bed and striped ticking mattress, a washstand and a cupboard, and a rag rug on the cold lino. There were stern moral pictures on all the walls. Lizzie held the candle up to a representation of a woman in the gutter guzzling from a bottle and clutching a crying baby, while an uncouth man carrying a pint pot beat his poor dog in the background. It was clearly preaching against the demon drink – a strange choice for rooms in a public house.

'It's not exactly cosy up here, is it?' said Lizzie. 'Still, I promise you it's clean. I have a sweep and scrub every week or so, for Matty's sake. She was Tobias's wife and my dear friend – and now I try to keep the place decent for her. I trot up to the churchyard every Sunday, and when all the folk have gone away, their ears still ringing with the sermon, I go and sit by Matty and we have a little chat just like we did when she was alive.' She shot me a look, as if daring me to laugh. 'I know it sounds daft like.'

'It doesn't sound daft at all, it sounds lovely,' I said. 'I talk to Mama in my head and she talks back to me. Well, perhaps it's only my fancy, but it seems as if she does. She told me to come here, Lizzie.'

'Well, that's extraordinary, because this is a harsh, hard village without much comfort even for those born and bred here. Still, maybe she has her reasons. Now, I'll get you clean linen from the press and settle you down for the night.'

We made up the bed together, Lizzie nodding with approval when she saw me tucking the sheets in with precision. Years of hospital training had stood me in good stead in some ways.

'I'll come in early tomorrow and make sure you get a proper breakfast,' said Lizzie. 'Goodnight . . .

9

Emerald?' She gave a little snort. 'Though that's never your real name!'

'It is now,' I said.

Lizzie left me with the candle. She insisted on leaving her shawl with me too, and I certainly needed it. It was only early autumn but the north wind straight off the sea rattled the windows and I had only the thinnest of blankets. I wound the shawl tightly around me and laid out all my precious possessions on the bed: my little books of fairy tales, Mama's brush and comb and violet vase, a fairground dog, and the fat manuscript in which I'd recounted all my adventures so far. I turned the page, and put the date, *Friday September 29th 1891*, at the top of the page.

My name is Emerald Star, I wrote, in my best hospital-taught copperplate. *I am here in Monksby!!!* But in spite of the three exclamation marks I could not feel excited. Doubt made my heart thump, my stomach churn, and had me fidgeting from one side to the other in that narrow bed long after I had blown out the candle. Had Mama *really* said Monksby? Was it perhaps Monksford . . . Monkslawn . . . Monkton?

When we curled up together during those sweet stolen nights at the hospital, we had whispered the stories of our missing years. I had told Mama about the cottage in the country that had been my home till I was five. I had told her about my dear foster brother Jem, though I found it painful talking about him then, because I thought he had forgotten me.

Mama wasn't so interested in any of my foster siblings but she asked endless questions about my foster mother Peg. I tried to give a truthful picture of that warm, work-worn woman but it was difficult remembering details. I just had an impression of her strong arms cuddling me close or giving me a royal paddling when I had been disobedient or overly fanciful. She frequently said I was more trouble than all her other children put together, but I knew she loved me dearly all the same. Mama could not see it that way when I told her tales of Peg. She sucked in her breath when I said I'd been paddled and became very agitated.

'How could any woman hit a tiny child, especially one as small and sensitive as you, Hetty,' she said fiercely, holding me close and rocking me as if the paddling had only just occurred. Poor Peg could do no right in her eyes. She asked what she'd given me to eat and poured scorn on my slices of bread and dripping.

'What sort of nourishment is there in chunks of bread and pig fat?' she said. 'No wonder you were such a little scrap of a girl with no flesh on your bones. And she was getting paid for your keep too! Didn't she ever give you any meat?'

'We had rabbit stew,' I said, licking my lips at the memory, but this didn't impress Mama either.

'Didn't she ever give you a decent plate of roast beef, or a proper chop or cutlet?'

This was unfair, because she knew they were simple country people and couldn't afford such splendid meals. Mama was totally unreasonable where I was concerned. She felt Peg had been a pretty poor mother to me – and frequently wept because she had lost the chance of mothering me herself for ten long years.

At first I had asked her many questions about her own past, but right from the start I could see she found it troubling to talk about.

She told me my father was called Bobbie and had bright red hair just like me and she'd loved him with all her heart – but he had left her to go to sea. I didn't know if he had left her because she was going to have his child, or whether he'd never known about me. It seemed cruel to question her because her voice always shook and her blue eyes filled with tears.

'He was a fine man, your father. All the girls in the village were after him, but he picked *me*,' Mama said proudly.

I wasn't so sure a truly fine man would get a young girl into trouble and then abandon her. Perhaps I wouldn't like this father at all if I ever found him – but I was sure Mama wanted us to meet.

'Go and find your father now!' she'd said to me, her dear voice clear in my head even though she had been dead for weeks.

I had no address – I didn't even have his last name – but I knew he'd grown up in the same village as Mama. She'd said it was called Monksby – or some such name. I hadn't quizzed her because her tears spilled again when she talked of it. I knew her mother and father had turned her out when they discovered she was having a baby – they could not stand the shame. I cried too at the thought of poor Mama, destitute and sick, making the long journey to London to leave me at the Foundling Hospital.

I fancied I heard her crying now, curled up beside me in the cold bed.

'I'm here, Mama,' I said, reaching out across the bare sheet and clasping thin air. 'You mustn't cry. I will be all right. I will find my father and I will love him almost as much as I love you, and we will live happily ever after – as happily as I can ever be without you.'

I squeezed tight, imagining the pressure of Mama's thin fingers squeezing back, and I fell asleep, our hands still clasped.

ALSO AVAILABLE BY JACQUELINE WILSON